Andrew Anastasios was born in Melbourne in 1966, the grandson of a water diviner. He began his working life as an archaeologist, excavating in the Near East and Turkey, where he met his wife Meaghan. He was a travel-writer, journalist and advertising copywriter before a line in a century-old letter sparked the idea for his first feature film script. Andrew is the co-writer of the international film *The Water Diviner*, and works from Australia as a screenwriter and producer.

Meaghan Wilson-Anastasios grew up in Melbourne before travelling and working as an archaeologist in the Mediterranean and Middle East. She holds a PhD in art history and cultural economics and lectures at the University of Melbourne. Meaghan balances her academic career with an unapologetically populist taste in entertainment, writing and researching for film, TV and the print media. She lives in inner Melbourne with her husband and their two children. *The Water Diviner* is her first novel, and she hopes it won't be her last.

* * THE * * *
WATER DIVINER

ANDREW ANASTASIOS AND
MEAGHAN WILSON-ANASTASIOS

BASED ON THE ORIGINAL SCRIPT
BY ANDREW KNIGHT AND ANDREW ANASTASIOS

PAN BOOKS

For Roman and Cleopatra, and the history that lives in you.

First published 2014 by Pan Macmillan Australia Pty Ltd

This edition published 2015 by Pan Books
an imprint of Pan Macmillan, a division of Macmillan Publishers Limited
Pan Macmillan, 20 New Wharf Road, London N1 9RR
Basingstoke and Oxford
Associated companies throughout the world
www.panmacmillan.com

ISBN 978-1-4472-9506-8

1 3 5 7 9 8 6 4 2

A cip catalogue record for this book is available from the British Library.

Typeset in 13.5/16 pt Granjon by Midland Typesetters, Australia
Printed and bound by CPI Group (UK) Ltd, Croydon, CR0 4YY

Visit www.panmacmillan.com to read more about all our books
and to buy them. You will also find features, author interviews and
news of any author events, and you can sign up for e-newsletters
so that you're always first to hear about our new releases.

When we leave this world, do not look for our tombs in the earth, but find them in the hearts of men.

Rumi

PROLOGUE

A match flares in the dark. It dies a swift, hapless death. A second, this one shielded by a cupped hand, licks a candlewick until it catches. As a halo of orange illuminates the dugout, a quick, frosty breath snuffs out the match. With strong manicured fingers a man prises open a fob watch, glued shut with grit and sweat: five minutes to five. He slips the watch into his tunic pocket. A second thought. He retrieves it, polishes the casing on his rough woollen sleeve and places it in a small metal trunk on his bed. Every instinct tells him he won't be needing the watch after this morning. If everything goes as expected, he won't be needing anything much at all.

The man shuffles around the small bolthole, picking up his meagre personal effects and packing them into the trunk. It surprises him how austere the world of even the most cultured man can become. When life is distilled down to its most basic elements, it's remarkable how little you really need. Some officers like to confect a home away from home, surrounding themselves with familiar comforts: their favourite cologne, a gramophone, coffee-making utensils, their library. He resists the urge. He never wants this to feel normal, never wants to mistake what they do here for civilised. Nevertheless, this lair has been his home since May, through a dysentery-wracked summer and a wretched autumn. Now a sodden winter is smothering his resolve. It snowed last month and an eighteen-year-old sentry was found frozen at his post in the morning. Not how you expect a man, young or old, to die in war.

He has packed the trunk in this way, the same scant items in the same order, eight times since they landed. He could leave it for someone else. For after. But the packing has become something akin to a rite, a ceremonial declaration. Everything is in order. *I am ready for the worst. I dare you.*

He flicks the pages of his diary, water stained, muddy and precious. He recalls his first entries, considered and self-conscious, every word a labour. Yesterday's entry – *I woke early. Bitterly cold. Reported to colonel.* After seven months of suffering, there's nothing left to say. He wipes the cover with his hand and drops it into the trunk, then places a family photo on top. In his palm he juggles a closed pinecone like a grenade before putting it, too, inside the chest. His shaving bowl, razor and brush follow. He lifts a woman's scarf up to his nose, breathing in the scent of his wife. Or the memory of her. Who knows for sure anymore? He wraps it around a sheaf of papers – a letter – then drops them into the trunk and closes the lid.

As he moves to the table where his revolver lies, the flickering candlelight catches his epaulettes and the hilt of the sword strapped to his side. He's a career officer, a major, a forty-seven-year-old man of quiet resolve. Now weary and taut, he is on the brink of ordering yet another pointless assault on the enemy trenches at Gallipoli. He has done this countless times before. But today, inexplicably, it unsettles him.

He knows this attack may well cost him his life. Which is nothing new. Snipers on both sides routinely target officers, to decapitate the lumbering enemy on the charge. Certainly he knows hundreds of his men will perish in the next thirty minutes for no particularly good reason. Whatever scant centimetres they advance this morning will be stolen back by the enemy tomorrow. With all the to-ing and fro-ing at Lone Pine, the front lines haven't moved for four months. There was a time when he was disgusted by the profligate waste of life. Now it just exhausts him.

Light filters through the coarse hessian curtain that acts as his door. He hears a guttural cough, a none-too-subtle reminder from his sergeant. He smiles to himself. Hat on, pistol holstered and sword slapping his leg, the officer pushes back the curtain and steps into the pre-dawn light.

A rugged face appears before Major Hasan. It is his staff sergeant, Jemal, a weather-beaten lion of a man and a veteran of too many campaigns. He speaks in Turkish, fog on his breath.

'Five minutes?'

Hasan looks past him and down the muddy Ottoman trench at his ragtag army. Whiskered grandfathers stand beside terrified teenagers, farmers beside bank clerks from Stamboul. Some wear full uniform, others are clad in a motley mismatch of civilian clothes tricked up with military-issue jackets, trousers or belts. The Ottoman Government is still recovering from the Balkan War and is desperately low on uniforms and supplies. Many of these conscripts are standing in the clothes of dead men, the blood washed away and bullet holes worn as lucky charms. Surely lightning can't strike twice. The fortunate wear boots – often salvaged from the feet of fallen comrades – but the rest have wrapped their bare feet in cloth against the cold.

'Wait for the sun,' says Hasan with a nod.

Jemal salutes and the message is relayed quietly along the trench with a whispered word or a gesture. Soldiers shake hands and kiss their comrades, fathers or sons on both cheeks. An imam, bearded and solemn, blesses men as they huddle around a brazier; the heat of the flames does little to disperse the frost of mortal fear.

The bone-chillingingly cold air is still. Silent. Jemal supervises as scaling ladders are raised against the trench wall and men line up at their bases. Their tension is palpable. Teeth chatter, not just from the cold. The acrid smell of urine and the stomach-churning sweet tang of the decaying dead in the ghastly stretch of land between the two front lines pollute the morning air.

Hasan spots a young boy, lost in an oversized tunic, his boots on the bottom rung of his ladder. He is determined to be first over the top. As the major strides towards him the boy looks into the mud, deferring to the senior officer.

'Soldier, what is your name?' asks Hasan sternly.

'Yilmaz,' the boy replies into the dirt, adding, 'from, Mardin, sir,' as an afterthought.

'Fetch my binoculars, Private Yilmaz from Mardin. They're in my dugout.'

'But Commander, I'll miss –'

'Do it,' demands Hasan, cutting him short.

4

Reluctantly Yilmaz gives up his place at the front of the line and makes his way along the trench. Major Hasan watches the boy disappear and then steps onto his ladder and chances a look over the top of the sandbags at the enemy line. The grim expanse of no-man's land is dusted with frost; infinitesimally small crystals reflect the first blush of dawn's pale light. A distant rifle cracks, shattering the unnatural silence, and Hasan ducks automatically. He composes himself and signals to an old bandleader, who is resplendent in his tattered velvet jacket and meticulously waxed handlebar moustache. A handful of drummers and trumpeters gather in a huddle, and the bandmaster thrusts a flag into the air. A trumpet wails and the band strikes up a discordant anthem, the signal to charge. In a chaotic, adrenaline-fuelled scramble, men surge up the ladders and over the trench wall crying, 'Allahu Akbar! Allahu Akbar!'

Hasan has timed the assault perfectly, using the rising Aegean sun to dazzle the enemy as his troops charge across no-man's land. Hasan climbs over the sandbags, with Jemal puffing beside him like a swimmer coming up for air. Ottoman soldiers cry out at the top of their lungs around them, expelling their fear and anxiety. Those with guns fire blindly into the dawn light before them. The rest brandish farm implements and handmade pikes, waiting for the man beside them to fall so they can seize his rifle and make it their own.

The Australian front line is barely the length of a tennis court away but the ground is sodden and uneven, and punctuated with craters and bloated corpses that form a gruesome obstacle course for the running men. And soldiers do fall, some tangled at the ankles by coils of razor-sharp wire curling out of the mud, others dropping into shell holes

5

filled with a hideous soup of stagnant water and disarticulated body parts.

In the confusion they can hear guns from the enemy trenches spit and buck. The band is charging across the field in a loose formation, still playing its defiant, dissonant song, but now a few instruments short. The bandleader waves the colours of the 47th Battalion like a red rag to a bull.

Revolver in hand, Hasan stumbles across no-man's land, Jemal at his side. At any moment he expects to feel the searing heat of a bullet and the mud in his hair as he is knocked onto his back. He knows his sergeant will be happy if he can just get his cavalier commander to the enemy trench in one piece. He can almost hear Jemal thinking, *Why can't the major be like most men of his rank and stay behind the line? That's what binoculars are for.*

They have caught the Australians off guard with the early hour. Hasan imagines them still huddled under their khaki coats like street children as the Turkish boots drop down beside them, spraying mud. Bayonets make for a rude awakening. In the last assault Hasan watched as most of his men were mown down by snapping machine-gun fire before they took a step. He lost count of how many fell back into the trench, killed before they even cleared the sandbags. *Are the Anzacs just waiting, biding their time, before launching an unholy barrage?* Ahead, Hasan can see the first wave of his attack nearly at the enemy line, bayonets raised and bellowing at the Australians, daring them to do their worst.

And then, through the December mist, it happens.

Suddenly the raging Turks all stop in unison. The sound of gunfire peters out. The yelling subsides as perplexed soldiers stand in silence and look down into the enemy trench.

Jemal nudges soldiers aside as Hasan makes his way through his troops to the edge of the trench. From high up on a sandbag he looks down in disbelief.

There is no one there.

Hasan, conditioned to always expect the worst, is suspicious.

'It's a trap. It must be.'

Jemal shrugs. 'If it was, we'd know by now.'

Hasan drops into the Anzac trench and Jemal joins him, both wary of booby-traps. Perplexed and confused, the men of the 47th watch on in silence.

A sudden blast from a rifle propped on the edge of the trench, and the men dive for cover. Jemal and Hasan barely flinch. The two men examine the unmanned gun, smoke still spiralling from its barrel. Hasan sees that it's been set up to shoot at the Ottoman front line automatically. The .303 is fired by a clever system of water-filled tin cans punctured so that they empty gradually, until they pull the trigger. He can't help but admire the ingenuity.

Jemal reloads the rifle and unscrews the stopper on his canteen, about to pour water into one of the cans. He pauses, looking down the barrel at a cluster of soldiers watching at the business end of the rifle, and waves them away.

'Move or be martyred,' he bellows.

The men have learned that an order from a man as rash as Jemal is ignored at their peril. They scramble out of the way as he empties his canteen into the can tied to the trigger. The gun fires with a loud crack. Jemal nods, impressed.

Hasan continues along the trench, passing a table set for a game of chess; one white pawn pushed two squares towards the enemy line. A note in English sits under the piece and reads, 'Your move, Abdul.' Hasan gives a wry smile. Another time, another place, he might have enjoyed meeting this chess player. Strange to think that in the midst of the dehumanising chaos of war, an enemy soldier found solace in such a civilised pastime.

Jemal appears, wielding a cricket bat like a club.

'A weapon?' asks Hasan.

'I watched them play this pointless game near the beach, between barrages.' Jemal holds the bat over his shoulder and swings it through the air before studying it intently. 'Whatever it was, they took it more seriously than the war.'

They are interrupted by a distant cheer, and peer over the sandbags to see the bandleader waving his flag and dancing. He is pointing out to sea. Hasan climbs a ladder and raises his binoculars to see a white wake cutting through the ink-black Aegean and trails of smoke from the departing Anzac troopships as they make a beeline for Greece.

As Hasan's men realise what has happened, shocked silence gives way to waves of celebration. Just moments before, they had resigned themselves to the inevitability of sudden and violent death. The release of tension ignites the gathered Ottoman troops like a lit fuse. Some men fall to their knees in silent prayer. Others weep and congratulate their friends for surviving. But most cheer and shoot their guns into the air, crying, 'Allahu Akbar! Allahu Akbar!'

Today, Hasan thinks, after months of being a passive bystander, God truly is great.

Hasan sits on a sandbag and leans his head back against the trench wall. He takes in the significance of the moment, and doesn't know whether to laugh or cry. After 238 dreadful days of staring at each other across the ditch, strafing each other with machine guns, picking each other off on the way to the latrines, mining each other's trenches, listening to each other's wounded bleed out in no-man's land, and finally tossing gifts of cigarettes and food from trench to trench, the invaders have skulked away in the night. He knew they must, before the winter floods washed them off the cliffs that they had clung to so tenaciously. This is a good thing; it is what they have been praying for. But for a moment he feels bereft – cheated. The enemy has defined him, given him his purpose. But now, to a man, they have suddenly stolen away under cover of darkness without giving him the opportunity to salvage anything positive from this cursed morass.

Yilmaz, the boy soldier, appears, running across no-man's land, out of breath.

'Sir, your binoculars. I could not find . . .' He trails off as he spots them hanging around the major's neck.

With a half-smile Hasan replies, 'Private Yilmaz from Mardin, today was not your day to be martyred.'

The band launches into a Turkish folk song as soldiers throw down their guns and start singing and dancing.

CHAPTER ONE

A man paces across a vast paddock, under a vaulting indigo-blue sky. He performs an oddly choreographed dance; first striding in one direction, then sidling in another; backtracking slowly before turning.

From beneath a dusty brim his eyes scan the rust-red soil. He is blind to the beauty of the sunrise as the first long fingers of rose gold stretch across the Mallee plains, glinting off the strands of parched summer grass.

He stops abruptly, and peers down at his clenched hands like a churchgoer who has forgotten the words. How, he wonders, has he just noticed? Knotted, with skin like bark, they are hands much older than his forty-six years.

In each fist he clasps a short length of brass tubing, polished to a warm patina from years of use. A foot-long length of wire bent into an L-shape protrudes from each tube, like grasshoppers' feelers. As the man moves, the antennae swivel and scout. He follows their lead, weaving across the paddock and watching for the moment when they converge and cross. It will be right there that he will find it, but he never knows how deep down it will be.

Joshua Connor is as tough and unyielding as the land he calls home. Tanned like hide, he is tall with the broad shoulders and well-muscled chest of a man conditioned to long days labouring under the Australian sun. He has neither the time nor the inclination to place any stock in life's mysteries. To him, water divining is just something he can do – just as it was something his mother could do, and her father before that. Take it back a few generations and they would have been called water witches. A bit further back in time, and most likely they would have been burned at the stake. But here, today, in the dry and unforgiving Australian outback where water is life or death, Connor's strange gift is as precious as it is inexplicable. Unyielding and irascible, he is not the most popular man in the district but no one would ever deny that Connor's baffling ability to sense hidden subterranean water has saved many a local family.

Connor pauses and lets the feelers settle, then veers in an arc to his right. His thick-tailed sheepdog shadows him cautiously; he has long since learned to keep a reasonable distance. Any sudden change in Connor's direction could earn him a kick in the ribs. Their boot and paw prints snake through the red soil behind them like plaits, tracing this strange ritual right across the paddock.

The man points to a lonely cluster of Mallee trees, bloated at the base with thirst like dead sheep in a drought. He talks to his dog as he would to a smart child.

'It's here somewhere. Those buggers don't survive on air alone.'

The dog sits patiently in the dust as the sun scales higher above the horizon, the first sting of its rays burning the dawn chill from the air. Connor wipes a bead of sweat from his brow with the back of his hand. *You don't need any special gifts to know today is going to be a scorcher.*

'Let's get this over and done with, mate.'

Connor studies the wires as they slowly rotate, swinging one way and then the other. They settle, pointing along parallel paths to an outcrop of rocks.

'See, soil's different over there. Rocks close to the surface.' He heads in the direction the wires indicate, adjusting his path as they sway to and fro. Now he takes smaller steps, barely shuffling, until the wires swivelling in the brass tubes converge and settle in a cross. Funny, he thinks to himself, how a cross can mean treasure, salvation or death – it just depends.

Connor marks the spot with his heel, digging into the earth four times – one for each point of the compass.

'Right there, boy. Stay.'

The dog settles down on his haunches. He's in for a wait.

Connor begins the punishing walk back to his horse and cart, squinting his blue eyes against the caustic morning light. There is nothing easy about this land. As the ground warms, a raucous insect orchestra strikes up; Connor strides out in time to its beat as the piercing trills cut through the air.

The mare stands patiently in the shade of a ghost gum, stamping her hooves and flicking her ears to ward off the black tide of flies that rises and falls around her. She knows the routine; it's been a long time since Connor last had to tie her to a hitching rail. She's not one to wander off. Wander where, anyway?

Dry as a temperance meeting, Connor sips from a canteen, jumps onto the seat and takes up the reins.

'Time to earn your keep, you old nag.' He pats her rump affectionately and flicks the reins. As the horse begins to move Connor turns her, swivelling the cart around to face the distant spot where the dog stands guard.

The mare picks up pace, casting a red wake of dust into the clear morning air. Connor enjoys the speed, the cool rush of wind against his face. He looks back – the airborne dust, thick as smoke, obscures their path. The cart clatters and jolts as the contents shift – gnarled branches tied in bundles, heavy ropes, a block and tackle, a square canvas bucket, shovels and a pick.

The dog sees them approaching, shifts nervously. It wouldn't be the first time he ended up under one of the mare's hooves.

'Steady, girl.' Connor draws the reins up, bringing the cart to a halt. He jumps down and bends to scratch the dog roughly behind the ears.

'Good boy. No one'll get past you, will they?'

Connor unloads the cart, carefully placing his equipment in neat piles, stalling. He straddles the marker in the dust and lifts the pickaxe above his head.

'Let's hope it's not too deep this time, eh?'

The dog shifts quickly to the side. Connor brings the iron crashing down into the unyielding ground. The impact jolts him, reverberates up his arms, making his teeth clack together.

Connor lifts the pick again, smashes it down. And again. Begrudgingly the brick-hard earth begins to give; small red clumps shift aside as he drives the pick deeper. Enough loose soil now for the shovel. Connor plunges the spade into the dirt, ropey muscles along his arms and back tensing as he clears the first bucket of what he knows will be many more.

He peers down into the bottom of the shallow hole, anticipating the telltale darkening of the soil, the gradual seep of water into the dust, which he knows will tell him when he's close.

Connor glances at the dog, who sits transfixed as always by his master's every move.

'A man can hope, can't he?'

The sun lifts higher above the endless horizon. Connor feels the rising heat against his skin and the first trail of perspiration running between his shoulder blades, down his back and under his belt.

He bends and lifts the pick again.

'Best make yourself comfortable. It's going to be a fight today, mate.'

For Connor the day disappears like a mirage through eyes that sting with salty sweat. Down the hole, he reckons the hours in buckets of dirt, blisters and feet below the surface. One, two, three . . . Each time he emerges from the dark, damp well, blinking like a boobook owl, he tracks the shimmering sun across the sky, sees the shadows lengthening. Fourteen, fifteen . . . Gone is the midday cacophony of parrots and cockatoos as they swoop and soar across the plains. As dusk approaches, Connor is serenaded by the buzz of crickets and the mocking call of a kookaburra perched on a gnarled tree nearby. Night is on the counterattack.

The dog peers down at his master, at work deep beneath the surface now in a neatly excavated hole. The walls of the well are reinforced with a scaffolding of Mallee-scrub branches, interlocked and methodically lashed with rope to hold back the brittle, crumbling earth.

Aching and spent, Connor bends, his large frame restricted by the confines of the well. He winces as he lifts the canvas bucket full of muddy red soil, attaching it to the block and tackle. He climbs up the bracing timbers to the surface and lifts the bucket, hoisting the rope hand over hand, calloused palms raw. Connor empties the cool, damp earth onto the hot dust that still holds the warmth of the sun's rays.

He pauses, hands on hips, bone tired. Looks down at the dog, now lying on his side, snapping at flies.

'Don't want to take over for a spell, do you?'

Connor breathes deeply, clambers back down into the pit. He crouches, feeling the soil between his fingers. *It's wet. No doubt about it. Can't be far off now. She's a tease.*

'Time to show it who's boss,' he mumbles.

He grabs a long shaft of steel leaning against the wall behind him – almost as long as Connor is tall, and flattened at one end to a chisel-like point. He lifts it above his head and slams it into the mud.

The earth yields. A vein of red stone cracks, and water belches out like a busted fountain. Connor raises the steel and strikes again, letting out a conqueror's roar that is lost on a dog, a horse and a barren and empty landscape.

Distracted for a moment, his mind baked, Connor doesn't notice how quickly the water is rising. Up to his knees already. It never comes this fast.

He grabs for his tools, blind hands fumbling beneath the water. He reaches for the ladder, tossing the shovel, bucket and pick up to the surface.

Not far enough – the pick catches on a protruding branch and tumbles back down the shaft into the swirling red water.

Could leave it. Should leave it. But how am I going to replace a pick out here in the middle of nowhere?

Connor curses and scrambles back down the well. He ducks into the water to retrieve the pick.

As he surfaces again, his eyes stinging with water and silt, Connor stretches, fingers searching for a beam. It doesn't seem fair that this has happened at the dead end of the day when he is spent. His weary hand grasps a branch and he levers himself upwards. Suddenly the branch shoots clear of the wall, slamming into Connor's forehead and dazing him. He falls back, grappling desperately for a handhold as the rising water undercuts the scaffolding and the branches tug at him with sirens' claws.

The dog yaps madly around the collapsing hole. Connor struggles to keep his head above the surging water. White stars exploding in his eyes from the clout to his head, he fights the grey fog that threatens to descend on him. He looks up at a perfect circle of sky, fringed by a ring of twisted branches. As the blood runs from his gouged scalp all he sees is a crown of thorns.

He feels the water cleanse the day's sweat and dust from his skin. He lets go, a soporific detachment washing over him.

He is done fighting.

Surrender.

He shuts his eyes, accepting the inevitable. And yet. There. The water, rising to the surface, places salvation within reach; the lip of the well is now just above his head.

Connor's survival instinct kicks in. Submission, whether to fate, chance or a higher power, has never come naturally to him. Connor brawls with this mean landscape every day. He reaches out and grabs the edge, hauling himself to safety. He collapses on solid ground with a wet whack. The dog licks his bloodied face, whining, and Connor shoves him away.

'Thanks for all your help back there, mate.'

❖

In the early evening light, Connor stands under a make-shift shower in his long johns. From a corrugated-iron tank perched on a stand, a stream of clear, restorative water pours over him. He peels back his sodden underwear and the sun-warmed water turns red as it sluices the dust from his chest and back. He rubs his hair, wincing as his fingers find the jagged wound on his scalp. He picks the dried blood from his hair, not wanting to alarm Eliza.

Behind him a windmill, cobbled together from a cart-wheel and flattened kero tins, clanks and murmurs as it pumps water from the deep well below.

Connor looks across the yard towards their unassuming home. He built it with the same hands that now struggle to hold a cake of soap and push it round his underarm. He had paced it out, carted the red brick and iron sheeting from Horsham, dug the postholes, split the shingles and papered the walls. He recalls riding all the way to Adelaide to pick out the wood-fired stove. He laboured by day and slept under the stars by night to build this home – all for the family that he had hoped was to come.

The home faces north to catch the sun in the depths of winter when chilling winds blow across the plains from the south, and is shielded from the summer sun by a deep verandah.

How many times had Eliza told the boys about the day their father stood back, hands on hips, and judged his work done? He had dressed in his Sunday best, ridden into town and pledged his troth to Eliza, his childhood sweetheart. When she'd seen what he had built her out here in the middle of nowhere, she'd understood how much this hard, bashful man cared for her, and wept.

'Who . . . *Dad*?' the boys laughed.

Connor glances towards the bay window. Eliza stands silhouetted against the lace curtains, backlit by the flickering light of the kerosene lantern, absently picking at tendrils of hair falling around her temples.

Connor turns off the showerhead, dries himself, and passes along the concrete path past a row of well-tended yellow and red roses. A tyre swing hangs from an ancient peppercorn tree. A colony of boys' clothing swings in the evening breeze, pegged neatly on the washing line like fruit bats. Shorts, overalls, shirts and socks – some so small it's impossible to imagine them fitting a human being.

Connor tosses his sodden clothes into a copper washtub, grabs a dry outfit off a hook near the flywire door at the back of the house and dresses – slowly and deliberately. He grabs a comb from a chipped enamel mug sitting on the back stoop and runs it through his hair.

There's a moment of quiet as the day gives way to night, and the water diviner drops his shoulders and exhales for what feels like the first time today.

The screen door swings, screeches and slams.

'Sounds like that hinge could do with some oil. I'll get onto it tomorrow morning.'

Eliza sits at the table, hunched over and immersed in the job at hand. She tilts her head towards Connor and gives a papery smile. Although she still has the fine complexion and clear green eyes he first fell in love with, the grey streaks in her hair belie her relative youth and signal an advancing frailty. She seems to be disappearing; folding in on herself. The sharp line of her fine nose and dark hollows beneath her jawline become more prominent every day. Where once she had filled her pin tucked, tightly waisted dresses with womanly curves and soft skin, now she stitches new seams into her clothes to disguise her diminishing frame. When Connor has occasion to embrace her, she feels as insubstantial as an armful of chicken bones.

The day is not over for her. She works with brush and cloth to polish a line of schoolboys' boots to a mirror-like shine, her knuckles stained nugget-brown.

'Lizzie. . .? Everything all right?'

She doesn't glance up, trying to avoid his gaze. 'Dinner's waiting.'

Connor looks towards the table where a solitary, uninviting meal sits; cold pressed ox tongue, mustard pickles and some slices of bread. Next to the plate sits a small brown paper–wrapped parcel, opened but face down.

He moves towards the table. 'Lizzie – what's this? Who's it from?'

Eliza rubs at one small boot and holds it up to the lantern light.

'For goodness' sake. Arthur's worn through the toe of his boot again. What on earth does he do to them?' Her face softens as she looks up at Connor. 'The boys are all in bed. They're waiting for you to read to them.'

'I'm bone tired, Lizzie.'

'You mustn't disappoint them, Joshua. It's their favourite part of the day. They waited up specially.'

Connor concedes with a resigned nod and drags his waterlogged body down the hall towards the bedroom door.

❖

Connor lowers himself carefully onto the end of one of the three single beds. He smiles and takes a small blue leather-bound volume from a bedside table. He opens it and begins to read *The Arabian Nights*, the boys' favourite.

Prince Hussein called to the man and asked him why the carpet he wished to sell was so expensive, saying, 'It must be made from something quite extraordinary.'

The Merchant replied, 'My Prince, your amazement will be all the greater when I tell you that it is enchanted.'

Connor's voice, honeyed and sure, drifts through the room and down the hall.

'Whoever sits on this magic carpet and closes his eyes may be transported through the air in an instant to wherever his heart desires to be.'

Connor closes the book and rests his hand on the hollow place in the mattress where his son should lie.

Moonlight shines in the window and illuminates the three empty beds, cold and unjumped-on, the white pillows missing sleep-tousled heads, the neatly made starched sheets unrumpled by sweaty slumber.

He is alone.

※

After he composes himself Connor slips out of the bedroom, closes the door and makes the desolate walk back to the kitchen table. Eliza sits, arms crossed, her heart burnished raw like the shoes lined up before her. Connor takes the seat opposite, with the small, brown parcel and years of arrested grief perched between them. His dinner sits, untouched, at the other end of the table.

Connor has been reading to empty beds now for four years, ever since the first telegram arrived from the army telling them that 'regrettably' Henry was missing, presumed dead.

'Read to him,' Lizzie beseeched. 'I'll close my eyes and imagine him back here safely. He's just lost. Not dead.'

Connor read to comfort her. It seemed to be the only thing he could do to help. Within a fortnight the second telegram arrived; young Edward had gone missing on the same day as his brother. The message had been lost, sent to a Connor family in Queensland. Connor imagined the relief that family felt when they realised the telegram was not for them. He wanted dearly, desperately to be that Mr Connor of Brisbane.

When Lizzie saw the postmaster arriving at the front of the house with a third piece of pink paper clutched solemnly in his hand, she ran out the back door, pulling at Connor's arm and begging him to hide too.

'Don't let him deliver it. If he can't deliver it it can't be true.'

All three boys had been lost on the same day. Connor is certain that it was the cruelty of the disjointed arrival of the letters that began to unhinge Lizzie. Each time the couple held one another on the bed. Lizzie wailed until she was hoarse and her eyes were too bruised to cry. He shook uncontrollably; swallowing his grief and feeling it ricochet through his chest bruising his ribcage from the inside. By the third telegram he was too shell-shocked to grieve properly. He read Arthur's name with grim resignation, gave one involuntary guttural cry and waited for the flood of emotion. It did not come. He was cauterised from the inside out.

For the next year Lizzie lived in sleepless limbo.
'I'm *presuming* they are not dead. That's what the letters say. Missing. Not dead,' she would declare whenever he made the mistake of speaking about any of the boys in the past tense.

Initially Connor read to an empty room to offer Lizzie some peace. When he tried to give it away she shrieked at him and accused him of wanting the boys dead. He realised that for her the storytelling had transcended comfort and was now a liturgy, in the same way the shoe polishing had become a ritual. Long after Connor surrendered hope that their sons were still alive, Lizzie maintained her belief. In her troubled mind, to read was a declaration of faith.

Connor reaches out, feels the crackle of the wrapping paper and coarse twine and the unmistakable form of a book hidden within. He turns it, glances down and sees the opened end and the all too familiar mark of the Australian Imperial Forces. *No. How? Why now after so long?*

He places it back down on the table, avoiding the subject.

'So, I hit water at fifteen feet. Bit brackish, but good pressure . . . a bit too much pressure, actually . . .' Connor looks up, sees tears welling in Eliza's eyes as she stares at the package.

'They didn't even wipe the mud off . . .'

'Lizzie, it's been four years . . .'

Her eyes flash. 'You think you're so clever. But in the end, it counts for nothing. You find water, but you can't even find your own children.'

Eliza stands, shoving the chair to one side, toppling it with a crash that echoes through the empty house.

'Why can't you find them? You lost them!'

In this forlorn home in the middle of nowhere with the nearest neighbours many miles away, she retreats, sobbing, to the only refuge available to her. The door to their bedroom slams.

An all too familiar wave of helplessness washes over Joshua Connor. It's been a long time since he's known how to soothe Eliza's grief. He picks up the parcel on the table and unfolds the paper wrapping. Enclosed within is a muddy, dog-eared diary. Connor gingerly folds back the leather cover and smoothes the brittle pages within. Interleaved between a haphazard collection of handwritten letters, rough sketches, cartoons and maps is a crumpled photograph. A studio shot. Three handsome young men in A.I.F. uniforms, arms proudly draped over each other's shoulders, smiling broadly.

Art, Henry and Ed had been the pride of the district. Tall, long-limbed, blue-eyed, and all handy with a football and a cricket bat.

'We're the only three brothers in Australia to score centuries in the same day,' they boasted, without a skerrick of proof. When challenged Art would retort, 'Well, I've never heard of any others, have you?' as if that should be verification enough.

In Lizzie's eyes, her boys died perfect. But Connor prefers to remember them warts and all, and enjoy their imperfections. Arthur, the eldest, would be twenty-five years old now. He inherited his father's stubbornness and sense of honour along with his mop of brown hair. As his son matured Connor wondered if the boy's bull-headedness would ever evolve into the kind of perseverance and backbone a Mallee farmer needs. Not that it is of any conse-quence now, but Connor had looked forward to seeing what sort of man Art would become.

Henry was two years younger than Art. Sandwiched between his brothers, he'd always fought fiercely for his fair share of attention and approval. More solid and muscular than Art and Edward, Henry was their enforcer on the football field, rushing to his brothers' defence if they caught a stray elbow or fist from an opponent. He was fearless. Connor would never forget the day he found Henry, aged about twelve, standing on the shed roof preparing to jump down into a dray full of hay. It had to be a twenty-foot drop; at least four times his height.

'Don't be a fool,' Connor yelled. 'You'll break some-thing.'

'No I won't,' Henry cried as he launched himself. 'I've already done it four times!'

He knows it is irrational, but Connor runs his fingers over the photograph, imagining the light stubble on his boys' cheeks and their coarse hair. He recognises the glint in Edward's eye, the cheeky little bastard. When he enlisted at seventeen he lied about his age. Lizzie threatened to write to the army and report him but he talked her round.

'Mum, don't bother. By the time you write to them and send it, and then they write back, I'll be eighteen anyhow.'

For Connor age means nothing. Seventeen or seventy, Art, Henry and Ed are still his unruly, wilful, larrikin boys who were going to follow in his footsteps and work this farm. That had been the plan, anyway. Until they were shot dead somewhere called Gallipoli.

He has become accustomed to feeling their loss as a sharp pain that pierces his gut. It's too much to bear. Connor slips the photo back into the body of the diary and turns to the front page.

He reads the inscription: *Arthur Connor: My Grand Tour, 1915.* Connor will never forget waving them off, young bulls in spring, like it was a holiday. A restrained hug, a scant few words and Privates Art, Henry and Edward Connor pushed and shouldered each other as they mounted their horses and then raced each other out of sight and over the horizon, leaving a cloud of dust in their wake.

The early diary entries are detailed, expressive. A letter slips from between the pages along with a small photo of a pretty girl with long brown hair, happy eyes and a bright smile. It is Art's sweetheart, Edith. On the next page, a pressed gum leaf.

Connor flicks to the end of the diary. The entries become briefer; cursory. Going through the motions. The page falls open at the final entry.

5 August. Lone Pine. Hot as Hades but maybe worse.

CHAPTER TWO

P *urple thunderheads roil shorewards. Sheets of lightning strafe the gloom. Or are they flashes of shell fire?*

A young man lies wounded amongst hundreds – perhaps thousands – of bloodied combatants. Around him mud and gore spatter in gruesome clumps. The battle rages; a deafening clamour. Shattered nerves, shuddering. Thunderclaps, or mortar rounds? Impossible to know.

Wasted limbs seized by uncontrollable tremors. His face bloodied, he winces in agony.

Rifles repeat and flash. Bayonets clash and then disappear inside khaki and skin. Dying screams cut through the bedlam. Bullets whistle, thwacking into flesh like stones hitting water. Incendiary devices flare. The muddy ground shakes from the thud of artillery shells as they hail from the sky.

He squeezes his eyes shut, presses clenched fists against his ears to block out the noise.

Inaudibly, he murmurs, 'Tangu. Tangu.' Louder now, 'TANGU!'

A squelching sound, like a boot extricating itself from the mud.

Unsurprised, the soldier feels the ground shift. Invisible to those around him, he begins to rise up, levitating above the chaos. Lifted skywards atop a small, mud-soaked Turkish carpet, he weaves through ghastly battlefield tableaux, skimming just above the heads of the soldiers below.

He looks down dispassionately, observing the now silent scene of devastation. He passes an Ottoman soldier in the basket of an observation balloon who pays him no mind.

Clean air.

Silence.

He gazes up at the stars as the carpet rides the gentle currents of the breeze, out over a calm, moonlit sea.

CHAPTER THREE

The dog yelps desperately at the screen door, scratching and scrabbling at the fly mesh with his paws. Connor starts awake, stiff from a night spent asleep in the armchair. Art's diary falls from his leg onto the rug as he stumbles to the door. Something is terribly wrong.

Connor rushes through the house to the kitchen. The customary morning smells and sounds – the clatter of pots and pans; the thud of plates and cutlery landing on the timber table; wood fire crackling in the stove; bacon grilling on the griddle – are absent.

The small room is empty and cold, the embers in the fireplace dead and black.

'Eliza! Lizzie!'

He has a shadow of a memory, of Lizzie's light footsteps on the floorboards and her frail lips kissing his forehead as he slept in the chair. *Was it real or imagined?*

He flings open the screen door and is momentarily blinded by the early morning sun. The dog barks, charging to and fro along the concrete path, leaving muddy paw prints. Seeing Connor step outside, he bolts towards the windmill and dam, looking back to make sure his master is following. A sick feeling of foreboding grips Connor.

'Lizzie? Lizzie!' he bellows. 'Lizzie!'

He sprints desperately across the yard and vaults the low fence of the rose garden. He is oblivious to the thorns ripping at his shirt and skin. As Connor scrambles up the dirt levee surrounding the dam, he registers the neatly folded pile of clothes stacked in the dirt. His heart sinks. *No. Not now. Not more.* Disbelieving, he feels the dust shift beneath his boots, the morning sky's blue dome spinning above his head. Connor's mind scrabbles hopelessly for possible explanations. *Swimming? Washing?* But in his heart he knows the truth.

'No! Lizzie?'

Connor reaches the rim of the dam and straight away sees Lizzie floating just below the surface, the rust-stained water casting her body in a translucent sepia light. She lies face down, arms outstretched. Her long hair is loose and fans about her head like a halo; her petticoats billow and encircle her splayed legs. The water in the dam is stirred by a warm breeze, barely perceptible waves breaking the surface and gently rippling along Eliza's drifting body. The movement is strangely peaceful, causing her fingers to sway and wave.

Connor bellows and charges down the embankment into the water. He wades out to Eliza with mud tugging and sucking at his boots. The water is shallow at first but with every step the dam floor drops away until the water reaches his chest. He reaches out and takes Lizzie's cold hand, turning her and drawing her to him. He pushes the hair from her face, presses his lips to her forehead and sobs.

'Oh, God! Lizzie, no! Please, no! What have you done?'

Connor stands in mute grief then, cradling his wife as water laps against his torso. It's his fault. He let his guard down momentarily. A tear splashes into the weak tea-coloured water of the dam. The war has claimed another victim.

The sun begins beating hard on Connor's head before he wades towards the edge of the dam and sits on the muddy bank. He nurses Eliza's limp body in his arms, pressing his cheek to hers as he rocks back and forth. He stares at her once pretty face for a moment, her translucent green eyes now dim, her soft, carmine lips turned grey. He gently picks sticks and gum leaves from her hair.

The dog sits by his side. A flock of scarlet-winged black cockatoos swoops past, cawing and startling the chooks that peck at grass seeds in the dust.

Connor looks up at the unforgiving heavens and wails.

❖

'Dear Lord, give me strength . . .' Father McIntyre murmurs angrily to himself, shifting uncomfortably in his vestments.

Any other day, the searing heat alone would have been enough to plunge the priest into a foul mood. But today he has caught sight of something through the arched window on the side of his humble church that displeases him no end. Since his exile to this godforsaken parish, there is no shortage of things that cause him displeasure. There are veritable plagues of them.

'Why today, of all days? In this blessed heat?'

He fans at his face with a bible, but the leaves of the Good Book prove to be quite ineffectual against the infernal heat of the Mallee summer. Sweat beads on his head, trickles down the strands of hair pasted to his scalp and pools in the tissue paper–like folds of his neck. He tugs at his sodden clerical collar and scratches, a vicious heat rash doing its best to worsen his mood even further.

Although he possesses the meagre frame of a penitent, beneath the oppressive weight of his cassock even his gaunt thighs find a way of chafing against one another. The coarse fabric and the slick of sweat irritate his legs to the point of utter distraction. Tonight he'll pass the time popping the white eruptions of pus but for now he has little choice but to stay put and play the part of the country pastor. That means dealing with the man standing waist deep in a pit outside.

Beside the whitewashed timber church is a small cemetery shaded by a gnarled and ancient peppercorn tree, its branches laden with plump, pink fruit. Between the weatherworn timber crucifixes and carved headstones, Joshua Connor swings his pick with a regular rhythm, putting the tools of his trade to a much grimmer task. His horse and cart stand beside the grave; in the back, poking out from under a tarpaulin, is a long handcrafted coffin. McIntyre can see that Connor has planed the raw timber planks, bevelled the edges, polished it all with linseed oil and fashioned a simple cross to affix to the lid.

Connor's muscles strain under a pale blue shirt as he puts down the pick and hefts his shovel. Dark circles of perspiration form under his arms as he shifts the dark red soil into a neatly formed mound teetering on the edge of the grave.

Father McIntyre watches through the church window with growing agitation.

'Who in blazes does he think he is?'

To his relief Connor climbs out of the freshly dug grave and heads towards the church, sparing the priest from having to go out into the furnace to confront him.

McIntyre hears stomping and the scraping of boots. The door of the weatherboard church creaks open, allowing a blast of searingly hot air to blow into the open hall. McIntyre points to the door and winces.

'Mr Connor . . . if you wouldn't mind . . .?'

Connor turns awkwardly and closes the door before entering. The priest draws his thin lips into a semblance of a smile as he grits his teeth, the sound of his molars grinding together setting his nerves on edge. He assumes the outward appearance of a holy man: hands clenched tightly before his sternum, head tilted slightly to one side, and what he considers to be an expression of benevolence and understanding pasted to his face. Connor shuffles towards him, looking out of place. He stands before the priest, shifting on the spot, like a boy caught skulking out of Sunday School.

'Mr Connor . . . Joshua. You have been through a difficult time. These things are sent to try us.' He shakes his head. 'However, you can't just come here and start digging in the churchyard without so much as a by-your-leave.'

McIntyre swirls his hand in the water of the baptismal font. He wrings out his handkerchief and mops his neck.

'You understand, my son, in all conscience, I cannot bury your wife if she took her own life. Our Lord is the giver of life and He alone can take it away. Consecrated ground is His promise to the faithful.'

Connor scoffs, hands fixed defensively on his hips. 'She fell in the dam and drowned. So your conscience is clear.'

The priest has seen enough of human failing over the years to doubt Connor's story. Besides which, one of the few indulgences he allows himself in this hellhole is to participate fully in the very fertile local gossip circle. And it didn't take long for word of the true cause of Eliza Connor's demise to become the focus of many a hushed conversation over morning and afternoon tea. He's determined to make sure that Joshua Connor knows he can't pull the wool over his eyes.

'Three sons killed. That's quite an ordeal for her – for both of you. But as the book of Job teaches us, God sets us these trials for a reason. Many families in the parish have made similar sacrifices for King and Country.'

Momentarily distracted by a locust picking its way across the lectern, McIntyre turns back to see the flush of anger in Connor's face.

'Father, we've had our fair share of trials. You owe her this much.'

Incensed, Father McIntyre straightens his back and rises to his full height. He places his bible on top of the locust and presses, listening for the crunch of its armour and the soft pop of its belly.

'You know, you have some nerve coming in here and making demands. You haven't stepped inside this place for four years. No confession. No communion. You are all but lost to God.'

'Yes, and when my time comes you and God can feed me to the pigs for all I care. But this woman, Eliza, you knew her. She was here every Sunday, listening to your preaching. Don't damn her for my failings.'

There's no hiding the fury in his voice.

'I've dug the grave, I made the coffin. All you need to do is say some words and throw some dirt.'

In spite of his anger, Father McIntyre knows this is not a man to cross. He decides to change tack. He looks out to the graveyard where Connor's horse stands, hitched to the cart.

'That cart out there – paint it and it would make a useful benefaction for our community. As an offering to God, you understand.'

McIntyre can tell the message isn't lost on Connor. The pound of flesh. Connor smiles wryly.

'He's taken everything else. He might as well have that too.'

❖

An unspoken deal done, the two men meet at Lizzie's graveside later in the day. A group of locals turns out to watch as Father McIntyre races through the burial rite: Lizzie's older sister, Ivy, and friends who understand her grief firsthand. His duty done, the compromised priest hurries away with almost indecent haste, clutching his censer. The musty tang of incense lingers in the air as the mourners drift from the graveside.

Not ready yet to leave Eliza's graveside, Connor watches a swarm of young children dressed in their Sunday best, blissfully unaware of the solemnity of the occasion. They play hide-and-seek amongst the gravestones as their mothers stand together and converse quietly in the shade of the gnarled peppercorn tree. For ones so young they have donned mourning black far too often. Their fathers now exist only as stern-faced, uniformed men in black and white photographs, their loss ever-present as a faint yet unrelenting sense of anxiety.

Rainbow is now a town of widows and old men and wraiths in greatcoats with dead eyes and hair grey too soon. Absent is the banter and idiotic laughter of young men, the reckless canter of their horses or the shrill tweet of an umpire's whistle on Saturday afternoons. When the faces began appearing in the local paper surrounded by wreaths, the town fell silent, the joy bled away.

An old man struggles to his feet from one of the chairs arranged by the side of the grave to salute a young soldier who limps past, leaning heavily on his wife's arm. The veteran nods his head, acknowledging the tribute, but averts his face, ashamed of the disfigurement that is only partially disguised by an unconvincing tin prosthetic device.

Connor watches him pass, and remembers the young man as he was before the war. He feels a gentle touch on his arm. Edith, the girl who would have been his daughter-in-law, follows his gaze as the veteran continues his agonising struggle across the cemetery.

'Anytime I feel my heart breaking, I think of what could have been – what Art might have been like if he'd come back to us like that. Sometimes, I think it is better that he died at his beautiful best.'

She shuts her eyes and murmurs a prayer, then kneels and places a sprig of something green and fragrant into Eliza's grave.

'Rosemary. To remember.' She looks up at Connor, her bright blue eyes shining with tears. 'We've made scones and tea for everyone. Will you . . .?'

'You're very kind, Edith. But I think I need to sit with Lizzie a while.'

She smiles sadly. 'Soon, then?'

Connor nods vaguely. Edith reaches up and gives him an awkward hug, then slowly walks back to the path to join the other mourners as they leave the churchyard.

Connor kneels by Eliza's grave, head bowed.

'I will find them, love. I'll bring them home to you. I promise.'

Back at home, Connor sits in the darkened room, furniture shrouded in sheets, curtains drawn. Motes of dust sparkle in the narrow shafts of sunlight shining through chinks in the blinds.

Ivy and her sons helped him pack up the house. He has given her all the things Eliza held dear: the blue and white willow-pattern china; a ruby cut-glass vase; the delicate porcelain figurine of a shepherdess with cupid's-bow lips; her sterling silver–backed mirror and ivory hair comb.

He stands, turns and looks around the room one last time, then pushes open the screen door and farewells the only home he has known for twenty-five years.

Connor looks at the pits on either side of the path where the ladies from the church have claimed the rosebushes. Edith is going to plant one of them at Eliza's graveside. Connor knows those roses were the only things left that had made his wife smile. The dog sniffs at the ground and cocks his leg on the upturned earth.

'It was the only sensible thing to do, old fella. They won't last long out here without me to look after them.'

He bends down and scratches the dog roughly behind his ears.

'C'mon mate. Let's get you some dinner.'

The dog looks at Connor quizzically. He knows the daily routine and the sun is still high in the sky – much too early to be eating. But never one to turn down a meal, he trots after his master to the back of the house, tail wagging.

Connor throws some offcuts from a sheep carcass he butchered a few days ago into the dog's bowl.

While the dog tucks into the unexpected bounty, Connor walks to the small shed near the tank stand and fetches his rifle. Sitting on the back steps, he loads it – slowly and deliberately.

He stands and walks over to where the dog is licking the bowl clean. Connor bends and gives him one last scruff on the head.

'You're a good fella. It's a bit like the roses, you see. Except you're not much use to anyone other than me. Never were any bloody good as a sheepdog. You understand, don't you, mate? There's no place for you where I'm going.'

He places the barrel of the rifle against the dog's head, looks away and fires.

Connor hears the thud as the dog's body slumps into the dust. Too shell-shocked to grieve another loss, he drops the rifle and walks away without looking back.

CHAPTER FOUR

An open horse-drawn carriage bumps across undulating ground towards a military checkpoint. Major Hasan and Sergeant Jemal are seated in uncomfortable silence on the bench seat, jolting and knocking awkwardly against each other. A third man, Lieutenant Greeves, sits opposite Jemal, wearing the distinctive slouch hat and khaki uniform of the Anzac troops. Sergeant Jemal is wearing a traditional cloth *kabalak* on his head and the brass Arabic numerals of the 47th Regiment on his lapels. For the duration of the trip from Kelia Bay, he has been flicking black agate *tesbih* beads with one hand and tidying his prodigious moustache with the other. His brooding brown eyes do not leave Greeves.

At the barrier, a uniformed soldier draws himself up and raises his hand, signalling the driver to halt. As the two Turks watch on, Greeves alights from the carriage and salutes, his softly corpulent belly straining at the gilt buttons of his tunic. The man at the barrier returns the greeting and introduces himself as Sergeant Tucker.

'Lieutenant Greeves, Sergeant. Here to escort Major Hasan Bey to Lieutenant Colonel Hilton at the War Graves Commission.'

Greeves' flat vowels betray his New Zealand heritage; Hasan has learned to recognise the accent. Greeves passes a sheaf of official papers to the sergeant.

Sergeant Tucker narrows his eyes and glares at Greeves' passengers. 'I know who he is.' He hawks a sticky gob of phlegm from the back of his throat and spits it into the dust. Jemal rises in his seat, indignant, but Hasan places a calming hand on his arm and speaks in Turkish. 'No need. We have already beaten them once.'

Tucker examines the paperwork, his dark eyes darting between the typed document and the Turks in the cart.

'Right. Everything seems to be in order.'

After Greeves heaves himself back into the cart, Tucker jumps in and sits opposite Hasan. Struggling to retain his military bearing as they make slow and ungainly passage across the uneven ground, Hasan fixes his sight at some point in the indeterminate distance, avoiding Sergeant Tucker's unwavering and antagonistic stare.

Jemal is less diplomatic. He glowers at the angry sergeant and grumbles to Hasan in Turkish under his breath, 'So we need an escort in our own country now. This is madness. Why bring us back here?'

Hasan makes no attempt to answer. After all that passed four years ago, he never thought he would return to this accursed place. *All that remains here is death.*

The good-natured Lieutenant Greeves tries to ease the palpable tension between his fellow passengers. He flicks open a silver cigarette case and offers it to the Ottoman soldiers. Jemal raises an eyebrow and takes two, slipping them into his breast pocket without thanking him. Greeves extends the cigarette case to Hasan.

'Cig-a-rette?' He mimics lighting and smoking a cigarette. 'You want smoke, sir?'

The carriage hits a pothole, and the cigarettes become
airborne.

'Damn. Sorry, sir.' Greeves scrabbles to retrieve them
as they roll and bounce across the floor. He abandons his
efforts when he realises that the majority of the cigarettes
have landed in Hasan's lap.

Hasan contemplates the well-meaning lieutenant coolly
and does nothing to assist him.

The carriage continues its progress across the broken
earth. They pass over a ridge and despite himself, Hasan
is taken aback by the beauty of the Aegean shore that
stretches out before them, heavily wooded islands visible
in the far distance and sunlight reflecting on the gentle
waters. During the many months they spent entrenched on
this hideous escarpment, he rarely had the opportunity to
appreciate the view.

Shouts and the clatter of equipment draw Hasan's attention to their destination, a makeshift encampment on the
side of the ridge. Village labourers lead trains of donkeys
to tents where soldiers unload supplies and equipment.
Clerks officiously check off lists as uniformed men struggle
past, heavily laden with picks, shovels, buckets and timber.

As the cart slows, Sergeant Tucker vaults to the ground
and Hasan watches him make his way towards an officer
who is directing the bustle in the camp like a ringmaster.

Tall, broad-shouldered and suntanned, Lieutenant Colonel
Cecil Hilton is just thirty years of age. He directs the local

workers in broken Turkish, switching quickly to English to fire off an order to one of his men. It's unusual to find such a young man in command of such an important commission, but his aptitude and intelligence marked him for early promotion.

Hilton oversees the hive of activity on the hillside and asserts his authority gently but firmly to ensure the organised chaos does not descend into utter bedlam. He strides purposefully towards an open area where two paint-spattered soldiers are hard at work, painting hundreds of wooden crosses white and, by default, half the hillside. Neither Private Dawson nor Private Thomas notices the approach of their commanding officer.

'God Almighty, Dawson!' marvels Thomas. 'Could you be more cack-handed? How you managed to survive four years on the front I'll never know.'

Dawson puts down his brush and strikes a pose. 'I put a lot of it down to good looks.'

Lieutenant Colonel Hilton coughs, his blue eyes crinkling at the corners and his mouth hiding a smile beneath his militarily precise moustache. 'I take it neither of you were house painters back home?'

Dawson laughs. 'It's hard to believe, I know. But no, sir. Never lifted a paintbrush in my life till now. Thinking about taking it up when I get back home though.'

'When they're dry, send them up to Baby 700 in the cart.'

'How many are you wanting, sir?'

'Whatever you've got.'

A puffing Sergeant Tucker approaches Hilton and salutes. 'We've got company, sir. It's him.'

Hilton watches as the horse-drawn carriage draws to a halt. An uneasy quiet settles over the Anzac soldiers who

41

have gathered around to inspect the new arrivals. Hasan stands, arranges his sword and belt and alights from the cart, brushing cigarettes from his lap.

Tucker glowers and murmurs under his breath to Dawson. 'Four years ago they would've given me a bloody VC for shooting that bastard.'

In contrast to the Anzacs' angry reception, the Turkish villagers throng around Hasan, doffing their hats and bowing, awestruck to find themselves in the presence of a celebrated war hero. Hasan nods his head, acknowledging their greeting.

Hilton approaches Hasan. Even if the Turkish major was not wearing polished black boots, a dress sword, and a breast full of impressive medals, his dignity and noble carriage would mark him as a man of high rank.

Lieutenant Greeves stands at the major's side and salutes. 'Lieutenant Colonel Hilton. May I present Major Hasan Bey? Major Bey was commander of –'

Hilton corrects Greeves. 'No, Lieutenant. It's just "Major Hasan". "Bey" just means "Mr".'

Greeves' round cheeks flush. Embarrassed, but seeming not to comprehend Hilton's explanation, he continues. 'Right. Yes. Thank you, sir. So, Mr Bey here was in charge of the 47th Turkish Regiment. Apparently he gave our boys what for at Lonesome Pine, sir.'

'We all know who *Major* Hasan is. Thank you, Lieutenant.' Hilton turns to Hasan.

'*Merhaba. Hoş geldiniz.*'

Hasan smiles, his eyebrows raised, clearly taken aback by the greeting in his own tongue. '*Hoş bulduk. Türkçe biliyor musunuz?*'

An uncomfortable silence descends as it becomes apparent that Hilton has exhausted his conversational Turkish. Hasan holds his gaze. Hilton is forced to break the deadlock.

'English?'

'No, I'm Turkish. But I speak French, German, Greek and a little English. What would you prefer?' Hasan replies.

Hilton swallows. 'Let's stick with English for now. How was your ride out here?'

Hasan ignores the question. He looks across the desolate ridges and deserted beaches. 'I see you have finally taken the peninsula.'

Hilton smiles. 'Yes. Lost the battle, won the war. Chai?'

❖

The two men perch on folding canvas chairs inside Hilton's tent. They have little to say to each other as they drink tea and swat flies. Looming above them, pinned to a board, is a large map of the Gallipoli Peninsula.

Hilton coughs, businesslike. 'We've started working this area . . .' He gestures at the map with his teaspoon. 'From the Nek to Hill 971. I assume they briefed you fully at the War Office in Constantinople? We would appreciate your help locating our dead.'

Hasan raises an eyebrow. '*Your* dead?'

'We lost ten thousand Anzacs here at Gallipoli. We still don't know where half of them are.' Hilton's voice betrays his anger. 'Some were buried properly but a lot of the graves have been lost or washed away since we evacuated . . .'

'You didn't evacuate. You retreated,' Hasan corrects the Anzac officer. 'So now you build your cemetery on our soil?'

'I have a duty to honour them, and that's what I'll be doing – with or without your help.'

Hasan studies Hilton. 'You were here?'

Hilton answers with a brusque nod. 'First Light Horse.'

Hasan seems to hesitate, to relent. 'What do you need of me?'

Hilton draws a deep breath and returns to the map, taking advantage of the detente born of shared experience. 'The land has changed, but you know this area better than any of us. I'm hoping you could help us locate the units we lost track of.'

'I'll need a horse.' Hasan finishes his tea and stands, moving towards the tent's door. He pauses. 'You know, we lost seventy thousand men here . . . at Çanakkale. For me, this place is one big grave.'

Before Hilton can reply, Hasan turns and walks out into the daylight.

◆

Hilton rides on horseback along the ridge, at the head of a trail of mounted soldiers. The view across the Dardanelle Straits, the gateway to Constantinople and the Black Sea, is idyllic. Gentle waves glitter as a cluster of small, brightly painted fishing boats bob in the wake of a white steamship bound for the city.

Behind Hilton, Greeves urges his horse into a trot and draws alongside Sergeant Tucker and Privates Dawson and Thomas. He throws his left arm out in an expansive gesture, indicating the perfect panorama below.

'Dunno what you fellas were belly-aching about. It's the Garden of bloody Eden here!' As one, Thomas, Dawson

44

and Tucker give him a dead stare and keep riding in a grim procession.

Hilton reins in his horse briefly, allowing Hasan to catch up with him. Hasan indicates the summit.

'If your troops had taken this hill we would have been finished. You nearly did it on the first day. It would all have been over so quickly.'

'How close did we get?'

Hasan points to a spot some fifty yards away. 'Here.'

Hilton shakes his head incredulously.

Hasan continues, 'When you landed there were only two hundred of us here. There were two thousand of you.' He stops for a moment. 'But we had more to lose.'

As they speak they nudge their horses on towards the crest of the hill. They halt suddenly. To a man, no one utters a sound.

In stark contrast to the lush approach, spread out below them is a nightmarish landscape. Barren and pockmarked with shell craters, the scorched terrain is knee-deep in the detritus of war: used shells, fraying and faded packs, shattered ammunition boxes, rusting cannon and skeins of barbed wire. But the most unsettling aspect of this surreal and apocalyptic tableau is the endless and tangled harvest of sun-bleached bones protruding from a field of rotting, shredded khaki uniforms.

The unmistakable pall of death drifts towards them on the warm Aegean breeze as a murder of crows takes wing.

Sergeant Tucker turns to Greeves.

'There you go, sir. Your Garden of Eden.'

CHAPTER FIVE

The boy teeters on the edge of a vertiginously steep dirt mound. A rough and rutted path leads down the hill, dropping away beneath the front wheel of his rusty bicycle.

Long brown hair falls across his brow. He sweeps it aside. Glacier-blue eyes squint. He looks down to where his brothers wait on either side of the path below: Henry on the left, Ed on the right.

Braced and ready. In neat piles at their feet, sticky clods of horse shit.

'C'mon, Art. No more muckin' around. It's time,' Henry shouts.

'Ready . . . Steady . . . GO!'

The boy smiles and launches himself over the edge of the mound, careening down the hill at breakneck speed.

Ed and Henry whoop and laugh, chucking their ammo with deadly accuracy.

He picks up momentum as he flies down the hill. Darts, weaves, tries to duck, but his brothers chalk up more hits than misses.

'Woohoo!' A war cry. Victorious. 'Six! I got him! Art — you're a goner!'

Freckled from head to toe with shit, the boy laughs, throws his hands sky high. The bike hits a small, rickety ramp.

The boy and the bike part company, airborne.

He spreads his arms and legs, cruciform against the cornflower-blue sky. His brothers cheer, a new volley of dung flying his way. A sting and slap to the guts as he belly whacks into the murky waters of the dam.

His brothers' peals of laughter ring even underwater.

The cloudy water reveals nothing . . . He feels around . . . mud . . . Is that . . . ? Yes, feels like a bottle . . . more mud . . .

That's it. The handlebar.

The boy emerges from the water, fist raised in victory. He drags the bike with him, laughing so hard he nearly chokes.

Ed and Henry roll on the muddy bank, laughing fit to split.

The water laps at the shore.

CHAPTER SIX

An insistent clanging, clear in the morning air, summons the passengers on deck. The engine chugs, sending vibrations shuddering through Connor's corner of the four-berth cabin. The ship dips and rises, waves slapping against its sides as it drives through the choppy swell.

He sits on a small bed, flicking through Art's diary. Gently, he takes the photo of his three sons from between its well-worn pages and slips it into his jacket pocket. He presses the book between his palms; the leather is now warm and yielding. Connor has come to know every crease and fold better than he knows his own hand.

Beside him sits his small, neatly packed brown suitcase. He is travelling light. Besides the clothes he is wearing he has a pair of trousers, two spare shirts, underwear and socks and a handkerchief. His personal effects are equally scant: a leather toiletries bag containing a comb, a razor and a shaving brush. He has also packed Lizzie's gold locket, inside which is a lock of her hair. At the beginning of the journey it still carried her scent and Connor opened the clasp in the mornings and took a deep breath so he could rise with her. Now, after six weeks, all he can smell below deck is bilge water and coal. He places Art's journal carefully on top of his clothes, next to a small blue book, its boards tooled and inscribed with the familiar elaborate gilt lettering, *The Arabian Nights*. He closes the case and snaps the latch.

From a distance, Connor hears the mournful low call of a foghorn, and wheeling above, the now familiar cawing of sea birds.

But today, cutting across the sounds of life at sea to which he has become so accustomed, there's something else. A melodic yet discordant trill. Not quite music, yet still musical. A voice . . . perhaps hundreds of voices.

He moves to the porthole. On this side of the ship there's little to see. Faint lights glitter along the distant shore, and the inky shadow of hills are outlined against the early dawn sky. The source of the sound is unclear.

Connor grasps a brass door handle damp with sea mist, turns it, and steps out onto the deck. He looks towards the ship's prow. His fellow passengers stand in a cluster at the rail.

The sky behind them glows peach as sunrise approaches, illuminating the city that lies ahead. On the horizon, Connor sees an endless procession of domes and thin, pointed towers reaching heavenward. Teetering ruined walls encircle the steep hills and stretch out of sight along a low, sweeping plain.

Connor turns to a deckhand. 'What's that sound?'

'Can't rightly say, sir. Haven't been to Constantinople before. Who knows what they're on about? Bloody infidels, pardon my French.'

Seagulls swoop and squawk, skimming the small schools of fish left floundering in the wake. The ship banks to the left towards a narrower channel and heads for the dock. On either shore, myriad sea vessels cluster in an impenetrable mass, bobbing and banging together in the waves. Rigging creaks as a thousand sails sway in the wind; motor launches roar, kicking up sea spray and carving a wake that tips the brightly painted caiques off course. Captains and crew members gesticulate as small fishing boats dart expertly between the larger ships, narrowly avoiding collision.

As his steamer approaches the wharf, Connor counts more people than he has ever seen in one place. They throng along the docks, climbing on or off boats, loading and unloading cargo, scurrying from one place to another like ants on a dead beetle. Behind this waterfront circus lies the city. Nothing in his forty-six years living in rural Australia could have prepared Connor for the pace, or the chaos, of modern Constantinople.

Buildings on a scale Connor can barely comprehend cover the steep hills, dwarfing the thousands of people who scuttle in their shadows. Ancient domed mosques, a twin-tiered aqueduct and grand palaces create a baffling visual maze of colour and texture.

Connor feels a nervous anticipation rising in his gut. He clenches his fists, lifts his shoulders and inhales a long deliberate breath.

The city may have been built by the Greeks, Romans and Byzantines, and the British are in charge now. But for five hundred years it's been Ottoman.

For Joshua Connor, it is, and will always be, enemy territory.

Connor grabs at the railing to steady himself as the boat slams against the side of the dock. Sailors toss weathered, salt-stained ropes to shore where dockhands loop them around massive brass bollards, arms straining as they struggle to secure the bucking ship against the temperamental ebb and flow of the current in the Golden Horn.

The boat's arrival attracts a hoard of vendors and touts. A thousand voices babble in countless tongues, guttural and incomprehensible. Porters shove and scrabble, elbowing each other aside to grab at the cases and trunks being lowered from deck to shore.

Beetle-browed, swarthy men shout, waving at the disembarking passengers. Laden with implausibly enormous loads, these human beasts of burden take off at alarming speed towards donkey-drawn carts and covered hackney carriages led by pairs of well-groomed horses.

Connor hangs back, grasping the handle of his own small suitcase in a determined grip. The air is warm, sultry. Waves slap against the dock, sending spray into the air. It beads and dries, crystalline, on Connor's hands. He closes one fist and feels the powdery salt crumble in his palm like Mallee dust. He sidles down the gangway, his wide-brimmed hat set squarely upon his head. He does his best to avoid the grasping hands and shouts of the rabble squabbling for custom below.

'Mister, mister!'

'Sir! Here, sir!'

'Welcome Constantinople, sir! My name is?'

Weaving between their legs is a scruffy-headed boy, dodging repeated clips to the ear from competitors. He has fixed on Connor, knowing that the more senior touts will

fight over the well-outfitted, well-heeled travellers in pref-
erence to the tall, solitary man who steps down onto the
dock clinging to a single battered suitcase.

'Mister, hello for you. Very clean, very cheap. Hot water
I have. My name is, sir?' The boy waves a creased photograph of a two-storeyed building under Connor's nose.

Ignoring the child's entreaties, Connor presses into the
mass of humanity. He clutches his case to his chest and
edges towards a rudimentary desk set up on the dock
that seems to serve as the local customs office. A Turkish
official wearing a fez and pince-nez glasses takes his prof-
fered passport and inspects it in a cursory fashion, one
hand stroking his luxuriant moustache. At his side a jaded
British officer leans back against the wall, indifferent to the
chaos that reigns around him.

The official stamps Connor's document with a flourish
and hands it back, then gestures to the next foreigner in line.

Connor stands firm, palms pressed against the desk.

'Gallipoli? The boat to Gallipoli is where?'

At his back, the persistent cries of the young boy continue
unabated.

'Sir! Sir! Best hotel in Constantinople. Hagia Sophia,
Blue Mosque, Grand Bazaar. Sir! Sir?'

Eyes hooded, the Turkish official peers at Conner over
the rims of his pince-nez.

'*Ne?*'

'Gallipoli. Come on. GA-LLIP-OLI. Don't tell me you
don't know where that is.'

The kid breaks free of the pack and comes to stand at
Connor's side, tugging at his sleeve. He sticks the photo in
front of Connor's face.

'Clean sheets, sir. Hot water. No Germans.'

Connor's patience is wearing thin. He feels fury and frustration building behind his eyes.

'Not now! Clear off!'

He turns back to the official, whose arm is outstretched to reach for the next passport.

'You understand? GALLIPOLI!'

The man's impassive Turkic face is uncomprehending. Connor looks to the British soldier at his side, disturbing his reverie.

'Excuse me. Can you help? I'm going to Gallipoli.'

The soldier stares at Connor incredulously.

'No you're bloody not. No one goes there without a permit. Check with the War Office. Sultanahmet.'

'Where?'

'Old City. Up the hill.' He indicates a vertiginous, cobblestoned street with an idle flick of his wrist.

The child holds up his photo. 'Sultanahmet. We go.' He grabs Connor's suitcase from his hand and darts off into the crowd.

The soldier watches him disappear. 'I'd watch your case if I was you. Shifty little bastards, the lot of them.'

Connor charges after his luggage. 'Oi! You! Come back!'

Still struggling with his sea legs, the ground shifts beneath Connor's feet. He fights to quell a rising tide of panic. The child has melted away into the amorphous mass of people jostling and shoving each other along the docks. He has made off with nearly everything Connor owns.

How could I be so bloody stupid?

Instinctively he slips his fingers into his breast pocket. Relief. The photo. His boys are still there. Then he remembers.

Art's journal.

Connor feels sick to the stomach. He's pushed to one side as a group of regal-looking men outfitted in brocade turbans and billowing robes sweeps past. Servants and porters wearing peculiar baggy trousers and ornately decorated silk sashes follow in their wake.

Connor catches his heel and falls backwards on a worn marble step turned grey from the passage of hundreds of years of feet. He stumbles, throwing out a hand, and finds purchase on a steep stone staircase behind him. He finds his feet and bounds up it. There, elevated above the tumult at street level, he can see the child tearing across the open square. He is heading towards a two-storeyed building, its façade a lattice of coloured stone like red and white humbugs. Connor sees his suitcase held aloft, like a trophy, as the boy scampers towards one of the three massive arches that make up the grand entrance.

Connor vaults down the stairs, two at a time. An elderly man sits on the bottom step, a tin of wheat in his hand. At his feet, a flock of grey pigeons coo and cluck, pecking at the grain the man tosses across the grey stone pavement. Connor charges past and the birds erupt in a feathery cloud, soaring skyward. He stumbles through the crowd towards his prey, eyes fixed on the boy's narrow shoulders and scruffy, thick black hair. The farmer darts and weaves past vendors selling plump cobs of buttery corn and others with trays full of circular bread rings stacked in pyramids on top of their heads.

Reaching the building, the child glances back. Seeing Connor in hot pursuit, he runs inside.

'Oi! You! Get back here!'

Connor sprints into the arcade, slowing as his eyes adjust to the dimly lit interior. A warm and intoxicating cloud washes over him. Temporarily stupefied, he stops in his tracks. More scents than he can process at once — a riot of alien aromas — waft through this space. Heady, pungent, the fragrance is so thick he can taste it at the back of his throat. An earthy smell, moist and loamy like damp soil; another as woody as freshly hewn pine; scents heavy with the bitter tang of incense, and the lilting sweetness of a handful of jasmine crushed in the palm.

Sacks filled with neatly stacked cones of coloured powder — marigold orange, raspberry red, buttercup yellow, moss green — line the narrow passage. High above, arched windows admit columns of light that are given form by the fragrant dust that fills the air.

Connor becomes aware of a sudden silence. A young man wearing a long blue robe gazes at him cautiously, frozen mid-action with a scoop of blood-red powder poised above a set of scales suspended from a timber brace. On all sides, people stop what they are doing, scrutinising the foreign invader. Connor pushes forwards, wanting more than anything to be out of this place. His head spins, his senses strung as tight as piano wire. Peering along the hazy corridor, he sees the little thief's embroidered red vest as he darts ahead.

Connor gives chase. Faces turn towards him silently, watching him pass. Black eyes, green eyes, eyes the colour of amber; skin as brown as a buffed pair of work boots, skin pale and translucent as porcelain; ancient backs as bent as a bow, gnarled hands clutching walking canes; ramrod-straight backs in gilt-buttoned woollen military tunics;

thickly kohled eyes pooling black beneath fringed and embroidered headdresses; faces hidden behind diaphanous veils; shapeless hooded forms gliding through the market in groups.

Ahead, daylight is framed by an arched doorway. The boy looks back, sees Connor, and raises his hand. A victory salute? Rage rises in him like bile.

He's mocking me? I'll show the little bastard.

Connor bursts into the bright spring sunshine and looks ahead up a steep cobbled street. Striped awnings lend it the appearance of a country fair. But that's where the familiarity ends. Stalls spill into the street, stacked high with produce: flimsy timber crates stuffed with squawking birds and squealing rabbits; copper urns, tankards, jugs, pots hanging from hooks; dried vegetables strung like garlands; skeins of rainbow-coloured silk stacked in teetering piles; baskets of unidentifiable dried flowers and fruits; handcarts piled high with plump and glossy vegetables. And, everywhere, people. So many people.

The boy has slowed and is now dragging Connor's case along the cobbles.

Pressing forwards into the crowd, Connor elbows his way past merchants who grab at his sleeve, gabbling loudly. He shakes them off.

'No! Get out of it, for Christ's sake!'

His leather-soled boots slip on the cobbles as he charges up the steep hill, watching as his suitcase disappears around a corner. Rounding the bend, he runs straight into a street festooned with washing hanging from lines, which zig zag festively up the hill. Branching off the central lane is a bewildering network of tiny alleys. Not a sign of the boy.

He looks around desperately and spots an attendant at a street café who stands stoically, eyes on the foreigner. Connor turns to him.

'A boy? My suitcase?'

Confounded, the man shrugs his shoulders, raises his eyebrows and clicks his tongue against the roof of his mouth. No.

Well. That's that, then.

Connor stops, hands on hips, unsure what to do or where to go next.

'Where you going, sir?' Behind him, the boy waves from the entrance to one of the myriad lanes.

Realisation washes over Connor and his anger slowly subsides. *Not a thief, then.* Overcome with relief, he strides over to the child and takes his case firmly from his grasp. He turns and starts to walk down the hill.

'Hey, sir! Wrong way. Hotel this way.'

Connor looks back at the boy. Weary to his core, resigned and reluctant, he submits. 'What's your name?'

'Me? Orhan, sir. My name is?'

'Pardon?'

'My name is, sir?'

'Oh. My name. My name is Joshua Connor.'

'*Merhaba*, Joshua Connor Bey. Welcome my city.'

'So, Orhan. Do you really have a hotel? With hot water? I really need a bath.'

'Yes, Sir Joshua Connor Bey. Best hotel in all Constantinople. Come!'

Orhan leads Connor through a maze of tiny streets that wind their way up a hill. They pass between tall, timber terraced homes with the upper storeys overhanging the street, poised as if ready to topple at any moment. Connor looks up at the sliver of sky visible between the rooftops where swallows swoop and chirrup.

Rounding a corner, they pass a row of barbers set up in the street. Well-dressed men lean back in armchairs, crisp white robes protecting their lapels from the foamy lather the barbers apply liberally to their chins. One strops a cutthroat razor along a heavy leather strap affixed to the leg of the chair and pulled tight with a sinewy forearm. Further up the hill, a wall is covered in a filigree of hastily scripted Ottoman slogans. For Connor, their meaning is obscure, but the scorched effigy of a soldier wearing a British Army uniform and lynched from a grapevine nearby makes the message clear. Tales told by the boat's captain on the voyage out were unequivocal; tempers in Constantinople are frayed, driven to fever pitch by the unwelcome Allied occupation in the wake of the Great War. Besieged by the Greeks to the west, the Russians to the east, and set upon by English and French troops in their capital, the Turks are on the brink of rebellion or civil war.

Orhan grabs Connor's sleeve and drags him up another laneway. He gestures towards a grand mansion on the crest of the hill ahead.

'There, sir. My hotel.'

The once opulent building has seen better days. The approach is shaded by towering trees – chestnut, cypress, plane – all that remains of what must have been, in its prime, a well-tended and manicured garden. Fresh rose-pink and white paint disguises the deep fissures in the concrete render covering the brickwork on the lower storey. But the mask slips above street level. Here, the old paint fades and peels and the plaster is riven by a crazed lattice of cracks and crevices. A spill of weeds cascades from the mossy tiled roof and pigeon-dropping stalagmites teeter above the top edges of the window frames. At the entrance, a faded oval sign is penned in curlicue Ottoman script and English: '*Otel Troya* – Troy Hotel.'

Although the building now lacks any pretension, Connor can't quell a hot flush of intimidation. He has seldom seen, far less entered, such a stately building.

'Sir! You are welcome!'

Orhan darts up the stairs and holds the front door ajar, gesturing for Connor to enter.

He raises his hand to his head, mops the beads of sweat from his brow. It was Lizzie – always Lizzie – who gave him strength. She would have hooked her arm in his, held her head high and led him through that door. She was just a country bride, but when she entered a room she was a queen. Heads turned to watch her pass. While Connor stood back, stoic, silent, Lizzie held court. Where he stumbled and faltered, confounded by small talk and social niceties, Lizzie warmed to strangers and they warmed to her. Within minutes of meeting someone, she'd lean in, resting a gentle hand on their forearm, inviting them into a conspiratorial aside. When the evening ended and they climbed back up into the buggy to take the long ride home, Lizzie would do so having made a handful of new friends. She had a warmth about her that was foreign to Connor. He is a man who finds more comfort in solitude and silence than in the company of others.

Standing on the hotel's bottom step, he is petrified. He feels the void at his side. She is never far from his thoughts.

But now, he needs to feel her hand on his, gently urging him forward.

'Come in, sir! You are home!'

He shuts his eyes, mounts the stairs.

If only I were.

CHAPTER SEVEN

The foyer of the Otel Troya is silent.

It has taken four years but the war has quietly, unwittingly suffocated this hotel. Keys hang on hooks behind the counter like cocoons; dusty, dormant and waiting for the long winter to pass. Walls that once were white are now tobacco-yellow and the lace drapes are stained and beginning to fray. A group of Thomas Cook tourists wave from a picture frame behind the reception desk. Beside it a photograph of an Ottoman patron with a proud moustache, and another of a band of musicians brandishing their instruments, recall happier times at the Troya. Absent are the familiar aromas of oriental hospitality: roasted coffee beans, eggplant baking and lemon cologne liberally splashed on the hands of guests. All lingering traces of the life that once filled these rooms have been trampled into the fraying rug at the base of the stairs. Despite the bleak times, the hotel ledger lies optimistically open on the desk, pen poised by its inkwell. A vase of pink damask roses staves off the musk of dust and desperation.

From upstairs comes a giggle and a hurried 'Shh.'

A woman bedecked incongruously in blonde wig, black beaded cocktail dress, stockings and patent leather high-heeled court shoes backs out of a doorway and into the first-floor hallway. Natalia is hopelessly overdressed for the morning, let alone the job at hand. She is carrying one end of a rolled-up carpet. A nudge from the opposite end punches her in the midriff and pushes her into the corridor, tottering in her heels.

'Wait. Give me a moment,' she blurts out through a mouthful of blonde hair. She speaks schoolgirl French with an Eastern European accent. 'Who is going to buy this moth-eaten old rag anyhow?'

'Quiet,' comes the reply, also in French, from inside the room. 'It is my father's favourite. We cannot let him hear us.'

As the rug snakes its way into the hall the door opens wide to reveal a small study with an oak desk and captain's chair. On one end of the desk is a brass microscope surrounded by teetering stacks of glass slides. The study walls are lined with half-empty bookcases, the gaps like forgotten moments or stolen memories. The rug is not the first thing to have been excised from this collection. Nor will it be the last.

Ayshe stands in the doorway clad in a long fawn dress and coarse cotton scarf. She is strikingly beautiful. Her grace, the poised way she holds her head high and her lilting French betray her privileged upbringing. Despite this, she labours without complaint.

Struggling to get a good grip on it, Natalia drops the other end of the rug.

Ayshe laughs and exclaims, 'You are like a drunken sailor. You keep steering me the wrong way!'

'Do you speak this way to all your hotel guests?' Natalia asks.

The Turkish woman replies with a smile, 'Yes. Come on! Pick it up.'

'So much bother! I wouldn't give you a piastre for it.'

'It is silk, Natalia,' Ayshe explains in a whisper. 'The highest quality, from Baluchistan.'

The Russian woman grins lewdly. 'It reminds me of a man I had from Baluchistan. He nearly split me in two!'

'I don't want to hear!' Ayshe says, feigning embarrassment and trying to quell her laughter.

'Ayshe Hanim, this is not a time of silk,' explains Natalia, gently. 'It is a time of bread. That is what everyone is queuing up for. You can't eat silk carpets. You should hang on to it.'

'I'll take what they give me. I don't have a choice.'

Ayshe casts her emerald eyes along the corridor and listens for the shuffle of her father's slippers on the boards. All clear.

'They are only things, Natalia. Just things . . . Now, go left,' she whispers. Natalia goes right. 'No, *your* left.' They choke on their laughter as they edge towards the staircase with the rug hanging limply between them.

Natalia teeters on the steps, only the weight of the carpet keeping her from tumbling backwards down the first flight and through a wooden screen.

'Careful. If I roll an ankle I might have to spend the rest of the week on my back.'

The two women look at each other from opposite ends of the rug, worlds apart yet united in compromise. The young Turkish beauty selling off her family's belongings and the older, overdressed Russian widow bartering with the only thing she has left to her. They smile, a gentle smile of understanding and affection, before bursting into uncontrollable laughter.

'On your back. Oh, you poor thing,' Ayshe manages to blurt out.

'Could be worse,' replies Natalia as she drops her end and sits on the steps to gather herself.

The front door rattles. The two women stand and smooth their dresses with their palms. Natalia straightens her wig with a tug and automatically curls her fingers through the side locks. A serious man in his late thirties, wearing a burgundy fez, a suit and a self-important moustache, lets himself in. He swoops across the foyer to the counter with a proprietary air and speaks in Turkish without raising his eyes or his voice.

'I heard you two chirping from the street. What if there had been guests, my dear?'

'I don't see any, do you, Omer?' replies Ayshe flatly, the light mood ruptured. 'I asked Natalia to help me.'

Natalia retreats upstairs, knowing where this conversation is heading. 'It is fine, Hanim. Now the big man of the house is here you don't need my help.'

As part of his morning routine Omer glances at the guest register, closes it, and then checks the keys. There is only one missing from its hook, the same one as always.

'That Russian woman brings shame on this household,' he blurts out, loud enough for Natalia to hear before she reaches the sanctuary of her room. She doesn't speak fluent Turkish but Ayshe knows she will recognise the disapproving tone.

Ayshe cuts Omer off before he has a chance to wind up.

'You know we don't have the luxury to judge. She brings

in money. Sometimes it is that simple.' She points to the buckled rug on the stairs and deflects him. 'Here, will you help me with this?'

Omer softens, genuinely concerned.

'What next, Ayshe? The beds? The sheets? How do you propose paying the creditors when there is nothing left to sell?'

He holds her gaze as he takes off his suit jacket and places it on a hook. 'Ayshe, what then?'

She shrugs and the corners of her mouth turn up ever so slightly in good-natured resignation. It is in Allah's hands. She has no real plan and knows it. She presents a good front to the world, but in her quietest moments, she struggles to control the quavering sense of anxiety that has embedded itself deep in her heart. Allah may have something in mind for her, but she wishes he would give her a hint of what that might be.

'Leave this to me,' sighs Omer as he shoulders the carpet and carries it out through the breakfast salon and into the courtyard.

Ayshe stands alone in the foyer and looks at the glass evil eye hanging on the wall, its black pupil set in a pool of indigo blue and pearlescent white. Momentarily she imagines herself drifting in a great expanse of water halfway between Europe and Asia. She treads water, waiting for the tide to turn in her favour, but every Stambouli knows the currents in the Bosphorus are fickle and treacherous.

Suddenly what sounds like the Sultan's Army crashes through the front door. Orhan. Despite herself, she smiles. Her eleven-year-old son is one of the few things remaining in her life that still give her joy. He is an only child and it is a mystery to her how one small boy can make such a racket. His eyes gleam with a level of unbridled excitement usually reserved for such occasions as watching a firework display; a rare event these days.

Scarcely able to breathe, Orhan runs to his mother and wraps his arms around her waist while he blurts out his news. 'Mum, mum. I found a foreigner. An Englisher.'

She holds Orhan tightly and inhales the scent of sea air and spices from his hair. She pictures the route he has come home by, along the wharf at Eminönü and through the Egyptian Bazaar, running up the hill past men smoking outside the coffee house.

'My clever little man. I could eat you,' she replies, now also excited.

Ayshe looks up as a long shadow crosses the stoop, preceding a tall, broad-shouldered man who steps through the open door.

❖

Connor removes his hat and wipes his brow with his forearm. He is sweaty and puffing from the ascent up the hill and still struggles with a debilitating sense of displacement. He hesitates as his eyes adjust to the soft light, letting them wander over the faded glory of the Troya. This place has seen better days, that much is clear. He spots Arabic calligraphy on the wall beside a photograph of a man sporting a moustache, uniform and fez, but the hotel does not feel as alien as Connor had feared. Almost European, he dares to think. Although in truth his expectations are grounded in exotic bedtime tales of harems, crusades and caves of riches that open on command. For him, the Constantinople he has passed through is a closer match to how he imagined this city. But he has no reference point for the modern – if somewhat down-at-heel – hotel he has just entered, far less the breathtakingly beautiful woman standing before him.

The woman seems to sense his hesitation. 'Hello. You are welcome. I am Orhan's mother, Ayshe Hanim.'

The boy wriggles away from her. Her warm smile cuts through the fog of Connor's grief and apprehension like a spotlight. As Ayshe steps towards him, smoothing her slim-fitting dress and tucking a stray lock of hair back under her scarf, this Australian farmer is completely disarmed.

'Yes. Ah, I need a room . . . Your boy said you . . .'

Ayshe smiles. 'You are from England?'

'I am from Australia.'

'Australia?' Ayshe bristles, visibly thrown by the revelation. Her warmth evaporates like mist on morning breath. She tilts her chin up defensively and raises her eyebrows. 'I am sorry, Orhan has made a mistake. We have no rooms free.'

Connor looks past her at the board of room keys behind the reception desk and then glares at Orhan. The boy looks puzzled; confused.

Dumping his case on the floor, Connor raises his voice, fatigue and pent-up frustration threatening to bubble over. 'Your son has dragged me halfway across this wretched city with the promise of a room –'

Before he has the opportunity to finish the sentence, a smiling man appears from the adjoining salon and pushes past Ayshe. 'Welcome to the Troy Hotel, sir. Where Achilles himself would have stayed – if he had visited Constantinople.'

He pauses in his patter, anticipating a laugh that does not materialise. 'We are busy but I am sure we can find you a room.' He opens the hotel ledger and runs his finger down the page.

'Ah, yes. You are in luck. The boy was right. Our best room is now vacant. Mr . . .?'

'Connor. Joshua Connor.'

'Welcome, I am Mister Omer. Can I have your travel document, please? I will register you immediately, while the room is still available.' He smiles, pen poised over the book.

As Connor hands over his passport Ayshe spits her protest at Omer in Turkish. The man scribbles quickly and responds in Turkish through a frozen smile. He hands Connor his passport and a key. 'You are most welcome, Mr Connor.' Connor has no idea what has been said, but feels less than welcome.

'Your room is upstairs and on the left. The break of fast is at eight o'clock in the morning. Would you like for her to bring you coffee or tea now?' He nods to Ayshe.

'Thank you, no,' replies Connor. He picks up his case and heads for the stairs, one hand on the balustrade as he turns, recalling Orhan's sales pitch on the docks. 'Your son mentioned hot water and a bath.'

Orhan's jaw drops and his olive complexion blanches. As the father of three sons who were known to be liberal with the truth at times, Connor recognises the shamefaced look immediately. Not for the first time today Connor concedes that the kid has had the better of him, but he's too exhausted to make a fuss. 'No worries, it'll be just like home, then.'

Omer is not so forgiving. He cuffs the boy over the back of the head and snaps at the boy in English, apparently for Connor's benefit, 'It is shameful to lie. You are a spoilt mother's boy!' Orhan cringes in the corner of the lobby, tears welling in his eyes.

Connor intervenes, almost a reflex. 'No, it doesn't matter. Really. I probably misunderstood.' Orhan may have led him a merry chase this morning, but he feels a strange camaraderie with the bright-eyed and persistent child.

The Turkish man bows his head and holds his right hand to his chest. 'Sincere apologies, Mr Connor. It is not our way. You are our guest here, and it is our duty to make you welcome.' He points to Connor's suitcase and cuffs Orhan once more, lest he missed the point. 'Orhan will help you with your bag. It is his duty.'

With his head bowed in shame, eyes fixed on his shuffling shoes, Orhan leads Connor up the stairs to the room. His chatter has dried up and the case the boy sprinted with through the streets as if it were as light as a feather now suddenly seems laden with bricks. They approach Room 6 and Orhan slides the key into the lock.

'This your room.'

Connor takes his suitcase from the boy and pushes his way into a sparsely furnished room. He fishes a coin out of his pocket and presses it into Orhan's hand. The remorseful boy tries to hand it back but Connor nods and smiles.

'You seem to know where everything is around here,' says Connor. 'Tomorrow, can you take me to the War Office? I will pay you.'

Orhan's face breaks into a broad grin and his hooded eyes reclaim their spark. 'Yes you will.'

Connor watches Orhan race back along the hall and disappear down the stairs, three at a time. He wonders if you are still a father when you have no sons left.

❖

Ayshe swings a wicker carpet beater in a fury. Decades of accumulated dirt explode in smoky clouds from the weathered Baluch carpet, which is suspended over a clothesline in the hotel courtyard. She whacks at it with impotent rage, tears of frustration cutting runnels through the dust that has settled on her cheeks. Finally she steps back from the rug, her anger beginning to abate.

She stands in what remains of a magnificent garden surrounded by an ageless stone wall. When this building was her childhood home Ayshe would help the gardener, Ali the Bent, weed the beds and plant seeds and bulbs that erupted in a riot of colour long after she had forgotten them. Tulips, hyacinths, narcissus, irises. It was in this garden that she first learned that miracles seldom happen without someone getting their hands dirty.

The courtyard has gone to seed, in every way. Small, tenacious tufts of grass appear between the flagstones, and tree roots growing beneath the paving lift the stones erratically. A build-up in its pipes means that the fountain that once spurted and gurgled merrily during hot, dusty summers has slowed to a trickle and does little more than stain its marble basin with streaks of rust. Wicker chairs, stacked in a far corner, quietly unravel.

Ayshe has fond memories of the garden in its prime, small tables set neatly with lace-edged napkins and delicate china cups as guests reclined in the dappled shade of the stately trees. But beauty has made way for necessity. Tethered to a tree is a nanny goat, named Şafak for a new dawn. Orhan helps milk her each morning. Tomato seedlings are staked along the back wall and cucumbers wind their way amongst the endive and Greek lettuces.

In the time of Sultan Abdulhamid II, Ayshe's father would often drink coffee and read the newspaper out here in the mornings before heading off to work. This morning he sits on a stool throwing seed to chickens that scratch around his ankles. He is dressed in a faded three-piece suit, a fez and leather slippers. From under his thick eyebrows he eyes his daughter suspiciously. As Ayshe takes a deep breath and prepares to launch one last violent assault on the carpet, he pipes up.

'I know this carpet from somewhere. Pasha... Pasha...' He struggles to recall the name. 'A pasha gave it to me. His son. I cured his son.'

Ayshe pauses. 'Noblemen are in short supply nowadays, Father.'

'I haven't seen it for years. Where did you find it?' Ibrahim asks as he nurses a hen and absent-mindedly begins to pull feathers from its tail. The bird squawks and flaps its wings in alarm but Ibrahim holds its claws and continues to pluck.

Ayshe smiles sadly to herself and gently takes the bird from him. 'We haven't killed it yet, Father.'

Chapter Eight

Connor sits on the edge of his double bed in trousers and a singlet. There is a reassuring familiarity about the room, which, like the foyer, is unexpectedly European. It is decorated with care and restraint: a hardwood bedhead; a tallboy with turned legs topped with a delicately embroidered runner and a small silver salver bearing a heavy, cut-crystal tumbler and a decanter of fine Scotch whisky; bedside tables with marble tops and teardrop handles. The drapes are made of lace and the mattress is draped in an embroidered woollen bedspread. He could be in any Continental capital were it not for the lilting song that at this moment ripples across the city and through his open window. It is not one voice but a multitude, a breath between each call as they echo one another. For him it is strange-sounding and arcane; the only thing he can liken it to is the distant pealing of a bell.

Spread out on the bed is a hand-drawn map of the Dardanelles, copied by Connor from a newspaper back in Rainbow. In black ink are the foreign places that became household names in Australia during the war, for the very worst reasons: Suvla Bay, Gallipoli, Hell Spit, Krithia, the

Nek, Lone Pine. The letters 'A', 'H' and 'E', one for each son, appear in various locations with dates scribbled next to them as Connor has tried to trace his boys' movements over the four months they were at Gallipoli. Art's diary lies open and Connor reads, checking and crosschecking against the map.

There is a light knock on the door. Connor slips his arms into a shirt, pulls it up his back and hastily begins working on the buttons. He opens the door half-expecting to see the boy grinning at him on the other side. Instead it is Ayshe, struggling to hold a copper basin of hot water in a towel. The steam has made her face flush and a tiny rivulet of sweat trickles down her forehead and soaks into her eyebrow.

'Please, allow me,' says Connor, reaching for the basin instinctively.

Ayshe breathes heavily with the effort but refuses his help. 'It is very hot. Be careful, please.' She sidles carefully past him and deposits the basin on top of the chest of drawers.

Connor immediately regrets the fuss he made downstairs. 'Really, there was no need.'

'My son is no liar,' Ayshe states firmly. 'He promised you.'

Connor smiles, a little bemused by her prickly demeanour. 'He seems like a very resourceful lad.'

'Yes, he is,' she replies, softening slightly. 'You have sons too?'

Connor's answer is unexpectedly abrupt, even for him. 'Yes. Three.' He retreats to the window, suddenly uncomfortable with Ayshe, for being Turkish, a woman, a mother, beautiful, prying, defiant – and for being in his room.

'What's that noise?' he asks as the call to prayer trails off.

'This is your first time in Constantinople, Mr Connor?' she asks, rhetorically.

'What are they selling?' he asks, to remove any doubt.

'God,' she quips. 'It's a call to prayer.'

'The bathroom is down the hall when you want to bathe.' She casts an eye over the books and papers on the bed and spots the ornately bound blue volume of *The Arabian Nights*.

'Your guide book is out of date, I'm afraid,' she says dryly.

'I'm not here to sightsee.'

An awkward silence descends, which Ayshe breaks by beating a hasty retreat from the room. As she leaves, she speaks without glancing up at him. 'You should make time for the Blue Mosque at least. Even in my "wretched city" it is a beautiful place to find God.'

He may well be in desperate need of divine intervention, but Connor has neither the time nor the inclination to seek God on these shores.

'I didn't come for Him either,' Connor grunts. 'I am on my way to Gallipoli.'

Ayshe stops in the doorway, her almond-shaped eyes narrowing. Just the sound of the word seems to harden her.

'You mean Çanakkale, Mr Connor. We call it Çanakkale. There is nothing there but ghosts.' She composes herself and leaves, calling over her shoulder, 'My son cannot help you tomorrow. I need him here.'

Connor watches Ayshe stride towards the stairwell, holding her head aloft and arms swinging. As he closes the door, he is uncomfortable, confused by the Turkish woman's coolness and undisguised disdain. If he needs to stay in Constantinople for any length of time he might have to look for another hotel.

Connor removes his shirt and singlet and dips his cupped palms into the water basin. The steam rises up and wets his cheeks. He realises it has been weeks since he has had hot water to wash in, and relishes the moment. He brings his hands up slowly and feels the wave of heat on his eyelids and lips. He rubs his forehead all the way to the hairline, the sides of his nose, the inside of his ears and the back of his neck. To his surprise he finds red grit from home still lodged in places that he would swear were clean. *I'll always wear the mark of where I come from, ingrained, no escaping it.*

Long after the water in the basin has turned cold, a paste of olive oil soapsuds and dirt clinging to the sides, Connor awakes with a start. He has fallen asleep face down on his map, allowing every contour to project itself on his mind. The evening prayer call, shriller and more urgent this time, exhumes him from a deep slumber and discombobulates him. Where is he? What is the time? Where are they, where are his sons?

The farmer gathers himself on the side of his bed as his mind slowly finds its way through the fog of lost sleep, along an outback rail line, a turbulent sea and through the labyrinth of Constantinople. A glance out the window tells him the city is lurching towards the end of the day, like a runner chesting the tape. The afternoon has sprinted by.

Connor sniffs and confirms he needs a bath. He needs to be at his best tomorrow. He gathers his towel and his flat leather toiletries bag, and steps into the hall, careful to lock his door behind him. *You never know with these Arabs.*

He makes his way along the low-lit corridor, looking for a bathroom sign. He rounds a corner and sees a distinguished Turkish gentleman sitting on a bench beside a closed door, several bathroom towels stacked beside him. The older man nods and smiles at Connor, politely letting the Australian know he must wait his turn. Connor returns the nod and sits, ramrod rigid with his towel on his lap. He doesn't have to wait long before the door handle rattles from inside the room and a sheepish-looking Turk appears. The man hurries off, pushing his fez down on his head and buttoning his coat as he goes. Right behind him is a woman.

Connor's jaw drops. He has never seen a woman dressed, or undressed, like this; not on his wedding night, and certainly never since. He wants to fix his gaze on the floor but his eyes betray him and dart upwards. The woman is dressed in a red silk robe over lace underwear, and wears a long black wig that drops over her shoulders in the shape of a heart. In spite of his searing discomfort, Connor steals a glimpse at her shiny red lips, the line of her full bosom and the curve of her hip.

The enthusiastic suitor sitting next to Connor springs from the bench and greets the woman with a formal bow. He says something to her in Turkish and Connor catches her name: Natalia.

She smiles, opens the door wider and guides the man into her room. Over his shoulder Connor sees not a bathroom but a bedroom. On the dresser sits a mute audience of wig stands, each modelling a different colour of styled baroque wig. Elegant brass candlesticks and a samovar stand on a small dresser in front of a silver icon of Saint George lancing a dragon.

76

Natalia finds and holds Connor's gaze with a provocative smile. He fights the urge to let his eyes roam and feels himself blush. She seems surprised but pleased – about what, Connor can't fathom. Her eyes move to Connor's towel and shaving kit and the penny appears to drop. She smiles and says in heavily accented English, 'He spend twenty minutes complaining about wife, then five minutes later, he finish. You have bath and come back?'

Connor realises his mistake and is thrown. Instead of retiring into her room, Natalia leans against the doorframe, a grin on her face. Mortified, Connor cannot bear the indignity any longer. He stands and scurries away, tugging at an imaginary hat brim and apologising, though for what he is not sure.

Chapter Nine

Early morning light streams over the terracotta-tiled rooftops as the cries of gulls and kestrels echo through the cobbled streets.

Connor stands on the marble stoop of the Troya, watching the city wake from its slumber. Two men struggle to control a rickety handcart laden with fresh bread still steaming from the oven as they attempt to negotiate the steep street. On the opposite corner, a stone fountain deeply etched with garlands and grapevines spits sparkling, clear water from an ornate copper spigot. Connor resists the urge to cross the street and dip his cupped hands into the basin to taste the water. A gaggle of women cluster about the well, chattering like sparrows as they bend to fill their buckets with water for their households. In procession, they disperse through the streets, carrying two buckets apiece at each end of a brace balanced across their shoulders.

A small child – no older than ten, and most likely considerably younger – walks past the hotel, carrying on his head a tray of the same circular bread rings Connor saw on the docks yesterday.

'*Siii-miiiit*!' the boy cries, looking at Connor expectantly. He slows. '*Siiiii-miiiitttttt*!' The smell of the fresh bread has set Connor's stomach rumbling.

'How much?'

The boy looks at Connor, confused. '*Sii-miit*!'

Connor raises his voice, thinking that perhaps the boy hasn't heard him. 'How much? For the bread? Money? How much?'

The boy smiles crookedly, embarrassed.

For goodness' sake. What does he think I'm saying?

'Sir, Connor Bey!'

Orhan appears round the corner, from the courtyard at the back of the house.

'Connor Bey. Is *simit*. Bread. You want?'

'Er, yes. I am feeling a little peckish.'

'Peckish? What is peckish?'

'Hungry. Yes. I would like a . . . *smeet*, you say?'

'*Si-mit*.'

'*Simit*. Yes. How much is it?'

'I pay now. You pay later.'

Orhan darts into the hotel and reappears with a coin. He gives it to the *simit* vendor and takes two from the carefully stacked tray balanced precariously on his head.

'Here, Connor Bey. Eat.'

Connor takes the bread ring, still warm and covered in golden sesame seeds. He bites into it – the centre is soft and slightly sweet.

'Delicious.'

'You like, Connor Bey?'

'I do. It is good. Thank you.'

Connor and Orhan sit in silence on the top step eating their *simit*s.

'Last night your mother told me that you cannot take me to the War Office. Can you show me which road I need to take to get there?'

Orhan looks over his shoulder into the hotel foyer.

'Mother said that? No. It is all right now. I can go. Lots of roads to get to Topkapi. You will get lost. I show you.'

'Good. No time to waste. Let's go.'

'Yes. I am good guide. Come!'

Connor brushes the sesame seeds from his chest and lap, sets his hat atop his head and strides down the hotel steps in Orhan's wake. Rested and recalibrated, he has found his purpose again. Now he knows exactly what he must do.

❖

As they round what seems like the hundredth corner, Connor has absolutely no idea where he is. He's always had a good sense of direction, an instinct for the right bearings. At home he can navigate by the sun and stars, but here in the opposite hemisphere he feels disoriented and off beam. Right now, he wouldn't even be able to point north, far less find his way back to the hotel they left only minutes ago. The network of tiny alleys and lanes that wind up then down and round these hills seems planned only to confound travellers. Orhan was right. Without his assistance, Connor would have been irretrievably lost in this labyrinth.

Somewhere nearby Connor can hear raised voices, furious chanting, and the ringing sound of many feet running along cobbles. He looks downhill along a narrow street in the direction of the uproar, and catches flashes of an angry mob rushing along an adjoining street. They are some distance away but there's no mistaking their fury. Men stop and shriek at something hidden from Connor's view. Some join arms and surge together, only to be pushed back by unseen forces.

'Orhan, wait. What is happening down there?' Connor begins to move down the side street, curious to see what's going on.

Orhan grabs Connor's sleeve. 'No, Connor Bey. It is better to stay here. These men are very angry.'

'Why? What could make them so furious?'

'The Sultan. The British. The Greeks. The war. Everything.'

Connor wisely changes course, moving away from the riot.

'Let's keep going on our way then. That seems to be the best idea.'

'Yes, sir. You come this way. We go to Topkapi up here.'

They walk on in silence, the sounds of the clash receding into the distance.

Orhan's brow is furrowed. 'Connor Bey, Ottoman people are good people. You do not worry. You are Australian. Not British. British and Australian are not same.'

Connor pauses. 'No. Not always, I suppose.'

❖

Connor and Orhan pass between a row of teetering, three-storeyed timber homes, garishly painted, with upper levels that peer out over the street like nosey neighbours. Towering above the rooflines on his left Connor can glimpse a monumental crenellated stone wall. Ahead he sees another long wall constructed of the same curious red humbug–style brickwork he had noticed the day before in the spice market.

Orhan gestures beyond it. 'There! Connor Bey! Topkapi Palace.'

'What about the War Office?'

'Yes, is here. Inside.'

Stepping out into a broad plaza, Connor looks towards an ancient and fortified gateway at its apex. The entrance to Topkapi Palace is now guarded by sentry boxes occupied by soldiers wearing British Army uniforms. The modern military paraphernalia – rifles, ammunition, bandoliers, khaki jackets, armoured vehicles – strikes a discordant note against the white marble Ottoman entrance, set with emerald-green panels inscribed with ornate gilt Arabic lettering.

Connor approaches the British guard. Ginger-haired, with peeling skin on his nose and a rubicund complexion, he's not well suited to a Mediterranean summer. The soldier's otherwise impassive face registers a wince of disapproval at the sight of Connor's companion.

'Can I help you, sir?'

'I want to go to Gallipoli. I'm told I need a permit.'

The soldier scoffs. 'Don't like your chances.'

Connor hands the sentry his passport. 'Where do I go?'

'Worth a try, I guess. *He* won't be going any farther, though.'

For a moment, Connor is unsure who the soldier is talking about.

The guard flicks a dismissive hand at Orhan. 'No wogs.'

Orhan is unperturbed. 'I wait, Connor Bey.'

'No, you have helped enough. Thank you. You go back home. Thank your mother for letting you come.'

Orhan stands his ground. Connor is puzzled by his persistence until he remembers the question of payment. He fishes in his pocket for a coin and hands it to the boy. Orhan smiles.

'I wait. You need guide for getting back to hotel.'

'Fair enough. I may be a while.'

'I wait.'

Connor steps through the arched Topkapi gateway into an expansive courtyard. He stands, hands on hips, and does the reckoning in his head – big enough to fit twenty houses the size of their family home. Maybe more. In the centre of the courtyard is a lawn populated with a forest of exotic trees. Junior officers and clerks bustle along the paths that dissect the forecourt like spokes on a cartwheel. Once the imperial residence – the Sultan now prefers to live with his wives and concubines in the European-style Dolmabahçe Palace on the Bosphorus this labyrinth of chambers, salons and reception rooms now serves as an impromptu War Office.

A young uniformed British guard approaches, his hobnailed boots clicking against the flagstones like tap shoes.

'Sir, can I be of assistance?'

'Ah yes, I am from Australia,' Connor begins.

'From the colonies?' the guard interjects, amusing himself.

'Until you need us, then we're all one Empire. Now, I want to go to Gallipoli. Who do I see?'

Cheeks flushing, the guard replies, castigated. 'You need a permit, sir. The Travel Permit Office is down there. One, two . . . eighth door on your right.' He points Connor along a colonnaded verandah dotted with small wooden doors.

Fists tight, Connor follows the marble columns until they disappear behind a white stucco pavilion that reminds him of an oversized wedding cake. A sign on an open door reads 'Travel.' Connor pokes his head in apologetically but is greeted with a small, unprepossessing, windowless space that could only have been an Ottoman storeroom. In the centre is a simple timber desk holding up heroically under a hill of files. On top of the table a black metal fan turns, teasing the loose paperwork, the only hint that someone might be returning. A name plate reads 'Lieutenant Sinclair Bryant.' On one side of the desk stands an abandoned swivel chair with a cushion embroidered in a regimental flag and a lion. Connor smiles at the ignominy of someone resting their backside on the company colours.

Against the wall are two uninviting wooden chairs that immediately remind him of primary school in the town of Birchip, on the very edge of the Mallee: twenty-four kids of all ages crammed into the timber schoolroom – the youngest up front, the eldest at the rear – and the balding Mr Dirk, who would make miscreants bend over with their palms on the seat of his empty chair while he whipped them across the backs of their legs. On what became his last day of school, twelve-year-old Connor caught the switch in his hand on the third lash and wrenched it from his teacher's grip. He snapped it into four pieces before Dirk's open palm struck him on the jaw. The next blow was a back-hander that caught his nose and the classroom exploded in red. Connor recalls his father coming home after speaking to his teacher and not being able to hold his knife in his right hand at dinner.

Connor sits on the edge of a chair and places his hat on the seat beside him. He leans forwards, his elbows on his knees, and lets the fan cool his sweaty hair. Three times he hears footsteps on the marble paving outside and stands to greet the lieutenant, only to see a blur of khaki pass across the doorway. On the fourth occasion Bryant appears, a tall and wiry man in his late twenties with hollow cheeks and an aquiline nose. He balances a tray with a teapot and milk jug in one hand and holds his walking stick in the other.

'I'm terribly sorry. I had no idea anyone was waiting,' he says as he puts the tray on the desk and offers a twiggy, ink-stained hand out to Connor. 'Sinclair Bryant, Lieutenant . . . Tea?'

'No, no thank you,' replies Connor impatiently. 'I want to go to Gallipoli, tomorrow.'

'What for? There's nothing to see there,' says Bryant dismissively. 'Did you fight there?'

'My sons, my three sons,' explains Connor. 'They're still there.'

'Ah.' Bryant has no idea what else to say. 'You do realise where it is?'

Connor nods.

'Unfortunately I can't help you. I don't have the authority to issue permits to civilians. Only military personnel, you understand.'

Connor sits back in the chair and sucks in the still air through his clenched teeth.

'So why in God's name did they waste my time by sending me to you?'

Bryant shrugs. 'I can't be sure. Possibly just trying to help.'

'Some help. So can you tell me who I need to speak to?'

'I'm not sure there is anyone,' explains Bryant. 'It's an unusual request. Unique.'

'There must be someone. Who's your boss?' demands Connor, rage and frustration building in his gullet.

Bryant withers under Connor's steely gaze. He scribbles a name on a piece of paper and hands it across the desk.

'I would suggest you see Captain Brindley. He may be able to help you.' He does not sound very convincing. 'Across the quadrangle,' he adds. Connor can see he has put a crease in Bryant's day and the lieutenant is keen to be rid of him.

Standing, Connor grabs his hat and points at Bryant's walking stick. 'I thought you might understand better than some.'

'I'll never understand, Mr Connor,' says Bryant bleakly. 'Ever.'

Connor stands, grabs his hat and leaves Bryant to his tea and files.

He is halfway across the vast courtyard, cursing under his breath, when he stops. He is suddenly aware of the midday sun beating down on his hat and shoulders, like a stinging slap on the back from a mate in a crowd. While everyone around him seems to be scurrying for shade Connor turns to feel the warmth on his face. He closes his eyes and opens his palms, grounding himself properly for the first time since he arrived. It is a relief to commune with something so elemental and familiar when he has done little more than slip on cobblestones since he arrived. A parade of British,

French and Turkish soldiers pass by, most too preoccupied with the business of ruling to give him a second glance.

❖

Captain Charles Brindley is leaning back in his desk chair, contemplating the ornate ceiling. Since he learned that Muslim artisans leave a deliberate flaw in everything they create – because only Allah is perfect – he has been looking for the errant brushstroke or misplaced tile in the intricate dome above. It has been three months, but he is determined to find the chink.

Brindley's aide-de-camp appears in the doorway with another man, a civilian, behind him. 'Sir, there is a Mr Connor to see you. From Australia.'

Curious, Brindley lowers his gaze and beckons Connor into the princely reception room that is now his office. The desk and a pair of generic filing cabinets do little to fill this expansive space or subdue the exuberant decoration. Brindley imagines himself as a khaki smudge on a background of gilded architrave, mirrored arches and niches detailed in the signature blue and white tiles from Iznik. A rich green and burgundy runner leads Connor towards the captain's desk.

During the war Brindley had been a military censor for the Gallipoli Peninsula, fighting his battles with a blue stamp on the Greek island of Imbros. From a hexagonal tent, nicknamed 'the big top' because what went on in there was a circus, he would paw through the mail leaving the trenches. His job was to excise sensitive information from the soldiers' letters, to put a thick black line through anything that might give away front-line locations, reveal details of an upcoming offensive or damage morale by being overly graphic. The last thing the army needed was to discourage men from enlisting.

For the men who wrote frequently, Brindley followed what happened in the lives of their families back home. If he ever did the mail run to the peninsula or bumped into men on leave on Mudros he had to stop himself asking after their wives by name, or querying whether they had heard from their brother in France or had decided on a name yet, for a newborn.

Many times he would be reading the last letter a soldier sent home, not knowing they were already dead. The last missive their families would receive from a missing father or son was a tissue-thin piece of paper filled with half-sentences, folded in an envelope stamped with the blue censor's mark. Only Brindley had seen into their hearts as they faced oblivion, and when necessary had put the sword to their last well-wishes and desires, killing them over again.

Brindley is not impervious to the beauty that can sometimes come from catastrophe. If ever he needs reminding he opens the pages of Homer's *The Iliad*. With the letters, as in life, Brindley was generally efficient and unsentimental. Every once in while, though, a line would jump off a page and its honesty and poetry would leave him gutted. Against his better judgement he would let it go through to its intended recipient. Who was he to tamper with perfection, God-given or otherwise?

As Connor approaches, Brindley rises, smiling, and leans over the desk to shake his hand. 'Charles Brindley. You're a long way from home, sir.'

'Joshua Connor. So are you.'

'Indeed.' Brindley is amused at the older man's direct-ness and offers him a chair. 'What can I do for you?'

The two men drop into seats either side of the desk. 'I want to go to Gallipoli, to find my sons,' says Connor, in no mood for idle talk. 'They didn't come home.'

Brindley runs his fingers over his well-groomed moustache, taking a moment to choose his words. 'The Dardanelles remain a very sensitive military zone, as I am certain you understand.' He straightens his tailored tunic. 'I regret to say, Mr Connor, we do not issue civilians with travel permits to Gallipoli.'

As he speaks a young Turkish tea boy skips down the rug and places two cups of tea, a creamer and a sugar bowl on the desk.

'Tea?' Brindley asks Connor. 'Not much chop I'm afraid.'

The boy hovers and Brindley waves him away, waiting until the boy has exited before continuing.

'Don't be deceived, Mr Connor – this is still enemy terri-tory. We might hold the city, but it will be some time before we bring order to the chaos.'

Connor reaches into his jacket pocket and slips a photo-graph across the desk.

He speaks slowly and firmly. 'Arthur, Henry and Edward Connor. From Rainbow, Victoria, southwest of Swan Hill. All three of them were in the 7th Battalion, A.I.F. They enlisted together on 7 July 1914 – thinking they were heading off to fight the Hun in Europe. I suppose we all thought that. Instead, they went to Gallipoli. They were all killed at Lone Pine on the same day – August the 6th – a year later . . .'

Brindley interrupts. 'I'm truly sorry. Truly. We do have the Imperial War Graves Commission working on the peninsula as we speak. They have a formidable task ahead of them. But when they find your sons, as I'm sure they will, I promise we will notify you.'

Brindley reaches for the photo, meaning to file it in the folder in front of him. Lightning fast, Connor leans across and pins it firmly to the desk with his hand.

'I have waited four years. I cannot wait any longer.'

'You must understand, these men on Gallipoli are experts,' Brindley replies. He can see that it falls on deaf ears.

'I intend to find my sons. All I need from you is a piece of paper and a stamp saying I can go there.'

Brindley cannot help but admire the man's devotion to his sons but his reply is blunt. 'I couldn't, Mr Connor, even if that was my inclination. Regulations do not allow it.'

'I can find them,' says Connor, fixing the captain with a hawk like glare.

'Oh yes?' says Brindley, his patience fast evaporating. 'How do you imagine you are going to do that? Along with your three there are sixty thousand sons of the Empire out there.'

He points his manicured finger over Connor's shoulder. The entire rear wall is devoted to a bank of primitive shelving that houses a colossal pile of service records and field reports, arranged by country. Already a light dust has settled on the top files in each pile. Brindley expects that the enormity of the task will sink in as Connor registers the signs that read United Kingdom, British India, Newfoundland, Australia, New Zealand and France.

Brindley is on a roll. 'Do you know what the army used to do with the rank and file dead after Crimea, Khartoum, the Boer War? A Yorkshire company called Thompson and Sons would come in and throw the lot in a hopper and turn them into blood and bone. You should see the gardens in Sebastopol. Best fertilised flowerbeds you'll ever find. This is the first war in which anyone has given a damn.'

Connor looks unmoved. 'My boys should be buried at home, beside their mother.'

Brindley picks up the photograph of the boys and studies it for a moment. He speaks softly as he hands the image back to Connor.

'Fine lads. That's the way you should remember them.' Brindley stands; the meeting is over. 'Go home, Mr Connor.'

CHAPTER TEN

Connor walks angrily through the white poplar-tree floss that blows in drifts across the street like a late spring snowstorm. Orhan falls into stride behind him. Connor nods to the boy but says nothing, still smarting from the frustrating exchange with Brindley.

Too late, Connor hears the unmistakable sound of strife. Rounding a corner, he and Orhan are swept up in a mass of angry protesters. Fists clenched and raised to the sky, the men shout in unison, marching away from Topkapi. Jostled, shoved and buffeted every which way, Connor has no choice but to go in the same direction as the mob. He begins to panic. The crowd is surging into an enormous square – it has to be more than four hundred feet wide and at least a thousand feet long – dominated by a central massive obelisk that seems to be a rallying point.

Deeply furrowed brows and gaping, spitting mouths turn towards him, sensing and now seeing an unwanted alien in their midst. It is Connor's turn to be the enemy. Jabs in his side become sharper, deliberate, no longer accidental. The smell of the crowd envelops him: rank and sour sweat; the stench of fear and fury. A man confronts him, his pointed finger spearing Connor's chest, his turgid face flushing with impotent rage. He is babbling, screaming, in words that are completely foreign to Connor. But there's no mistaking their meaning. Connor knows he is in grave peril.

He feels a small hand on his wrist, tugging at him.

'Connor Bey! This way!'

Orhan pulls Connor's distinctly foreign hat off his head and pushes it under his jacket. Miraculously finding a way through the rampaging mob as only a child can, Orhan leads Connor towards the edge of the pack. He finds himself pressed up against a long marble wall punctuated with arched windows. He is bumped and dragged along, his hip slamming painfully into the wall's hard stone lip. The press of the crowd pounds his shoulder into the metal grille that fills each arch. Orhan clings tightly to Connor, pulling him forwards towards an immense ceremonial entrance. He darts through it, leading Connor behind him.

In the courtyard beyond the gateway Connor is confronted by the most remarkable building he has ever seen. Sweeping domes trace delicate and airy crescents against the cornflower-blue spring sky. Six pointed towers, impossibly thin and unfeasibly tall, ascend to the heavens. He gazes up at one, head spinning.

Orhan is insistent. 'This way, Connor Bey! It is not safe. Come!'

Unenthusiastically, Connor allows Orhan to lead him to a hidden open arcade along one side of the raised platform on which the mosque stands. Scores of tiny brass taps protrude in a long row from the marble foundations. Seated on low rush stools before the running water, men quietly wash their bare feet, scooping water into cupped hands to splash over their heads and faces.

'Is this a public bathhouse?'

Orhan laughs. 'Not bath, Connor Bey. For Allah. We wash for Allah.' He takes a vacant stool and removes his slippers. 'Come! You wash too.'

'Why would I do that?'

'For the mosque, Connor Bey. To go in mosque, you must wash.'

Connor hesitates, reluctant to participate. Up and down the row of men performing their ablutions, faces turn towards him. Water spurts loudly from the pipes, filling a channel carved in the marble floor. He sits and marvels at such an abundance of water, gushing away. Such waste. Begrudgingly, he removes his boots, peels off his socks and immerses his feet in the jarringly cold cascade spilling from the tap.

'Head and face, Connor Bey!'

He fashions his hands into a scoop and catches some of the falling water. Mimicking Orhan, he tips it over his head and wipes his face, feels the icy chill trickle down his neck and chest. He licks his lips. The water is sweet, fresh, cold. Not at all like the water he coaxed up to the surface from artesian wells back home. This is mountain water, spring water, fed by melting snow and winter rains. It tastes of mossy forests and cool glades. It is everything that his water is not.

Weighted fabric curtains block the entrance to the mosque. Orhan moves ahead, holding them aside for Connor to pass. Ducking his head, he enters.

As his eyes adjust to the darker space, he notices something missing. Chairs. Benches. Seats. This immense space is completely devoid of furniture. There is nowhere to sit, other than upon the intricate patchwork of carpets that covers the entire floor. And then Connor looks up. The dimension, majesty and ethereal beauty of the soaring blue-tiled dome above his head are beyond anything Connor has ever imagined. He can only assume this is the Blue Mosque Ayshe beseeched him to visit. The glossy painted tiles are so vivid, the light so clear and the dome so high that it almost seems to disappear into the heavens. In one corner, a curious turreted tower stands; Connor presumes it to be something akin to a pulpit. And facing that in ranks, rows of men kneel on the floor, alternately raising their hands then lying, prostrate, face down.

Orhan has been watching him. 'You have a place like this where you come from?'

Connor pauses, lost for words, then answers dryly, 'Yes, but a bit bigger.'

He turns, pulls aside the curtain at the entrance.

'Come on. Let's go.'

Orhan and Connor slip out through the side entrance of the mosque and away from the riot. They can still hear the angry shouts and the roar of the mob that is yet to disperse.

The odd pair walks in silence. Connor is still trying to digest what he has seen.

Orhan, Connor is learning, is incapable of keeping quiet for long. The boy fills the dead air with his tour-guide patter. 'It was built by Sultan Ahmed.'

'I beg your pardon?'

'Mosque was built by Sultan Ahmed. He was very great man. It is three hundred years old. Very old.'

'Yes, that is very old.' Connor is distracted and in no mood for Orhan's chattering.

They walk across a large open plaza towards another monumental building. But unlike the sublime confection they have just visited, this building has an imposing corporeality to it, like a prison or a fortress. Heavy, rose-madder buttresses support a great, grey cupola.

Connor's unsolicited tour continues. Orhan is just beginning to warm up. He indicates the imposing edifice with a theatrical sweep of his hand.

'Hagia Sophia. It was church for Christians like you. But it is now mosque. This building is more old. Built by Emperor Constantine. He is why city is called "Constantinople".'

Despite himself, Connor is curious. 'So how old is Hagia Sophia?'

'One thousand years and five hundred years.'

'You mean five hundred years?'

'No – more than five hundred years. The English I do not know.' He writes the numbers in the air with his finger. 'One, five, nought, nought.'

'One and a half *thousand* years old? That cannot be right.'

'Yes, Connor Bey. That number.'

Coming from a land that was settled by the British a whisker over one hundred years ago, this time span is almost inconceivable. Nothing Connor has ever experienced in the wide, sparse expanse of his homeland could prepare him for the scale – the consequence – of this ancient city.

Orhan leads Connor down the hill away from the Sultanahmet district and through a neighbourhood of wooden terrrace homes, keen to put as much distance between them and the mob as possible. Between the rows of houses Connor can see the reflection of sunlight off water. Gaily painted fishing caiques are moored along the shoreline of the Sea of Marmara, bobbing in the waves as fishermen on board hunch over nets, untangling, repairing and stacking them in preparation for the night ahead. Further along, a wharf extends like a finger into the channel. Fishing lines suspended from thin rods sparkle like cobwebs in a rain shower.

From a stall to their left comes the sudden clamour of a bell and the baritone cry of a street vendor. *'Dondurrrrmmmmaa. Dondurrrrrmmmmaa.'*

Connor looks over to where a man wearing a tasselled fez and gold-embroidered velvet vest is pounding something in a tub with a great wooden paddle, intermittently clanging a bunch of cowbells hanging from his stall. He is a butterball of a man, sparkling eyes set deep in a face which has the dimensions of a pumpkin.

'What is that man doing, Orhan?'

'He sells *dondurma*, Connor Bey. Ice-cream.'

'Real ice-cream? Do you like ice-cream?'

Orhan looks at Connor incredulously. 'Yes, I like ice-cream. Everyone likes ice-cream. Do you like ice-cream?'

Connor thinks back to the number of times he has tried the iced confection; a handful at best. In the stinking hot backblocks of the Mallee, it is a rare luxury.

'Yes. Yes I do. Should we try some?'

'Yes. I would like an ice-cream. I am a bit . . . peckish?'

Connor laughs and hands the boy a handful of coins.

'Is this enough?'

'Yes, of course. You give me too much.' Orhan returns most of the money. 'This is money for two ice-creams. You wait.'

Connor watches the boy negotiate with the vendor, gesticulating, shoulders shrugging. He returns with two freshly made hot waffle cones crammed with an implausible quantity of gooey ice-cream. Orhan hands one to Connor with a look of deep satisfaction. 'He would not give me good price, but I made him give us extra *dondurma*. We have big *dondurma*.'

As they walk, Connor looks at his own daunting scoop and wonders how to tackle it without making a mess of his only jacket. He smiles, watching the irrepressible joy that illuminates the boy's face. Orhan's black eyes gleam, and his round cheeks and cleft chin are now covered in melted ice-cream. Connor can't help but think back to enjoying his own sons' delight in such simple things, a time before the world of men intruded on their lives. The memory is tainted with regret. He wishes he had treasured those times more. Now, Connor feels thwarted in his attempt to honour those memories, to bring his boys home.

He sets his jaw.

He has never been one to pay much mind to what other people tell him he can and can't do, sometimes to his own detriment. Just because he is away from home, in unfamiliar territory, he is not going to start now.

Connor needs time to think. Finding his sons' bodies isn't going to be as straightforward as he'd imagined. He pictured the stiff-necked British officer pontificating from across his desk. *'Go home Mr Connor.'*

Damned if I will.

CHAPTER ELEVEN

Connor lumbers up the hill towards the Otel Troya with Orhan darting around him like a swallow, chattering between licks of his ice-cream. As they approach the hotel entrance Connor notices Orhan's voice trailing off and the boy falling in behind him. Connor is reminded of a sheep dog when it senses danger. As they step inside, a glowering Ayshe appears from the salon with her hands on her hips.

Connor watches a rapid-fire exchange in Turkish between the two. He doesn't need to speak the language to know that the boy has done the wrong thing and is now trying to charm his way out of it. Ayshe is fuming and when Orhan holds out the coins he has been paid she turns and looks straight at Connor. 'Mr Connor, I told you my son had work to do here at the hotel, that he could not help you.'

'But Orhan said you had changed your mind and that he could ...' Connor looks at the chagrined boy whose eyes are boring holes into the floorboards as the ice-cream runs over his fingers and splatters on his boots. 'I am sorry,' Connor concedes.

'He is eleven years old,' spits Ayshe. 'What else would he say? I thought you had boys.'

She turns to Orhan and speaks to him in measured English. Connor knows it is for his benefit and feels its sting.

'Now, give Mr Connor back his money.'

'But I'll do the chores now. Whatever you want me to do,' beseeches Orhan.

'Give it back.'

'But Mama, I got it for you,' he whimpers offering her the money and trying to kiss her through his pistachio-flavoured moustache.

Ayshe barks out a final command in Turkish and storms upstairs.

With tears of shame in his eyes, Orhan hands the money back to Connor, who is still stunned by Ayshe's anger. He can't fathom what he has done to offend her or why on earth she is so thorny.

'No . . . you keep it. It'll be our secret. But that is the second time you have lied to me. Don't do it again. I can't be friends with a man who lies to me.' He pats Orhan on the shoulder and the boy disappears into the salon, giving his mother a wide berth.

❧

Later, in his room, light from a kerosene lantern spreads in a warm glow across the small escritoire where Connor pores over a map of the Sea of Marmara and the Darda-nelles. The enormity of his task is daunting. Almost one hundred and fifty miles away by land, there's no clear way of getting there, and although there's always the sea route, that will be next to impossible without transport on a British ship.

He stands, turns and starts pacing, playing his options through in his mind. From downstairs, sounds disturb his reverie.

Connor steps into the corridor, curious. Music echoes along the hallway. He walks quietly down the stairs, not wanting to intrude; the tinkle and trill of a piano played competently with just an occasional discordant note and a great deal of laughter lifts his mood. Halfway down the staircase is a landing that features a wide, open window overlooking the salon. The opening is covered by a dark, elaborately decorated timber screen, carved so that Connor can see into the room through its lattice, largely unobserved by the people in the room below.

In the centre of the tiled floor below, Natalia has one hand at Orhan's waist and the other extended and holding his. She guides him around the room, spinning and dipping in a pantomime parody of ballroom dancing. The Russian woman is wearing a multi-tiered petticoat as flouncy as meringue, with her natural auburn hair pinned back simply into kiss-curls around her crown. Lifting her feet ludicrously high between steps and bobbing her leading arm up and down emphatically, Natalia is in her element.

It seems that Ayshe has made peace with her son. At the piano, she pounds the keys theatrically, her head turned towards the dancing couple to follow their comedic circuit of the room. Connor can't help but find his gaze drawn to her delicate waist and the feminine swell of her form as she leans forwards over her hands. Propriety requires that he avoid fixing his eyes on Ayshe when they interact at the hotel desk or in the salon, but here he finds himself in a position to appreciate her beauty fully. In profile, her straight, delicate nose dips to full lips now parted as she laughs, head thrown back, at the sight of her son and the Russian woman dancing with such aplomb. Her dark eyebrows form a low arc above almond-shaped eyes as green as freshly unfurled spring leaves. Ayshe's hair, black as ebony, is usually secured tightly in a bun at the nape of her neck, but now it is loose and cascades like a silken veil over her shoulders.

Connor recalls a time when his own home rang with the sounds of such *joie de vivre*. He'd never forget the circus that ensued when Lizzie decided it was time to teach the boys how to dance. All three of their boys had asked lady friends to accompany them to the Rainbow church social. The only catch, as Lizzie pointed out to her eager sons, was that the ability to make a passable attempt at a waltz and a foxtrot was fairly important when attending a dance. Art, Henry and Edward had never shown any interest in learning something they deemed to be a little too ladylike for their liking. But with her mind made up and the dance only a matter of weeks away, Lizzie took it upon herself to teach them.

The first obvious impediment was the lack of music. Connor begrudgingly stood in for the orchestra, stamping out the rhythm with the heel of his boot. The second hurdle was the shortage of female dance partners. This incited a playful tussle between the three boys to reach agreement on who would dance with Lizzie and who, of the remaining two boys, had to play the part of the lady. Despite his protestations this duty fell to Ed – being the youngest was a dreadful affliction because he always ended up with the short end of the stick. As Connor watched his sons trip and stumble round the room like newborn foals finding their feet, he laughed fit to split. The boys played up deliberately, much to Lizzie's exasperation, which made Connor break into such uncontrollable peals of laughter that he could no longer keep the beat going.

Thanks to Lizzie's persistence and unflappable patience, by the time the boys entered the Rainbow church hall, arms proudly hooked through those of their pretty and fresh-faced partners, they could make a respectable pass around the floor.

The sound of the song ending and Ayshe and Natalia laughing and chattering in another language draws Connor back to the present. The scene of domestic whimsy before him plunges him into bittersweet melancholia.

Connor realises that Natalia has fixed her gaze on the screen that is concealing him, and he catches her eye. He immediately draws back onto the landing and pads gently up the stairs, fearing exposure and humiliation, acutely ashamed at having been discovered by the Russian woman. He returns to his room and closes the door quietly, hoping that she will keep his presence to herself rather than share it with Ayshe. It seems a feeble hope given that the women appear to be friends, but the thought that Ayshe might think he is prone to sneaking around the hallways, spying on private family moments, fills him with nervous apprehension. He finds his anxiety a little perplexing. There is no real reason why he should be concerned about what the Turkish woman thinks of him. He can't rightly explain why he felt compelled to put himself at risk of exposure by indulging in such inappropriate voyeurism. Alone, lonely, he just couldn't look away.

Back in his room he walks over to the decanter of Scotch whisky on top of the timber tallboy and pours himself a generous portion. Without returning the decanter to the tray, he throws the drink back in a single draught. Connor isn't much of a drinker back home, and the alcohol hits him immediately, burning his throat and making him wince, then spreading with a warm glow through his gut. Without another thought, he pours himself a second hefty slug and walks to the door of his room. After the trying day he hopes a strong drink and some fresh air will help hone his thoughts.

Connor makes his way to a pair of French doors at the end of the hallway, which open out onto a small terrace overlooking the garden and the city skyline. Small pools of light illuminate the streets, and windows are aglow with lamplight as Constantinople prepares to turn in. The smell of wood fire is strangely comforting as night creatures buzz and trill in the sultry spring air, and the narrow lanes echo with the clip-clop and creak of beasts of burden dragging cartloads of produce homewards.

From the great mosque on the hill the call to prayer rings out, lilting and musical, but also strangely forlorn. Connor has no truck with the God peddled by Father McIntyre and his ilk, a supreme being who seems intent on inflicting needless suffering and loss on his subjects as thanks for a lifetime of penance and servility. He doesn't know much about the heathen God, Allah, but judging by his demands on his people – compulsive bathing and attendance at church five times a day – he's no more reasonable than the Christian God. The plaintive carolling ringing out from the mosques across the city sounds to Connor like the cries of men desperately seeking something. *Does God hear their pleas?* Connor doubts it.

He drains the last of his whisky and turns to go back inside. He senses her before he sees her; hears the tinkle of her fine gold bracelets and charms, and detects a sweet and exotic scent – cinnamon and citrus rind. Natalia leans against the doorjamb, one hand resting on the swell of a voluptuous hip. Her full lips, plumped and daubed with rouge, curl seductively into a broad smile and her blue eyes, rimmed and highlighted with heavy kohl, are hooded and inviting.

As with their embarrassing encounter outside her room, Connor doesn't know where to look. Natalia's soft and ample breasts swell above the line of her satin corset, skin as white and flawless as anything Connor has ever seen. She makes no attempt to cover herself with the diaphanous gown she wears draped over her shoulders and loosely held together at the base of her neck by a black, silk ribbon.

Connor moves to step past her, sidling into the hallway, but Natalia stops him, gently taking his hand in hers. Her fingers are soft and supple, childlike next to Connor's weathered, calloused shovel of a hand; her touch feels as delicate as a sparrow alighting on the branch of an oak tree.

Across the city, one by one the imams reach the climax of their performance, helping men move one step closer to God. Connor draws breath, wanting, needing; conflicted, confused. Yet at the same time, not wanting, not needing, fighting a desire he feels strongly is wrong, trying to accede to the disquiet that is shrieking at him to retreat from this uninvited advance. But the smell of her is overwhelming, intoxicating. Her soft touch is warm and promises release. Release, and relief. Connor doubts he's ever needed it more.

Natalia takes Connor's rough-hewn hand in hers and draws him into her room. The light is low and a scarlet scarf draped over a lamp casts a red glow over their faces. As Connor relaxes into the warmth of the room his eyes settle on the objects he glimpsed through the doorway at their last encounter – the last vestiges of Natalia's once different life that scream a silent agony. On the dresser are the wigs; Connor imagines them as disguises – places for Natalia to hide for a short time and become whoever she wants to be. Connor has only this one scarified skin.

Standing close to him, Natalia tugs on the satin bow at her throat and her sheer gown drops to the floor. Every muscle in Connor's body is poised to flee but his eyes are riveted to her breasts, rising and falling with her quickening heartbeat.

He catches himself before he is completely lost in her.

'No . . . Sorry, I can't.'

Natalia reaches for his shirt buttons with experienced fingers. Leaning in, she kisses his neck and chest as he is intoxicated with the scent of cinnamon in her hair. She coos something in Russian in his ear, her voice soothing and mesmerising, then pushes her hands inside his shirt and runs her nails playfully across his back. She slides her fingers inside the waistband of his trousers and circles slowly towards the front, where she searches blindly for his belt and buttons. Natalia speaks in breathy broken English. 'It's all right . . . It's all right. You are a man. A man alone. I can take away your lonely. Let me do for you.'

Connor closes his eyes and surrenders.

Natalia's hand finds its way inside his pants. He tries to speak but cannot. She begins rubbing him, gently at first, and watches his face. He is simultaneously aroused and repulsed by his own weakness.

'No, please. I shouldn't,' he pleads.

'Yes,' she says, 'this is best for sadness,' and then purrs softly in Russian, whispered words that break down all his resistance.

She moves her hand faster and faster as Connor's breathing becomes shorter and more urgent. He stares at the row of wigs behind her. Then in one brief, humiliating moment his thighs stiffen and he groans.

'Yes,' she says in English. '*Da.*' She places her ear against his bare chest, as if listening to his heartbeat. Mortified and confused, Connor does up his belt and shirt and lurches for the door, desperate to be in the sanctuary of his own room.

'Stay,' says Natalia, but in vain. He hurries past her.

Connor backs into the hallway and, to his horror, encounters Ayshe standing only metres away, extinguishing a lamp. As if things are not strained enough with her. The heat of disgrace washes up his neck and cheeks. Ayshe's look of surprise betrays her. It's clear she had thought better of him. Connor watches her gather herself, nod formally and rush away. He barrels round the corner into his room; ashamed, confused, guilt ridden – and feeling more vital than he has for years.

Lizzie was the only woman who had ever touched him there, and never quite in that way. When they were together she had lain quietly under him, knees up while he pumped her. For Connor, their union was always marred by Lizzie's unspoken sense of duty. Nothing was ever reckless or free, for either of them.

After the news of the boys they had hardly touched each other. He had tried once or twice to be closer to her, but Lizzie could not bear the intimacy. It was as if she felt their union might somehow be an assault on the memory of the beautiful boys they had made together. When they'd died she'd been stripped of her motherhood, and had stopped being a wife too. So it has been four years since Connor has felt a woman's skin on his, and he feels doubly guilty. He has been unfaithful to his wife's memory – and worse, the encounter has awakened a dormant longing in him.

Connor peels off his clothes and falls onto the mattress. Despite being emotionally and physically drained, his night's sleep is fitful and broken. What has defined him for half his life, his family, is evaporating away from him like a dam in drought.

CHAPTER TWELVE

The salon curtains are open but the cheery morning light does nothing to lighten Connor's mood. Exhausted and embarrassed, he sits at a small table set for one. He avoids Ayshe's disapproving eyes as she attends to a silver haired Turkish man in a suit several tables away. They are the only two people here at breakfast. Connor recalls Omer's performance on the morning he arrived in Constantinople, referring to an imaginary list of guests in search of a vacant room; there is no hiding the fact that the Troya is desperately quiet.

Connor has packed his case. He plans to find another hotel, especially after last night's encounter. There does not seem to be much point in waiting around in Constantinople. But without a permit to go to Gallipoli he cannot be certain how far he will get. This muddle churns through his mind as he fixes his eyes on the tarnished chandelier hanging from the ceiling, and counts the missing crystals. Suddenly Ayshe is standing before him holding a tray.

'Last night . . .' he begins, not certain why he feels he needs to explain. 'Never in my life have I done anything like that.'

'I am not your wife. Tell her,' replies Ayshe directly. 'Here is your breakfast.'

She sets a plate down in front of him and glides off towards the kitchen. Yesterday, keen for an early start, Connor had a simit on the street with Orhan so this is his first Turkish breakfast and already he can see it bears no resemblance to the breakfasts he is used to. Some of the ingredients he cannot even put a name to. What are those black pellets with the wrinkled skin, and this soft white substance that crumbles under the fork? It tastes salty and smells like wet wool. He recognises the tomato and cucumber but pushes them around the plate, wondering if he has come down at lunchtime by mistake.

❖

Ayshe reappears with Turkish coffee on a tray just as Connor puts one of the black olives to his tongue. From the kitchen doorway she spies him spitting it back into his hand and putting it discreetly back on the plate. As he does, her father slides into the chair beside him. She pauses for a moment, enjoying Connor's discomfort as Ibrahim begins to chat to him conspiratorially, from behind his hand.

As she approaches the table she hears Ibrahim speaking earnestly, in French, and cannot help but smile to herself.

'I am glad you are here Professor. Sultan Mehmet's second son has haemorrhoids the like of which I have not seen before.'

'What's he saying? Who is he?' Connor asks Ayshe.

'This is my father, Ibrahim. He thinks you are French.' She kisses her father's forehead and places a miniature cup and saucer before him.

110

He continues to speak to Connor in fluent French. 'The anus has prolapsed so much that it now resembles a bunch of grapes. Passing stools is most painful for his young Excellency. It must be all the rich food.'

Ayshe pauses. 'He hopes you are enjoying your breakfast. He noticed you are not eating.'

Ibrahim leans in. 'Would you consider assisting me in lancing and draining the nodules? It would be a great honour.'

Connor smiles and nods, completely at sea. 'I am. Delicious. Thank you.'

Ayshe smiles and Connor seizes on the momentary amnesty. 'I wonder, sorry, would you have a boiled egg — from a chicken?'

The smile slides from Ayshe's face. She swoops on the rejected breakfast plate and marches to the kitchen before she says something she will regret.

Ayshe slams the food down on the kitchen table, close to tears. The Australian has no idea how expensive it is to find fresh food in the city since the war. Or how demeaning it is to have to coax and beg for the honour of paying the inflated prices for it. She resists the urge to race back into the salon and tell Connor just how lucky he is to have cheese at all.

If it were not for a grateful former patient of Ibrahim's who lives on the outskirts of the city, there would be far less. Since the occupation began, to add insult to injury, the British — *his* British — spirit away any produce that arrives from the outlying villages, to feed their troops.

111

Orhan, who is sitting at the other end of the kitchen table with Omer, jumps up to seize some of the village cheese.

'Orhan, we are not done. Finish this last *surah*, then you can eat,' says Omer firmly as he pushes the open Koran towards the boy. 'You haven't taught him anything, Ayshe.'

'I can't bear that room anymore,' she cries. 'It used to be so full of laughter.'

'The life your father promised was a mirage, Ayshe. You cannot pretend to be European anymore.'

'What are you talking about? This building stands in Europe.'

Omer smiles sympathetically. 'We are clinging to the edge of a continent that does not want us. Surely the war has taught you that much?'

Ayshe is in no mood for a lecture and opens the door to the courtyard.

'Orhan, go and find me one egg please, son.'

Orhan takes flight, pilfering a piece of cheese on the way past. Before Ayshe can follow Omer takes her gently by the arm and turns her to face him.

'Ayshe. You are a Turkish woman. A proud and beautiful Turk. It is time you behaved like one. You know what is expected of you. You must do the right thing now, if only for Orhan.'

She smiles with lips tightly clenched, knowing in her heart he is right. Before she can reply Orhan returns holding up a single egg in triumph.

'Look! They try, but they cannot hide them from me!'

Ayshe exchanges the egg for a hug. 'Thank you, my courageous hunter.'

She fills a saucepan with water from a terracotta urn partially recessed in the floor in the corner, and places it

112

on the stovetop. She lowers the egg in with her fingers and waits, listening as Orhan repeats the prayer, '*Al-hamdu lillahi rabbil 'alamin . . .*'

When Ayshe returns to the salon with the boiled egg, wrapped in a cloth to keep in the heat, Ibrahim is still deep in conversation with Connor. The Australian has no idea what he has agreed to and when Ayshe appears his relief is palpable.

'Oh, thank you. I am sorry, I didn't mean to put you to so much trouble. It's just that I usually have eggs – at home.'

She places the egg and a spoon down in front of him without ceremony.

'You are a guest.'

Ibrahim breaks his chatter momentarily to quiz Ayshe in Turkish.

'Where is his wife?'

'I do not know, father.'

'Ask him,' he urges, as Connor cracks the top off his egg and smiles, everything opaque to him.

'No. You ask him if you are so interested. But you'll have to learn English. He speaks nothing else.'

A look of confusion washes over Ibrahim's bristly face. 'English? This is not Professor Doctor Emile?'

'No. It is not him. He is not a doctor,' she explains gently before turning to Connor.

'Your wife? He is asking where she is.'

Connor sips the grainy coffee and winces. The cup looks like doll's house crockery in his blunt fists.

'She's dead.'

Suddenly this enigmatic man makes sense to Ayshe; his harrowed look, the prickly personality. How could she not have recognised the melancholic ache of loss? Then the revelation comes to her in a gasp.

'And your sons, too?'

Connor says nothing, but the look on his face speaks for him. His armour is breached and he is run through.

'I see it in his eyes,' Ibrahim whispers in Turkish, and so now can she.

Ayshe has seen enough bereft parents in the last four years to know that men and women grieve differently. Men must act, keep moving, stay ahead of the sorrow that will swoop on them like a hawk if they stall. Helplessly they try to restore order to life, realising too late that when a child dies the parents' world is turned irreversibly on its head. She knows that if she were to lose Orhan she would be adrift, off beam, forever.

Where she was once Ayshe, daughter of Ibrahim, she is now Ayshe, mother of Orhan. Her son defines her. It is the same for Connor, and now even in death his sons give him purpose, no matter how futile, misguided or irrational it might seem.

She offers an olive branch.

'Without papers you cannot go to Gallipoli. They won't let you off the boat. You must take the ferry to the town of Chanak, then find a fisherman – pay him enough and he will sail you across the Straits. He will have no need for British permits.'

Ayshe sees the black veil of frustration and anger slowly lift from Connor's face. She has given him a way forward, tenuous as it may be. She has offered him hope as naturally as if she had handed him a lamp in a darkened room.

Connor nods in gratitude, his face softening. For the first time since he arrived at the Troya, Connor is not looking at Ayshe as if she is an enemy. Pleased for that, Ayshe leads her father by the arm to the courtyard.

CHAPTER THIRTEEN

The stench hits him like a punch in the face.

Rainbow is over two hundred miles from the sea, and Connor's entire life until coming to Constantinople has been earthbound and landlocked. He knows the smell of shit and dirt, stone and fire as well as he knows anything, but despite the long weeks on the boat getting here, the scents of the sea are still utterly alien to him. During the journey over, he came to appreciate the invigorating tang of sea spray and the caustic bite of salt drying on hot canvas. But the wharves in Eminönü are working docks where men of the sea labour ceaselessly, leaving behind malodorous fish guts rotting in the sun and seaweed stagnating in the shallows. He will never become accustomed to these rank and briny smells.

Nearby, Orhan stands with a group of sailors, gesticulating wildly. Connor knows better than to attempt to follow what's being said as he finds the language completely obscure, and is unable to identify any familiar sounds, far less break down individual words. To his ear it is a meaningless, guttural babble. Even the emotional timbre is utterly ambiguous to him. A conversation that sounds like it's about to end up in fisticuffs is just as likely to culminate in raucous laughter and cheek kissing as it is bloodshed.

'These men have ferry going to Chanak. From Constantinople to Chanak is not far – eight, nine hours.'

'What about Gallipoli? Can they take me to Anzac Cove?'

'This man here,' Orhan indicates a pimply, friendly looking youth, 'he is Metin Abi. He has brother in Chanak who is fisherman and he has boat. You give him ten shillings and he take you to Sedd-ul-Bahr and then to Ari Burnu, your Anzac.'

Connor shakes the young sailor's hand, and the lad smiles and doffs his hat before turning to join his shipmates.

'He find you when boat arrives in Chanak, and take you to his brother. Now, we get ticket.'

All around them, porters and passengers push past hollering touts and street vendors plying their trade. Although Connor is not overwhelmed by the same sense of claustrophobia and agitation he experienced upon his arrival in Constantinople, he is still disconcerted by the crush of people and the frenetic pace and activity that surround him.

Darting into the crowd, Orhan heads for a small booth where he negotiates the purchase of a ticket for the Chanak ferry.

'Connor Bey! Connor Bey! Here! Your boat is here!'

Orhan raises his hand and gestures towards a passenger ferry swaying in the ebb and flow of the Golden Horn's fickle currents, its smoke stack billowing white clouds of steam into the morning air. Sailors in crisp white uniforms, caps set jauntily atop their heads, scurry around the floating leviathan, tying and untying ropes, loading and unloading supplies and baggage from a teetering stack sitting on the dock, and securing the gangplanks to allow the growing queue of passengers to board.

'Here, Connor Bey. Your ticket.' Orhan passes Connor the hand-written bill of passage with a wide smile.

Without Orhan's assistance, Connor knows he would have found it impossible to negotiate his way to Gallipoli, let alone work out how to get to Anzac Cove. He turns to the boy, reaching into his pocket for some change.

'Thank you, Orhan.' He extends his hand, coins jingling in his palm.

Orhan refuses Connor's offer. 'No. No money. I help you, you help me.'

'How can I help you, Orhan?'

'It is good fortune you come to my hotel and you are going to Çanakkale.'

Orhan takes something from his pocket and hands it to Connor, pressing it into his palm. It's a photo of a fine-looking Turkish man in military uniform sitting pensively in a chair. Standing by his side is a beautiful woman with a swan-like neck and sparkling eyes, her hand resting on his shoulder. Connor feels a jolt of surprise when he recognises the woman as Ayshe. On the man's knee sits a young boy. Orhan.

'Connor Bey. Please. You find my *baba* in Çanakkale. The war is finished but he did not come home. You tell him he must come home now. *Annem* – my mother – needs him.'

As the penny drops Connor's heart sinks for Orhan. He fights the urge to wrap the boy up in his arms. He knows better than anyone that after four years, Orhan's father is not coming home, but he cannot let his face reveal it.

'This is your father? Who is the man at the hotel?'

Hawking a gob of phlegm from the back of his throat, Orhan spits it to the ground in an expression of disgust.

'Omer Bey is my uncle. Baba's brother.'

The last of the passengers are filing onto the ferry as the horn sounds, booming and echoing from the ancient walls of the city. Connor is flustered, taking the photo and hurrying aboard, then glancing back at the boy and raising an awkward hand in farewell. Orhan waves enthusiastically, his hand like a pennant flapping in the wind.

'You find him. Ask him when he come home?' he calls out.

Connor is lost for words.

For some time after the ferry pulls away from the Golden Horn and begins its journey through the Sea of Marmara towards the Dardanelles, Connor is deep in thought. Orhan's revelation casts his time at the Troya in a whole new light. Suddenly Ayshe's latent hostility towards him, right from the time he tried to check in, makes sense. If her husband died fighting Australians at Gallipoli, then every time she looked at Connor, she would have seen the face of her husband's killers. How it must have galled this proud Turkish woman to have to feed him, have him sleep under her roof, and worse, watch him with her son.

He can only wonder at why she has not told Orhan the truth. Perhaps she still harbours some forlorn hope that Orhan's father might one day return. Her anger tells Connor she is not in denial; not really. It is possible she wants her husband to fade from their lives rather than be wrenched away from them.

Blinded by his own grief, Connor failed to recognise that when he looked at Ayshe he was glimpsing into a

119

wellspring of shared sadness. What Connor mistook for enmity towards him was Ayshe's anger at the indiscriminate brutality of life.

Ayshe is a widow, the man in the hotel her brother-in-law. Connor is puzzled. It shouldn't change anything. And yet, inexplicably, it seems to change everything.

The photo rests in his hand, a glimpse into a distant, and far happier, past. He takes Art's journal from his case and slips the photo inside.

Putting his hat and case neatly on the luggage rack above his seat, he carefully lays the journal on the bench beside him. Outside the ferry's misted-over windows he can see the rolling, forest-clad hills that plunge dramatically into the inky Sea of Marmara. The gentle rise and fall of the ferry passing through the swell is soothing, and lulls him to sleep, his head resting on the wall behind him.

CHAPTER FOURTEEN

*I*t starts as a sensation.

Hairs prickle at the base of the neck. Nerves tingle, on edge. Something's wrong.

It's the silence that makes them uneasy.

The Mallee is so quiet it hurts city dwellers' ears. Its unsettling and heavy quietude is so pervasive it seems to have a voice; buzzing, pressing on eardrums. Those sounds that hum constantly in the city are absent. No buildings, no walls, no lanes for the interminable cacophony of engines and ceaseless chatter to rebound off. Here in the middle of nowhere, endless plains soak up sound.

But those who live here can hear the desert speaking in tongues. Chirruping insects, cawing birds, reptiles slithering and scuttling through the dry undergrowth and across the red sand.

Now, though, even they hear nothing.

The world is holding its breath.

Then they hear it. A searing roar far in the distance.

Something's coming. Something bad.

The boys stand in the middle of the field, unsure where to go, what to do, unsure what's approaching. Art has a .22 rifle slung over his shoulder, and his brothers carry between them a brace of dead rabbits.

'There!' Art, his eyes scanning into the distance, has spotted it. He points. It's as if the horizon is disintegrating. Where just moments before a razor-sharp line separated red earth from blue sky, now the division is unclear. A heavy haze of what looks like smoke from a scrub fire, but red as ox blood, is billowing, roiling, barrelling across the plain. It's travelling fast. Far too fast.

In a heartbeat, it swells from a line drawn along the horizon to a wall that obliterates everything in its path.

Art howls. 'Run!'

In the middle distance, a small group of Mallee trees hugs the ground. The boys bolt towards it at breakneck pace. The tangled limbs and sparse foliage won't offer much protection. But this far from home, it's the best they can hope for. They're a way away, but they might just make it.

Art looks back. The solid wall of dust is nearing at an impossible speed, gaining on the running boys with every stride.

Might get there. If we're lucky, he thinks.

A sudden exclamation and cry from behind. 'Art!'

He looks back over his shoulder. Ed has stumbled, lies writhing in the dirt clutching his ankle. Art turns and races back, Henry in his wake. They reach their brother as the storm engulfs them. Art draws his brothers to his chest, trying in vain to shield their faces from the apocalyptic torrent of dust and gravel that rips at them horizontally, driven by a wind fiercer than anything he's ever experienced.

A looming shape appears through the haze. Through eyes squinted tightly into slits, Art can just recognise the outline of his father atop his mare, wheeling to a stop beside where he and *his brothers crouch in the whirling heart of the tempest. Connor vaults to the ground and slaps his horse's rump. She gallops into the distance. He carries a thick woollen swag beneath his arm. Battling to keep hold of it in the gale, he unfurls it and lowers it over himself and the boys like a tent, using Art's rifle as a pole. The three boys and their father huddle beneath the blanket as the blood-red dust consumes them.*

The wind screeches and howls. Connor turns to Art. 'Good on you, son. You didn't leave your brothers behind.'

He sees the look of fear in Ed's eyes. 'What's that magic word, Ed? The one that makes the carpet fly?'

For a moment, Ed forgets where they are; he smiles. 'Tonga.'

Art laughs despite himself. 'Tangu, you wombat.'

Connor wraps his arms around his boys. 'That's it. Tangu. The name of Prince Hussein's magic carpet.'

The storm outside screams like a banshee. But Art, Henry and Ed are safe. They can smell their father's skin, his hair. Nothing can touch them as long as he's here.

'Close your eyes, lads. Let's get out of here. Hold tight. Ed – I can see you peeping! Only works if your eyes are closed. You don't want us falling off, mate, do you? Now, all together . . .'

As one.

'Tangu!'

CHAPTER FIFTEEN

'God, you woulda hated to see this with skin on it. Look at the jaw on this geezer – he was half cow!' Private Dawson is holding a human skull, Yorick-like, inspecting its pendulous mandible.

Lieutenant Colonel Hilton has been working too long on this peninsula and seen too much carnage to brook any levity when it comes to the dignity of the fallen. He snaps at Dawson, 'Private! Bit of respect or I will have you on report!'

Dawson, shamefaced, puts the skull down. 'Sorry, sir. He was probably a very good-looking man.'

Hilton turns and walks towards the summit of a low ridge. As he departs, out of the corner of his eye he sees Dawson salute him with a disarticulated arm. He decides to let it slide.

From the peak, Hilton surveys the soldiers at work below. They fan out across a shallow gully the size of a rugby pitch, moving methodically from one side to the other as they prod the ground with rifle-cleaning rods, looking for the telltale friable soil they find in patches where bodies decompose beneath the surface. There is no shortage of soft soil.

Men dig into the side of the hill, exhuming bones stained umber by the minerals in the earth, some still wrapped in decaying khaki uniforms that disintegrate as the soldiers lift them from the ground. Remains that have lain exposed above the surface since the conflict ended have been bleached to a blinding white by the Aegean sun. They lie in tangled clumps surrounded by the rubble and refuse of war: boots, the leather cracked and peeling; canteens, crushed and flaking; ammunition casings and rifle clips, rusting and packed with dirt.

Further along the ridge, a man sits on a folding canvas stool, hunched over a large sketchpad that rests in his lap. A thin stick of charcoal held delicately between thumb and forefinger, his eyes dart from the tableau unfolding in the gully beneath him to the sketch that is taking shape on his pristine white paper. Hilton walks over, peers down at the artist's impressionistic and idealised interpretation of the sombre scene before them. The small, crude white crosses dotting the hillside become monuments of consequence; the dusty, weary soldiers working amongst them transformed into Homeric heroes, biceps bulging, noble brows furrowed. Hilton watches, marvelling at the strange alchemy that transforms monstrosity into beauty.

Hilton turns to see Major Hasan climbing the hill towards him. It's been a month since the Turk returned unwillingly to Çanakkale, and the two men have reached a peaceful accord based on a growing mutual respect.

'*Merhaba*, Hilton Bey.'

'*Merhaba*, Hasan Bey.'

Down the slope, Sergeant Tucker has been sifting through the soil. He hails Hilton and holds up a red and purple arm patch.

'One of ours! Sixth battalion, sir.'

'A name tag?'

'Not yet.'

'Keep looking.'

Hilton turns to his Turkish companion.

'You never told me what you did before the war.'

Hasan smiles sadly. 'This is Turkey – there was no "before the war".'

The men stand in silence for a moment, then Hilton hears a call from the gully below. It's Private Dawson, who is standing looking in the direction of the shore through a pair of binoculars. 'Ah, sir? We expecting company?'

Hilton strides down to join Dawson, who hands him the binoculars and points to a spot far below on the rippling black waves curling towards the sand. A small fishing boat is approaching the beach, rowed by a single man working the oars as another man stands at the bow. Incongruously, the tall, broad-shouldered man at the front of the boat is wearing neat pants, a suit jacket and tie, and a broad-brimmed hat. In his hands he's holding a small brown suitcase.

❖

Connor vaults from the bow, the beach just a few feet away. The water is deeper than he expects. Scrabbling with his bare feet to find purchase on the slippery pebbles, the waves soak into the trousers he has rolled above his knees. Attempting to keep his pants dry is an impossibility; one hand holds his boots and socks above his head, the other his suitcase. He wades through the water past the carcasses of wrecked landing craft, shattered timber crates and hollow, spent ammunition shells, feeling the cut and tug of sharp objects digging into the soles of his feet.

Reaching the shore, Connor puts down his luggage and looks up. Looming above him is a heavily eroded cliff, pockmarked by craters where shells have blasted away great chunks of earth, and deep scars where men have gouged paths and trenches that zig and zag up to the summit. The beach isn't much to speak of – only a couple of hundred yards long – and the cliff face is so close that Connor's head spins as he looks up at the escarpment. He shuts his eyes, steadying himself, but the imagined sounds of war intrude – the crack of rifles and pounding of guns, bullets whizzing and whipping through the air, explosions, the soft, wet thud of targets hit, the harrowing screams of dying men. Connor shudders, opens his eyes. All is quiet save the lapping of water on the stone beach and the unmistakable sound of horses' hooves.

Four men on horseback in military uniform are cantering along the beach towards him. Connor notices that one of the men is wearing an Ottoman uniform. The tall man leading the charge draws his horse to a halt and dismounts, marching determinedly, if a little awkwardly, towards Connor. His high black boots, polished to a mirror-like shine, slip and sink in the wet pebbles. The man's lips are pressed into a thin line of frustration, and his high cheekbones are flushed with anger. Without breaking stride, he snaps an order at the men who accompany him. 'Don't let that boat go anywhere!'

While the men hail the fisherman, who has turned his boat and is hoisting the sail, preparing to return to Chanak, the tall man advances on Connor.

'Lieutenant Colonel Cecil Hilton. Who in the blue blazes are you?'

Without turning to look at him, Connor addresses the soldier.

'This is where they landed?'

Hilton is incredulous. 'I beg your pardon?'

'. . . Sitting bloody ducks. What idiot would land an army here?'

'I asked you who you are, sir!'

'Joshua Connor. From Rainbow – hundred miles south-west of Swan Hill.'

'Surely they told you this was a restricted zone?'

'Someone may have mentioned it.' Connor shakes his head, trying to digest the Herculean task that faced his sons when they landed here in 1915. 'Back home the papers kept telling us we were winning.'

'Mr Connor, is it? I'm at a loss. You've turned up here unannounced. For what? A tour? A pilgrimage? We are trying to work here, putting names to ten thousand dead men.'

Connor looks up to the gullies in the escarpment above them, where tiny figures work amongst a growing field of white crosses. 'Good. Because I'm only looking for three.'

He can see Hilton's attitude soften immediately as the extent of Connor's loss registers on the soldier's face. 'Your sons?'

Connor nods.

'There are eight square miles of collapsed trenches, bomb craters and barbed wire around here,' Hilton explains gently, 'and more than enough unexploded shells to blow us all to high heaven. You simply cannot stay.'

From his coat pocket Connor draws out his map of the peninsula. He jabs his finger at the creased paper.

'Yep, I know it's tricky. But I know where my sons were killed. Here at Lone Pine. Around 7 August.'

Hilton's reply is firm and clear. 'You don't understand what you're asking. Those battles in early August were some of the most intense and bloodiest of the whole campaign. Finding your sons amongst the thousands of bodies at Lone Pine is a fool's errand.' Hilton draws himself up. 'Rest assured, Mr Connor, I aim to identify every man out there, including your sons. But you *cannot* stay. Sergeant! Escort Mr Connor back to his boat!'

'Don't bother.' Connor folds up his map angrily, shoving it back into his pocket. 'Thanks for all your help.'

As Connor turns to leave, the Turkish soldier steps towards him, holding something in an outstretched hand. With a shock Connor realises it is the photograph of his boys. The Turk is staring at it.

'Your sons,' the man murmurs in accented English, lifting his gaze to meet Connor's. 'It fell from your pocket.'

This man is the enemy and everything about him sets Connor's teeth on edge. The despised Ottoman uniform, the flourish of his elaborately coiffed moustache, his dusky complexion and eyes as black as pitch. That he has in his hand the photograph of Connor's sons – the sons who were cut down by Turkish bullets in this cursed terrain – only makes it worse. Connor snatches the photo wordlessly from the man's hand and storms down the beach to where the fisherman waits.

Dusk descends upon the Aegean as gently as a sheet of silk. It's one of the things about this land that Hilton has come to appreciate. He sits on a camp chair, hands intertwined behind his head, legs outstretched and resting upon a log, and watches the sky as it glows an implausibly peachy pink. The distant lofty purple peaks on the island of Imbros float on a mauve sea. Everything is still, impossibly calm. Not so much as a puff of wind.

From behind him drifts the clatter and chatter of the soldiers settling in for the night, tending fires and heating army rations. He hears footsteps, the crunch of heavy boots on gravel. Hilton looks over his shoulder at Tucker.

'Sir, something you might want to see.'

Hilton reluctantly gets to his feet and follows the sergeant over to the cliff's edge. He looks through a pair of binoculars at the beach below. A small fire flickers on the pebbly beach. Sitting on his haunches, lifting the lid on a billy, is the pigheaded Australian father, Connor.

Hilton is astonished. He is caught halfway between anger and admiration – there is no faulting the resolve of the stubborn fool.

'Damn.'

'Want me to arrest him, sir?'

'And then what? No. Take some food down to him. And a blanket.' Hilton turns and walks back to the camp. 'We'll sort him out tomorrow.'

CHAPTER SIXTEEN

Water sprays in curtains as a group of naked soldiers splashes about in the sea. Warm, briny droplets bead on forearms and foreheads tanned as brown as boot leather, in stark contrast to their fish belly–pale torsos. Greeves bobs about on his back like a barrel, his corpulent midriff providing an easy target for Tucker and Dawson, who skim flat skipping stones across the waves at his roly-poly profile.

'Incoming!' Tucker launches a missile, flattened and burnished by the tides. It hits its target, glancing off Greeves' gut.

'Steady on, fellas!' the New Zealand lieutenant protests, on his feet now, arms flapping impotently at his sides. The temptation's too great. Greeves is bombarded with a barrage of pebbles, shells and dried seaweed from shore, most hitting the mark.

Hasan sits some way back from the water's edge, coolly observing the Anzac soldiers gambolling in the waves. He has half an eye on his sergeant, Jemal, who is absorbed in his work at the base of the cliff, gently fanning a small stack of glowing embers. Rummaging in his mess kit, Jemal takes out a brass cylinder ornately engraved with foliate designs and unscrews it. Hidden within is a hinged, detachable handle that he removes and sets aside. He fills the bottom half of the cylinder with glossy, chocolate-brown coffee beans and screws the lid back on before attaching the handle to the lid. Jemal rotates the handle vigorously, nodding his head when he deems the job done and opening the grinder to appraise its contents. He holds the open bottom half of the cylinder to his nose, smiling with satisfaction. Meticulously, he measures the correct amount of coffee into a tiny copper pot that has a small amount of water in it from his canteen, along with a teaspoon of precious sugar. He rests it on the embers until the coffee begins to froth – a thick, bubbly foam – then pours it into a delicate, gilded coffee cup. Jemal inspects the coffee critically and raises his bushy eyebrows, satisfied with the product of his labour. Holding the fragile cup in his mitt-like hand, he treads apprehensively across the beach towards where Hasan sits.

'Coffee, sir?'

Hasan raises his head. 'Yes. Thank you, Sergeant.'

Jemal's eyes are fixed on the coffee, careful not to spill a drop into the saucer, as he hands it to his major.

'Health be on your head, *effendi*.'

Hasan responds with the customary reply, 'Health be on your hands.'

He takes a small sip of the piping-hot drink, savouring the bitter sweetness as it slips down his throat. Hasan sighs, shuts his eyes for a moment.

Further up the beach, a solitary figure stands, shin deep in the shallows, trousers rolled above his knees. Hasan and Jemal watch Connor as he bends and picks up a handful of pebbles and sand, running it through his hands.

'Are all Australians this stubborn?'

Hasan looks up, following Jemal's line of sight.

'It is a matter of national pride for them. You would fit in well there.'

Behind them they hear the crunch of hooves on the beach. The two Turks turn to watch Hilton dismounting his bay mare, leading her over to where the men sit.

'Not swimming?'

Hasan smiles wryly. 'We have bathhouses for that.'

'Sergeant!' Hilton hails his second-in-command.

Tucker bounds up the beach, stark naked, whippet thin and ungainly. He draws to a halt in front of Hilton.

'Let's split the men. I'll take the Nek, you take half a dozen chaps up to Quinn's Post.'

Tucker snaps to attention with a textbook click of his waterlogged bare heels, hand raised to his forehead. 'Sir!'

'Don't salute me like that, Sergeant.'

Grabbing a towel, Tucker covers himself and saunters down the beach to rouse the troops.

'Gordon, Mac, Les, Larry and Len! It's not Bondi! Rattle your dags. You're doing Spooks Plateau!'

Hasan looks again at Connor, who is now crouched by the water, chin covered with a thick lather, holding a small mirror in one hand and a razor in the other. 'What are you doing with your farmer?'

Following his gaze, Hilton winces. 'He stays here – out of our hair till the supply ship comes.'

'Maybe we could help him.'

'You *know* what the chances are of finding his sons.'

'We have the day they were killed, I know the area.'

'We both know it – half my regiment is still there, but I couldn't tell you whose bones are whose. Why tip everything on its ear for one farmer from the Mallee who can't stay put?'

'Because he is the only father who has come looking.'

Hilton screws up his face, exasperated. They both know that the major is right; where they choose to dig today is of little consequence – it will make no difference in the scheme of things. Hilton relents, shouting out to Tucker and the motley gang of soldiers now drying themselves on the beach. 'Sergeant! Change of plan.'

<hr />

A spent cartridge sits warming in the palm of Connor's hand, one of the infinite number that wash back and forth in the gentle waves that lap the shore. Hilton stands before him, his fists clamped testily on his hips.

'There's a supply ship back to Constantinople in two days; you may stay with us till then.' Hilton has capitulated, but his tone of voice makes it clear he's none too happy about it.

'Two days isn't enough,' protests Connor.

'Two days, two years; whatever it is you are looking for, you won't find it.'

'I can find things that other people can't.' Connor replies.

'I hope you can see underground?'

'Sometimes. I find water, I'm good at that.'

Hilton turns and begins walking back down the beach towards his men. 'This isn't water . . . Two days.'

Connor looks up at the escarpment, a glimmer of hope in his eyes.

'We'll see,' he murmurs. 'We'll see.'

A line of mounted soldiers snakes along a goat trail, up a gully between a scatter of scrawny bushes and mean grasses. The horses' hooves turn over clods of dry dirt, exposing lead bullets, the odd tin can and flecks of bone. At the head of the column is Hilton, who rides beside Major Hasan. Jemal rides alone behind them, tugging on the reins and kicking to keep his horse from straying or stopping to gnaw on grass roots.

A string of ten Anzacs follows. Tucker leads with Thomas and Connor riding behind him and Dawson trailing at the rear. As they reach the crest of a ridge they wind past a ghastly monument to the calamity of the campaign – a mound of hundreds of human skulls meticulously stacked like apples on a fruit stand. Beside the pile are neat rows of pelvises, scapulas, femurs, radii and ulnas; a medical student's dream. Protruding from the hideous collection is a rough wooden sign in Arabic.

Thomas turns to Connor. 'Don't worry, mate. Those are Abdul's. Not ours.'

Connor's gaze is firmly fixed on Hasan and Hilton. He is offended by the relaxed way in which they converse. As far as he knows, the Turks are the enemy.

Tucker doesn't take his eyes off the despised Ottoman officer for a moment. The first and last time he shook hands with a Turk was here at Gallipoli, at Johnston's Jolly. The day – 24 May 1915 – lives in him like an inoperable piece of shrapnel, impossible to dig out. Five days before, the Turks launched a disastrous counterattack on the Anzac line. Turkish bodies were piled up in no-man's land, so high the Turks had to stop advancing. His .303 was so hot from firing he had to wrap his hand in an undershirt to slide the bolt or remove the clip. The next day both sides agreed on a truce to recover the dead, who had been lying amongst the wild thyme and myrtle for nearly a month, swelling, rotting and liquefying in the spring sun.

The day of the armistice was uncommonly grey and overcast. The whistle sounded at 7.00 am and men on both sides tentatively poked their heads over the sandbags. Before long the land between their lines was teeming with officers and gangs of soldiers spiriting away the dead on stretchers, their faces covered in a vain attempt to mask the stench. Tucker was cutting the ID discs off the corpses and recording their names before they were dropped into shallow graves. Plenty he could put a face to when he read the name etched on the tag.

The day was eerily quiet. It was the only time he recalls the peninsula being silent for any length of time. When he could not sleep in his dugout he used to play a game, timing the interval between gunshots, mortars or artillery. Any sort of ammo fired anywhere along the line – as long as you could hear it – counted. In a perversity peculiar to war he would lie awake hoping for a shot, giving no thought to where the bullet might finish up. Or in whom.

On the day of the truce the officers were tramping up and down the line trying to stop any fraternising with the enemy. Tucker still managed to swap a tin of jam for a green plum, using hand signals. He was so delighted by the fruit that he forgot himself for a moment and shook the young smiling Turk by the hand. While their hands were locked the Turk turned and started spitting Turkish at one of the Australian medics beside him.

Tucker and his mates had always been a bit dubious about John James, who spoke a bit of Turkish and wore an Ottoman medal on his chest like some morbid souvenir. The Turks took offence at this too, crying bloody murder and accusing him of looting from a dead hero.

James was indignant, explaining in broken Turkish that he had earned the Sultan's Award for fighting shoulder-to-shoulder with the Turks against the Russians a few years earlier. Watching James and the Turks shaking hands and kissing cheeks made Tucker realise what an imprecise gesture a handshake is, and he vowed never to bother with it again. When 4.00 pm came that day, they all clambered back into their trenches to start killing one another again.

Connor breaks into Tucker's reverie. 'Who is the Turk? What's he doing here?'

Tucker turns and speaks under his breath. 'That's "Hasan the Assassin" – saw us land, saw us off. The dog wiped out half my battalion, including my brother. He would've killed your sons, for sure.'

In an instant Connor has spurred his horse with a swift kick to the flanks. Just as the horse takes off, Thomas reaches out and grabs a fistful of its bridle, and reins both horse and rider in.

He has obviously caught the gist of the conversation. 'Whoa there, you two. Where are you going? We're all best mates now. I get to serve the Major breakfast every morning. I always add a bit of Anzac allspice.' By way of illustration, Thomas hacks up a spit ball and fires it onto the ground beside Connor.

Tucker watches Connor settle but can see the Australian father is emotionally charged. The enemy now has a face, a target for the years of pent up anger and grief. Like the jam tin grenades that Tucker and his brother used to hurl at the Turkish line, Connor was set to explode without warning.

CHAPTER SEVENTEEN

The loose chain of horsemen winds around the rim of an enormous mine crater and up the adjacent ridge.

'Wouldn't have wanted to be standing here when that went off,' Tucker calls over his shoulder to no one in particular.

At the summit the party reins to a halt near a fledgling Turkish pine. The scraggly tree stands four foot high with its thirsty limbs hanging limply, most of its needles lying about the base of its trunk.

'Gentlemen . . . the Lone Pine,' Tucker announces.

'Not the original?' asks the gullible Dawson.

'That one was blown halfway to Brisbane during the battle,' answers Tucker as he empties his canteen at the base of the tree. 'More like Son of Lone Pine.'

'We call this place Kanli Sirt. Bloody Ridge,' Hasan says quietly. 'There was a whole forest here before.'

They all struggle to picture it as they look out over the grim plateau of tangled barbed wire, eviscerated sandbags, collapsed trenches and, everywhere, grim bone fragments sprinkled across the landscape like shredded coconut on a cake. Hilton dismounts and notes that there is not a bush or clump of grass growing that would reach the top of his leggings.

In the distance there is a rudimentary obelisk fashioned by the Turkish survivors of Lone Pine from concrete and spent artillery shells. A memorial to their friends who lie in the mass graves on the fringes of the battlefield.

'Do you remember much detail?' Hilton asks Hasan.

'Unfortunately. No one who fought here will forget it,' says Hasan without explanation.

He stands up in the saddle and looks into a series of trenches, framed with rotting sandbags and eroded by the flash floods over winter.

'That was our front line there,' he tells Hilton, and then jabs his heels into his horse's ribs and trots towards it. Jemal pulls alongside him, looking unsettled. Clearly this is not a place he wants to revisit.

'It can't be worse than the last time,' Hasan assures him with a smile.

'No. But scabs will still bleed if you pick them.'

Connor watches the two Turks and fights a rising wave of resentment. His anger, originally directed at a nebulous beast called 'The Turk', is now keenly focused on the man he has already begun to think of as the 'Assassin'. The enemy has a face, and every time Hasan smiles it is another bullet in the memory of Connor's boys. In his more rational moments, Connor can distinguish between war and murder. But since arriving on the peninsula, those moments have become few and far between, and more often than not he feels as if he is thrashing around in a dim well somewhere, grappling for a slippery rope.

Hilton, standing beside Connor's horse, sees the farmer's grim expression and accurately reads his thoughts. 'It's strange to think of him as something other than the enemy,' he says in a low voice. He swings back into the saddle. 'Takes a bit of getting used to.'

Connor can't imagine becoming accustomed to it, ever.

❖

Hilton gives the command to start at the Turkish trenches and work their way across no-man's land. The party drifts towards Hasan and Jemal, who are already standing on the sandbags above the trenches that hold such painful memories.

Hasan drops down into the trench and lands awkwardly. He grabs at a splintered piece of timber that leans against the trench wall and steadies himself. He hears a sound akin to a rolled-up carpet landing behind him, followed quickly by Jemal's colourful curses. The sergeant dusts himself off as the two Turks walk the line together. At one point the trench has partially collapsed and they must duck under fallen timbers. Almost everything useful has been souvenired by the local villagers and goatherds long ago, for use in rebuilding and extending their homes. The two men barely recognise the place that was their home and hell for six unbearable months.

Jemal reads the sun, now high above them, and mutters to Hasan.

'Give me a moment or two.'

He wanders into an adjoining communication trench and lays his tunic on the hard earth. He turns to face southeast and begins his prayers. Bringing his hands up to the sides of his head, with palms forwards and his stubby thumbs behind his ears, Jemal is ready to listen to his god for the first time in months. He places his right hand over his left in front of him and looks down, exhaling hard before bending in half.

Jemal hurries through the *rakats*, emblazoned in his mind from boyhood; he kneels and bows until he feels the coarse wool of his tunic against his forehead and nose. Amongst friends he calls himself a broken Muslim – he prays only sporadically, but like everything else, he does it with gusto. He says a personal prayer to honour his dead men, his hands cupped in front of his chest; more like a conversation with Allah than a prayer. He surprises himself when he feels the splash of a warm tear land in his palm. He wipes his face, stands and shakes out his tunic.

He finds Hasan looking out over the sandbags in a way he would never have dared when they'd last occupied these defensive lines. Tucker and half a dozen of the Anzac soldiers have fanned out from the top of the trench, doing an initial sweep for unexploded grenades and mortar shells. They move quickly and methodically. Twenty yards out from the trench they hammer a line of stakes into the hard ground and run a white rope between them. Tucker gives a whistle – the all-clear – and the rest of the party joins them.

❖

Hilton's men break into small teams. After three months, their macabre task has become run of the mill for many of them. They examine the scattered bones and shapeless bundles as if they are doing little more than picking vegetables in a market garden. They spread out across the broken landscape, lugging hessian sacks, labels, notebooks and spades, passing smokes between them and chatting. Every day they argue over football codes, lay bets on just about anything and give blow-by-blow accounts of their conquests during nights on leave.

No one dares talk about families – some of the men haven't been home since they enlisted – and they never bring up the war. What's the point? It's not like they weren't all there. Hell, they're still in it. They know what went on and why what they are doing now is important. If it was their remains lying about, they would want someone bagging them up and giving them a proper burial.

'It is impossible to care for so many, that's all,' Hilton once heard one of the rank and file telling his mate. He knows what he means.

After six months fighting at Gallipoli and another two years on the Western Front, Hilton expected that he would be inured to death, his senses and emotions cauterised. At least now there are just the blanched skeletons to deal with, not the fly-blown bodies that used to swell up and pop like paper lunch bags in the sun. The smell reminded him of sheep carcasses lying in the paddocks during the drought, buzzing with the sound of unseen flies and the waxy skin rippling over the maggots feasting below.

On the hottest days he would give the order and men would fire single rounds into the bellies of the dead to release the putrid gas before the bodies exploded. Inevitably what started as a grim necessity descended into a sport. There was always someone to take a wager on the longest shot or the most spectacular splat.

'Battle can bring out the best in men, but the waiting around has had the exact opposite effect,' he wrote to his wife in the middle of the summer of 1915.

Dawson hovers over an assemblage of weathered bones. The only clue to their nationality is a hobnailed boot with a collection of toe bones rattling around inside like a gruesome game of jacks.

'You couldn't lend us an arm, could you?' he asks Thomas. 'I've almost got a full set here.'

'Left or right?'

'He's not choosy.'

Thomas picks up a long, thin bone – a radius – and flings it across the ground to Dawson with a nod. No point in burying half a bloke.

The two men approach a shallow shell crater with a puddle of rancid water in the bottom. Grim-faced, they inspect the sodden uniform and sallow bones sticking out of the water.

'Oh, crikey,' complains Dawson, crinkling his nose at the fetid stench.

'Anzac soup.'

'Your turn,' says Thomas, pushing Dawson into the hollow and throwing him a bag and a short-handled entrenching spade.

Dawson bends down and fishes around in the water with his hand. 'He's still got hair. He must have been washed out of his grave over winter.'

He lifts his hand out of the rank puddle holding a small brass button embossed with the unmistakable map of Australia and an Empirical crown.

'Guess that answers that,' says Dawson, and starts to lift the gruesome remains onto the end of the spade. 'Hold the sack open.'

'Wonder if he was much of a swimmer?' asks Thomas, grinning from ear to ear. He looks up and is skewered with the disapproving eyes of Connor, who is watching from the Turkish line. Thomas' smile withers and he dips his head. 'Not much of a sense of humour, this old bloke.'

<hr>

Hasan scrambles out of the trench and walks along the sandbags as if they are castle battlements. Hilton keeps a respectful distance, taking notes as Hasan speaks.

'We were here,' he explains to Hilton. 'Your men were over there.' He points across the plateau.

'We had a machine gun here,' he continues, waving his hand emphatically. 'Another here. And one more there. We were close enough to see you – so many blue eyes. *Maşallah*. It is very lucky in Turkey to have blue eyes . . . Everywhere, that is, except here.'

The young Anzacs hear Hasan's wavering voice across the battlefield. One by one they stop working and drift towards the trench to hear him better. He takes a breath to calm himself and undoes the top button of his tunic. He locks eyes on the blue-eyed audience and smiles thinly, before continuing.

'We built a roof over the trench. I ordered them to cut down the pine trees on the ridge, and lay them side by side, like this,' he explains, showing how the rough-hewn trunks were fitted.

145

'The roof was to protect us from shell fire. Instead we made a trap for ourselves.'

Jemal stands in the trench, looking down the line and listening intently. Back when the timbers were in place the trench was twilight dark. Shafts of sunlight penetrated the gloom through gaps between the pine planks. When the Anzacs attacked in those early days in August, Jemal had expected them to run over the roof and on to the second line of trenches. When he heard men stomping heavily back and forth along the roof he knew they had made a terrible tactical mistake. When the men saw gun muzzles and bayonets poking through the gaps in the timber they panicked. It was like shooting fish in a barrel. Not content to stab and shoot mercilessly into the dark tunnel, the Anzacs began tearing at the timbers like rabid dogs. When the gaps were wide enough they wrenched their bayonets from the ends of their rifles and without hesitating, dropped down into the dark.

'You came in from two sides, here and here, and then from above,' Hasan says quietly. 'Inside it was bayonets, hands . . . teeth. It was so dark and close we didn't always see who it was we struck and slashed. We tore flesh off each other like mad men'

Jemal witnessed the most brutal and desperate fighting of his life in that tunnel. Men from both sides clawed at each others' faces, bit pieces of ears and noses off, pulled hair out by the handful and jabbed bayonets into each other's flesh at close quarters. He saw an Australian grab a Turkish boy by the face and force his thumbs into his eye sockets. The digits came out dripping gore the colour of strawberry jam. Another Australian swung his bayonet with his right

146

hand while he held his own entrails in place with the other. Eventually the guts slipped through his fingers and landed on the trench floor where the man stomped all over himself as he parried. Jemal finally battled his way into the sunlight covered in gore and blood, not sure if it was his own or not.

'Three days we attacked and counterattacked,' Hasan continues. 'We only stopped because we could no longer climb over the bodies.'

CHAPTER EIGHTEEN

An eerie quiet.

From nowhere, three figures cut through the plumes of impenetrable steel-grey smoke. Eyes white, flashing. Teeth bared.

Three young men. Tall, broad-shouldered. Boots catching on the rough-hewn timber planks.

Sharpened steel slashes through gaps in the boards. Bayonets jabbing, stabbing at them as they leap and stumble along the trench line.

Shots.

Close.

Too close.

A tug on Henry's jacket – the bullet pierces his sleeve but miraculously misses his flesh.

Ahead, a breach in the timber roof. Henry doesn't hesitate. Pulling the bayonet off the end of his rifle, he drops straight down and disappears. Shrieks. Hideous cries.

Art and Ed follow him into the blackness. Wet, blood-sodden darkness. Can't see. But the sounds. Grunts, things tearing, unholy slaughterhouse screams.

Eyes adjust to the dim light. Dirt falls through the cracks, sharp-edged sand beneath eyelids, tears streaming down filthy cheeks. Thin slits of light penetrate the gloom, revealing Dante's inferno.

Hands turn to sickles, ripping flesh from bone, tearing away bleeding chunks of scalp still attached to skeins of hair.

Henry is in the thick of it, his blade slicing and flashing like a scythe. Ed, pulling hair by the handful, digs his teeth into a young Turkish soldier's cheek. Henry blocks a knife as it thrusts towards his younger brother; slips his bayonet easily into the attacker's throat. It chips the spine as it severs the Turk's windpipe, blood mixing with bubbles of air in a hideous foam.

Art's back is to the wall. Slammed into a corner with nowhere to go. An Ottoman soldier has his rough hands around his throat, clamping it shut. Stars burst before his eyes – he can't breathe. He claws for a hold, desperately scratching at the man's face. Art's thumbs find the eye sockets and he pushes. Resistance, then a yielding as one eyeball pops out. The Turk stumbles back, his eye hanging down onto his cheek from the nerve. Drawing breath, blinded by blood and fury, Art reaches out, grabs it and pulls.

The three Connor boys run from the apocalyptic underworld towards the light. Plastered head to toe in gore, they scramble to the surface, clambering up a pile of bodies; tangled and severed limbs form a ghastly ladder.

Light. Air.

Suddenly, the Turks counterattack. A wave of enemy soldiers charges towards them.

The rifle. Art grabs it, aims, and starts to fire.

'Retreat! Get back to the trenches!' he howls, half-battlecry, half-plea.

The boys. Have to get the boys out of here.

'Retreat!'

CHAPTER NINETEEN

'There was no honour in this.'

As Hasan continues, no one notices that Connor has wandered across no-man's land towards the Anzac Line.

The major's words are flooding his senses. His eyes are fixed on the map that he holds out in front of him as his feet feel their way over the uneven ground. He steps deliberately over the rope barrier and into the red zone, not yet cleared of shells and mines. He folds the map and pushes it into his jacket pocket. Instead he reads the land, scanning the contours and feeling for the slightest ripple or vibration in the earth.

With his divining rods the subterranean water feels like a wave lapping at his subconscious, ebbing and flowing faster and faster until the rods cross. Today he feels like an exposed nerve. He is the rod and his instincts are tuned to a shapeless disquiet in the air that swells into a fitful quivering the further he walks. It turns him left and then right and his breathing quickens. Trance-like he begins moving in familiar, ever-decreasing circles, honing in on the source of the agitation.

Behind Connor, Hasan continues, visibly shaken, his eyes unfocused. 'As long as Allah grants me breath, let me see nothing like those days again. At night we would hear injured men crying for their mothers and pleading for water. They begged to be shot. Our snipers would finish them so we could sleep.'

Hilton surveys the faces of his men who have now all worked their way within earshot of Hasan. He notes that Connor is absent. Probably just as well, he decides. Could be a bit much to hear it like that. Tucker catches Hilton's eye, dips his hat brim towards Connor and lifts his eyebrows.

Hilton spins, alarmed, and catches the farmer taking two small steps forwards and another to the right and then pausing with his hands outstretched.

'What the devil does he think he is doing out there?' asks Hilton.

'Not sure, sir. The suicide waltz?' quips Tucker. 'Do you want me to bring him back, sir?'

'No, I'll go.' He is furious with himself for ignoring his gut and allowing Connor to accompany them. The man is clearly a loose cannon. Hilton crosses the rope barrier and carefully follows Connor's footprints out into no-man's land. As he does, he realises with surprise that the farmer is following a complex and deliberate pattern, not succumbing to the wild meanderings of a father driven mad by grief.

Connor stands still now, his eyes closed as his heart pounds in his ears. His fingers are stinging, a searing heat like a thistle burn piercing his skin. He smells eucalyptus and hears the creaking of a windmill. He feels a hand on his shoulder and opens his eyes. Hilton offers him his canteen.

'Civilisation can be a bloody thin veneer, Mr Connor. Come back; it's dangerous out here.'

'They are here,' says Connor, his voice raw.

'Yes, we're still looking but we –'

'No, they are *here*.' Connor looks directly at the ground and marks the dirt with the heel of his boot, digging it in four times – north, south, east and west. 'I need a shovel.'

He strides purposefully back towards the rope, leaving Hilton in no-man's land, not sure what he has witnessed and no idea what to believe. One thing is for certain; Connor means to dig with or without their help.

Hilton yells out. 'No, Mr Connor. We do all the digging here.'

❖

Dawson scrapes back the soil with the end of his entrenching spade and exposes an unmistakable porous ivory line. He has been scratching away the earth beneath Connor's mark and is barely a foot below the surface. He lets the spade fall beside the shallow pit and drops onto his hands and knees to brush the dirt from around the bone. He chances a furtive look at Tucker, who stands above him supervising with an amateur archaeologist's eye.

'No shortage of those out here,' the sergeant says. 'Could be anyone.' He struggles to sound convincing. This is exactly the spot where the farmer said to dig.

'Give him a hand, Thomas. But be bloody careful.'

'More careful than usual?' asks Thomas.

'A lot more.'

Thomas traces around the bone, taking shallow bites of topsoil with the spade until the blade catches on webbing, decomposing fabric and more bone.

Hilton and Connor are twenty feet away. The area has been checked and the rope line adjusted so that Connor's marker and footprints now lie within the safety zone. Connor is pushing stones around with his toe when suddenly he stops. As if sensing a shift in mood at the pit, he looks up, but Tucker smiles and shakes his head. He does not want to give the farmer false hope. Tucker knows his own father would never have made the trip to find him.

Hilton shares Tucker's doubts. A wild goose chase, he thinks to himself. An engineer by trade, his world is ordered by the mathematical formulae and the laws of physics that keep bridges from collapsing, hold domes aloft and, perversely, launch small projectiles from a narrow metal tube at a velocity sufficient to pierce skin. So he does not know what to make of Connor or his strange gift. Finding water in this way is absurd enough, but trying to find dead bodies – not only does it defy logic, but Hilton finds it difficult to think of it as a gift from God. He hopes that by indulging Connor the obstinate father might come to see that the search is futile. He gives the farmer a patronising smile.

Over at the hole, Tucker taps Dawson on the shoulder.

'What's that, there?'

Dawson picks through the gritty soil and bone fragments and his fingers settle on a flat round object. If it is a button or a coin they will at least know the soldier's nationality. Dawson presses the object between his thumb and index finger and breaks off the dry clay. He spits on it and wipes the disc on his sleeve.

'Shit.'

He passes the A.I.F. identity disc to Tucker. The sergeant has a pretty good idea what it is going to say before he reads it, but he is still stupefied. He pauses, happy that something in the world can still astound him.

Hilton watches Tucker walk towards him, fist clenched shut around something; the tight look around the sergeant's mouth tells him it must be something important.

'It's impossible,' Hilton catches himself mouthing under his breath. 'Impossible.'

Tucker presses the disc into the lieutenant colonel's palm. Incredulous, Hilton looks down and reads the name. Confirming what Connor already knows, Hilton addresses him reverently. 'It's your son. It's Edward.'

Connor is silent; there is nothing to say. His eyes are fixed on Dawson and Thomas, who are carefully lifting spadefuls of fabric and disarticulated bones into a hessian bag. The thought of seeing the ransacked body of his son is almost too much for Connor. But the thought of not witnessing his disinterment is inexplicably worse.

'I wouldn't,' Hilton warns him, but it is too late.

Connor staggers towards his son's shallow grave. He hovers over Dawson's shoulder just as the unsuspecting soldier lifts Edward's skull out of the soil and wipes it with his cuff. Confronted with the hollow remains of his son's gentle face, he looks into blank sockets where mischievous eyes once flickered and begins to quiver, his knees giving way beneath him. As Dawson wipes away the sticky clay the cause of death emerges: a single gunshot to the forehead. Dawson and Thomas exchange knowing looks. Tucker appears at Connor's shoulder and takes him by the arm to steady him. Dawson shakes his head, cautioning Tucker not to say anything, but the sergeant is already in his ear.

'The bastards executed your boy,' he whispers hoarsely. He points to Hasan. 'He gave the order not to take prisoners.'

Connor fixes his gaze on the Turkish commander, who has been watching the search for Connor's sons with keen interest from a respectful distance. White rage builds behind Connor's eyes and his heart threatens to burst, blood rushing and buzzing in his ears. He can barely think. Connor turns and begins to move towards Hasan, fists clenched together like maces. The farmer's pace and fury build to a charge as he hurtles towards his son's murderer.

'Stop him!' shouts Hilton, but the soldiers around him are deliberately slow to respond, reluctant to halt Connor's attack.

'I said stop him! Now!'

The Australian soldiers are spurred into action by their commander's order, but it is too little, too late. Thomas tries a rugby tackle and Connor fends him off with his palm. A solid-looking soldier places himself between Connor and Hasan. Connor props and straight-arms the man across the collarbone, knocking him onto his back. Hasan stands unflinching, casually and deliberately unclipping his holster as Connor descends on him. The Australian expels a mournful bellow, that of a bull in a slaughterhouse, and lunges at the major. As he does a fist comes from nowhere and catches him on the side of the jaw. A second punch lands up under his ribs and knocks the wind out of him. As he lies in the dirt on his side, gasping for breath, a well-aimed black boot buries itself deep into his stomach. Dazed and sucking in dust Connor sees the ursine form of Jemal looming over him – Hasan's last line of defence. Puffing

155

from the exertion, the wild-eyed sergeant places his boot on Connor's chest and shifts all his weight behind it.

'You butchered my sons, my beautiful boys,' Connor roars at Hasan.

'Perhaps, Mr Connor,' concedes Hasan. 'But you sent them. You invaded us.'

Before Connor can reply, Hilton and the Australians are standing over him.

'Take him away and put him under guard,' Hilton orders Tucker. His men pick Connor up and escort him back to their camp. A horrified Hilton turns to Hasan, already anticipating the diplomatic fallout and the deluge of reports, in triplicate.

'I am most terribly sorry.'

'He has two more sons,' observes Hasan, surprisingly unruffled by Connor's outburst. 'We should keep looking.'

CHAPTER TWENTY

A guard stands outside a bell-shaped tent, a rifle leaning against his leg while he rolls a cigarette. He lights it inside a cupped hand, protecting it from the warm evening breeze blowing off the sea. A lamp hanging off the central pole makes the tent glow like a paper lantern. Inside a man sits rigidly on his stretcher, casting a hulking shadow on the canvas.

Connor has hardly moved since he was detained. Shell-shocked, his stillness belies the tumult in his head. Just as the artesian springs call to him from beneath the soil, he knew the boys would help him find them. Their bond, thicker than water, drew him like iron filings to a magnet. Of that he is sure.

Finding Edward has tapped a well of grief and blind rage buried deep within him that, till now, he hoped and believed was dry. All the bruises and loose teeth are a small price to pay for his son's remains. Although he thinks he should now feel some inner peace, a sense of urgency remains; a quavering certainty that the job is not done. Not yet.

He hears the shuffling of feet and the rattle of a rifle as the guard snaps to attention. Hilton pushes back the tent flap and enters.

'We found Henry too.' He announces the news quietly.

'Lying beside Ed,' says Connor. It is not a question.

'How on God's earth did you know they were there?'

'So you haven't found Arthur yet?' Connor asks, his voice a low mumble, head bowed.

'No. We have combed the area thoroughly, but haven't –'

'There's no way Art would leave his brothers,' Connor assures him as he looks up. 'He must be there.' But as he says it, somehow he knows he's wrong. Art is not there; he is lost.

'We will keep looking, but we'll give Edward and Henry a proper burial tomorrow,' offers Hilton.

'I promised their mother I would find them and bring them home.'

Hilton crouches down on his haunches and lowers his voice.

'Connor, this is their home now; it isn't enemy ground anymore. They're amongst friends, probably the closest they ever had. Leave them here and they always will be. Take them back – they'll be just a couple of dead blokes in the corner of a cemetery.'

Conner pictures the Rainbow churchyard and finds it hard to argue.

'Lizzie wanted them buried in consecrated ground.'

'How much blood do you need for it to be consecrated?' pleads Hilton. 'Let us bury them here where it means something.'

Connor concedes with a resigned nod. He knows Hilton is right, but the thought of abandoning his sons here on a desolate Turkish hillside makes his heart ache.

As Hilton pushes the tent flap back to leave, he turns.

'We lost over two thousand men in those four days at Lone Pine. The Turks lost seven ... We didn't take too many prisoners either.'

'So you forgive them?'

Hilton pauses. 'I don't know if I forgive any of us.' He steps out into the night.

Inside the tent Connor takes the photograph of his boys from between the pages of Art's journal and holds it up to the light. That bastard Brindley was right – this is exactly how he wants to remember them. He knows he should find some solace in locating two of his boys. It is more than anyone could reasonably expect – a small miracle, really. But Edward's execution will never leave him now. He can only imagine his boy, wounded and bleeding, his tongue swollen for water, waiting expectantly for the stretcher-bearers. Instead a band of Turks moves across the field, collecting boots and weapons and finishing off the wounded. Connor can see the welcoming smile of his son when he hears the approaching footsteps, and then the look of confusion and horror as the gun is raised. The anger wells up in Connor again and he heads for the door. The sentry stands five feet away, his gun raised.

'There's nothing to be done out here, Mr Connor.'

Connor nods and backs down.

'You're right, son. Nothing at all.'

He lies down on his camp bed and begins a long, sleepless vigil until morning.

Dressed in a loose black cassock and the cylindrical hat peculiar to the Eastern Orthodox Church, a Greek priest stands like a charred tree trunk on the hillside. Beside him is a novice holding a gold cross on a staff and swinging a censer that creaks back and forth, feeble plumes of incense smoke puffing from its perforated brass dome.

Connor breathes in the pungent aroma that has an oddly narcotic affect. He stands in front of a small group of Anzacs, led by Hilton and Tucker, who have gathered around two newly dug graves. Out of respect the men wear their tunics and slouch hats, some decorated with the emu plume of the Light Horse Brigade. They stand quietly, glancing up occasionally from their boots to the two white crosses and back again.

As the sun warms their backs and they listen, uncomprehending, to the Greek liturgy, the solemnity of the occasion hits the Australian soldiers. It's easy to lose sight of the human scale of their endeavours on this lonely and grim peninsula. All day they labour in the dirt, exhuming the remains of fellow soldiers; classifying, crating and carting the dead. But they have never buried someone they knew, or stood by the grave of a dead man with someone who loved him most in all the world. They have never looked upon the deep, grey lines of grief carved in those faces. This man, who has travelled halfway across the world to find his sons, is barely distinguishable from their own fathers; it could be their body lying in the damp soil; it could be their father standing with hat in hand, mouth quivering, wiping tears from his eyes with the back of a rough hand.

This is a day they will never forget; not when they depart this shore and return to loving families in their great Southern Land; not when they age and watch grandchildren grow to adulthood. Today, they really understand why they are here, and they are honoured.

The priest chants through his long black beard as he blesses the ground by dipping a sprig of rosemary into a bowl of water and flicking it over the freshly turned soil.

Greeks and Turks have lived together on this coastline for centuries: Christians and Muslims worshipping side by side, fishing from the same seas, scratching the same soil, speaking the same languages. Constantinople has been in Ottoman hands since 1453 but the Greeks still think of it as part of Greece. Half the city's population is Hellenic. They tell and retell the stories of Alexander cutting the Gordion Knot and Agamemnon and Odysseus sacking Troy as if they were modern history.

Of all Turkey's neighbours, the Greeks know better than any what it is like to stand by as an Empire slowly slips through fat fingers. They have watched the weeds grow between the pavers in Athens, the womb of democracy becoming a political backwater. Greece has become a subject taught in universities, not a living, breathing culture. But the hope that this Aegean coast may be Greek again burns in their hearts like the embers that glow in the censer.

The priest comes to an abrupt stop, gives Connor a solemn nod and hands him a sprig of rosemary as he moves away. Before today Connor had never heard of the Eastern Orthodox Church. He's not sure that it matters which calendar you use, or whether you believe in the Immaculate Conception. The minutiae of religious dogma are obscure to him. He certainly can't imagine what bearing these trivial details can have on someone's relationship with God. Although Connor knows not a word of Greek or Latin, he is certain that God would speak them both. Connor's

God – the God of the Mallee – is an Old Testament deity, a god of the desert. He is combative, vindictive and casual with life. He is a god for the times, when the principles of turning the other cheek and loving thy neighbour have fallen from favour.

Hilton crosses himself and then motions to his men to withdraw. They leave Connor standing between his two boys. Only now with everyone gone can he bring himself to read the words painted on the crosses: 'Pte H.K. Connor #718, 7th Batt. A.I.F. Aged 19 years 11 months, RIP.' 'Pte E.R. Connor #719, 7th Batt. A.I.F. Aged 18 years 4 months, RIP.'

Connor pulls the familiar blue-covered *The Arabian Nights* from his jacket and sits cross-legged between the mounds. Breathing deeply, he begins to read.

> *. . . and the Sultan turned to his young Prince and said, 'you have travelled far and wide to kingdoms never imagined. After all your rich adventures, the magic carpet has carried you on the four winds to this, your home.'*

His voice cracks as he realises the word 'home' no longer means anything for him. He steels himself, determined to finish his personal liturgy.

> *And the Sultan assembled all the court musicians and the court dancers in great celebration for the safe return of his son.*

Connor closes the book, wipes his eyes with the heel of his hand and sits. Even when the sun falls, bleeding over the horizon, Connor stays with his eyes fixed on the graves. In all likelihood he will never return to Gallipoli. This may be the last time he ever spends by his sons' side. So he stares with an intensity that burns the graves into his mind's eye: the freshly painted white crosses, the neat lettering, the shell casings sticking out of the turned soil. A stereoscopic image to take home with him. He knows the decision to bury the boys here is the right one for them, but the thought of leaving them here makes him feel as if he is losing them once again, forever.

He shuts his eyes and places the palms of his hands on the cool soil.

'I found our boys, Lizzie. They're safe now.'

But there's no escaping the horrible reality that Art is still lost. Connor opens his eyes and gazes over the darkening sea.

'I will find Art,' he pledges. 'I'll find him for you.'

CHAPTER TWENTY-ONE

Jemal marches through the Anzac camp. The grave robbers – his nickname for them – are just stirring. The cook has the fire stoked and water is coming to the boil. A blackened pot of porridge hangs on a tripod above the flames. Jemal will be giving the thick sludge a wide berth today. He has just come from Chanak and has fresh *simit*s under his arm.

As he approaches Hasan's tent he hears the low rhythmic rumble of the final *salawat* prayer. He pictures Hasan standing in the half-light. He will turn to look over his right shoulder at the angel recording all his good deeds, then over his left at the angel transcribing the bad ones. Jemal opens the paper under his arm, takes a bite out of a *simit* and waits. He laughs to himself. The angel on Jemal's left would have run out of ink last night.

'Bring those in here. Don't think I can't smell them,' comes Hasan's voice from inside.

Jemal steps inside as Hasan rolls up his prayer rug, sits on his bed and begins to pull on his boots. He motions Jemal to a stool.

'Here is your telegraph,' says Jemal as he hands Hasan a sheet of paper. 'One whole day I wasted standing in line, drinking shit coffee.'

'And one whole night too,' adds Hasan knowingly. 'I understand there is a brothel near the post office.'

'So I hear.'

Jemal's mood becomes serious.

'The Greeks have taken Smyrna. I heard in town. The British sat in their ships and watched them do as they please. We have to do something. People are waiting for you to show your hand.'

'What hand is that? I don't have one. It is the British who hold all the cards. They will decide how much of our country we ultimately keep.'

Hasan turns his attention to the telegram. The discussion is at an end. A frustrated Jemal watches his commander and friend scan the telegram, and cannot contain himself.

'Why do you care about this farmer?' he blurts out. 'He wants to kill you.'

Hasan is up and out the door of his tent before Jemal finishes. The Turkish commander strides through the camp and makes a beeline for a tent on the far side – the tent with a sentry at the door.

❖

Connor is preparing to leave. A photograph lies on his open case, but it is not the portrait of his three sons. A young Orhan smiles at him from the sepia print. His handsome father, already mourning what he has not yet lost. And Ayshe with her delicate features and luxuriant dark hair looks wistful but still breathtakingly beautiful. After a war that claimed millions of lives, Connor wonders how many photos like this one there are scattered across the world; mute records of families irreparably shattered, pictures that will be torn up in despair, fingered until they fall apart or lost in drawers to fade. How many boys like Orhan will have no grave to visit, just a photo like this one to cry over?

He hears the sound of boots scraping the ground outside and quickly pushes the photo into Art's diary and shuts the case. Hasan appears in the doorway and Connor immediately takes a step back.

'Please forgive my intrusion, Mr Connor.'

'Yes, what?' Connor is defensive, unsure why the Turk has appeared in his tent, and is expecting the worst.

'What is the name of your eldest son?'

'Connor. The same as mine.' He is annoyed.

'We have no family name in Turkey,' explains Hasan carefully. 'What is his first name?'

'His *Christian* name is Arthur,' says Connor.

Hasan ignores the implied slight. He has seen more than his fair share of religious and cultural persecution in his thirty years as a soldier; certainly far too much to be bothered by such a distinction.

'And how do you spell this?' he asks.

'A–R–T–H–U–R. Arthur.'

Hasan follows the spelling, comparing it with something written on the paper he is holding in his hands. He looks up, a disappointed look on his face.

'I am sorry I have troubled you. I thought . . . Please travel with God.'

Hasan turns to leave and Connor stops him.

'I am sorry,' he says stiffly. 'For my outburst yesterday.'

'There is a Persian saying,' Hasan says, 'which translates as, "May you outlive your children." It sounds like a blessing, but it is the worst curse one can place on the head of a man. You would not even wish it upon your enemy.'

Hasan pushes the flap aside, but before he can clear the tent Connor asks, 'Why did you ask about Arthur?'

Looking uncomfortable, Hasan holds up the telegram, which contains a list in Ottoman Arabic. He explains, 'I had this list sent from Constantinople. There is a name here that is your family name. But the first name – the Christian name – it is another man. I am sorry. I did not mean to raise your hopes.'

'What is this list? What other man?' Connor must know.

'There are three initials. None of them 'A' for Arthur. They are R – F – R.'

'R – F – R . . .' Connor plays with the sounds. *Surely not. It's too much to hope for.*

'Ar – F – ar. Ar – Far! That's it. Arthur! That's him! It *has* to be him!' he exclaims. 'That's his name. Tell me – what is this list?'

There is a long, considered pause as Hasan looks directly at Connor and chooses his words very carefully. 'If this *is* your son . . . *If* . . . then we took him prisoner. He did not die here.'

The news hits Connor like an uppercut to the solar plexus. He gasps, scarcely audible, 'Oh God. What?'

'He left Çanakkale alive.'

Connor is so overcome he cannot speak. Hasan pushes through the doorway, leaving the father to contemplate the possibilities alone. Connor steadies himself against the tent pole, his reality turned upside down in a heartbeat.

CHAPTER TWENTY-TWO

The trill and wail of a *ney* flute penetrates every corner of the Troya, vying with the forlorn sounds from the strings of the *kemençe* and *oud*. A group of earnest musicians is perched on worn, bentwood chairs arranged on the small bandstand in the corner of the salon. They wear brocade, embroidered vests, sashes round their waists shot through with gold thread, and red fezzes on their heads, the tassels swinging in time with the music.

Ayshe and Natalia have scrubbed every corner of the room and aired and washed the old lace drapes until they are closer to white than they have been for many years. It has been a very long time since the hotel has hosted such a large gathering. The sound of the music and chatter streams out to the darkening street through open windows and a balmy, soft breeze enters the room, carrying with it the smell of pollen and the sweet scent of Judas Tree blossoms.

Against one wall is a low, timber daybed bedecked as if for a sultan. Cobalt-blue, carmine-red and ochre motifs shimmer on a rug so finely woven it folds and billows across the platform as if it were a sheet of satin. Plump cushions made from brightly coloured *kilim* fabric are stacked in a pyramid and threadbare gold curtains festoon the daybed frame. At the centre of the tableau sits Orhan, resplendent in a white satin suit with a broad red sash diagonally across his chest, clutching a silver-topped sceptre and reclining regally against the cushions. Despite the prestige of his central position in this large gathering of family, friends and neighbours, he shifts and fidgets in some discomfort.

The music changes tempo; fingers plucking the strings of the *kanun* resting on one musician's lap begin to move at an impossible speed and the man slapping out rhythmic beats on the *kudum* drum with the palm of his hand picks up pace.

Ayshe twirls to the music, smiling, as her father Ibrahim guides her around the dance floor. She moves adeptly, head held high and feet intuitively following the rhythm, vestiges of many hours spent in her husband's arms a lifetime ago. Many eyes follow her as she whirls around the room. Her chartreuse chiffon dress skims her slim frame and falls in soft folds about her legs, its hemline rippling to expose her delicate ankles. At her throat she wears a double strand of pearls – all that remains of her mother's once opulent collection of jewellery. Whenever Ayshe lifts it from its velvet-hinged box and feels the satiny orbs between her fingers, she recalls helping her mother clasp them about her neck as she and Ibrahim prepared for a grand ball.

The music builds to a crescendo, then ends. Ibrahim bows formally and extends his arm to his daughter to lead her to where her son sits. A queue of people waits to greet Orhan, showering him with gifts, which he places on the daybed beside him. One old man holds his hand over his heart and nods his head, sagely. 'All is over and done. It will grow better by God's will.'

Ayshe leans towards her son and cups her hand beneath his chin. 'Look at my little man. You are a miniature version of Turgut. Just as cheeky, and every bit as handsome as your father.'

At the opposite side of the platform, Omer asserts his role as benefactor in the proceedings, one hand tucked into the pocket of his vest, the other resting proprietarily on the edge of the daybed. As the guests file past his nephew, Omer greets them and nods gravely, accepting their good wishes and extending due acknowledgment for their attendance at this important family gathering. Between greetings, he conducts a covert conversation with the imam who stands beside him.

'Of course, my irresponsible brother made no provision for the *sünnet* – so again it falls to me.'

The imam nods sympathetically. 'Allah sees your goodness. Even in this time of strife this does you credit.' He looks at Ayshe standing proudly beside her son.

'Why is she still not wearing the clothes of grief?'

'She still pretends he is alive. God give him peace.'

Shaking his head, the imam continues. 'The boy needs a father. Especially now he is a man. He needs guidance and he needs to know the truth.'

'I have made it clear that I am prepared to take her as my second wife and become the master of this house. Fatma agrees. I can afford it.'

'It would be the best outcome. The boy carries your blood.'

Omer raises his eyebrows, looking pointedly towards Ayshe's father. The imam follows his gaze.

'Ibrahim Pasha's fortune is gone along with his mind, and this place groans under the weight of debt. Allah willing she will soon see reason.'

The imam places his hand upon Omer's forearm. 'God will show Ayshe her duty. *Inşallah.*'

❖

The rush of heady anticipation that hits Connor at the sight of the pink hotel on the hill surprises him. Since learning that Arthur might have survived he has felt as if he could walk on water from Europe to Asia. But this nervous flutter in his gut is something else, something inexplicable. He can't remember when he last felt this childlike excitement.

The setting sun is kind, casting the Otel Troya in a flattering light, disguising the peeling paint and disintegrating plaster. Despite a few wrong turns he was set straight by locals who pointed him in the right direction, and eventually he managed to find his way up the hill through the labyrinthine network of lanes and alleys. He hadn't even thought about how to find the hotel on the long trip back to Constantinople; he'd assumed that he'd run into Orhan waiting at the wharf to pick up affluent and eager new arrivals. He hadn't realised that the boy timed his recruitment drive at the dock to coincide with the disembarkation of ships from abroad, summoned by the expectant horn that signalled their arrival in port. The British military supply ship, by comparison, represented slim pickings for the touts, who gave it a wide berth, so he was left to find his own way back through the spice market to the hotel.

He hesitates now, unsure how he'll be received after his last visit. But this place is all he knows in this foreign city. He steels himself and climbs the front steps.

Connor stands at the entrance to the salon, mesmerised by Ayshe's incandescent beauty. She laughs loudly and surprisingly raucously as she shares an exchange with a woman of a similar age. Her hair is held back from her face in an elaborate chignon and pinned with a jewelled barrette, emphasising her high cheekbones and green eyes that gleam like gemstones.

Realising belatedly that he has stumbled on a private party, Connor begins to back out of the room, but looking up from his makeshift throne, Orhan catches sight of him. Barely able to contain himself, he flings his hands into the air with excitement and beckons to Connor from across the room.

'Connor Bey! I am man now! Come, join us!'

As Connor approaches, Orhan leans towards him and whispers urgently, 'Did you find my father?'

'Sorry son, no luck.'

Ayshe turns from her companion and locks eyes with Connor. Excusing herself, she moves across the room towards him. For his part, Omer observes the Australian's arrival cautiously. His face reads like an open book: he doesn't like the way Connor is staring at Ayshe, and he certainly disapproves of the looks she is giving him.

Ashamed by his undisguised appraisal of the Turkish woman, Connor averts his gaze as she approaches, his expression apologetic.

'I am intruding. Is it his birthday?'

Ayshe smiles. 'No. His *sünnet*.'

Connor looks puzzled. Ayshe furtively makes a snipping action with her fingers. None the wiser, Connor mimics her gesture, raising his eyebrows quizzically.

She nods. 'Yes.'

'A special haircut?'

Ayshe shakes her head, surreptitiously pointing downwards. The penny drops and Connor flushes, embarrassed. A circumcision.

'Ah. Right. Of course. Oh, bloody hell. It's a private thing.'

Ayshe is puzzled. 'No, it's a celebration.'

He is awkward, uncomfortable. 'I have had a long journey. I need to wash – if you are not full?'

'We may have a room.'

He nods his head, grateful. 'Thank you. Good night, Orhan. Happy – ah . . .'

Orhan pipes up, 'Do you want to see my scar?'

'No, mate. But thanks.'

Ayshe struggles to conceal a smile as she escorts Connor into the foyer and fetches him a room key. 'You found Çanakkale?'

Since leaving the peninsula Connor has vacillated between elation and utter disbelief. On the one hand he doesn't want to allow himself to believe what seems impossible; on the other he can't fight the desire to submit to hope, knowing that he will overturn heaven and earth to find his son. The urge to share the news with this woman is overwhelming.

'I have news – possibly good news – but I am not yet sure what to make of it –'

Omer is suddenly between Connor and Ayshe, eyes flashing and mouth set in an angry line, interrupting their exchange. He turns to Ayshe and snaps something at her in Turkish. Then he spins on his heel and graces Connor with an obsequious smile. 'Mr Connor. Welcome back to Stamboul. You are always welcome.'

173

Mumbling a reply, Connor hurriedly excuses himself. Climbing the stairs, he unlocks the door in the narrow corridor and steps into the same room he stayed in before. He opens the drapes and unlatches the window, leaning out to hear the sounds of the city that he recognises with a new familiarity – street vendors crying out, the clip-clop of horses and asses on the cobbles, and the mournful calls of gulls soaring about the rooftops.

He places his small, battered case on the bureau and opens it, taking Art's precious journal from where it lies nestled carefully between his neatly folded clothes. Removing his boots and shirt, he lies down on the bed, ankles crossed, with the diary on his chest.

The day Art was born had been oppressively hot, north winds blowing down from the desert to tear limbs from trees and set willy-willys spinning erratically across the Mallee. Connor walked up and down the verandah, waiting, pacing impotently as he heard Lizzie cry out. More than once he went to burst into the bedroom, needing to help, wanting to stop her pain. Each time, he stopped himself, until finally, with a blood-curdling wail, he knew his son had been born. Lizzie's sister, Ivy, stepped out of the room holding Art, who was swaddled firmly in a cotton sheet, tiny fists clenched so tightly they were white, little face contorted, wrinkled and shrieking. She handed Connor his son, and in that moment he knew fear, awe and love with an overwhelming and unimaginable intensity. It was deep, all consuming and utterly terrifying. That feeling never went away, and when he and Lizzie lost their boys, he had thought his heart would stop.

But now there is hope.

He shuts his eyes and dares to let it cradle him.

CHAPTER TWENTY-THREE

*S*unbeams strobe on the two men's faces as blades turn languidly in the bright morning light.

Far below and beyond where they work on a precarious platform beneath the vast sails of the windmill, the boundless, barren land is flat and featureless, and overwhelmingly beautiful. The scale of this land — the clear sky that arches over the red soil like a dome — is expansive and at the same time oppressive; it makes the products of human enterprise seem feeble, inconsequential.

The men work in silence, absorbed in the task at hand. Art spins a wrench to secure the bolt that holds the oily gear in place as Connor guides its teeth into alignment with the smaller cog.

Heavy metal parts, a rickety timber perch teetering a bone-breaking distance from the ground. So many things can go wrong.

Connor glances at Art. 'You right with that?'

His son smiles. 'Yeah, I reckon I can handle it by now, Dad.'

With the gear locked back into place, the pump rod resumes its perpetual motion, driven up and down by the movement of the windmill's blades as they spin in the morning breeze. Connor and Art down their tools and sit on the edge of the platform, *legs dangling side by side, Connor's clad in his well-worn work pants, Art's in new, khaki military-issue breeches and woollen puttees binding his leg from his ankle to just below his knee.*

Somewhere in the indeterminate distance, Connor's property ends and his neighbour's begins. He half-raises his arm and points off towards the horizon. 'I'm thinking I might buy Clive's place. He's getting out. Give us plenty of land — so there won't be any arguments between the three of you when I'm gone.'

Art laughs. 'We argue now and you're still around. You'll probably outlive us all anyway.'

A voice from far below. Henry, eager to head off.

'Oi! Come on, Art! You won't win any medals up there!'

Art draws a deep breath and turns to his father. 'Time to go then, I guess.'

Connor is silent. Yes. It's time. He and his eldest son climb down the windmill's frame, jumping to the ground at the bottom with a resigned finality. Connor shakes his boys' hands, claps them on their shoulders. Ed and Henry are champing at the bit to head off. Art is less exuberant.

They mount up and gallop towards the horizon at break-neck speed, one last salute as they disappear. Connor watches them till all that remains is the haze of dust left in their wake.

Everything left unsaid.

CHAPTER TWENTY-FOUR

'Help! Help, please, Mr Connor!'
Ayshe stands in the hall rapping on Connor's door. She is still dressed for the party, but her hair is dishevelled, her eyes wide and terrified. She puts her ear to the door and listens for movement. Nothing. She knocks again.

'Mr Connor! Please!'

A key turns from inside and the door swings open. Connor appears in trousers and a singlet, shoving his arms into the sleeves of his shirt. He looks disoriented and confused, like he has forgotten where he is.

'I thought I was dreaming. What is it?'

'Please help! My father!' Ayshe begs.

Ayshe leads Connor along the low-lit corridor to the French doors that open onto the terrace. There they look towards Ibrahim who stands, swaying, on the very edge of the pitched tiled roof in his dinner suit, bellowing in Turkish at imagined foes in the street two storeys below. The only thing that stops him from toppling head first onto the cobblestones is his tenuous hold on a rusted pipe.

He shakes his fist furiously as he shouts, tottering and swinging out over the street.

'What have you done to my country, you fat, spoilt buffoons with your thousand wives and syphilis sores?'

Ayshe is desperate. She leans over the balustrade, beseeching Ibrahim in Turkish and holding out her arms towards him. Eyes shut, head thrown back, his daughter's pleas fail to reach him through the fog of delirium. She turns to Connor.

'He's too strong. I beg him – but he's inside his head.'

It is only a matter of time before her father loses his footing and falls. She watches as Connor assesses the danger. He swings his legs over the terrace rail and steps carefully onto the mossy, terracotta-tiled roof. As he transfers his weight, his boots slip suddenly, immediately dislodging two tiles that skate down the steeply angled incline and plummet to the street below with an ominous crash.

Ayshe grabs Connor's arm. 'Be careful! Do not frighten him!'

Looking back at her, Connor seems a little put out by her apparent lack of concern for his welfare. He begins to edge his way carefully towards where Ibrahim teeters, a hair's-breadth from calamity. The old man continues to rant and rail.

'What have you done to our city? What have you done to your people?'

'What's he saying?' Connor calls out to Ayshe as he continues to sidle towards the old man.

'He cries for everything we have lost.'

Her father continues to wail. 'Caliph of the Faithful, Emperor of the Ottomans! Seize the sword of Osman, restore our fortunes!'

Reaching Ibrahim, Connor gently but firmly takes his arm and says calmly, 'Why don't we sit here for a while?'

Ibrahim turns his head and looks deeply into his eyes, uncomprehending. Ayshe watches on with trepidation as Connor carefully seats himself on the tiles and indicates for Ibrahim to join him. The old man looks out across the city and sighs. Bending his knees and guided by Connor, he reaches out behind him and rests his hands on the rooftop, lowering himself down to find a seat beside the Australian.

Once settled, Ibrahim speaks. 'Yes. Yes. Good. Let us watch the parade together . . .'

This is not the first time Ibrahim's manic nightscape has been populated by apparitions and phantasms. The pomp and splendour of the Ottoman court fill the streets in his mind's eye with a triumphal march. 'How magnificent . . .'

Ibrahim turns to Connor and his daughter with tears in his eyes.

'We shall not see the like of this again.'

After coaxing him back onto the terrace and into the house, Connor helps Ayshe escort Ibrahim to his room. While she settles her father to bed, Connor waits outside, sitting on the steps at the top of the landing. He tells himself she may need his help again. As he sits there listening to the low murmurs coming from behind the heavy timber door, he wonders at the growing attraction he has for this woman. When he married Lizzie it was for life. He was sure he would never feel this way about anyone else. But he can't help feeling abandoned, that Lizzie chose to leave him.

And now, the quiet strength and determination of this Turkish woman, her resolve, and her deep love and loyalty for her son and her father, triggers something long buried in Connor's subconscious.

The door opens quietly and Ayshe steps out into the hallway. She turns to Connor apologetically.

'He had a great mind once. My father was a physician at the Sultan's court.' She pauses, lost in memories.

Looking up, they lock eyes. Connor feels his heart leap.

'I thank you for your help, Mr Connor.'

'Joshua, please.'

'Thank you, then, Joshua.' She turns to leave.

'Wait, I have something of yours.' Connor strides down the hall. Opening his door, he scans the room, spying Art's diary on the bedspread where it slipped from his chest when Ayshe woke him. The journal falls open at the spot where he had placed the photograph Orhan gave him before he left for Chanak.

When he returns, Ayshe has found a seat on the top step of the stairway where she leans wearily against the timber balustrade. Connor hands her the photo.

'Orhan asked me to look for your husband at Gallipoli.'

Smiling sadly, Ayshe gazes closely at it.

'I hate this photograph. Turgut is a musician – never a soldier. What did they think he would do – waltz them to death?'

'How long were you married?'

'I am married – ten years . . . My mother had arranged for me to marry someone else but my father fought her.' She laughs. 'He told her: "Why would we want our daughter to be as miserable as we are?" and she agreed.'

Ayshe looks into the distance. 'It is not easy to marry for love here.' She smiles resignedly. 'Maybe my mother was right – Turgut was mad. Bills up to the roof not paid, music all hours, parties, lazy friends – oh, but how I miss the chaos.'

Connor takes a seat on a step further down the staircase, leaning his strong back against the wall with his legs bent and feet resting against the balustrade.

'I wish my mother had arranged my marriage for me.'

'You did not love your wife?'

'I adored Lizzie. But I was so bad at courting. So clumsy. It took forever.' He recalls his awkward attempts at attracting Lizzie's attention. Widely recognised as one of the district's best catches, she had no shortage of suitors. He could never quite understand why she chose him.

'Everything I said would offend her. My tongue would stick to the roof of my mouth. I think she only married me out of impatience.'

'But it was happy?'

'Very. Until the boys were lost. In the first year, every week she would head into town – twenty miles – and wait for the train. Just in case. Now I've found two of our sons she would be more at peace. It is good to know where they are – they're not lost or nameless anymore.' At last Connor had the opportunity to share his exciting news. 'And I have been told my eldest boy was taken prisoner . . .'

'So he is alive?'

'I have no idea. No one else seems to think so.'

'But you have hope?'

'Hope is a necessity where I come from. It's hard country, the Mallee – most of it just dust.' Connor laughs. 'My wife used to call me her Mallee Bull. A big, dumb brute – impossible to shift. I believe things when I see them.'

Ayshe gets to her feet. 'That is good news, then.' She turns to re-enter her father's room. 'Good night, Mr Bull.'

❖

She sits on the end of Ibrahim's bed, holding the photo in her hand. Ayshe looks at her husband and son and weeps, tears streaming down her cheeks and falling in dark pools on her chiffon gown. Her father twitches and murmurs, his visions continuing to pursue him in sleep.

She knows she no longer has any choice. Steeling herself, she wipes her eyes with the back of her hand. Standing, she moves to the head of her father's bed, bowing to kiss him lightly on the forehead.

Ayshe speaks to him under her breath.

'I understand why you prefer to be lost in the past, Father. But unfortunately it's a luxury I can no longer afford. Forgive me.'

CHAPTER TWENTY-FIVE

Hasan shifts impatiently in a hard timber chair. The anteroom in Topkapi Palace is decorated in gauche and lavish Rococo style, from a time when the Ottoman sultans sought to mimic the gaudiest French and Italian fashions of the day.

For centuries the Turkish rulers have felt compelled to prove their bona fides by outdoing their Continental counterparts. In the early years of the Empire, with incalculable riches flooding into the city along the Silk Road and the spice routes, the opulence of the Ottoman court was without equal. But once the Western European powers rose to prominence, keeping up with the neighbours became a very expensive exercise. Nowadays the sultans seem to spend most of their time successfully frustrating their treasurers and viziers by sapping the public coffers.

Hasan has never understood the fixation Turkish rulers have with being European, when in reality they were and are so much more. Ultimately their vanity has been the undoing of the Empire.

Today he wears his finest tunic, braided trousers, gleaming knee-high boots and a dress sword that rattles against the chair leg whenever he shifts his weight. A cylindrical woollen hat, his *serpuş*, rests on his knee. On his left breast he wears the Harp Madalyası medal for Gallipoli veterans: a silver crescent over a red enamel star. The Germans he fought with nicknamed it the Iron Crescent after their own medal of honour, the Iron Cross. The European compulsion to believe they invented everything mystifies Hasan. Above it hangs an impressive medallion with a seven-pointed star and an enamel centre decorated with Arabic calligraphy. It is the Order of Osmania, one of the Ottoman Empire's highest honours, but today its significance escapes the low-ranking French and British officers who bustle in and out and eye Hasan with suspicion.

Sultan Mehmed V, a man whose own jacket breast groaned under the weight of self-awarded medals, had bestowed the Order of Osmania on Hasan. He pinned the medal on his tunic, kissed him on both cheeks and headed off to bed feeling poorly. A week later the Sultan died, only months before the war ended. Hasan imagines that Mehmed died of a broken heart, unable to bear the imminent downfall of the Empire.

After half an hour of waiting Hasan is becoming tetchy. Things would be different if Jemal were here. Which is exactly why Hasan elected to come alone. His staff sergeant has many fine qualities but diplomacy and patience are not amongst them. He smiles at the thought of Jemal huffing and bellowing indignantly on his behalf; a raging bull in a bazaar. Yet as his frustration rises, Hasan is beginning to wish he had brought him.

The chanting that seeps in from the street momentarily distracts him. Constantinople's Christians – half the city's population is Greek and Russian – are cheering the British soldiers. The Greeks, especially, imagine this is the beginning of the liberation of the city that was once the capital of Greek Byzantium. Heated conversations in *kafeneions* across Constantinople begin and end with, 'What do they expect? This city was founded by the Greek king, Byzas – 'twas all Greece, you know.'

Hasan's countrymen have taken to the streets in protest. How dare the British dissolve their parliament? How can Sultan Mehmed VI be so chicken-hearted as to allow it? What happened to the man who wields the sword of Allah? His predecessors had honorifics like 'The Conqueror,' 'The Warrior' or 'The Thunderbolt.' Mehmed has the heart of a librarian or an accountant. After Friday prayers, when the city's disillusioned Turks have had time to stew on the events of the week and their disappointment boils over, Hasan overhears the nicknames they have coined for Mehmed: 'The Worrier,' 'The Puppet' and 'The Thundercloud.' Even in dire times his countrymen have not lost their sense of the absurd.

Nor have they lost their penchant for theatre. Black bolts of fabric are draped from the minarets of the Blue Mosque, mourning the death of young Nationalists hanged by the British for attempting to smuggle arms out of the city. Perhaps the fabric billowing in the breeze signals the hastening death of democracy in Turkey. The despair rises in Hasan's throat like acid and he can sit no longer. A small group of French officers file into the room and occupy the remaining seats. They look him up and down with smug smiles, whispering with each other behind raised hands and sniggering like schoolboys. When an adjoining door

185

opens and they are ushered in, it is the last straw for Hasan. He yells through the open door.

'I have an appointment with Admiral Calthorpe. How much more of this must I endure?'

Hasan hears a distant door slam followed by the clatter of boots on marble approaching at speed. Captain Brindley appears at the door in front of Hasan, speaking formally without a hint of sincerity.

'I apologise, Major. I really do. But Admiral Calthorpe will have to reschedule your meeting. Something rather urgent has come up, I'm afraid. Perhaps Tuesday next week? Would that suit?'

'Yes – if your admiral could also reschedule the Greeks,' spits Hasan sarcastically. 'Perhaps ask them to tear Anatolia apart the week after that.'

'Major, we are simply trying to restore order here,' says Brindley lamely. 'And your friend Mustafa Kemal and his Nationalist rabble are not helping.'

His insult cuts fast and deep. Hasan's thoughts immediately go to his young countrymen swinging outside the palace walls, hanged for daring to challenge the division of their homeland, its various parts handed over to the highest bidder. But rather than anger, a sudden wave of self-loathing washes over him. He realises he has been played for a fool. Any hope he'd harboured that his cooperation at Çanakkale might have made the British more amenable to Turkish interests and aspirations has been shattered.

'If we don't help ourselves, who will?' Hasan asks – of himself as much as Brindley.

Brindley holds his hands together, palm against palm, in front of his chest, head bowed and eyes closed patronisingly.

'Allow us to handle the Greeks through diplomatic channels, Major. You can rest assured we have no intention of giving this marvellous city back to them.'

'And the rest of my country?' snaps Hasan, now incensed.

'Come, now, Major; let's not have another war.'

His sanctimonious tone is too much for Hasan. 'It's the same war,' the Turk yells. 'It hasn't ended.'

Hasan's sword hilt crashes against the doorjamb as he storms from the room. Thrusting his jaw forwards with fury, he marches double-time down a long corridor, trying to put as much distance between himself and Brindley as possible before he does something regrettable. At least now he knows where he stands. And he knows what he must do.

Outside, Connor is walking towards Brindley's office beneath the colonnaded verandah when he sees Hasan crashing towards him with his fist clenched tight around the hilt of his sword. Connor smiles and holds out his hand.

'Major Hasan, hello. Can you tell me . . .'

The Turk flashes him a murderous look. 'No. I can't tell you anything. I have finished helping.' He barrels past without stopping.

Bewildered, Connor watches Hasan stride into the distance. He thinks of a hawk riding a current until it disappears in the shimmering midday sun. He could swear the two men had left Gallipoli on good terms. Nothing seems straightforward to Connor in this country. When he turns back, an agitated Captain Brindley is standing before him, grimacing like he has a mouthful of broken glass.

'Ah, Mr Connor. Welcome back. Do you have your passport with you?'

Connor fishes his travel documents from inside his coat and holds them out. Brindley inspects them cursorily and then tucks them into his own tunic pocket.

'Thank you.'

Before Connor can object Brindley is marching away.

'This way. Now.'

Brindley's tone is ominous. All Connor can do is follow, riding in the officer's wake until he tires or his anger subsides sufficiently to explain what the hell is going on. Connor is here to find out what he can about the Turkish prison camps Hasan mentioned. He is sure the British must have a map – names of survivors, lists of men registered for Red Cross POW packs, something like that. But the further Brindley marches into the labyrinth of offices and storerooms, the more unsettled Connor becomes.

They climb a narrow set of stone stairs and Connor pauses at the top to look through a timber screen into a small courtyard below. Guards have barricaded a wooden gate with crates and barbed wire and stand with bayonets poised. It seems like overkill to Connor.

'You can never be too sure,' warns Brindley over his shoulder.

The captain cuts through a room where four junior officers sit chatting and smoking while a fifth man pushes on typewriter keys with his index fingers and curses the carbon paper that is caught in the roller. They snap to attention and salute as Brindley passes and waves his fingers across his forehead.

As Connor closes on Brindley the officer turns to face him.

'You were specifically ordered not to go to Gallipoli.'

'Well, I'm not in your army.'

Brindley continues curtly as he walks. 'That man . . . the man you attacked – yes, we heard all about it – is a Turkish war hero. He was there on our invitation, to help our expedition down there. The sole reason you are not in prison right now is that he refused to file a complaint. From what I've heard, he had every right to.'

Connor has no intention of apologising to Brindley. It was a dispute between two men. It had nothing to do with the government or the army. Nor was he going to give Brindley the satisfaction of an explanation. They are passing an open double doorway. Across Brindley's shoulder, Connor catches a glimpse inside of a table covered in rolled-up charts and maps. He stops abruptly.

'He told me my son was taken prisoner. Show me where the prison camps were and I'll be out of your hair,' promises Connor. It doesn't seem an unreasonable proposition.

'All the prisoners of war were repatriated,' says Brindley bluntly. 'If he did not come home, the sad reality is that he is dead.'

'So you're telling me there was no one too sick, or too badly injured that –'

Brindley cuts him off, slamming his peaked cap against his leg in frustration. 'No, there is not, Mr Connor!' But he can see that the Australian is unmoved. He grabs Connor by the arm, and frogmarches him into the adjoining map room.

Connor finds himself staring up at a vast, hand-painted map that occupies almost an entire wall. Laid out before him is the Ottoman Empire at its zenith. The piece is so immense and exquisitely detailed in gold leaf that it could only have been commissioned by a regent determined to awe visiting dignitaries with the extent of his domain. Snakelike Arabic calligraphy edges the map's border, as elegant as it is utterly impenetrable to Connor. However, it seems an overzealous British bureaucrat has nailed small signs with the English translations alongside the map and each of its features. Connor reads, 'Sovereign of the House of Osman, Sultan of Sultans, Khan of Khans, Ruler of Rulers,' it reads. 'Commander of the Faithful, Successor of the Prophet of the Lord of the Universe, Protector of the Holy Cities of Mecca, Medina and Jerusalem, Emperor of Constantinople and the cities of Damascus, Cairo and Baghdad, of Cyprus, of Rhodes, the Black Sea, Greece, Albania, Tunisia, Georgia, Turkistan and many other countries, forts and castles.'

Brindley steps closer to the map and speaks without turning to Connor.

'The Ottomans had one of the biggest empires of all time.' He points. 'From the gates of Vienna to Mecca, from Casablanca, here, to Tehran – and right now you'd be hard pushed to find a more dangerous place on earth, Mr Connor.'

Connor's eyes dart across the wall. Even to his untrained eye, this is much more than a map. The brilliant blue seas, the lush green lands and the golden desert sands affirm God's greatness, while the fortified cities with their magnificent domes and minarets show the Sultan's dominion over man's greatest creations. The Ottoman Empire brings together earthly and heavenly treasures and the Sultan is both ruler and Allah's curator.

Beside each castle or city are wandering gold lines that make up their Arabic name, plus the small sign giving their

English translation. Connor spots Constantinople, then quickly finds Baghdad, Damascus, Aleppo and Jerusalem. It dawns on him that renaming the locations is the first step on the way to controlling them.

Brindley continues with his lesson in local politics as a corporal arrives, snaps to attention and hands Brindley a large brown envelope.

'The Bolshies want the Black Sea; the French and the Italians want the Aegean.' He moves to the centre of the map and stabs at it with a blunt, well-manicured forefinger. 'And here in Anatolia, where, incidentally, the prison camps were, the Greeks are turning the place into a bloodbath that makes Gallipoli look like a rugger match. Where, pray tell, in all this would you like us to start looking for your missing son?'

Connor's attention is piqued by Brindley's mention of prison camps. He steps forwards and starts running his index finger in a circle over central Anatolia.

'So, you say the prison camps were in this area here? Would the Turks have records? We could ask.'

Brindley loses his temper, shouting now. 'The camps are gone! All gone. He's gone, and so are you.'

He thrusts the large envelope into Connor's hands. 'This is your ticket for a steamer to Brindisi on Thursday morning, compliments of the British Government. Make sure you're on it!'

Taking control of himself, Brindley adds a hollow, 'Good luck,' as an afterthought. He calls to the corporal who now stands in the doorway. 'You! Show Mr Connor to the gate, and assign a guard to his hotel. Make sure he doesn't miss his steamer on Thursday.'

'Sir!'

'And if he puts a foot outside Sultanahmet – arrest him.'

The corporal marches over to Connor and begins to lead him by the arm. As they pass Brindley, the officer puts his palm flat on Connor's chest and leans in so that their hat brims almost touch.

'Say by some miracle, your boy, Arthur, is alive,' Brindley speculates. 'Have you bothered to ask yourself why he has chosen not to come home?'

After a moment of frozen silence, Connor shrugs himself free of the corporal and storms out, and Brindley feels a momentary pang of regret. Brindley is not a cruel man but he knows he has been reduced to his absolute worst by Connor's stubbornness and unrelenting optimism. In difficult times, personal traits such as these are exasperating indulgences.

The truth is that Connor is in the worst hell already – forced to leave Constantinople without knowing the fate of his son Art.

That reality is far worse than anything Brindley could say to him.

CHAPTER TWENTY-SIX

'Thursday morning. Bright and early,' says the corporal as he marches Connor towards the main gate of the War Office. As an afterthought, he adds a gentle warning. 'He's a stickler. He means it.'

Connor drops his shoulders, defeated and deflated. He knows that when he boards the ferry, the blast from its horn as it leaves port will signal the end of any hope he might have of finding his missing son. The thought of returning home not knowing what has become of Art has already begun to eviscerate him.

As he is nudged into the street Connor notices that the rallying crowd has started to disperse. Their anger is still palpable as small clusters of men make their way down the hill towards the city wall, waving their arms and arguing impotently amongst themselves.

Connor pulls his hat down over his brow, thrusts his hands into his coat pockets and fixes his gaze on the stone road under his feet as he picks his way from Topkapi. No man built like Connor, or dressed as he is, is going to simply blend in here. He has never felt more foreign or vulnerable. Connor curses himself for not bringing Orhan to help him find his way back to the Troya.

In the distance he sees Major Hasan's familiar woollen hat weaving its way through the crowd of fezzes and crocheted skullcaps. The Turk is the only person – out of all his own countrymen and supposed allies – who has seemed willing to help him. Perhaps, away from the War Office and the watchful eyes of the British, the major could be convinced to tell him more. One thing is certain, Connor has nothing to lose.

Hasan moves through the crowd easily as Turks step aside for him, occasionally taking his hand and kissing it or exchanging the poetic greetings that are a central part of public life in Constantinople.

'Peace be with you.'

'May peace, mercy and God's blessings be upon you too.'

During one of their lengthy walks around the city, Orhan had attempted to translate some of these greetings for Connor, and tried to explain the protocols.

'A man riding a horse should greet a man walking, but a man walking should greet the man sitting down. If they are in groups, the smaller group greets the larger one. If you are entering a house you should give the greeting too. It is in the Koran. And when you meet someone who has had a haircut or a shave, you give the blessing that you hope it lasts for hours. If someone gives you food, they wish you good eating, and you wish health on their hands.'

Suddenly to Connor his regular 'Hello. How are you?' and 'Good, and how are you?' seemed thoroughly inadequate.

Further down the street, Hasan moves briskly and with purpose under the shop awnings that line the pavement.

He curses as he steps over the filth mounting in the gutter, including a putrid dead dog, and crosses to the other side. The British and French are having a pissing contest over who is in charge of Constantinople's municipal services: the sanitation, the fire fighting and policing. Meanwhile the rubbish clogs the streets in fetid piles and waterways, and fires sweep through entire neighbourhoods of wooden homes until they burn themselves out. Half the population sees the Christians as saviours. But history shows that will only last as long as it takes for children to start dying from cholera or burning in their beds.

Hasan passes a wall and reads the question painted in Turkish across it. 'Where are they?' Below are the names of prominent politicians, army officers and newspaper editors – all well known for their Nationalist loyalties. Hasan has heard that many have been exiled to Malta. Others have simply disappeared. There are persistent rumours of British soldiers knocking on doors in the middle of the night and taking these men away. Worse, there are whispers that the Sultan's advisors are compiling the lists of 'agitators' – selling out their own citizens to maintain the status quo. Hasan would never dream of doing such a thing but still he feels compromised. Peaceful cooperation and reasonable discussion have not brought the Turks any closer to securing their country. The Allies have mistaken this collaboration for weakness and have run roughshod over Turkish aspirations for nationhood. So the time for compromise has passed.

❖

Hasan turns sharply into a narrow lane. Connor reaches the corner just in time to see the Turk disappear down a short flight of steps that lead to a basement door. Hasan raps on it with his knuckles and slips in. Connor darts across the road and stands at the top of the stairs, weighing up his options. Suddenly he feels a muscular arm go round his neck and a sharp object press into his side. He recognises Jemal's menacing rumble in his ear.

'So I get to kill you after all.'

'I need to speak to Hasan Bey. I know he is here.'

Without a word, Jemal pushes Connor down the stairs and holds him against the wooden door. He knocks three times with the hilt of his knife and Connor hears the turning of the lock. Jemal forces Connor through the half-open door, knocking a young Turkish man on the other side onto his backside. Jemal roars at him in Turkish. Connor finds himself in a small windowless basement with a vaulted stone ceiling. The room is scattered with tables and chairs where men sit in clusters, reading papers and drinking coffee. Cigarette smoke is trapped in the airless room and hangs like a fog above the tables. Connor's appearance takes the Turks completely by surprise. Their robust chatter stops abruptly as they spring from their seats, grasping for knives and guns. Chairs are overturned and rock back and forth on the uneven stone floor. Water sloshes across the tabletops and a coffee cup falls and shatters on the flagstones as its saucer is kicked under a nearby table. Connor sees that the men surrounding him are wearing civilian clothes but have the scars and dead eyes of soldiers.

Before Connor can even begin to guess who these men are, Jemal kicks him behind the knees and the Australian drops to the floor. Connor feels a sudden, violent tug on his hair from behind and a cold blade across his throat. Finally, after years of despatching animals on the farm, he finds himself on the wrong end of the knife. Every creature dies differently: sheep bleat and then lie down in resignation, chickens scratch and claw to the last, and rabbits, perhaps because they are born wild and innocent, look at you with genuine confusion and surprise. He thinks he knows himself but Connor has often wondered whether, come his time, he would die a sheep or a chicken.

He is surprised to realise he is not afraid. He knows that if Jemal wanted to kill him he would already have felt the burning line across his throat and the warmth of his own blood running down the inside of his collar and mingling with his chest hair. From his prone position he scans the desperate faces of the twenty-odd men in the cellar. There has been plenty of talk of Nationalist rebels. He presumes that is what unites this group of men. But Connor is surprised; Hasan has been cooperating with the occupying forces. It makes no sense that he would throw his lot in with the freedom fighters.

As they overcome their initial shock, the men relax and begin lowering their weapons. Hasan emerges from amongst them, bewildered.

'It's no accident that he's here. He followed you all the way from the War Office,' announces Jemal in Turkish.

Hasan's confusion transforms to anger. 'Who sent you?' he demands of Connor in English.

Jemal tugs harder on Connor's hair. 'He must be a spy. Let me kill him.'

With nothing to lose now, Connor speaks up, struggling to breathe as Jemal stretches his neck taut.

'No one will tell me what camp they took Arthur to. I just need the name of the camp. Records . . . Surely your army has records.'

Hasan stares at the Australian on his knees, wondering if he really has his measure. He looks deeply into Connor's blue eyes, searching for a hint of guile or deceit. Connor stares back, and there is nothing but determination in his gaze. No matter how crazed and mulish he might be, somehow Hasan is sure the Australian is not going to sell him and his men out. Connor is just as furious with the British as he is. The Turk signals to Jemal that he should release Connor.

'He will get us all hanged,' spits the sergeant as he releases his handful of Connor's hair in disgust and pushes the farmer forwards onto his hands and knees.

'Please, Major Hasan, I am at a dead end,' Connor beseeches.

'Then we are in this same place together,' Hasan replies. 'Go. Now.'

Connor struggles to his feet and steps backwards towards the door. The young Turkish guard holds the door open momentarily as Connor slips out.

Inside, Jemal and Hasan watch Connor disappear.

'I have fought beside you for over fifteen years but I do not understand this. What do you want from this farmer? Forgiveness? Redemption?'

Hasan speaks in a low voice.

'You were there. Some things should never be forgotten.'

CHAPTER TWENTY-SEVEN

Kestrels dip and flit in the wake of the ferry as it cuts through the choppy waves and surging current that intersects the deep, shadowy waters of the Bosphorus.

Ayshe sits on the long bench in the spring sun and idly tosses small fragments of *simit* to the wheeling birds that hover within arm's reach, sparring to grab the pieces of bread from her hand. Receding in the distance are the spires, domes and bustle of Sultanahmet. Ahead are the forest-clad hills of the Asian side of Constantinople, a city split between two continents.

Is it any wonder we forget who we're supposed to be half the time?

'The city is like twins, only with different parents,' Ibrahim used to tell Ayshe when she was a child, years before his dementia set in.

It is only a short ferry ride across the Bosphorus, but the other side is a world away. The last time Ayshe can recall visiting Asia was when Turgut was still alive. Omer and Fatma's daughter, young Fatma, had just been born and they crossed the waters bearing neatly wrapped boxes containing sticky baklava from the Greek baker and opalescent green pistachio *lokum* dusted with icing sugar. Turgut passed the time telling stories. Ayshe could never tell if he was concocting a fanciful tale based on nothing more than his fertile imagination, or if he was telling her something that was true. It was one of the many reasons she loved him.

'Ayshe, *janim.* Do you know why this is called the Bosphorus?'

'No, Turgut. But I'm sure you'll tell me.'

'Well, it all began in an age long gone and forgotten with the ancient Greek god, Zeus. He was many things – King of the Gods, mightiest of all. But he also had an eye for the ladies . . .'

Ayshe jabbed him firmly in the ribs. 'Turgut!'

'What? Don't blame me! I can't change history – who am I to argue with the gods? Anyway, Zeus had an eye for the ladies. One day he caught a glimpse of a beautiful, nubile nymph, Io, who was frolicking in the lush olive groves outside the walls of the city of Argos. She had soft, wide eyes flecked with gold, clear skin as white as freshly fallen snow and long, slender limbs. She was, dare I say, almost as beautiful as you, my wife.'

Turgut did the unthinkable then, lifting Ayshe's hand to his lips and kissing it gently. Other passengers sitting nearby clicked their tongues disapprovingly and turned away from this public display of affection. Ayshe blushed and died a thousand deaths inside, but she was also exhilarated by Turgut's lack of restraint.

She pulled her hand gently but firmly from his grasp.

'You are just using this as an excuse to embarrass me, then?'

Turgut bowed his head and held his hand to his heart.

'Apologies, my lady. May I continue with my tale?'

She nodded, smiling.

'Zeus was transfixed by the bewitching young maiden and determined to seduce her. The one thing standing in his way was the rather inconvenient matter of his wife, the goddess Hera, who was jealous and vindictive and didn't look too kindly upon Zeus' dalliances.'

'Understandably.'

'Quite. Zeus – did I mention he had an eye for the ladies? – decided that the only way he could protect Io from his vengeful wife was to transform her into a heifer, which he did – a beautiful white heifer with a coat that glimmered like satin, and still with her gentle eyes flecked with gold. But Hera was wise to her husband's ploy and set a trap for him. I would not recommend doing such a thing to a husband, but Hera did. She demanded the beautiful white cow as a gift, knowing that Zeus could not refuse without revealing his guilt, and then set a hideous monster with one hundred eyes by her side to watch over her. Zeus was not to be thwarted; he commanded his son, the cunning and swift-footed Hermes, to slay Hera's guardian, which he did –'

'Begging your pardon, oh great bard, but what does any of this have to do with the Bosphorus?'

'Patience, *janim*. I'm getting to it. After Hermes killed her all-seeing sentinel, Hera was furious. She sent a gadfly to torment poor Io. The parasite pursued her from one end of the Mediterranean to the other, before she reached these shores and crossed from Europe to Asia, and eventually found peace. This is the very spot she passed from one continent to the other. So this is the "Bosphorus" – it means "cow crossing" in Greek.'

He nudged Ayshe and indicated one of the women who had clicked her tongue at them.

'Today we are re-enacting this historic moment. You see that old cow over there, with the sour face and black scarf . . .?'

Ayshe smiles at the memory.

As the ferry sounds its horn on the approach to the Kadıköy terminal, Ayshe reaches up to the silk scarf that lies across her shoulders and is tied beneath her chin like a shawl. She unravels the knot and lifts it to cover her head and veil her hair and forehead, intertwining the ends behind her neck and draping it back across her chest. She fingers the embroidered edge of the fine fabric, feeling the intricate lace pattern she had laboured over under the watchful eye of her mother as she had prepared her trousseau. When the contents of her dowry chest were laid out for the inspection of neighbours, friends and her husband's family in the week before she wed Turgut, the quality of her needlework was more than a reflection on her own suitability as a wife; it was a matter of family pride and a mark of her mother's competence as a matriarch. A quietly petulant Ayshe had been compelled to unpick and redo countless lengths of lacing because her mother deemed it too clumsy or uneven. Ayshe had found the whole time-consuming process frustrating and pointless; she cared little for handiwork and had known that her inability to make lace would not deter Turgut's stubborn determination to make her his wife.

Sure enough, their life together had been full of laughter and joy, and very little needlework. Yet when he left her to go to war, to defend their homeland, he left her nothing. She has struggled for the last few years, trying to survive without him. Though she resists it, it is sometimes difficult to quell the resentment that rises at the back of her throat as she recalls Turgut's spendthrift squandering of her father's fortune. If he had been more frugal, given some thought to the future, she would not now be forced into this untenable situation. But in spite of everything, she finds it hard to be angry with him for long.

The ferry bumps against the wharf and sailors leap from the deck to secure the boat. Ayshe stands with her fellow passengers and treads carefully down the steep stairway to the lower deck, where she waits for the crew to extend the gangplanks. Unlike the streets on the European side of the city, where people of many races and religions mingle and there is a quiet acceptance of a more liberal way of life, all the women waiting to board the ferry at Kadıköy have their heads covered, some with their faces completely veiled, and stand meekly behind their men, whether they be husbands, sons, fathers or brothers.

The dutiful faces of the mute women gazing up at her remind Ayshe of the purpose of her visit to the Asian shore and fill her with a sickening sense of dread.

My gadfly awaits me on this side of the Bosphorus.

She knows a quicker way, but Ayshe decides to follow a circuitous route through the Kadıköy markets in a desperate attempt to stave off the inevitable. Although it's late spring, she is pleased to find a small café still selling *salep*. Ignoring the disapproving sideways glances she attracts from people passing along the bustling street, she seats herself alone at a small, outdoor table and sips the hot, creamy drink, savouring the scent of the cinnamon on top.

On the opposite corner is a fishmonger, his trays and racks heaving with marine creatures: a glistening, pink octopus splayed across a vertical board, its tentacles extended and pinned to display its size; a tray stacked high with small squid the colour of pearls; straw baskets overflowing with glittering, slippery fish. But there is something else the fisherman has just laid out, which is shielded from Ayshe's view by the scrabbling hordes of women elbowing each other out of the way to get at it. Her curiosity gets the better of her, and Ayshe finishes the last of her *salep* before crossing the street to see what is causing the near riot.

She asks one of the scarfed women standing on the outer edge of the scrum.

'*Hamsi! Hamsi* is here!'

Ayshe can't believe her luck. The *hamsi* season is almost at an end, and the plump anchovies have all but disappeared from the markets – this late in spring it's a miracle to find any at all. But the tiny, oily fish are Ibrahim's favourite. She pushes her way to the front of the pack and manages to get her hands on two pounds of the fat, silvery fish. Tonight, they'll have *hamsi pilav* – she'll line a dish with butterflied fillets, fill it with savoury rice and bake it till it's fragrant and golden brown. Hopefully that will help her father throw off the deep depression that has consumed him since the incident on the roof of the hotel.

Taking her paper-wrapped parcel, she continues through the market, past *turşu* shops stacked to the roof with huge glass jars of pickled cucumbers, cauliflower, beets, carrots, cabbage and chillies, gleaming like gems and suspended in vividly coloured brine; and stalls selling countless varieties of olives and cheeses displayed in hessian bags. She stops at a store where the window is filled with a baffling display of sweets and cakes; many are unfamiliar to Ayshe. Stepping through the front door she is struck by an intoxicating bouquet of smells: rosewater, orange blossom, roasted hazelnuts, crushed pistachios, warmed honey, sugar syrup and toasted almonds. She buys a selection of baklava and asks the shopkeeper to package it in a gift box.

Walking back out onto the street, she knows she can no longer avoid the true purpose of her visit. Ayshe takes a turn into one of the many small lanes that branch off the main street. It is a balmy spring day, and the sun warms her back as she trudges up the gentle slope towards the residential area of the district. Under just about any other circumstances, a bucolic day like today would lift her spirits, but what she knows she must confront at the top of the hill only deepens her black mood.

There. She has not forgotten the way, nor, unfortunately, has her hesitancy clouded her sense of direction. She finds the immaculately maintained, two-storeyed timber home, bay windows jutting out above the pavement, stoop swept and windows sparkling clean – one of many in a long row of terraces sweeping up the wide boulevard. The turquoise-blue paint is fresh, with window frames and edgings meticulously picked out in white.

A neighbour who is sweeping the pavement, hunched over a handle-less straw broom, pauses to stare unashamedly as she approaches the door of the neat blue house. Ayshe from Europe hesitates. She knows that once she enters, she will have committed herself and her family to an irreversible course of action. The well of despair at the thought of it is so bottomless, so inescapable. But she is well past the point where she has any choice.

Fighting her desire to flee, she climbs the steps and knocks at the door.

She hears light footsteps along the hallway. The door opens.

'Ayshe Hanim, *hoş geldiniz*.' Fatma is a statuesque beauty, with almond-shaped azure-blue eyes set above high cheekbones and well-defined, full lips. Despite her attempts at modesty, the deliberately shapeless dress she wears fails to disguise her feminine curves. Ayshe leans in to kiss her sister-in-law on each cheek. '*Hoş bulduk*, Fatma Hanim.'

Like Ayshe, Fatma's hair is covered by a scarf, and her face is bare. She extends a hand, inviting Ayshe into the house. Ayshe steps over the threshold and slips off her shoes; she is committed now. She presents the package of baklava to Fatma, who offers the obligatory words of thanks and places it on the hallstand.

The two women's relationship has always been polite and civil, if somewhat strained. Although of a similar age, they could not be more different. Fatma shared Omer's disapproval of Turgut's and Ayshe's lifestyle, condemning them as dissolute and irresponsible, and with two daughters' dowries to worry about now, she resents the money that flows from her family's coffers to support her dead brother-in-law's wife and son and their degenerate existence. To her, Ayshe's arrogance is staggering. To think that a woman, a widow, can run a business, sheltering a prostitute under her roof and mixing with foreign men, even on the European shore, is beyond belief and reason.

For her part, Ayshe has never had much respect for her sister-in-law, dismissing what she sees as Fatma's servile docility and smug piety as antiquated and irksome. But today the tension between the two women is heightened. Fatma regards Ayshe coolly. She gestures up the stairs with an elegant wave of her wrist. 'Come.'

At the top of the stairs, she points to a closed door.

'That is the number one bedroom.' Walking further along the narrow corridor, Fatma opens the door to a second room.

'We thought this room would be suitable for young Orhan.'

Against one wall is a small, neatly made bed covered with an embroidered satin quilt. On the floorboards lies a small red and ochre prayer rug; the only adornments in the room are two framed Islamic texts that hang on the wall above the bed. Sunlight streams into the spacious room through open lace curtains. Ayshe moves over to the window and looks out at the street below. In the distance, above the rooftops of the neighbouring houses, she can see the Bosphorus and, beyond that, the pointed spire of the Galata Tower in Beyoğlu and the lush green gardens and terraces of Topkapi Palace on Seraglio Point. She feels a bitter pang of nostalgia at the sight of the opposite shore.

Ayshe turns to Fatma, who stands in the doorway, hands clenched together tightly, knuckles whitening. 'It's a beautiful room, Fatma. But what about your lovely daughters? Where will they sleep now?'

Fatma smiles thinly in response. 'They will share a room for now, but they will both marry soon enough.' She turns and walks back into the hallway, opening a third door. 'Your father may sleep here.'

Like the first room, it is neat and contains a single, narrow bed. But it is tiny, with barely enough space to pass around the foot of the bed, and much more spartan than the extravagant, lushly carpeted bedroom that Ibrahim currently enjoys. The single window opens onto a narrow enclosed external stairwell and only admits an insipid grey light. Ayshe can't hide her disappointment. The thought of her father in this dark and poky room amplifies her growing disquiet. Sensing her misgivings, Fatma attempts to reassure her.

'It will be a different life for Ibrahim Bey. But the girls will take good care of him.'

'Perhaps he could take Orhan's room?'

Fatma shakes her head firmly.

'Omer always prayed he would have a son to fill that room.' She walks to the end of the hallway and opens another door. 'Here – you will be next to your father.'

Ayshe walks into the room that's intended for her. Like her father's, it is dark and small, with most of the space occupied by a double bed. She edges around to the other side and turns to face Fatma, who is standing tensely with her arms crossed and her lips pressed tightly together.

'This will be your room.' She shifts uncomfortably. 'Omer will join you on every third night.'

For a moment, Ayshe puts her own qualms to one side. If this scenario represents an unimaginable upheaval for her and her family, it must be doubly distressing for Fatma. Thanks to Omer's sense of familial obligation, her world is about to be turned on its head. Her own daughters' position in the family is to be usurped by another woman's son, and she will be compelled to share her husband in the most intimate of ways with someone she neither likes nor respects. Ayshe speaks to Fatma softly.

'And you are comfortable with this arrangement?'

Fatma turns and leaves the room, avoiding the question. 'Omer is a good man and a fine husband.'

Wordlessly Ayshe follows Fatma back down the narrow staircase to the salon.

Omer sits in a high-backed armchair in the sunlight-filled front room, newspaper held in front of him. One of his daughters enters from the back of the house with a coffee in a small cup balanced on a silver tray, which she offers to him. He accepts it with thanks and a restrained smile, sips the hot drink and gives a nod of approval. By the window, Fatma and Omer's other daughter is bowed over a fine piece of linen, painstakingly picking out decorative designs on a tablecloth intended for her trousseau. Fatma moves over to examine her handiwork, and murmurs words of encouragement.

Standing in the doorway, Ayshe feels like an unwelcome interloper. Omer acknowledges her arrival with raised eyebrows and a proprietary wave, inviting her to enter. Fatma quietly ushers the girls out of the room so that Omer and Ayshe can discuss matters in private.

Folding his newspaper and placing it on the small, inlaid wooden table beside his armchair, Omer stands and faces his widowed sister-in-law.

'You have seen the new arrangements? And everything is satisfactory?'

'It is a good home.' There is nothing else Ayshe can say.

'Yes. It will be done, then. First you must observe the traditional period of mourning, wear your black, and then we can be married. I will come after prayer this evening and we will tell Orhan.'

Ayshe's stomach clenches with anxiety and her heart begins to pound.

'No. Allow me one more day. And I will tell him in my own way, please.'

Well accustomed now to Ayshe's avoidance of the inevitable, Omer is not surprised, but nor is he particularly pleased by the delay. But in the spirit of peaceful accord, he agrees to the concession.

'As you wish.'

She leaves the room and farewells Fatma and her daughters. Fatma is still cool and reserved, but the two girls show her appropriate deference and affection. She walks out of the house and back down the street towards the ferry that will carry her back to her own home, fingernails digging raw half-moons into her palms as she resists the urge to run, and fighting the tears that she feels pooling in her eyes.

One more day. That's all we have left to us. One more day.

As Ayshe returns to the European side of the city, she is rent in two by the knowledge of what she must do, and crippling despair weighs on her heart as heavily as a lead curtain. She keeps her thoughts to herself and goes through the motions when she arrives home, but is testy, more easily vexed. Cursing silently to herself, she fumbles as she fillets the tiny silvery hamsi she brought home from the Kadiköy markets. She tears the delicate flesh and makes a mess of a dish she has made more times than she can count. Even the joy that gleams in her father's eyes when he sees the glistening dome of baked fish and rice does little to lighten her mood.

Snapping at Orhan and punishing him for some minor infraction, she sees his open-mouthed look of shock and is unsurprised when he comes into her room later that evening long after he has gone to bed, black hair tousled and sweaty, eyes wide, face blanched from the assault of nighttime demons. She lifts the coverlet and he crawls underneath, snuggling against his mother's side, his heavy head resting on her bosom and his shoulder wrapped in her slender arm. Her mind wanders to their home-to-be and she finds it hard to picture them lying together like this in her new room. She lies there in the dark on her back for some time, feeling the sweet rise and fall of Orhan's breath.

But she is too unsettled to sleep. After she is sure her son is in a deep slumber, Ayshe gently swings her legs over the edge of the bed and steps onto the cool floorboards. Moonlight floods into the room, falling on a framed photo of her standing with Turgut, sombre and serious on their wedding day. Beside it is an image she much prefers: Turgut as a wild-eyed musician seated on a bentwood chair, his *oud* resting across one knee, and on the other a young Ayshe, in her mid-twenties, her carefree hand resting on his shoulder.

She stands and walks over to the dresser, taking a wrapped parcel from the bottom drawer and opening it carefully. The stiff brown paper crackles like wildfire. She takes the contents gingerly in her hands before turning to face the full-length mirror in the corner. The long, black widow's dress unfurls like a shroud as Ayshe holds it against herself.

She looks at her moonlit reflection and silently weeps.

CHAPTER TWENTY-EIGHT

'You hold that there. Hold it tightly – don't let it move about, or I might slip and whack your finger . . .'

Orhan's brow is furrowed, his tongue pressed against his top lip, as he concentrates and attempts to follow Connor's instructions.

'Right. That's good. Now – keep it steady, and I'll bang the nail in.' Connor raises the hammer and brings it down with a strong and efficient movement, driving the nail into the plank Orhan holds against the frame of the chicken coop. Since he arrived at the Otel Troya, the free-ranging poultry have irritated Connor's farmer's instinct for live-stock management, and, finding himself with some time on his hands, he has recruited Orhan to help him construct an A-frame pen for the hotel's feathered residents. Besides, it is an excuse to do something useful.

At the bench top in the kitchen that overlooks the courtyard, Ayshe absent-mindedly takes small mounds of cumin and coriander–spiced rice and rolls them neatly and firmly within grapevine leaves, packing them tightly inside a pan lined with slices of fresh tomato. Her hands move instinctively – her attention is elsewhere. She gazes at her son and the broad-shouldered Australian man working quietly in the yard. Connor's sleeves are rolled up to his elbows, and she can't help but notice his muscled forearms flexing as he raises the hammer. Golden hairs glint against suntanned skin, and a light sheen of perspiration shines across his forehead.

Ayshe's feelings for Connor have caught her by surprise, softening in a way she could never have anticipated. For so long, Australia and its menfolk had loomed like a spectre in her imagination, a mute target for her grief, loss and bitter fury. She had no one else to blame. When the Çanakkale campaign ended, Turgut had simply not returned. He did not write. There had been no knock at the door from a uniformed messenger delivering condolences from the Ottoman army, or a list or newspaper with his name printed in an inventory of dead and injured. Just silence. For a while, Ayshe had maintained her faith that he would come back, experiencing waves of blind optimism, then frustration and, finally, desperation. Until the day she acknowledged to herself that he was gone. On that day, she turned her impotent rage on those men who had travelled halfway across the world to invade her home. The Australians – their accursed Anzacs – had carried the weight of her heartbreak. It had been an effective diversion for her. Until this man came lumbering through her door and challenged all the things Ayshe thought she knew, disarming her with his quiet resolve and lack of guile. Any lingering animosity she still harboured disappeared when she saw the close bond forming between her son and the Australian.

As liberated as she is, the world of men is opaque to Ayshe, but watching Orhan with Connor she can see that it is governed by rules that transcend language, age and geography. It has been many years since Orhan has had a strong man in his life whom he also admires. Her son adores his grandfather, but as Ibrahim's mind disintegrates, Orhan coddles him as he would a baby brother. Even when Turgut was still with them, he was so distracted by his music and social life outside the family home that Orhan never interacted with his own father in this way. They had fun together, went on adventures, but Orhan was still young.

Watching her son with Connor, she is struck by a horrible realisation. Her son detests his uncle, and even if Orhan lives beneath the same roof as Omer, he will never feel the same warmth towards him. If she is brutally honest, she doesn't want Omer choking her son's spirit with his dour counsel. This thought brings her back to the present, and she flinches at the thought of what she has promised to do today. She had resolved herself to her fate yesterday. But when she woke this morning and caught sight of her black widow's dress hanging in the wardrobe like a carrion bird, she still couldn't bring herself to put it on.

Natalia works by Ayshe's side, adding to the growing stack of *dolma*. She interrupts Ayshe's reverie, murmuring to her under her breath in French.

'He is handsome, don't you think?'

'I do not think about other men. I am married.' Ayshe's cheeks flush; she is embarrassed that the Russian woman has caught her gazing at Connor.

'No, of course ... It has been four years for you, no? There must be cobwebs up there.'

Ayshe raises a hand and laughs, feigning indignity.

'Natalia ... please!'

'Don't pretend you don't miss it . . .'

'I miss my husband. That is different.'

'Would your husband want you to wither and weep and marry into misery? Is that who he was?'

The women watch Connor as he gently directs Orhan and heaves the pieces of timber into place, his strong chest straining against his shirt.

'His equipment is all there, Ayshe Hanim. In need of practice, but all there . . .'

'Enough, Natalia,' Ayshe retorts. 'Too much. Go and eat your breakfast.'

'He is cut, too.'

Ayshe claps her hands over her ears in mock horror. Glancing into the courtyard, she sees that Connor and Orhan have finished their work. They turn to walk back into the hotel, stopping at the trough to wash the sawdust from their hands.

'Shush, you disgraceful woman. They're coming.' Ayshe hurries Natalia from the kitchen; the Russian woman sashays out, hips wiggling.

Orhan bursts through the door, blurting out in Turkish, 'Mother, Connor Bey is coming with us to the cistern. He wants to see it!'

Ayshe looks into Orhan's upturned face, alight with anticipation. Shaking her head, she addresses him in Turkish. 'No. It is just you and me today. Special treat.' Ayshe turns to Connor and reverts to English. 'I am sorry, Mr Connor. This is not possible.'

Connor nods his head in understanding.

'It would not be proper,' she adds.

'Of course. I am going to the Red Cross this morning anyway.'

Ayshe feels a small hand in hers, senses Orhan's disappointment. His excited expression has imploded into one of utter dejection.

'Little one, it is not possible.' But as she says it, Ayshe's will breaks.

'Well . . . Mr Connor, where we are going is near the Red Cross. Perhaps if you were to follow – perhaps twenty paces behind. Then there would be no shame.'

The boy whoops with delight. 'Come, come, Connor Bey. Come get your hat. We go. We go now.' Orhan leads Connor from the kitchen by the hand, the big man following awkwardly but willingly in the child's wake.

Ayshe can't see any real harm in allowing him this one, small indulgence. The boy's world is going to be shattered soon enough.

❖

A war veteran, still clad in the well-worn but patched and clean remnants of his Ottoman uniform, sits at a spinning whetstone, pumping the treadle to keep the glistening disc whirling. He lays the edge of a wooden-handled knife against the stone, sending sparks flying. Connor pauses to marvel at his adroit handling of the razor-sharp blade and notices the recent nicks on the man's fingers. Finished, the veteran brings the knife up to his ear, flicks the blade with his thumbnail and listens to it like a tuning fork. Perfect. He calls out the name of the knife's owner and looks up, and Connor sees a burn scar melting down the man's face and two milky, sightless eyes.

Along the wall of the busy alley, a gaggle of shopkeepers sit in a row on low, rush-bottomed stools beneath the eaves of their stores, inhaling deeply on their cigarettes and gossiping. As Ayshe moves past them she joins in the banter; although Connor has no idea what she says, the tone of her voice and the gales of laughter that follow her leave little doubt that she is popular in her neighbourhood. One of the men stands and, doffing his cap, bows theatrically. Ayshe curtsies and laughs easily, continuing on her way with Orhan in her wake.

The lane is steeper here, and a narrow flight of wide steps makes negotiating the slippery cobbles less perilous. Connor walks a short distance behind the woman and her son, an unwitting voyeur. He can't tear his eyes away from her; he finds it impossible not to be entranced by Ayshe's elegant curves and the fluid and graceful way she moves. Her head is held high on a ballerina's long neck, and she places her feet daintily as she walks. Mounting a step, she lifts her skirt slightly, offering Connor a glimpse of her lithe lower leg and delicate ankle. He feels the unfamiliar thickness in his throat that accompanies desire. Connor's encounter with Natalia has sparked something within him that has lain undisturbed for what seems like an eternity.

Ayshe and Orhan turn into a dead-end lane and approach an enormous open doorway edged with an ancient mossy lintel and fluted columns. They slip inside and Connor follows. Immediately he is struck by a familiar and welcome sound. Water. Dripping, gushing, trickling, flowing water. And the smell: a dark, green scent that permeates the cool air. As his eyes adjust, he sees shafts of light penetrating the gloom from cracks and holes in the cistern's roof. The beams of sunlight shine on an immense forest of massive columns as fat and tall as the oldest river gums back home.

They glitter on a body of water that stretches back into the darkest depths of the cistern.

He can't help but utter an exclamation of surprise.

Ayshe explains. 'This is Orhan's favourite place. It is Roman. And still the best water in the city.'

The volume of water here is unfathomable. Connor picks up a shard of terracotta from the jumble of broken chunks of marble and shattered ceramic that crunch underfoot, and tosses it as far as he can into the vast pool. He can tell by the hollow plonk it makes as it strikes the surface of the water that the reservoir is very, very deep. He kneels by the edge and dips his hand into the pool, then lifts it to his lips. Like the water at the Blue Mosque it is sweet and cool.

'It doesn't come from beneath the ground,' he observes.

Bending, Ayshe uses a small pannikin to fill the large urn she has brought with her from the hotel.

'No it comes from the mountains along the aqueduct of Valens that runs through Constantinople. It always runs, even in the middle of the hottest summer.'

Connor turns to Orhan. 'Do you know how to find water?'

Orhan looks puzzled at what seems to be a patently obvious question.

'When it rains, it comes from the sky.'

'Where I'm from it's like the desert, and sometimes it doesn't rain for years. We have to find water that's fallen through cracks in the earth. There are rivers and lakes under there. You have to find them'

'How do you find it under the ground?' Orhan looks sceptical.

The Australian pauses. His strange gift seems so normal to him that he rarely gives it a moment's thought. At home, his neighbours accept his ability to divine water without question. He can't think of the last time he was asked to explain it.

'That's the trick. You have to feel it. It is like the earth talks to me.'

Orhan's brow creases.

'First I look for clues above the ground – like old river beds or big rocks. If I see trees growing, then I know there must be water somewhere down there. Then I *really* start looking, and I use my hands. And it is like they can see underground.' Connor struggles to think of a way to describe it to the boy. 'When you are trying to find something in the dark, you use your hands, don't you?'

Orhan nods, transfixed by Connor's every word.

'It's just like that. The things buried deep beneath the earth are sending me messages, and I can hear those messages with my hands. When I find the spot I dig down to the water.'

'And you find water every time?'

Connor laughs at the thought of the number of failed attempts he's made over the years.

'No. I've dug a lot of wells that just end up being holes in the ground.' He steps behind the boy and rests his hands on his shoulders. 'Here. I will show you. Shut your eyes.'

Orhan obediently lowers his eyelids. Connor gently raises the boy's arms so they are extended in front of him. 'Now hold out your fingers and move slowly in a circle. That's it. Slowly.'

Watching from alongside, Ayshe is moved by the unexpected tenderness with which Connor rests Orhan's hands in his own rough-hewn palms. He turns the boy's hands over and runs his fingers lightly down the veins that pulse blue at his wrist.

'Can you feel it here? Tingling?' he asks.

Sneaking one eye open to peek up at Connor, Orhan looks disappointed.

'I cannot feel it. Just your hand.'

'Come on. Close your eyes. No – don't open them! Can you feel it now?'

'No.'

'Are you sure?'

'No, Connor Bey. I feel nothing.'

Connor bends and scoops some water into his hands, splashing it playfully into Orhan's face.

'Can you feel it now?'

Orhan shrieks with delight and splashes Connor back. They go tit for tat until water drips from their hair and soaks their shirts. Eyes glinting, a mischievous idea strikes them simultaneously. Together they turn towards a grim-faced Ayshe.

There's no doubting their intentions. Ayshe stands firm and places her hands on her hips. 'No! Absolutely not. That would not be proper.'

Connor gathers himself, conscious of propriety and feeling like a clumsy oaf. 'I am very sorry.'

Out of nowhere a wicked smile flashes across Ayshe's lips and she flings the pannikin of water into Connor's face. She bolts back out of the cistern, shrieking with laughter, her son in hot pursuit.

Blinking, Connor wipes the water from his eyes and watches them leave, his hair dripping and his heart pounding.

'I wish I could be of some help, but we only forwarded relief packages to the prison camps – with bars of soap, blankets and such. We didn't have any direct contact with the soldiers. It wasn't our war, you see.'

The Red Cross nurse has overcome her initial surprise at Connor's sudden entrance and very bedraggled appearance. Hair still damp and shirt and pants sodden from the water fight, he cuts an unconventional figure. He attempts to smooth down his hair with his palms, but the light brown strands stick up in errant, unflattering clumps.

In a corner of the courtyard visible through the door of the old hospital a fire burns brightly in a huge metal drum, fuelled by a mountain of old manila folders and files fed into the flames by two Turkish workers.

'We're packing up here,' she explains. 'Heading home.'

'But what about the prisoners of war?' Connor persists.

'To tell you the truth, sir, there weren't many of those. And those who did come through here couldn't wait to go home. Most of them hadn't seen their families in years.'

'Is there anywhere else ... any other people ... who might be able to help me?'

The nurse sees the desperation in his eyes. She lowers her voice, speaking soothingly.

'The ones who lived couldn't get out of this place quickly enough. If your son hasn't come back to you ... well, I'm very sorry to say it, but it's likely he didn't make it. The camps were brutal places, I'm told.'

Connor stares into the rising flames despondently, watching them consume page after page of military records, sending ash and black smoke billowing into the sky.

He is overwhelmed, broken.

CHAPTER TWENTY-NINE

The coffee sits, muddy and unappetising, by Connor's hand.

I suppose in time I might acquire a taste for it. He takes a sip. *Unlikely.*

Two solitary Turkish men sit at single tables in the salon. One reads the newspaper while absently fiddling with a lavishly coiffed moustache. The other gazes pensively out into the garden, tapping a manicured fingertip on the tabletop. With four guests in residence, including its permanent habitué, Natalia, the Otel Troya is busier than it has been in many years.

Ayshe moves about the salon, serving her guests an afternoon tea of rosewater *lokum*, dusted with icing sugar on tiny silver dishes, and sweet Turkish coffee. Connor is consumed by his thoughts, trying to plan his next step. Ayshe returns to his table, pointing to the cup by his side.

'Take good care. Your fate is in there, you know.'

He lifts the cup and saucer, and offers them to her.

'No one else has been able to help me. Maybe you can tell me what to do next.'

'It is a silly peasant game.' She laughs and hands it back to Connor.

'And you have to drink it first! But make sure you only drink from one side of the cup, otherwise it will not work.'

Throwing back his head, he grimaces as he consumes the thick, grainy coffee in a single gulp.

Ayshe holds out her hand and sits in the seat opposite Connor. 'Here . . . give it to me.'

She places the saucer on top of the cup and slides it back across the table to Connor.

'Careful. Hold the saucer on top and make three circles in the same direction as a clock turns. Like this . . .' Ayshe mimics holding the cup, hands rotating at chest level. Amused, Connor plays along, following her instructions.

She takes the cup back and quickly flips it so it sits, inverted, on the saucer.

'Now we wait.' She smiles. 'You know, we decide everything here by coffee. Business, holidays, even our husbands.'

'And that works?'

'Of course, it is the best way. When two families come together to arrange a marriage, the young girl serves her parents coffee. If it is sweet, they know she approves of the match. If it is bitter – go away.' She waves a dismissive hand. 'The more sugar, the deeper her love.'

'. . . And with your husband?'

'I used the whole bowl of sugar.' She laughs at the memory. 'I thought my parents were going to be sick.' Ayshe shifts in her seat, seeming suddenly conscious of the disapproving glares of the other guests.

She changes the subject. 'Now. Your coffee. What does it tell us?'

Ayshe lifts the delicate bone-china cup and gazes at the smear of coffee grounds in its interior. 'I see a stubborn man . . .'

'No, you must have someone else's cup,' Connor retorts.

'No, I see a farmer who eats only boiled eggs, even in a city where there is a woman . . . see, there she is,' Ayshe points into the cup. 'A woman who is the best cook in all of Turkey.'

'That is a lot of detail in a very small cup.'

Ayshe lowers her voice and leans in conspiratorially. 'Everything is in the coffee. The cup never lies.'

'Does it say if this cook is beautiful?'

She flushes and leans back in her seat, her gaze darting to the two Turkish men in the room. The Australian locks eyes with her.

'Tell me what it really says,' he urges her.

No longer playing, Ayshe peers intently into the cup. Suddenly she rises to her feet.

'It is all peasant nonsense.' She takes Connor's coffee cup and saucer and walks quickly away.

❖

As she hurries towards the kitchen, Ayshe is alarmed to see Omer standing in the doorway. As promised, he has arrived to set things straight with her son. But the dark expression on his face tells her that he has witnessed her exchange with Connor, and he is furious. She pushes past him and walks quickly down the hallway, her brother-in-law following in her wake.

Once they reach the privacy of the kitchen, Omer turns on her. 'You are not dressed in black? Where is Orhan?'

Ayshe slams the coffee cup down on the bench and spins to face him, arms crossed defensively across her chest. After a night of troubled sleep during which she picked and unpicked her options, she knew there would be no easy path for her or her family. But after watching her son at the cistern this morning and seeing how happy he could be, and knowing that a life with Omer and his wife would be constrained by duty and starved of love and levity, she has made up her mind.

'Until I'm certain Turgut is dead, I can't . . .'

'Do you take me for a fool?'

'No, and your offer is most generous.'

Omer's fury rises to fever pitch. 'We both know – everyone but Orhan knows. My brother is in Paradise!'

Ayshe's voice lifts to match his, her fear and frustration building. 'I am not ready to re-marry.'

'You came to my house and we agreed. You would now humiliate me in front of my wife and daughters?'

'I cannot be any man's second wife.'

'Then you will never marry again. Who else would take you as well as your father and son? And you think only of yourself, but this marriage is not for you. It is for Orhan. He needs a father. He will become my son.'

The grim expression of resolve on Ayshe's face leaves Omer in no doubt that she is not going to change her mind.

'I have a duty to my brother! It is our way!'

Ayshe shakes her head. 'No. It is your way.'

'This charade can't continue. It is wrong.' Omer steps into the hallway and calls out to his nephew. 'Orhan! Come!'

Ayshe has done everything in her power to avoid this moment for the past four years. The thought of it – knowing what it will do to her son — makes her knees buckle. She whispers, 'Please. Not this way. I beg you.'

Omer glares at her venomously. 'It's your pride that has done this. Orhan!'

Ayshe knows that Orhan always dreads heeding his uncle's call — most of the time it is accompanied by a clip to the ear and a volley of stern words. And the scene he confronts when he arrives in the kitchen — his mother's blanched face and eyes glistening with tears, and Omer's mouth set in a grim line, black eyes glinting — doesn't bode well. He moves to his mother's side and takes her hand.

'What have I done?'

She looks down at him. 'Nothing, cherub. Go away,' she urges him. 'Leave us.'

Moving across the kitchen, Omer takes the boy's other hand. 'Orhan ...' He speaks gently, but with resolve. 'Your father is dead. He has been dead for four years. Your mother has lied to you.'

Ayshe speaks over Omer, attempting to drown out his words. She takes Orhan's face in her hands and looks into his eyes. 'Don't listen, my darling boy. Don't listen.'

Pushing Ayshe's hands away, Omer draws the boy to face him. 'Do you understand?'

The blood drains from Orhan's face. 'Mother? ... Please?' He searches his mother's face, and can see from her grief that his uncle has spoken the truth.

Omer continues as Ayshe grapples to put a hand over his mouth. He flings her aside.

'Your father is a martyr, Orhan. Be proud.'

His mouth wide with horror and disbelief, Orhan breaks away from his uncle and runs into the hallway in tears.

Ayshe screams. 'You will never have him. You will never have me or this place!'

'You think you are too good for me and my home?' Omer spits. 'You are no better than the slut upstairs!'

Years of accumulated anguish and grief explode in the pit of Ayshe's stomach. She strikes Omer on the cheek with the flat of her hand and shrieks, 'That is why Allah never gave you a son!'

❖

The sound of raised Turkish voices finds its way into the salon. Connor stands and moves towards the doorway, unsure what to do. There's no doubt at all that Ayshe is in distress, but she's in the kitchen with her brother-in-law; it's a family matter. Connor knows from bitter experience he can expect no thanks for interfering in private affairs. He is standing awkwardly in the hallway, hands buried in his pockets, when Orhan barrels into him.

'Steady on, mate! What's the matter?'

Orhan flings his arms around Connor's waist and buries his face in his shirt. Connor encircles the boy in his arms, patting his back. In the kitchen, the barrage continues. Connor can't understand exactly what's being said, but there's no mistaking the fury and vitriol in their voices. Orhan covers his ears, trying to block out the hate.

The stinging sound of a slap rings through the hotel, followed by a scuffle, pots falling to the stone floor. Connor can no longer restrain himself. He squeezes Orhan's shoulder. 'Stay here, son.'

He marches into the kitchen in time to see Omer bring an angry open palm down on Ayshe's face. Her knees give way and she slumps to the floor, one hand clutching the side of her face. Her brother-in-law has her by the arm, his thin fingers digging into her soft, white forearm, as he raises his other hand to slap her again. Hot rage explodes behind Connor's eyes. He propels himself forwards and swings the crook of his elbow around Omer's neck, dragging him away from Ayshe and flinging him to the floor. Shocked, the Turkish man kneels on the tiles. With two hands, Connor grabs his collar and lifts him to his feet. He clenches his calloused fist, readying to strike, but before he can draw back his arm, Ayshe pushes her way between the two men and holds out her hands, pressing against Connor's chest, restraining him.

'Stop! Stop! You fool. This is not your business!'

Relinquishing his grip on Omer's crisply starched linen shirt, Connor stares at Ayshe, perplexed.

Fists raised, Omer squares up to Connor and glares venomously at the Australian, veins throbbing at his temples and the tendons in his neck strung out like piano wires as he grinds his teeth in fury. Without glancing away, he lashes out at Ayshe .

'Now I see. This is what you want. The enemy.'

Ayshe snaps back. 'It has nothing to do with him.'

'I have eyes. You were seen together at the cistern. My brother was a fool.' Omer spits a thick nugget of phlegm onto the floor. He straightens his collar and smooths down his heavily pomaded black hair, scornfully taking in Connor's well-worn work boots and labourer's hands. Omer continues his tirade.

'This donkey's son knows not one word of our tongue. And you? You disgrace this family.' Turning, Omer stalks out of the kitchen.

When Ayshe whips around to face Connor, he sees she is enraged. 'Go! You have offended his honour!'

Connor is confused by her reaction, and attempts to explain himself. 'He struck you.'

'Yes. But I hit him.' She scoffs. 'You understand *nothing*! You will never understand.'

'I thought it was the right thing to do.'

'Yes, you and your sons and your armies – all doing the right thing. Was it right to push us to war? Was it right to invade us? All you did was rob Orhan of a father and leave me with impossible choices like this.' She is deflated; grief-stricken and lost.

'Then please let me help.' Connor is taken aback by his own offer. He has been doing his best to suppress the growing attraction he has for this woman, the intoxicating rush of adrenaline that sparks in his blood when he catches sight of her. He isn't too sure what he means by his offer of assistance. But there is one thing he knows – at this moment there is nothing he wouldn't do to help Ayshe and her son.

She looks at him, aghast. 'So now you will rescue us?'

Connor stammers, 'I didn't mean it like that. I raised three boys . . .'

'And where are they now? This is not your world. Go home, Mr Connor.'

Lost for words, he leaves.

❖

With a tear-stained face and puffy red eyes, Orhan keeps vigil at the door of the hotel, watching Connor as he treads carefully down the narrow staircase and into the foyer, carrying his small brown suitcase, broad-brimmed hat on his head.

Connor sees the boy, but keeps silent. There is nothing to say.

Ayshe is nowhere to be seen. Connor takes his room key and places it carefully on the front desk. Without glancing back, he steps out into the cobbled street and the warm, spring sunshine.

The sudden impact of a wooden club against his spine sends Connor flying forwards. Another swing takes his legs out from under him. His knees crunch into the stone paving and he falls onto his hands, the pain shooting from his wrists and exploding in his shoulder sockets. An unseen assailant wrests his suitcase from beneath him, tossing it back onto the hotel's stoop where it pops open, its contents spilling in a cascade down the steps. Out of the corner of his eye, Connor sees Orhan rush down to gather his possessions – he is relieved to see the boy tuck Art's diary safely under his arm.

Hands hoist Connor to his feet – two men, one at each shoulder. Omer stands before him, wielding a club. He holds it by the end, drawing it back behind his shoulder before swinging it with full force into Connor's guts. The air driven from his lungs, Connor doubles over. A clenched fist swings up and catches him on the cheek, splitting the skin. He feels the warm flow of blood and tastes the iron tang on his lips. Another solid thwack hits the back of his head and he finds himself splayed on the street, face down, sharp-edged gravel digging into his cheek. Bruising blows from multiple sets of boots pummel his ribs; he curls into a ball to protect his midriff.

Inexplicably, the assault ends as suddenly as it began. Connor opens his eyes to find himself inches away from a pair of highly polished black riding boots.

Connor looks up, temporarily blinded by the late afternoon sunlight. He squints, confused. An imposing figure turned out in an impeccable uniform stands beside him, hands on hips. Connor focuses, shading his eyes from the harsh light with an upraised hand. There's no mistaking Jemal's hawkish nose and heavy brow.

The Turk shoots him a half smile. 'You missed a step, Connor Bey.'

CHAPTER THIRTY

He is outnumbered. But Jemal has never been one to be intimidated by a superior force. He stands with his arms akimbo, coolly calculating the odds of success should he be compelled to take on Connor's assailants.

Omer is flanked on either side by two burly men eager for a fight. Jemal decides it could go either way. There's no doubt the well-dressed Turkish man is livid. His eyes are murderous pitch-black obsidian blades that flick between Connor and Jemal. The Turk can see that Omer is infuriated by his arrival and eager to resume his assault on the Australian. But the authority vested in Jemal's Ottoman army uniform and its impressive array of medals makes him hesitate.

'You know him?' Omer spits. 'This man has dishonoured my family.'

Jemal raises an eyebrow, unperturbed. 'My orders are to take him to Major Hasan.'

Stepping forwards aggressively, Omer prods Connor in the midriff with his club. 'First we will teach him about honour.'

Connor smacks the stick aside with the back of his hand.

'All three of you will teach him – together?' Jemal scoffs. 'Why don't you leave questions of honour to those who fought for this country?' He bends and offers Connor his hand, helping the bruised and bleeding Australian to his feet. The two men turn to leave, and Jemal serves up one last parting shot for Connor's assailants. 'If you're looking for a fight, do something useful for your country. Join the Nationalists.'

Connor hesitates. 'My suitcase.'

Looking back over his shoulder, Jemal sees Omer pacing at the entrance to the Otel Troya. He puts a hand at Connor's back, urging him forwards. 'Connor Bey, I think it is better we leave now. You get your things later.'

Glancing back at Omer, Connor nods in agreement. Then, walking gingerly, Connor allows Jemal to lead him down the cobbled street.

'Maybe you should have been a diplomat, Connor Bey,' the Turk observes with a wry smile. 'Come. I take you to Major Hasan.'

<hr>

Steam billows heavenwards, roiling languidly around the small, enclosed dome. Sunlight shines through coloured glass discs set in the ceiling, forming hazy columns of light. In each of the four alcoves branching off the central room, elaborately carved marble fonts are set into the wall. Steaming water gushes from ornate brass taps into the basins and cascades in sheets across the grey and white marble floor.

Hasan, lounging along the low step that runs round the marble-tiled walls, wears nothing but a fine silk *peshtamel* secured around his waist. He dips his hand languidly into the basin to test the temperature. He retrieves a copper dish that floats in the basin and scoops up some of the warm water, pouring it over his head and rubbing his face and short-cropped hair with his other hand as it courses over his skin. Hasan offers the dish to Connor, who shakes his head with a tight smile.

The Australian sits self consciously, ramrod straight, beside the Turkish officer. When he arrived at the bathhouse with Jemal, he was ushered into a small, timber-lined changing room and given what he assumed to be a flimsy towel. When he stepped out of the booth clad only in his long johns, the hefty attendant clicked his tongue disapprovingly and took the towel from Connor's hands, manhandling him like a doll and wrapping it around his waist. And so Connor finds himself in the bathhouse clad in sagging, dripping wet long johns, with a checked red and white cloth wound awkwardly about his midriff.

On the enormous heated marble platform at the centre of the room, Jemal lies prostrate, his modesty barely preserved by a patently inadequate *peshtamel*, his limbs extended and his skin as pink as a pomegranate where a wiry masseur has pummelled and pounded his weary muscles. He groans. 'I need a woman.'

Hasan laughs. 'Your wife is in Erzurum!'

'Do not talk of my wife when I am thinking of sex.' Jemal rolls onto his side and sighs. 'My poor manhood. I used to have balls like a bull. Now they are dried chickpeas.'

A waft of cold air blasts clear through the vapour. The three men fall silent and look towards the opposite side of

235

the room where the timber door has swung open to admit two figures who inch slowly towards an adjacent alcove. An elderly man with silvery hair and shoulders like chicken bones has one arm encircling another, much younger man, who leans heavily against him. Connor watches as the two men settle themselves beside the font; the greying man guides his youthful companion so tenderly he can only be the boy's father. He picks up the copper dish and sluices hot water across the young man's chest. The youth's vacant eyes are black pools. Connor gazes at them absently, averting his eyes suddenly when he registers the angry red stump at the boy's shoulder socket where his right arm should be.

Jemal's expression is now sombre. He turns to Connor. 'I found your son's name on a list of wounded. They sent him from Çanakkale to a camp at Afion Kara Hissar.'

The purpose of Connor's audience with Hasan has, until now, been unclear. The longer Connor spends in this country, the more accustomed he is becoming to the protracted Ottoman way of conducting business, traversing a route as circuitous as a goatherd's track. Issues are rarely addressed directly, and resolution is never immediate. Any discussion is preceded by a frustrating and extended round of social niceties and the drinking of hot beverages. For Connor, who has never had any time, far less talent, for small talk, it's a cruel and unusual punishment.

This visit to the *hamam* is the worst example yet. But it seems that the expected protocols have been observed, and he will now find out why he has been dragged halfway across the city to sit here in wet undergarments.

'Afion . . . what?'

Hasan elaborates. 'Afion Kara Hissar. A town in Anatolia. It means "Opium Black Castle".'

'After Afion, we don't know. Winters there are hard.' Jemal groans as he rolls to the edge of the platform and swings his legs out to sit up on the edge of the heated marble slab.

'So he died there?' Despite the cloyingly humid air in the *hamam*, which sends sweat running in rivulets down his back and beading across his brow, Connor feels a frigid explosion of dread in his gullet.

Jemal wiggles the fingers of both hands and blows a puff of air from distended cheeks. 'From there, he vanished. I cannot tell. No more records. We are Ottoman, not German.'

Connor persists. 'Could he still be in Afion?'

Since learning of Art's capture at Lone Pine, Connor has held on to a gossamer-thin shred of hope that his son has emerged from the abyss and survived, but found himself lost, adrift. Connor has run through all the possibilities in his mind — there are so many reasons why Art may not have been able to return. Most of them are utterly implausible, yes. But in Connor's dreams, Art is well. He is alive.

'No.' Hasan speaks softly. 'There is much fighting in central Anatolia. No one would choose to be there right now. If he could leave, he would have gone already.'

Connor's shoulders melt, his strong spine sags. The sound of rushing water fills his ears; everything else dulls to a faint buzz. His heart stops for a moment, and then jolts in his chest. Steam fills his lungs. He is drowning. The evanescent hope that has been sustaining him since his trip to Gallipoli dissipates in the plumes of mist that fill the room.

Feeling his desolation, Hasan reaches out to rest a hand on Connor's shoulder.

'In the morning you are returning to Australia. But tomorrow we travel east to Ankara. Mustafa Kemal is gathering an army there . . .'

Jemal shoots his commanding officer a wary look. It is clear to Connor that he still thinks the Australian poses a grave danger to the two Turks.

Hasan ignores his friend and continues. 'We pass through Afion. If it has not been burned to the ground, I will ask if anyone remembers your son.' Hasan looks down at his feet, watching the streams of water that pool behind his heels and run between his toes. He watches it funnel into channels carved into the marble and disappear into the pipes running beneath the *hamam*'s floor, flowing as it has for centuries. 'But as a soldier and a father, I tell you – it is past praying. He is lost.'

❦

Connor sits slumped forwards over his knees on the low bench in the narrow changing booth, forearms leaning heavily on his naked thighs. His hands hang, impotent, between his legs; broad palms, strong, flat fingers, all riven with deep creases permanently stained with the red dirt of home.

Where to now? Is this really the end?

He seems to have exhausted his alternatives. The British are desperate to see the back of him, and with the way he left things, he can hardly expect a welcoming committee at the Otel Troya – the one place in this overwhelming city where he was beginning to feel comfortable. Worst of all, if Hasan and Jemal are right, there seems little hope of finding Art still alive.

The walls press in on him. The sound of incomprehensible babbling comes from outside the door and echoes around inside his head. The room is muggy and smells musty, heavy with the stench of wet skin, sweaty feet and damp hair. He shuts his eyes and transports himself to his dusty red plains, the vast sky an impossible blue and air so hot and dry it sears the lungs. The windmill turns with a hypnotic rhythm.

On his farm Connor knows and accepts the way of the land – doesn't fight it, instead submits to its sovereignty and marvels at its fickleness. He has no choice. Nature wreaks havoc on his small community – droughts that last so long that young children are terrified when they first see rain falling from the sky; fires that consume every living thing in their path, leaving fields of charred, contorted carcasses, blackened tree stumps and stubble where before vast plains of whispering wheat grew. But those disasters are familiar to him; they are old friends in adversity, even.

He wonders why he finds everything here so difficult, why he cannot bring himself to accept what seems obvious to everyone else. His boys are all dead. God knows it would be a relief to stop pushing, even for a moment, and just accept the truth.

But if Art died, terrified and alone, in a camp far from his brothers, his bones now lie in alien soil too, except they are untended and unmourned. The thought makes Connor feel bereft – physically ill, and quite desperate. He must find him.

A sudden, sharp rap at his door. 'Connor Bey?'

'Yes, Hasan?'

'Jemal has told me of the situation with the men at your hotel. Now we are dining at the *meyhane* you followed me to. Perhaps you should join us and return for your things later.'

Connor shuts his eyes. 'Thank you. Yes.' In the absence of anywhere to sleep that night, it was his only real option.

❦

'The invisible wind carries us throughout the world. Remember God so that you forget yourself ... *Mustafa Kemal!*' Jemal bellows, butchering Rumi. His eyes are closed, one hand upraised, clutching a tall, narrow glass filled to the brim with a cloudy liquor. The other men in the room, all huddled around small, marble-topped tables, raise their glasses and echo Jemal's raucous toast.

'*Mustafa Kemal!*' As one, they throw back their heads and down their drinks in a single hit.

'Who is he toasting?' Connor asks.

Hasan observes his sergeant fondly.

'Turkey's future.'

He offers the Australian a dish glazed with a foliate blue pattern that contains salty dried black olives. Connor shakes his head. 'No, thank you. Not to my liking, I'm afraid.'

Hasan indicates a dish of nuts sitting on the table. Connor smiles tightly. His misgiving is plain to see as he gingerly picks a whole pistachio from the bowl and pops it into his mouth. Before Hasan can stop him, Connor crunches down on the shell, wincing as it shatters against his tongue.

'It is called an *antep fıstık*. But you must open it first. Like this,' Hasan explains, picking a nut from the bowl as

Connor spits the shards from his mouth. The Turk digs his thumbnail into the tiny split between the two shell halves and pops the pistachio open. Connor makes another, more successful, attempt and pops the nut into his mouth. Surprised, he smiles as he bites down on the sweet and fragrant nut.

'This isn't bad. Delicious, really.'

Hasan watches the Australian, who wears his unease like an ill-fitting suit. Connor flinches and starts, his eyes darting from one side of the room to the other, totally at odds with his environment. But Hasan can tell that he is a man not easily diverted from his course.

In the *hamam* Hasan didn't have the heart to tell Connor the news from Anatolia. Every day, survivors flood into Constantinople, fleeing the massacres. They carry with them tales of atrocities and brutality that beggar belief. As the Hellenic army makes sorties into the Turkish country-side from Smyrna, Turkish and Greek neighbours turn on each other, and centuries of festering acrimony accrued for real and imagined episodes of dispossession and dishonour incite men to rape and disembowel; to tear flesh from bone. It's inconceivable to Hasan that anyone, least of all a foreign prisoner of war, would willingly remain in the midst of such mayhem. But he can't find it in himself to shatter what remains of Connor's hope.

Jemal staggers over to the table, wielding a bottle of raki like a weapon. He slops a generous serve of the clear liquid into three glasses, and adds a dash of water from a jug that sits by Connor's elbow, turning the alcohol a milky white.

'Now, raki becomes *aslan süt* – lion's milk!' Jemal extends one of the glasses to Connor. 'Drink, Australian!'

Connor lifts the glass to his nose and sniffs. 'That smells good. Like liquorice.' He takes a large sip and the air is driven from his lungs. He coughs, eyes watering.

Having taken a deep draught of his own raki, Jemal stands in the centre of the room, head tilted to the side and both arms held at shoulder height, one palm facing upwards to the ceiling, the other turned down towards the dusty floor of the *meyhane*. He begins to spin, clumsily and slowly.

'Outside, all is madness. We are drunk with it. Defeat. Pain. Grief. Inside – in the middle, all is quiet.' Jemal lowers his finger to his lips. 'Shh.'

Hasan shakes his head. 'Now he's a Sufi. He always finds religion in raki.'

Just as suddenly as he started, Jemal stops spinning and stands stock still in the centre of the floor. The men gathered in clusters around the room pay him little mind, remaining deep in conversation, brows furrowed and hands gesticulating emphatically. Jemal shuts his eyes and takes a deep breath. He begins to sing in a voice that is surprisingly melodious for such a bear of a man. He sways in time and claps the rhythm on hands held high. Faces turn towards him, smiling, recognising the tune, transported to the distant pine-clad mountains in the Anatolian hinterland through the force of Jemal's lyrical warbling. They begin to join in, tapping bottles and glasses with metal spoons, drumming on the tables and slapping their thighs. Jemal warms to the attention, begins to dip and dance as he sings. The song catches the room like a brushfire and other voices join his as he lifts the tempo, now stomping and chanting towards a crescendo. Men sway together, arm in arm.

Jemal spins back to where Connor sits with Hasan and pulls back a chair, collapsing into it. Hasan leans forwards, shouting to Connor above the din.

'He is an enthusiastic singer but the worst sergeant in the whole Ottoman Army. Three times I have saved this man's life. Never once in battle!'

Spilling more raki into their three glasses, Jemal affectionately goads Hasan.

'Look at him. Like a peacock with a big moustache and gold buttons . . . "I love my wife, I love my children, I have a big stick up my arsehole".'

Despite himself, Connor laughs.

Jemal turns towards Connor and whispers conspiratorially, 'Tonight we kill this man together, yes? You and me. We kill him with lion's milk. *Şerefe!* Forget!'

Connor raises his glass and takes a tentative sip. '*Şerefe.*'

Shaking his head, Jemal reverts to Turkish.

'I don't trust him. He doesn't drink like a man.'

CHAPTER THIRTY-ONE

The night is still and the air heavy. Connor finds his way along darkened streets; only a few lanterns glow in the windows of the terraced buildings he passes as he labours up the steep incline towards the crest of a hill. Shadows shift and melt as low-slung clouds of sea mist scud across the face of the moon. The tread of his heavy work boots rings and ricochets along the alleys, inciting a chorus of stray dog calls. He pauses, listens, certain he is being followed.

A single light still burns in the foyer of the Otel Troya. Connor can't see any movement on the ground level; it is late, and the household sleeps. He quietly mounts the steps, embarrassed by his furtive approach. This is not his way. He tries the lustrous brass door handle, polished to a rich patina by many years of frequent use. To his relief, it is unlocked and gives way, allowing Connor to push the door open. If the front door had been locked, he wasn't sure what he would have done – he probably would have had no choice but to wake Ayshe or Orhan, the thought of which mortifies him.

He edges into the foyer, looking around for his suitcase.

Moving towards the front desk, he notices a light on in the salon.

'Mr Connor?'

In the half-light, he can make out Ayshe seated in one of the salon's high-backed brocade armchairs. He draws breath. She is beautiful.

'I am so sorry I disturbed you. I'm just here to pick up my bag . . .'

Ayshe stands and crosses into the foyer, hand outstretched in protest.

'No, I'm glad you came. I was waiting, hoping you would return. I wish to apologise for all I said. I was angry. I meant none of it.'

Given the terms on which they parted company, this is not the reception Connor was expecting. He is struck with remorse.

'It is I who must apologise. I presumed too much . . .'

'It is difficult – even for those of us who live here.'

'You were right. I filled my sons' heads with heroic nonsense . . . God, King and Country . . . my rowdy, wilful and loving sons.' Uncontrollable grief wells up from a dark place. 'It was my job to steer them to manhood, and I failed them.'

She gazes up into his eyes. 'I measure a man by how much he loves his children, not by what the world has done to them.'

They both fall silent. Neither knows what to say.

Connor breaks the impasse. 'Well, if you can just direct me to my suitcase, I will bid you good night. I'm sorry again for troubling you . . .'

'But where will you stay tonight? You are leaving on the British boat tomorrow, yes? Omer won't return before then. You may have your room until the morning comes.'

Having resigned himself to the necessity of an uncomfortable night spent propped up somewhere down on the docks waiting for the sun to rise, Connor is relieved.

'Thank you. You are very kind.'

Ayshe moves towards the reception desk. She gestures apologetically at the mortal remains of Connor's suitcase, which sits on a small desk.

'Orhan and I tried to fix it, but the latch is broken. Tomorrow morning I will give you a rope to tie it closed before you leave.'

Crossing to where it lies, Connor lifts the lid, and relief floods through him when he sees Art's diary and the copy of *The Arabian Nights* sitting on top of the neatly folded but dusty clothes. He takes the diary and slips it carefully inside his breast pocket. Then he holds *The Arabian Nights* out to Ayshe.

'I won't need my guide book anymore. Do you think Orhan would like it?'

'I know he would,' she replies, taking the book in both hands and smiling wistfully.

Connor gathers the broken suitcase under his arm. 'Thank you again.' He moves towards the stairs. 'They will be here for me in the morning to make sure I'm on that boat. Good night to you.'

'Mr Connor?'

He halts.

'Before you go, may I ask one small favour of you?'

❖

Connor sits at the long stone bench that runs along the wall in the kitchen. Atop the chipped and pitted surface is an array of small dishes, some glazed and shimmering like gems, embellished with fluid brushstrokes of turquoise, emerald green and carmine red, others formed from rosy sheets of copper engraved and stamped with geometric patterns. Each dish contains something different and, presumably – hopefully – edible. Tiny purple cubes glisten, sprinkled with a finely chopped green herb; a swirl of buttery yellow is topped with a puff of rust-red powder and drops of a shiny green oil; bright red paste is flecked with orange flakes. Connor recognises an ingredient or two here and there, but he can't put a name to any of the dishes.

'No boiled egg, then?'

Ayshe laughs. 'No. None at all. Close your eyes.'

Connor obliges. She places something in Connor's fingers. 'Try this.'

He pops it into his mouth and chews. It's creamy – yoghurt, perhaps? But the sharp tang of pungent garlic is utterly unfamiliar to his palate, and the dried mint, though fragrant, is unexpected.

'It is called *cacik*.' Ayshe wants his verdict. 'So?'

'Yes. Well.' He swallows. 'Interesting.'

'I learned to make this from my grandmother using yoghurt from sheep's milk.'

'Are there no cows in this country?'

'None that I have seen,' she adds dryly, handing Connor what feels to him like a small cigar. 'Now try this.'

He bites into it and the deep-fried silky-thin *yufka* pastry disintegrates in his mouth. At its centre is a warm and tasty filling of tart cheese and chopped parsley. 'Oh. This is quite good!' he exclaims, surprised to find he likes it. Connor

247

smiles, opening his eyes. Ayshe returns the smile, and her green eyes glint. She's enjoying this.

'*Sigara börek*. It is my speciality. And Orhan's favourite.' Next, she hands him a fork. 'Now, dessert.'

Connor peers suspiciously at the malformed piece of fruit dripping syrup into the dish. 'And what is this, then?'

'Poached figs in rosewater with pistachio and spices. Smell the cinnamon, the way it warms you.'

Obediently shutting his eyes again, he takes a bite. 'Oh, my word. That is delicious. What's in it again?'

'A thousand years of loving food.' She hesitates. 'How is it that a man who can feel underground rivers cannot see what is before his eyes?'

Connor opens his eyes and looks at her. 'I see well enough.'

Ayshe holds his gaze and feels herself dissolving. 'Today, you did not presume too much.'

Her soft hand rests on the bench, fine fingers splayed out on the marble. Reaching out, Connor places his weathered hand on hers.

Ayshe lifts Connor's palm to her lips and kisses it, then places it gently against her cheek. Her heart races. She has never touched any man other than her husband in this way. But the sensation of Connor's skin against hers makes her want to arch her back, to yield.

'I have no room in my heart for two men. Since you have arrived, he is fading, and it scares me.'

Connor stands and gently turns her to face him. He bends his head and touches his lips to hers, wrapping his arms around her waist and drawing her towards him.

Ayshe tilts her chin and returns the embrace, lips parting slightly, softly.

Connor feels the soft pout of her breasts pressing into his chest, and the dip at her waist where his hands rest. Desire and passion are useless indulgences in the Australian outback, and Connor has never had the time or the inclination to succumb to either. But he wants this woman with an intensity that terrifies him. It rises from his abdomen up his torso, filling his chest and making it hard to breathe.

Ayshe takes his hand to lead him from the kitchen. 'Come.'

❖

The only light in Ayshe's room is the pale blue moonlight that floods through the lace curtains. It whispers across the starched white sheets and pools on the two figures that lie, outstretched, on the bed. On the floor, one pair of worn leather boots are cast aside, removed hurriedly with clumsy fingers and tossed onto the rug. Tucked neatly beneath the fringed edge of the woollen bedspread, the finely tooled burgundy court shoes are placed side by side, small leather buttons unfastened carefully, deliberately.

Ayshe and Connor lie facing each other on the small French bed, her head resting in the crook of his arm and her hand on his ribs. Beneath the crisply starched cotton of his shirt, she can feel his heart pounding, his breath racing. She shifts towards him and presses her cheek to his chest, tucking her head under his chin. She can smell him, warm and smoky, and feel his breath in her hair as he lowers his head to kiss the crown of her head. Inching her hands towards his waist, she slides her fingers along his smooth leather belt, searching for the buckle. Finding it, she fumbles.

'My fingers have forgotten.'

Connor takes her hand from his belt and lifts it to his lips.

'Please, we don't have to do anything. I am content to look at you.'

Although he desires her so much he can scarcely breathe, he knows it would be improper to push.

'I never thought I would lie with another man. But I can . . .' She hesitates. 'I can tend to your needs.' Turgut had been virile, and it hadn't always been possible for her to serve him as a wife should. It had been Natalia who had spoken to her of the other ways a woman could bring a man pleasure.

'Not if I can't tend to yours.'

She wrestles with her conscience and resists. 'I must not.'

Connor tries to hide the disappointment in his voice. 'Good. So we lie here.'

She turns her face up to his and kisses him tentatively as Connor presses his hand against the small of her back, drawing her hips to his.

Needing to feel his skin on hers, Ayshe reaches up to the tiny pearl buttons that hold her long-sleeved shirt closed. Fingers quivering, she pops them one at a time until the turquoise-blue silk falls open. As she exposes her perfect ivory skin, the curve of her breast, Connor is captivated. His voice catches in his throat, thick and husky.

'Oh . . . You are beautiful.'

He strokes her breast with his weathered, square fingertips, and Ayshe moans involuntarily. Opening her emerald-green eyes, she gazes at Connor as she lowers her hand and presses it against his groin, feeling him stiffen beneath his coarse cotton pants.

They lock eyes, hands now still. Ayshe breaks the silence.

'We should sleep now. It will be light soon.'

Connor kisses Ayshe lightly on the lips.

'Yes, we should.'

He lies back on the pillow, watching her as she closes her eyes. The moonlight skims the dip of her waist and the swell of her breast as she lies beside him. He wants to be with her, to tend her. But she is strong, so strong, and caught between two worlds, neither of which he can hope to understand.

Ayshe senses Connor's gaze and opens her eyes.

She kisses him and smiles.

CHAPTER THIRTY-TWO

She rocks and grinds against him as he bucks beneath her. His broad hands encircle her tiny waist. She rises and falls astride him, one of her hands resting against the hard muscle of his lower belly. She fingers the serpentine trail of short, dark hairs that cover his abdomen, feeling the sinews in his pelvis contract as he thrusts hard inside her.

A blinding flash. The deafening roar of artillery unleashed. The burning slash and splatter of shrapnel embedding in mud and flesh.

He looks up at her face. Hair falls across her brow, shielding her features from his gaze.

Another blast; the ground rocks beneath them. She doesn't flinch, is deaf to the mortal sounds of battle around them. Wet, persistent, she continues to slide along him. She bends forwards, then throws her head up, flicking her long hair back.

'Edith?' Through the haze, he is confused. Edith is in Rainbow. Edith should not be here.

He feels blood – hot, wet – coursing down his face. Raising a hand to his brow, he feels the wound: ragged, deep. Bone through mangled flesh. The apparition that is Edith continues to ride him. He is rising, swelling inside her as bullets and shells whiz by.

Turn to the left. 'Is that Henry?' His head is cleaved in half; the one, remaining bright blue eye is blank. Dull. Dead.

A cry. To the right. Ed. Gouts of blood oozing through his tunic, running in a sheet down the left side of his head. Not long for this world. Ed lifts a hand, beseeching, pleading.

Art turns away, fixes his eyes on the figure astride him, feeling himself pulsing, bursting. She lifts his bloodied hands to her breasts and he releases inside her, climaxing with a groan.

CHAPTER THIRTY-THREE

The woman lowers her skirt and dismounts the young man who lies prostrate on a soiled and frayed divan. The low bed is protected from general view by a crudely fashioned curtain made from a rough sheet of old hessian that she now draws back. She wanders off, disappearing into the darkened depths of the labyrinthine building.

Swaying, disoriented, the man swings his legs to the edge of the bed and waits for his head to stop spinning. He sits up, fumbling as he closes the front of his trousers and slides his feet inside a pair of worn leather slippers. He reaches for a faded khaki tunic emblazoned with A.I.F. regalia where it hangs on a peg. Clumsily putting one arm then the other into the jacket, he attempts to stand, tripping on one of the figures that lie supine at his feet.

The timber-panelled room is dimly lit, its floor a jumble of stained old mattresses and cushions and worn *kilim*s. It is difficult to see through the haze from the opium smoke, which rises in rings and whorls from the pipes that rest in the insouciant fingers of the men who sprawl on the floor in a tangle of limbs.

He finds his feet and weaves his way through the recumbent figures towards a wooden door at the opposite side of the room. Limping, he reaches for a stick that rests against one wall and opens the door, flooding the room with early morning light. Squinting his glacier-blue eyes against the sun, Art stumbles into the street, leaning heavily on his shepherd's crook.

Roosters crow to welcome the morning, their cries echoing along the narrow, dusty lanes. Chickens peck at loose grain in the street as a fat white cat with one green and one blue eye sits on a stoop, cleaning itself. An old woman wearing a black dress with a garish fringed scarf wrapped around her head is bent double, sweeping her front step and casting water from a cup like seed to keep the dust down.

Oblivious to the sounds of the town awakening, Art is in a waking dream. He lifts a hand to scratch at the lice that inhabit his matted, light-brown hair. An angry, jagged red scar crosses his forehead, and his trousers – baggy and white in the local style – are stained and ragged, held around his emaciated waist by an A.I.F. webbing belt.

He stops stock still in the middle of the street, spell-bound by the sight of a mangy dog so thin her ribs protrude from beneath her matted coat, feeding her three puppies. The dog lies, resigned, beaten, its eyes dim, as the three small dogs fight and tug at her nipples.

An interjection breaks into his reverie. A bovine man leading a donkey laden heavily with fat sheaves of wheat is trying to pass.

'Watch out! Watch out!'

Art staggers back against the whitewashed stone wall, raising his hands and responding in Turkish. 'Yeah, all right, brother. All right. Keep your bloody shirt on.'

The ground undulates beneath his feet. Slumping back against the wall as the man shakes his head and pushes his way past, Art shuts his eyes, feeling the wet night chill in the stones seeping into his spine as the rays from the morning sun warm his face. A noisome stench cuts through his opiate stupor. Across the lane, a young woman uses a huge wooden paddle to chop and turn bricks of manure, drying them in the sun for fuel. By her feet, a basket woven of dried reeds is slick with the remains of the dung, gathered in her home the night before, to add to the rancid muck — excrement from bird, beast and human alike.

He turns and starts walking up the hill to escape the foul miasma. Carefully placing one foot in front of the other, Art tries to maintain his purchase on the slippery and uneven cobblestones, one hand reaching out to steady himself against the wall, the other clutching the top of his wooden stick.

Another narrow street intersects the lane. The air here is full of the warm and yeasty smell of freshly baked bread. Through a plate-glass window, a stack of fat, golden brown loaves the shape of lemons teeters precariously. Outside the shop, a group of women stand in a cluster, waiting to be served by the flour-covered baker. Their heads are covered with brightly coloured scarves fringed with delicate lace edges. They laugh and chatter, their nut-brown faces deeply creased with wrinkles, enjoying the reprieve from the day's chores.

As Art limps past, the baker leans out from the stoop of his shop, raising his hand in greeting and calling him over. The young man sways and stumbles as he diverts his course, shuffling over to the bakery door where the women recoil and move aside as he passes. He takes the broken heel of bread offered by the baker, and acknowledges the gift with a hand raised to his brow.

'Health be on your hands.'

The baker smiles kindly, nods his head and responds with the customary salutation. 'Health be on your head.' The irony of the blessing is never lost on Art.

He slumps down in the doorway of the neighbouring shop and sinks his teeth into the crunchy crust, savouring the still warm, cloud-soft bread, and is surprised to find his stomach rumbling. He chews, rolling the salty-sweet dough around his mouth. Art's abject existence relies entirely upon the benevolence of others; he is a familiar presence in the streets of Afion and he survives on the alms offered to him by the shopkeepers and those who live in the small houses that line the streets – small gifts of food, clothes and the occasional coin. As the years have passed, his life force has dimmed to a flicker; his physical needs have been pared down so utterly through deprivation that sensations like hunger and fatigue no longer register on his blunted consciousness. He swallows, feeling the last of the bread passing down his throat and into his stomach.

A sound, clear in the morning air.

At first, Art thinks the pounding comes from inside his own head, a rhythmic beat yammering inside his injured skull. But then the haunting trill of the *ney* flute joins the drum. He leans on his crook and drags his body upright. Standing, cocking his ear, he begins to walk, trying to follow the direction of the sounds but at the same time wondering if the melody is real or a figment of his addled imagination.

He turns a corner; the music swells. To his left, a low stairway leads to a stone arch that opens out into a large terrace encircled by a high stone wall. The terrace is paved in tiny black and white polished pebbles painstakingly arranged in a chequerboard pattern. Here the drumbeats are louder, more persistent, as they echo around the four sides of the courtyard.

Mounting the wide stairway, Art treads warily and clutches the crumbly stone doorway with feeble fingers. The pebble paving is difficult to negotiate; the hard, rounded stones press uncomfortably into the soles of his feet, and his stick is next to useless on the uneven surface. At the apex of the courtyard is a massive building, its entrance graced by a colonnaded portico and the long wall facing Art punctuated by large arched windows. Through the windows, he can see movement. He edges towards the portico and approaches the door of the building, the sound of the music growing louder as he advances on the massive, carved timber doors that stand ajar.

The room is large, unfurnished. Beneath a soaring ceiling seven men are spaced like chess pieces in a ring on the tiled floor. Each spins slowly, rhythmically, arms outstretched at shoulder height, one palm facing the roof, the other the floor, his head tilted towards one shoulder and eyes gently shut. All the men wear long grey tunics with skirts so full they billow in heavy waves as they twirl, reminding Art of the movement of the swell far out to sea. Atop their heads are tall, conical felt hats. In the corner, the musicians, whose rhythmic melody was the siren call that drew Art to this place, sit on small wooden stools, nodding their heads slowly in time with the music. Most peculiarly, not a single man acknowledges Art's arrival. In their ecstatic state he is invisible to them.

The scene is so improbable that Art is unsure whether or not he is hallucinating. His grasp on reality is fragmenting. The horizon between the real and imagined universe is becoming increasingly porous; motifs and visions often navigate between his opium dreams and the world around him.

He drops his stick to the floor, his senses spinning as he watches the men whirling silently in a trance. Art is drawn to them; like a satellite he is pulled into their orbit. He staggers forwards into the centre of the circle and holds his arms out, closing his eyes as he is transported by the music, spinning and limping in broken mimicry of the dervishes around him.

For a heartbeat, the Sufi trance seizes him and Art is at the centre of his world. But there is no revelation awaiting him. All he sees is a black and hopeless abyss.

The music stops and the dervishes come to a halt.

Art looks up at the ceiling, tears streaming down his face.

CHAPTER THIRTY-FOUR

Connor sits bolt upright in the dawn light, breathing hard.

'He is alive!'

Eyes heavy with sleep, Ayshe awakens. She has been lying beside Connor, and fumbles to close her shirt as she sits up beside him.

'How can you know?'

The clear certainty in Connor's eyes leaves her in no doubt, and she realises something. 'But you have *always* known, haven't you? That is why you came here.' At last, Connor's unwavering determination makes sense. 'You did not come here chasing ghosts.'

Bending to lace his boots, Connor shakes his head, speaking as much to himself as to her. 'Lizzie never believed it. And to me, Arthur never felt dead. Not in the way my Henry and Ed did.'

Connor is interrupted by a sudden loud knock on the hotel's front door. He and Ayshe freeze like adolescents discovered. There is silence for a moment and then there is another round of hollow pounding that echoes through the foyer and up the stairs. An abrupt and impatient summons follows: 'Come down now, please, Mr Connor! We have a long walk to the dock!'

Ayshe looks up into Connor's eyes. 'You cannot go back.' They both know that to have come this far only to be frogmarched back onto a steamer bound for Australia is no longer an option.

'No,' Connor says with conviction. 'I won't go.'

❖

At the entrance, Captain Brindley balls his hand into an angry fist and pummels the door with greater force. True to his word he is here with his men to escort Connor to the wharf, to ensure that the Australian quits Constantinople as instructed.

The pre-dawn air has an edge to it, a crisp cold that scratches like a hundred fishbones at the back of the throat. A British private hops from foot to foot to keep warm. The corporal leans his rifle against the hotel wall and breathes warm fog into his cupped hands while his captain puts his ear to the timber door and listens for any movement inside. The prolonged silence makes Brindley even more agitated. He waits as long as his pride will allow and when he spots a smirk behind his corporal's cupped palms he explodes.

'Give me your gun!' he demands, and begins to bruise the elm door with the corner of the rifle butt. The repeated dull thuds reverberate through the empty foyer but the hotel remains still. Brindley feels like a dog worrying a tortoise that has retreated into its shell. And right now, he looks just as ridiculous.

Connor's impudence is staggering to Brindley. It confirms everything he despises about the colonials and their attitude to authority. It is no wonder that Anzac soldiers have such a flagrant disregard for rank, when they are all born of convict stock.

Brindley prides himself on being the product of a tradition steeped in glory and history, where rank and postings are purchased or come as a birthright. The British Army is founded on the twin principles of discipline and obedience. An order is an order, no matter how inane or misguided it might seem to the rank and file. Brindley and those around him know that their orders are part of a grand scheme in which every regiment plays a part, so he and his ilk obey unquestioningly even if he does not fully understand the intended consequence of his actions. It has worked this way for centuries. The cogs and wheels of the British military machine must work in perfect concert, or the entire framework will disintegrate. That is why the punishment for disobeying an officer is so severe: a recalcitrant soldier will face court martial and execution, in the most serious of cases. If men falter and the foundations crumble, the entire army can fall.

The colonials have a very different view, possibly because they are a volunteer army. Brindley and his peers refer to them as the 'irregulars', which the Anzacs seem intent on taking as a compliment. These men trek halfway across the world and go to war as if it is a great big adventure, with every expectation of returning home to their families and real lives in one piece, when the job is done.

Freedom of choice and the expression of will mean everything to the Australian soldiers. To them, Brindley has learned, respect is not a given, it must be earned. A man with a superior rank cannot automatically expect to enjoy due deference from the colonial soldiers in his command. At

Gallipoli and in France, Brindley encountered Australians who willingly followed their officers to the gates of hell and back, but only those commanders who placed a high value on their men's safety and who would never send them into battle if they weren't also prepared to join the fight. He read it time and time again in the letters he censored. They highest praise an Australian soldier could give his officer was that he was 'game' and 'led from the front.' It was no surprise when the Anzacs lost so many officers.

If Brindley is honest with himself, what galls him the most is that despite, or perhaps as a result of, this ingrained resentment of authority, the colonials make a formidable fighting force. It was certainly only their bull-headed grit that kept them from being swept off the cliffs of Gallipoli by the Turks. Their refusal to follow orders meant they concocted some singular plans of attack on the spur of the moment that often took the enemy by surprise. But it was not just here in Turkey. On the Hindenburg Line, it was quickly realised that the most effective way of exposing the chinks in the German defences was to let the Australian 'irregulars' off their leash.

The Anzacs learned some hard lessons on the Gallipoli Peninsula. Their trials had become legendary. Even Brindley had heard about the Light Horse at the Nek, anni-hilated in the August Offensive. It was only a few hundred men – nothing in the context of the war – but he knows that the obscenity of the squandered young lives still sticks in their collective national craw, and for that, the Anzacs blame the British.

So in France and Belgium, where the Allied solution to the stalemate was to order wave after wave of young men to throw themselves at the German machine guns, the Australians would simply refuse to go. The cavalier flouting of authority trickled down from the very top of the Australian command. In letters home, their officers admitted to sending orders back to British Command, stalling, querying and ultimately refusing to send their men over the top when they thought they didn't stand a fighting chance.

Brindley remembers having a run-in with an Australian officer who threatened to shoot any British soldier he saw retreating from the village of Villers-Bretonneux, as a deserter. He ordered his men to do likewise. Brindley objected, pointing out to the Australian officer that there was a significant difference between retreating and deserting.

'It's not up to you to play judge and executioner. There are rules,' Brindley insisted.

'Keep your shirt on, mate. I haven't had to shoot anyone yet.' The Australian smiled and then added, 'So the message must be getting through, eh?'

Villers-Bretonneux had been a turning point in the war, and the Australians' actions had made the difference between victory and an embarrassing retreat. The very thing that had infuriated Brindley about the Australian soldiers on the Western Front – the same thing that was making his blood boil as he stood here in the cold, dawn light outside the Otel Troya hammering on the front door – was what made these men such phenomenal soldiers. They would fight to the death for each other and for their cursed pride, and when issued with an order, they were almost always guaranteed to do the exact opposite.

He bellows, 'Connor, I am losing my patience.'

Still nothing.

'Break the damn door down!'

A thickset private with a rugby player's bullocky neck steps forward. He takes a short run-up and puts his shoulder to the door, which rattles on its hinges but doesn't give an inch. The door has been here for two hundred years and is not going to capitulate that easily.

❖

Connor pushes his arms into his jacket sleeves and checks his pocket for Art's diary, now the most precious object in his possession. His eyes settle on Ayshe. She is a vision: dark hair tousled from sleep, her green eyes wide, startled by the racket from downstairs. Her tongue rests against her top lip in concentration as she fumbles with the last of the tiny buttons on her silk blouse. She looks up, and their eyes meet in mute acknowledgement of so many things left unsaid, so many things left undone.

Ayshe feels a deep pang of regret. If the British were not hammering on her door, if she could overcome her crippling sense of propriety, she would give almost anything to succumb to desire, to feel this man on top of her, inside her. But it is beyond contemplation. It is something she can never – will never – surrender to.

Connor opens his mouth to speak but instead a sigh escapes and he finds himself speechless. He feels an unmistakable warmth filling his chest as they share a sad smile, the gentle flowering of a bittersweet love pierced by the cruel dart of inevitable loss. He is, and will always remain, grateful for the evening spent in Ayshe's arms, but now he knows he must learn to hold on to that memory, free from regret and without any need for atonement.

The pounding from downstairs is louder now, more insistent, the timber beams running beneath the floor transmitting the heavy thud as the front door is assaulted.

'Quickly, the roof,' whispers Ayshe.

She opens the bedroom door to find Orhan standing in the hallway, still in his cotton nightshirt and rubbing eyes puffy from sleep. The racket downstairs has woken him; the rest of the household won't be far behind. Ayshe puts her arm over his shoulder and draws her son to her side. He is momentarily surprised to see Connor in his mother's room, but does not question what somehow feels right.

'Connor Bey is leaving, Orhan. You must say goodbye,' she tells her son in English.

'When will you come back?' asks the boy.

Connor kneels down, takes Orhan's hand in his and shakes it. It is answer enough. Tears well in the boy's eyes as drowsiness gives way to grief. Yesterday, Orhan felt his father's shade slip through his fingers like smoke, and now he must face losing this strong, kind man who has somehow made him feel safe again. When he is with his mother and Connor, Orhan feels that he has found a way to keep his head above water again.

The boy throws his arms around Connor's powerful neck and squeezes him tightly.

'Goodbye, Connor Bey. Come back.'

Connor smiles and smooths Orhan's ruffled hair. 'You will be a great man – just like your father.'

They hear a dull thud and the groan of splintering wood downstairs. Orhan starts and clutches his mother's arm.

'It is all right, Orhan. Now, you must be strong. You are a man now,' Ayshe reassures her son. 'Go and open the door before they break it down.' As Orhan heads along the hallway she adds, 'And stall them if you can.' He gives her a cheeky smile and bounds down the stairs.

Orhan reaches the foyer just as the front door yields to the British assault and its lock is wrenched from its mount. Brindley steps through the breach followed by half a dozen soldiers who stumble around trying to get their bearings in the half-light. Brindley spots Orhan standing at the bottom of the stairs, skinny shanks sticking out from beneath his white nightshirt.

'Where is Joshua Connor?'

'You want room, mister?'

'Quickly. The Australian. What room is he in?'

'Very cheap. Hot water. No Germans.'

Brindley is in no mood for Orhan's banter. He grabs the hotel register and begins flicking pages.

'Australian? Connor Bey? He is on the first floor. I will show,' says Orhan.

Brindley pushes past the boy and mounts the staircase two steps at a time. He summons his men, who scuttle up the stairs behind him.

'Upstairs. Check every room!'

❖

Natalia hears the tumult from her room and springs out of bed in a panic to pull a gown over her nightdress. The sound of slamming doors in empty guest rooms is unmistakable as the soldiers work their way down the hall towards her.

Still half-asleep, she is overcome by an irrational and uncontrollable fear. Although Natalia knows that she is in Constantinople, the drumming of hobnailed boots on the floorboards drags her back into the darkest, most desperate recesses of her memory. Before the revolutionary guard came banging on their door in St Petersburg, Natalia begged her husband to flee. As a businessman he presumed he could negotiate with them. He was beaten to death on his own doorstep in full view of the neighbourhood as Natalia and her baby daughter, Elena, hid beneath the bed and listened to his dying screams. The bloodied, hobnailed boots thumped through their home until eventually they found them and wrenched them from their hiding place. As Natalia shrieked, holding her baby to her chest with one hand as she clawed desperately at her assailants with the other, Elena was torn from her grasp and thrown like a discarded toy out the second-storey window. After hearing Elena's cry trailing away to nothing, she was inured to the Bolsheviks' depravations. Nothing they could do to her could be worse. That was two years ago, and here again on her doorstep are the boots.

A fist hammers on her door.

'Connor. Are you in there?'

The door bursts open and two young British soldiers appear, cocking their rifles and shouting. Expecting to face down a reluctant Australian farmer, they are taken aback to find Natalia standing before them in her vermilion silk gown, surrounded by the trappings of an Imperial Russian salon. She stands stock still, petrified, with her eyes lowered, expecting the worst. Almost apologetically the soldiers step into the room to check under the bed and behind the door.

Her voice quavers, fat tears of fear welling in her eyes. 'Take what you want. Don't hurt me, please,' she cries in English. 'I have my papers. They are here. You want?'

Another soldier, one of higher rank, Natalia suspects, steps into her room, his meticulously groomed moustache bristling.

'Captain Charles Brindley, ma'am. I'm looking for Mr Joshua Connor.'

Orhan pushes past the British officer and stands in front of Natalia, hands planted firmly on his hips. He juts his chin forward, challenging the soldiers.

Brindley sighs. 'I just want Connor.'

Then, from above their heads comes the unmistakable sound of footsteps, followed by a scraping sound and the crash of a terracotta roof tile on the street below. The soldiers run from the room.

❖

Ayshe stands on the terrace that overlooks the peaked rooftops of Sultanahmet. Connor has straddled the balustrade and stands on the edge of the roof. The indigo night sky is now in full retreat as a halo of orange light appears over the top of the city wall, tinting the sandstone blocks amber and pink.

Blind to the dramatic skyscape, Connor takes Ayshe's hands and kisses her gently. With his rough, stubbled cheek against hers, she whispers a line of poetry in his ear, in Turkish.

'I shall wait. Will I ever know another night like this?'

'Pardon?'

She responds in English. 'I said, "Don't crack any more tiles".'

They hear the British pounding down the hallway towards them and steal another hurried kiss before Connor turns to scale the hotel roof. He scrambles up the steep incline towards the summit, the rounded red tiles crunching and shifting under his boots.

Ayshe hears frantic shouting from inside the Troya, 'Stop now! Stop him!' and turns to see a British officer barrelling towards the doorway, pistol in hand.

A soldier follows in his wake calling, 'Captain Brindley, sir, the roof!'

Cursing, Brindley marches the length of the hall, clearly determined not to let the Australian get the better of him. Ayshe slams the door shut and presses her shoulder against it but before she can turn the lock, Brindley crashes through and knocks her against the balustrade. He scours the roofline and spots the silhouette of his quarry straddling the peak of the roof, the distinctive wide-brimmed hat set firmly on his head. Brindley raises his gun and aims.

'Stop, Connor. Or, God help me, I will shoot!' His cry ricochets over the rooftops, startling sparrows from beneath the eaves and shattering the tranquillity of the streets below, still quiet in the early dawn. Ayshe hears the false bluster in his words as they rebound, echoing through the narrow laneways and bouncing off timber terraces. He lowers his gun. Brindley may be sorely tempted to pull the trigger, but he has no intention of shooting the Australian. Instead he watches him clamber over the apex of the roofline and drop from sight.

Brindley turns on his men in a rage. He points at the nearest private.

'You! Get up there! After him!'

As the soldier makes a half-hearted attempt to clear the balustrade, Ibrahim appears from a nearby bedroom, wearing a long nightshirt and clearly disoriented by the turmoil.

'Has there been another coup?' he asks his daughter.

Brindley pushes past the old man and sticks his finger into the breastbone of his corporal.

'This isn't the end of it. I want Connor on that boat! Today!'

❖

Connor slides down the reverse side of the hotel roof, clutching at the dry moss and the ends of the tiles and finally sticking a boot against the fascia board to bring himself to a stop. He takes a breath and leaps the small distance to the next roof, feeling the tiles snap under his boot as he lands. He scrambles up the next valley and over the roof ridge, his hands now red as the Mallee with tile dust.

He finds himself at the end of a narrow wooden gangway that joins the surrounding homes, built a century ago for bucket brigades to pass water along whenever house fires threaten to engulf the neighbourhood. Frantic voices shouting in English echo up from the street below as Brindley and his men pursue Connor at ground level. He jogs into the sun and notices the tiled roofs giving way to hewn sandstone blocks. Suddenly he finds himself running along an ancient rampart, the broken teeth of the city's crenellated wall beside him.

Connor stops, sucks in the fresh morning air and surveys the emerging cityscape to get his bearings. He singles out the towering minarets of the Blue Mosque and the succession of domes at Topkapi Palace. During his desperate dash across the rooftops, Connor's mind has been working clinically, measuring his options. Until a moment ago he had no idea where he was going. Now, no matter how he looks at it, there is only one place that makes any sense. But it is a path fraught with danger.

Shimmying hand over hand down a drainpipe, back braced against the adjacent wall, Connor finds his way down to street level from the dizzying heights of the ruined city wall.

Heart pounding and with a singularity of purpose, he straightens his collar as he merges with the people starting to move through the market. He dips his head and hunches his shoulders – a feeble attempt to blend into a crowd in which he could only ever stand out. He feels eyes burning into him as he tries to move quickly through the streets, sure that at any moment a voice will cry out, signalling his presence to his pursuers.

From the corner of his eye, he sees figures jostling, hears raised voices. He clenches his fists, his nerves tense as he anticipates a shout of recognition. Or perhaps Brindley, spying his distinctive hat across the heads of the shoppers. Connor resists the urge to run, knowing it will only attract more unwanted attention. He steals a glance towards the source of the hubbub. A rush of relief. It is only two stall-holders squabbling.

He has a sense now of the chaotic rambling of the lanes that wind up and down the hills of Sultanahmet, leading him one way and then the next. He has learned that the best way to negotiate the labyrinth is to follow landmarks. And so Connor peels off the main street and passes the row of barbers plying their trade before turning left at a three-storeyed mansion with an elaborately designed wrought-iron gateway. Every step he takes, he listens for the ominous sound of boots ringing on the cobbles behind him. The street dips down then branches into two, a marble-faced fountain at the intersection spurting water into a carved basin and running over onto the paving stones. Connor steps over the channel of water and takes the right-hand laneway.

A narrow strip of light is all that penetrates into the alley from between the uppermost levels of the terraces, tendrils of ivy hanging in curtains from the iron grilles that cover the bay windows. Connor sees the place he's looking for at the end of the lane. Set below street level, a haphazard row of timber steps – barely more than a glorified ladder – leads down to a basement door. A narrow strip of dusty glass barely a hand-span wide runs along either side of the worn timber door and emits a dull glow from a flickering light source burning within.

Yes. This is it. I'm sure of it.

Connor glances around him, fairly certain now that he isn't being followed. He carefully descends the stairway, standing at the bottom for a moment to gather himself and contemplate his next move. It's not too late to change his mind. He could still make his ship. Brindley wouldn't be too pleased, but what he is about to do will make the captain apoplectic.

The vision that came to him this morning is still clear, still palpable and still very real. Connor knows that if there is even the slightest chance that Art is still alive he must knock on this door. He takes a long deliberate breath.

Then he raps on the door quickly with the back of his hand and braces himself for what he expects will be a less than welcome reception. After a pause, the door opens with a creak and is held ajar by the proprietor Connor recognises from the previous evening. His dark eyes register surprise to see the Australian standing there. He is wary, and silent.

Connor is at a loss; he has no idea what to say. In the end he utters the one thing he can think of that may gain him entry to the *meyhane*.

'Mustafa Kemal.'

The doorkeeper raises his chin and steps back from the entrance, allowing Connor to enter the smoke-filled room. Jemal is in a corner, nursing a raki. He looks up and glares at Connor, eyes flashing.

'You, Australian! Can't leave us alone, eh?'

Hasan steps forward and stands before Connor, arms crossed at his chest. His Ottoman uniform has been replaced with a peasant's baggy woollen trousers, cotton shirt and embroidered vest. He gazes at Connor dispassionately, saying nothing.

'He is alive. I know it,' Connor rasps. 'So kill me – or take me with you.'

CHAPTER THIRTY-FIVE

'The train will slow for us.'

Connor kneels beside Hasan, Jemal and thirty or more of their Nationalist comrades behind a bank of long reeds just past the outskirts of the city, sharp pieces of flinty grey gravel digging into his knees.

At the top of the ridge where they lie in wait, the railway runs along a steep embankment. Further down the hill towards the port and the ramshackle hovels that cling to the outermost edge of the city like barnacles, a train approaches through a steep cutting, thick plumes of black smoke and white steam billowing into the sky.

There had been a moment in the *meyhane* when Connor was certain Hasan would give the order for Jemal to slit his throat. The mood in the room was grim and resolute, and he had braced himself for the worst. With the warped perception that comes at such moments, to Connor it seemed that hours, rather than seconds, or minutes at the most, ticked by as Hasan contemplated him coolly. But a brief flicker in the Turk's eye betrayed his decision, and Hasan's face softened in line with the slight relaxation of his military bearing.

Everything moved at breakneck pace after that. The men listened gravely as Hasan outlined a precise plan for reaching their rendezvous point. They departed the *meyhane* in small groups, leaving at random intervals; Connor had been assigned to a group of four that included both Hasan and Jemal. Jemal didn't hide his displeasure and distrust of Connor from his commanding officer, muttering under his breath in Turkish as they prepared to leave.

Ignoring his sergeant, Hasan brusquely explained the plan to Connor in English before they left the basement room. As he stood at the door, he turned to the Australian.

'You are not to speak as we move through the city. We will be doing our best to avoid British soldiers. But if we do pass any, do not converse with them. If you try to draw any attention to us, I will have no hesitation in giving Jemal permission to execute you.' He gave a wry smile. 'As you have surely noticed, he is eager for the task.'

After that, all the communications were in Turkish, with Hasan and Jemal giving Connor quiet instructions in English as required as they moved through the streets. When they rounded one corner and encountered a small British patrol, Connor's gut dropped. He anticipated the worst, expecting the soldiers to be on the lookout for him. But he was relieved when the only attention he attracted was barefaced stares at the curious spectacle of a European man in league with three Turkish peasants, a scrutiny that was easily diverted when Connor smiled and tipped his hat.

On the circuitous journey to the rail yard the quartet had passed under a mossy archway that cut through the Byzantine city wall. On the other side lay the stone-faced breakwater on the Sea of Marmara. As Connor made his way through the wall, he marvelled at the ingenuity of the fishermen who now made this place their home. Ramshackle huts made of driftwood and discarded sheets of metal had sprung up like weeds in the ancient breaches in the wall's defences.

It was on one of their first walks through Constantinople that Orhan had relished telling Connor that Mehmet the Conqueror had smashed his way through the city walls using cannon and driven the Christians into the sea. 'And Mustafa Kemal will do it again,' he'd added with a cheeky grin. Only now is Connor beginning to realise what Turks will risk in order to make Orhan's bold declaration a reality.

When they arrived at the wharf, Connor was surprised that the other members of the party weren't waiting for them.

'We are all leaving the city from different places,' Hasan explained. 'If we travel together, it will raise an alarm. The British do not want us to leave the city any more than they want you to stay.'

A bent and weathered fisherman stood waiting for them by the dock. He led them down the pier towards a blue and white caique that was tied to a bollard, bucking against it in the heavy swell, the low edges of its hull perilously close to the waterline. A chilly wind blew to shore across the narrow strait, and sea spray misted against Connor's face each time the waves slapped into the dock.

Jemal, a superstitious man, rapped his knuckles against a timber upright. '*Inşallah*, it won't be a bad crossing.' His face was pale, his usually gregarious nature strangely diminished.

'This man does not like travelling by water,' Hasan laughed, slapping Jemal on the back.

'It is not natural. Otherwise we would have scales and fins.'

During the crossing from Australia, as they'd passed through the tropical regions, Connor had experienced some monumental storms. At times the boat had seemed to tilt from end to end in waves that loomed above the masthead, solid blue-black walls of water that had threatened to teeter and topple onto the boat, shattering it into splinters and sending all on board to a watery grave. To a man whose entire existence had been earthbound, the mutability of life at sea was unsettling, the sensation of the deck constantly shifting beneath his feet more than mildly disconcerting.

He smiled at Jemal. 'I'm with you, mate.'

As predicted, the crossing from the European shore to the dock at Kadıköy was rough. The wizened fisherman blithely clung to the tiller, standing on bowed legs in the stern of the boat. Connor clutched the smooth edge of the bench seat that spanned the boat, knuckles white and teeth clenched as he fought the hot rush of nausea that washed over him.

Can't have them thinking I'm weak.

The passage seemed interminable. Each time he looked over his shoulder towards the Asian shore, they seemed to have made little or no progress. If Hasan was at all concerned by their circumstances it was impossible to tell; his face and carriage were impassive and unyielding. For his part, Jemal made no attempt to remain stoic; he spent most of the voyage bent double over the edge of the boat, dry-retching into the waves, all remnants of his breakfast long gone in a ghastly feast for the tiny, silver fish that darted about in the boat's wake.

When they finally made landfall, Connor clambered to shore with a conspicuous sense of relief. Jemal had all but fallen to his knees in thanks once he felt solid ground beneath his feet; he was so shaken by the crossing he felt a pressing need to down two shots of raki to steel his nerves. By comparison, the route through the streets of Kadıköy to their rendezvous point beside the railway line was uneventful.

Crouching now behind the reeds and brush on the ridge, the group watches as cargo is loaded into the long line of carriages and the Ankara train begins to snake up the steep incline from the station below.

'The sixth and seventh cargo carriages will be open for us,' Hasan reports.

As the train approaches their hiding spot, it slows to a crawl. Counting the carriages, Hasan shouts to Jemal, 'There! Those two!'

Jemal scrambles up the embankment to the track and trots beside the passing train, seizing the unsecured doors of the empty livestock carriages and sliding them open. He vaults inside the second carriage and signals the other men – all is clear. In a rush, they scurry up the gravel slope and grab the edges of the carriages, hoisting timber crates of guns and ammunition on board and tossing their packs up onto the wooden floor before leaping onto the train. Hasan waits until all his men are aboard before he turns to Connor.

'It's not too late to change your mind, Australian.'

Connor doesn't hesitate. 'Not a chance. I don't have anywhere else to go now.'

'If you insist.' Hasan waves Connor forwards and they clamber up the embankment and make a dash for the second carriage. 'Come on, then.'

❖

The air is implausibly crisp and clear as the train begins its slow ascent into the wooded mountains to the east of the town of Izmit.

The slatted doors of the railway car Connor is in are fully open on both sides, allowing cool air to circulate in the carriage in gentle waves, a relief after the heavy and humid air of the port. After leaving Izmit, the soldiers had changed out of their peasants' clothes and put their uniforms back on. Now, some of them sit with their legs dangling over the sides, quietly smoking and chatting. Others relax inside the carriage, backs leaning against the stack of crates that sit in one corner, cleaning their guns or seizing the opportunity to sleep, caps tilted over their eyes to shut out the light filtering through the open slats.

Connor sits on the side of the train that faces the downward slope of the mountain, watching the sparkling waters of the Sea of Marmara recede in the distance. He is mesmerised by the verdant forest before him. It is unlike anything he has ever seen before, accustomed as he is to broad, desiccated plains and the tenacious but flinty life forms that manage to survive there. The loamy, rich volcanic soil tumbling down these craggy slopes supports a profusion of living things. Groves of lilac arch above dense mats of bracken and blood-red lilies. Soaring trees form a lush canopy – dark green pine needles, broad emerald plane tree leaves and the scalloped leaves of the oak – that casts dappled golden shadows on the forest floor.

'Tell me, Australian,' Jemal says, hefting his bulk to the floor to sit beside Connor. 'What part of the Ottoman Empire did Australia get?'

'None of it. The war was never about land for us.'

Jemal scoffs. 'Always it is about land. English get Egypt, Palestine. France gets Syria. Even Italy gets a beach. You don't get land?'

'We don't need more land. We've got too much of that as it is. Australians didn't even know where Turkey was before the war. We weren't fighting for land. We fought for a principle.' Just saying it makes Connor feel hollow. A generation of Australia's youth decimated, the country's coffers stripped.

A costly principle, indeed.

Slapping his thigh with mirth, Jemal roars with laughter. 'You fight. You die. You get nothing. Good principle! We should make business with your country!' He translates for his fellow fighters who laugh along with him.

Jemal shakes his head, shouting out to Hasan who lounges against his pack in the corner of the carriage. 'His whole country must be from the Black Sea!'

Connor is confused.

'All Turkish people are brave and smart,' Jemal explains. 'But not in Black Sea, all people are stupid.' Without needing any encouragement Jemal launches into a story. 'Two men in Trabzon, Temel and Dursun. They fight and don't talk to each other anymore. One day Temel walks past Dursun with goat. "Where are you going with donkey?" Dursun shouts. "It is not donkey, it is goat!" Temel says. "Shut up! I not talking to you. I talking with goat." See?' Jemal cackles with laughter. 'Black Sea people are stupid like Australians!'

Suddenly, Jemal becomes serious. 'We did it for two battleships.'

'What?'

'We go to war for two battleships. Four million of your pounds. We pay your George King to build us two battleships. He steals our money, and keeps our ships.' Jemal snaps his fingers in front of Connor's eyes. '*That* is why Turks help the Kaiser.'

Connor shakes his head, frowning. 'The British didn't do that.'

From his corner of the carriage, Hasan snorts. 'They did, as a matter of fact. But it is old news. Governments will always find a reason to go to war.'

'And peasants like me do not need a reason. Being shot at is more exciting than watching sheep.' Jemal laughs. 'Me? I like war so I not have to sex my wife anymore.' He repeats this in Turkish to gales of laughter from his comrades.

The train surges on through the forest.

❖

Connor rests his head on a rolled-up hessian sack that smells of crushed oats and chaff dust. He dozes fitfully, lulled to sleep by the train's rhythmic clatter as it travels along the rails. Through the slats in the side of the carriage, the dappled light of the forest gives way to the white, clean sunlight of the great central Anatolian plateau, and the tracks begin to level out. The train accelerates as it leaves the mountains and starts to cross the wide, grassy plains.

The carriage begins to heat up as the sun beats down on its roof. Connor shifts, uncomfortable, but still half-asleep, disoriented and groggy.

A sudden thwack of wood against wood next to his ear startles him awake, and he sits bolt upright.

Jemal stands, legs apart, with his great mitt of a hand wrapped about the handle of a cricket bat.

'I found this wood in trench at Çanakkale, the same day your Australians ran away. All day, I watch them use it on the beach. Through bombs and bullets. They never stop. I keep it – to remember me of that victory day.' He holds it in both hands, spinning it over. 'You tell me. It is a game or a weapon?'

Connor holds out his hands, smiling. 'Both, in the right hands. Here, give it to me.'

A makeshift ball of rolled-up socks and string flies through the air, lobbed by Jemal towards Connor, who stands at one end of the carriage with the bat. Connor swats it away and it flies back to the other end of the railway car where six of the soldiers stand poised to catch it. Many an afternoon playing bush cricket in Rainbow stands Connor in good stead, and he skilfully places the ball at their feet, just out of range of their fingertips or a catch on the full.

'Ha!' Connor is excessively jubilant. The soldiers laugh, but Jemal glowers, unimpressed. He picks up the ball again and flings a full toss towards Connor's head. The Australian blocks the shot with the bat. 'No – that's not the way. You must use a straight arm. Otherwise it's a "no ball".'

Jemal advances on Connor, indignant. 'Englishers. Always with rules.' He reaches for the bat. 'Give me the stick now.'

283

The carriage jolts as the train slows suddenly. Hasan leaps to his feet and moves to the sliding door, briefly looking out before grabbing the handle and hefting it closed.

'Sergeant!'

He signals to Jemal to close the other. Jemal whips around, responding instinctively to the peremptory tone in Hasan's voice, and sprints to the other door, glancing out before sliding it closed. Back pressed to the door he addresses Connor, deadpan.

'We still want our battleships.'

The train is now crawling along at walking pace. Connor detects the heavy stench of ash, smoke and cinders thick in the air. There's something else, too; something sweet smelling that he cannot identify. He can't see anything, but intuition tells him whatever is going on outside the carriage isn't good. Any sense of levity quickly dissipates as Jemal directs the soldiers to ready their weapons. Faces grim, the men slide their rifle bolts and prepare to fire.

Peering between the narrow slats in the railway car door, Connor catches a glimpse of a village in the middle distance consumed by flames, thick plumes of black smoke rolling in torpid waves into the otherwise blue sky. He turns to Hasan. 'Greeks?'

Hasan nods, raising his eyebrows. 'Satan's Army, the partisans. A special regiment sent ahead to terrorise the villagers. We ruled the Greeks for four hundred years, now they think it is their turn again.' He takes his pistol from its holster and leans against the side of the carriage, sliding the door ajar slightly to afford a better glimpse of the passing country. Jemal moves to his side and raises his rifle.

They wait.

The landscape is a flickering patchwork of smoke and flames.

The train crawls along the tracks past villagers fleeing the carnage, their faces caked in dust and soot and their meagre possessions on their backs. For a short distance, a woman trudges beside them, her expression a blank mask of shock. She is bent double under the combined load of a baby bound to her back in a papoose and a carrier crammed full of squawking chickens in her arms. Five children walk by her side, hand in hand, tears staining their grimy little faces. A boy pushes a crippled old man along in a handcart. They see very few, if any, fit and able-bodied adult men.

Inside the carriage, Hasan and his men are silent and grim, their faces set. Connor clenches his fists in impotent rage. He has never been one to watch from the sidelines when others need help. The Mallee has left him no stranger to suffering. He has seen families left destitute from the ravages of drought, fire and flood; and, on one terrible occasion, he witnessed the shotgun murder of a gentle woman and her two daughters at the hands of her alcoholic husband. But he is overwhelmed by indiscriminate misery on this scale. It is almost impossible for him to conceive that other human beings are responsible for this pain. Back home, when a settlement was razed by a bushfire or inundated with water, everyone in the district rallied together to help the afflicted. Other than the occasional scuffle at the local pub, people rarely hurt other people.

A revelation hits Connor like a thunderbolt. *Australians are too busy fighting nature to fight each other.*

Australia has no borders with any other nations, no ancient rivalries with neighbours looming on the horizon like a powder keg just waiting for a fuse. Connor comes from a nation that has always fought other people's battles. His sons had to travel halfway round the world to find someone to fight.

Through the slats in the carriage, he sees a lone child wandering barefoot amongst the long grass on the side of the rails, clutching his hands together, face contorted in fear and grief. Connor grits his teeth and grasps the edge of the sliding door, unable to contain himself any longer. He prepares to leap from the train to help the child.

'No.' A slab of a hand lands firmly on his wrist. Jemal. 'You will die, Connor. And then we all die. For one child.'

Connor angrily pulls his wrist away from Jemal's grip. 'But he is alone. He can't be left by himself.'

He looks to Hasan who shakes his head grimly and adds, 'Maybe he goes to his uncle's village. Or he finds his father and mother. Maybe his brother is coming soon and will find him. Maybe, maybe not. This is war.' Jemal moves between Connor and the doorway as Hasan continues. 'There will be many more children like this if we do not make it to Ankara.'

Connor drops his arm to his side and slumps back against the wall. He can't deny the logic in Hasan's argument. But it flies in the face of everything he believes.

He turns from the side of the train and shuts his eyes, shielding his gaze from the parade of misery outside and fighting the tears that well up.

The train, which has been making painfully slow progress through a low cutting, suddenly comes to a halt. Hasan motions for the men to stay still and quiet, and signals for Jemal to investigate. Connor follows Jemal to the carriage door. The Turk slides it open far enough to peer cautiously outside. At first, it's difficult to see through the veil of thick black smoke that billows from the solid mass blocking the train's passage. When a gust of wind cuts through the ghastly fragrant miasma, Connor can barely fathom what lies before him. Countless bodies have been tossed onto the track and ignited. A jumble of charred and bleeding limbs and scorched skulls burned bare of flesh entangled with garlands of burning clothes form a gruesome barrier that almost reaches the height of the train's engine. Long hair, small limbs, large hands. Men, women and children.

The train driver has jumped down from his cabin and stands, disbelieving, before the apocalyptic tableau, his hands hanging helplessly by his side.

The silence is shattered by the crack of a single gunshot, and Connor sees the driver collapse to his knees, his head exploding in a grisly spray of arterial red.

'Inside! Now!' Jemal shoves Connor back into the carriage and slams the slatted door shut.

The men in the carriages hold their breath. Waiting. Listening. For a moment, all they can hear is the rustle of wind in the trees.

Then comes the ear-splitting chatter of machine-gun fire and the splintering rip of bullets tearing through timber. A wave of uniformed partisans appears along the top of the embankment, charging towards the train. Some race across the gravel with guns raised, firing and reloading rapidly, faces contorted and screaming in Greek. Others plunge down the slope on the backs of strong, stocky horses.

Hasan shouts directions to his troops, who drop to the floor to escape the barrage that peppers the carriage. Men shriek and jerk as bullets find their targets, ripping through flesh and chipping bone. The dreadful metallic smell of blood fills the train car as wounded men groan and clutch at bloodied limbs, gore oozing between their fingers to splatter on the dusty floor.

Keeping low, Connor reaches out for the injured man who has fallen beside him. The man's face is pallid, his lips almost blue as he feebly attempts to staunch the flow of blood from the jagged hole in his left thigh, the shattered bone visible through his shredded khaki uniform. Connor grabs a hessian sack and rolls it into a pad, then presses it against the gaping wound. He knows it is futile as the fabric soaks through in an instant, the blood from the man's femoral artery running in a sheet across the floor. As his heart tires and his blood drains, the man lies still.

The salvo lulls for a moment. Jemal levers open the door a fraction and takes aim at an partisan on horseback galloping past the train. The rider jerks backwards in his saddle and tumbles off the rear of his mount, half his head blown off.

Without explanation the Greeks withdraw from the train. All is still for a heartbeat. Then they hear the piercing whine and whoosh of an incoming mortar as it smashes into the carriage in front of them. A wall of heat and sound pummels Connor as the neighbouring railway car and most of the Turkish soldiers within it disintegrate in a hail of molten shrapnel.

Hasan, Jemal and the remaining Turks smash through some of the shattered slats with the butts of their rifles and return fire, felling some of their assailants.

Unarmed, Connor feels useless, helpless. He hears the rattle of the door behind them as it is forced open. Partisans pour in through the breach.

Hasan takes careful aim with his revolver and picks the Greeks off as they swarm into the carriage. Jemal spins on his heel and raises his rifle, shooting a partisan in the face, shattering it to a featureless pulp. Before Jemal has the chance to reload, a comrade of the man he just felled shoots him in the gut. The big man slumps to his knees, clutching his stomach.

The Greeks keep coming. They press into the carriage and overwhelm the surviving Turks.

Hasan raises his revolver, readying to shoot, but is brought to the ground by a rifle butt slammed into the back of his legs. He lies, prone, with the muzzle jammed into his cheek. By his side, Connor feels strangely detached from reality as another partisan snaps at him in Greek, forcing him to the floor, where he kneels, the soldier's rifle pointed at his head.

An officer vaults into the carriage. He barks out a volley of orders. Most of the remaining partisans seize the fallen rifles and boxes of ammunition, and drag and kick the surviving Turks out of the carriage onto the embankment beside the train.

The Greek officer moves towards Hasan and bends to examine him as he would a dog turd stuck to his boot. He picks at the military insignia on the Turkish man's tunic and tweaks the waxed tips of Hasan's moustache, sniffing the air and turning to address his troops in Greek.

Indicating Connor, Hasan lifts his head and speaks to the officer in Greek.

He then turns towards Connor. 'I have told him you are Australian and his ally, that you are my prisoner.'

The partisan leader examines Connor, sceptical. 'Australia?' He holds his hands in front of him, mimicking paws. 'Kangaroo? Speak English?'

Connor nods. 'Yes. Australian.'

The Greek officer waves away the soldier holding Connor captive. 'Australia, you stay in here.'

Then he points at Hasan and tosses one of the men a hessian sack, barking an order. He laughs and explains to Connor. 'We shoot Turk dog with his own gun. Then cut off his head, take to Smyrna.' The commander vaults down to the side of the track where his men are rounding up the remaining Turkish troops.

Jemal and Hasan are frogmarched to the door on the opposite side of the train and thrown to the gravel below. A wine-red stain covers the front of Jemal's tunic, and he lets out a loud, frothy exhalation of air as he hits the ground.

Connor is jolted into action by shouts and curses from outside the carriage, punctuated by the crack of a rifle and the ominous thud of a body hitting the dirt. Lifting himself to his hands and knees, he scrambles around on the floor of the railway car, pushing bloodied bodies and fallen crates aside in a desperate attempt to find a weapon. The partisans were too thorough. There is nothing.

As he searches, Connor sees through the slatted boards that at the base of the embankment, a burly partisan has forced Jemal to his knees. The front of the Turk's tunic and trousers are sodden with dark blood. An involuntary gush of urine runs down Jemal's thighs as he struggles to conceal his pain. His face blanches as the Greek soldier pulls his arms behind his back, opening up the wound in his gut. The other partisan checks his magazine, tugs on the bolt and presses his rifle into Jemal's brow.

Inside the carriage Connor's heart pounds as he continues to search for something to arm himself with. Then he sees it. Wedged between one of the fallen Turks' bodies and the side of the carriage. He hefts the man aside and grabs it. *Why not?*

He hears a distressed shout from outside. 'Anzac Bey!' Connor looks up as Jemal locks his rueful eyes on him through the open door.

'Don't invade a country if you don't know where it is.'

The soldier pulls the trigger and Jemal's lifeless body slumps forwards.

Connor feels his legs give way beneath him. The sound of gunfire continues on the other side of the carriage, accompanied by the soggy thud of bullets penetrating flesh.

❖

Standing beside his fallen comrade, Hasan closes his eyes and holds his hands before him, palms turned towards the sky, murmuring a prayer for Jemal and ignoring the order to kneel. A brutal whack to the back of his legs brings him to his knees and he struggles to remain upright.

The Greek slowly and deliberately reloads Hasan's revolver. 'Your head will be coming with us. It will be put on display in our headquarters.' He presses the muzzle to the base of Hasan's skull. 'Less damage to your face,' he explains.

Hasan doesn't flinch. Opening his eyes, he fixes his steady gaze on the partisan. He murmurs in Turkish. 'Allah, protect my family. God is great.'

The partisan responds with a Greek salute: 'Long live President Venizelos!'

There's a sickening thud, and the soldier jerks forwards. Hasan starts, anticipating the searing impact of a bullet in his brain. Instead, the Greek collapses, spasming and bleeding from the mouth and ears, his skull caved in. The Turk sees Connor standing motionless behind the soldier, clutching the cricket bat, its edge dripping with gore and sticky clumps of black hair. Spinning as he falls, the Greek reaches out and grabs hold of his attacker's shirtsleeve, pulling himself close. He coughs, spattering hot droplets of blood on Connor's face, who looks into the man's dying eyes with horror.

The other partisan is levelling his weapon, Connor in his sights. Hasan moves like lightning, grabbing his revolver from the mortally wounded partisan's grasp and shooting the other Greek soldier in the heart. The man drops, dead before he hits the ground. Moving quickly to Connor's side, Hasan holds the gun to the dying man's head and pulls the trigger.

Connor is looking down at the bloodied cricket bat in his hands, paralysed by what he has done. Hasan grabs him by the elbow and pushes him under the train. Looking out to the other side, they see the only two remaining Turkish soldiers shot point-blank in the head, their bodies slumping to the side in the gravel.

The sound of these last gunshots rings and echoes along the cutting. The Greeks pause. For a heartbeat, an eerie silence descends.

Their monstrous work accomplished, the Greek commander begins to bark out new orders. 'Gather up all their weapons and search their bags for gold. Hurry! Then get clear – we're going to blow up the engine.'

Crawling back out from beneath the train, Hasan glances up and down the track. Towards the rear he can see a group of horses tethered, their riders otherwise occupied on the other side of the train. Connor is going through the motions, his face white, still in shock. Slipping back under the train, Hasan elbows him in the side to get his attention. He gestures at the horses, whispers, 'There. Wait till I signal, then we run.' Turning, Hasan checks that the partisans are still occupied, rifling through the dead Turks' packs and clothes. 'Yes. Now!'

The two men scramble out and run, crouched over, towards the horses. On Hasan's whispered instructions, they untie them all, then grab hold of a set of reins each and swing their legs up into the saddles. As they accelerate, the Turk and the Australian scatter the other horses with slaps to their rumps, then spur their mounts up the embankment and away.

CHAPTER THIRTY-SIX

Connor is mounted on a tall white stallion. He feels the horse's muscles swell as his strong legs pump, propelling them up the steep, gravel-covered slope. Hasan is astride a stocky Anatolian bay that easily keeps pace with Connor's horse. As they reach the top of the slope, a sharp cry rings out from below. They have been spotted.

Bullets whiz past their ears, but as they launch themselves over the ridge and onto the plain, they are shielded from the Greek barrage. In the middle distance, a deep river valley cuts through the fields, and the two men dig their heels into the sides of their mounts and gallop at full tilt towards it.

The sounds and smells of death are far behind them when Connor and Hasan eventually slow their mounts to a walk.

The horses' hooves crunch through the opalescent, smooth river pebbles that cover the floor of the valley, washed to shore by the shallow but wide, fast-running river that cuts through the chasm. Stones bumping against each other in the water sound like hail on a tin roof. Above the gurgle of the crystal-clear water Connor can hear birds warbling and the soft sound of the breeze blowing through tendrils of bright green leaves hanging from willow boughs. The beauty around them seems almost absurd in contrast to the scene they have just left.

'Will they follow us?'

Hasan has been silent, lost deep in thought. 'Us? I do not think so. They have a whole country to plunder.' He shortens his reins and draws his horse to a halt.

'Our horses need rest.' Leaning forward Hasan slips his feet out of the stirrups and swings his right leg over the saddle to dismount. He drops to the ground and gently feeds the reins over the horse's ears, leading him to where the river eddies in a shallow and shady pool.

Connor follows his lead. The horses drop their heads to the water and drink deeply, flicking at flies with their tails and stamping their feet. Bending to grab a handful of wet sand, Connor scrubs at the blood that has dried on his hands, a rosy cloud blooming in the clear water where he washes it away. Dipping his hands into the river again, he scoops up some clean water and splashes it on his face, rubbing it through his hair to sluice away the dust and dried gore.

Connor sits heavily on the pebbly beach. As the rush of adrenaline that has sustained him begins to fade, he reels with horror at the thought of what he has done, is haunted by the dying man's face. He looks up at Hasan. 'His breath smelled of garlic and tobacco.'

From the pack hanging from his horse's saddle, Hasan produces a small bottle with a label on it, printed with heavy, black Greek script. He tosses it to Connor. 'I carry the breath of hundreds. Wash him down with this.'

Connor holds the glass bottle in a trembling hand and examines the clear liquid. 'Raki?'

'Ouzo. Same mother.'

Fumbling as he uncorks the bottle, Connor throws his head back and takes a deep draught. He winces as the thick, sweet aniseed spirit burns the back of his throat. After securing the horses' reins to a fallen branch in the shade, Hasan joins Connor on the warm pebbly beach and holds out his hand. Connor passes him the bottle and the Turk takes a swig. Then he turns to the Australian and hands the ouzo back.

'If not for you, I would have died today, Connor Bey. Yet at Çanakkale you would have killed me yourself.'

'I still might,' replies Connor dryly. 'But not before you show me how to get to Afion.'

Connor glances at the hollow eyes and sombre expression on his companion's face and is reminded of all the Turk has lost. He raises the bottle. 'To Jemal.' He takes another drink and passes the ouzo to Hasan so he can do the same.

Hasan takes the bottle and nods his head 'Thank you, Joshua Bey.' Connor notes that Hasan has used his Christian name for the first time. Hasan takes a swig. 'Buried not far from here is the man whom Jemal loved more than anyone, Nasreddin Hoca. He was a famous jester who lived hundreds of years ago. When Jemal was full of raki he would tell his jokes and laugh so much he would cry. His favourite was the story of the time the great Moghul emperor, Tamerlane, saw himself in a mirror and burst into tears when he realised how ugly he was. Everyone in the court told him how handsome he was, to make him feel better. All except Nasreddin Hoca, who had also burst into tears and was still crying. The emperor said to him, "I had a reason to weep, I am the lord of many lands and master of many slaves. But I do not understand why you should weep like this." Nasreddin replied, "My lord, you wept for two hours when you saw your reflection for an instant, but I have to see you all day long".' Hasan shakes his head. 'It is a miracle Allah turned a blind eye to Jemal for so long.'

'You believe in a heaven, don't you?'

'Yes. But he is not going there.' Hasan laughs. 'Jemal is Allah's one great chance to avenge himself on Satan.' He raises the bottle to the sky before downing another mouthful. 'Ah, Jemal. To your awful poetry.'

The two men sit in silence as the water rushes past and dragonflies hover and dip above its surface. Soft, white clouds appear motionless in the pale blue sky, and the air smells of moss, pollen and fresh grass.

Hasan drops his head. 'No. Even the poetry I will miss.'

❖

The great, golden plain stretches out in all directions, intersected by tiny, dusty tracks and the occasional rutted road. Connor and Hasan had followed the river valley, meandering along its deep cutting as the blinding sun began to descend towards the horizon, then turned and followed a narrow shepherd's trail as it zigzagged from the river up to the lip of the escarpment.

The landscape before them is strangely devoid of life. In the middle distance is a small cluster of low buildings constructed from rough fieldstones and capped with thatched rooves. But no smoke spirals from the chimneys, and there are no people to be seen.

Spurring their horses on, the two men canter along the track and cautiously enter the village. When Connor peers through the doors left ajar in the modest homes, he sees a chaotic jumble of household possessions: clothes, cutlery and bedding strewn about.

'Where have they all gone?'

'They knew what was coming and chose to leave before it arrived.' Hasan dismounts his horse. 'Come – we will find food here.'

Connor joins Hasan as they move through houses and courtyards, gathering staples left behind when the villagers fled. Honey, a stale loaf of bread, onions, a can of olives, tomatoes growing on a small plant in an empty oil tin at someone's doorway, and apricots and plums ripening in an orchard.

The sun is lower on the horizon now, its rays skimming across the yellow fields. Connor turns to Hasan. 'Should we rest here tonight?'

'No. The Greeks are too close, and they are moving in this direction. This village will be a target.' He slips his left foot into the stirrup and swings his leg across his horse's back. 'We should find somewhere else.'

As Connor mounts up, Hasan nods towards a range of low wooded hills visible beyond the expansive fields. 'Over there we will find shelter.' Kicking their horses into a gallop, the two men race across the plain towards the distant forest.

Connor's head rings with the deafening buzz of a cicada chorus as he passes beneath the dark canopy of pine trees lining the roadway. His horse's shoes clang as they strike the marble slabs that pave the ancient boulevard, crushing stands of wild thyme and oregano growing between the cracks and releasing a sweet scent into the warm, still air.

On either side of the road, the stumps of what once were majestic columns and their bases stand; all around them, fluted column drum fragments and enormous chiselled blocks of marble lie haphazardly in the undergrowth like the discarded toys of a giant child. Visible through the trees is a monumental wall constructed of massive rectangular stone blocks, each as high as Connor's waist. In places, olive trees with trunks so fat a man couldn't wrap his arms around them grow from chinks in the wall.

Connor turns to Hasan, who rides silently beside him. 'Greek or Roman, do you think?'

Hasan shrugs. 'Someone's empire.'

A steep hill rises to the left of them. From a distance, it appears as if someone has taken a bite out of its side. As Connor moves closer, he sees rows of stone seats arranged in steep tiers around the semicircular depression. Next to him, Hasan turns his horse off the paved road and onto a narrow goat track that meanders between the fallen ruins, heading for the amphitheatre. 'We can rest over here.'

The men tether and unsaddle their horses and cross the cracked marble floor of what was once the stage, their boots grinding through the fallen gravel that partially covers the paving. They move around the ruins, gathering branches and pieces of timber to burn.

The shadows are lengthening and the cool chill of night begins to cut through the heat of the day. Connor quickly builds a small fire in the lee of a fallen column drum. Hasan has a small pan taken from the village into which he chops some of the tomatoes and onions. He places the pan on the coals and sits with his back against the lowest row of seats, his legs stretched out on the paving. He offers Connor a small tin of wizened black olives after he has taken a few for himself.

Connor shakes his head, wrinkling his nose. 'Still haven't developed a taste for those.'

Chewing on the bitter olives contentedly, Hasan spits the pips onto the paving. His eyes are fixed on a faint light flickering far in the distance.

'The first Australian I met – not to shoot at, to talk to – was a thief.'

Connor laughs. 'That'd be right. We were all convicts, you know.'

'I met him at Lone Pine. This man waves a white cloth, calls out and walks straight across no-man's land. We see he is carrying something. A thousand Turkish guns are on him, two thousand Turkish eyes. But still he walks. He reaches us and drops one of our wounded into our arms.'

'Why the devil would he do that?'

'He was very brave. But very stupid.' Hasan raises his eyebrows, shrugs. 'He and I sat on sandbags and we shared a cigarette. And then he walked back.'

'And no one shot him?'

'No, they were too stunned. *I* should have, though. It was only when he reached the Australian trenches that I realised he had stolen my cigarettes.'

Both men laugh.

The flickering light on the horizon is suddenly joined by others. Tiny bursts of flame bloom against the backdrop of a perfect, glowing, peach-pink sunset.

Hasan points towards the source of the light. 'They're a day behind us, at the most. I will ride with you as far as Afion. But then I must go on to Ankara.'

Connor nods.

'Tell me, Joshua Bey. If by some miracle you do find your son, what will you say to him?'

It's a question that Connor hasn't even considered. His only thought is to find Art. Past that, he doesn't know what he'll do.

'I suppose ... I will tell him to come back home. It's where he belongs.'

Hasan nods, his brow furrowed. He changes the subject. 'The food will be cooked now.' He stands and moves to the edge of the fire, using a forked stick to lift the pan off the coals by its handle. He brings it back to where Connor sits and tosses him the loaf of bread. Connor tears off a fist-sized piece and breaks it into smaller morsels, dipping them into the pan of soft and sweet-smelling cooked tomatoes.

'Smells good.' The tomatoes have disintegrated into a thick and juicy sauce that soaks into the dry bread. It is delicious. Or perhaps he is hungrier than he thought.

The two men eat in silence, scraping the pan clean with their bread. The sun has long since dipped below the horizon and night envelops the mountainside.

Hasan passes Connor a saddle blanket. 'Now, we rest.' He gestures towards the ominous glow of fires on the horizon. 'But we will not be spending long here. Tomorrow we wake at sunrise and ride to Afion. From here, it is not far.'

Connor rolls up the saddle blanket and wedges it against the base of the amphitheatre's lowest step, moving his body towards the heat of the campfire. He rests his head on the blanket. The smell of horsehair and sweat is comforting and familiar. As the damp of night descends, he lifts his collar to protect his neck from the chill of the stones and buttons his coat up to his chin.

Although he never admitted it to Lizzie, Connor always enjoyed the times he was compelled to spend the night sleeping under the stars. If he was searching for water a long way from home and reached the end of the day without success, he would quietly rejoice when it became apparent that he would have to make a fire and roll out his swag to slumber under the expansive dome of the velvety blue night sky. The stars spun above his head and seemed to press down upon him. Lying on sand that was still warm from the sun's searing heat, he felt utterly inconsequential, his life meaningless when measured against the immensity of the universe. Humans have barely scratched the surface of the place Connor calls home. In the great southern continent, life is an interminable battle against natural forces that seem determined to wipe humanity from its face. And he likes that. Sometimes it is good to feel as if he counts for nothing in the scheme of things.

But here, even the sound of the night creatures is comforting. Crickets gently buzz and whirr; an owl hoots softly. Everything seems to move in concert with the deep breathing of the two men lying under the stars. *People belong in this landscape*, Connor thinks. Against his back, Connor feels the grooves worn into the marble by the passage of countless feet over thousands of years. The gravel that lies in drifts around the ancient stone platform is not stone crushed and weathered over millennia. Instead it is man made. He realised earlier as he bent down to gather firewood; what looked like chunks of bright orange and pale grey soil were actually fragments of ceramic. Some pieces were as tiny as match heads; other, larger pieces looked like the rims of shattered bowls or broken handles and spouts. So many people have moved through this land – discarding and abandoning so much as they passed – it is no longer possible to distinguish between the creations of man and things born of nature.

He loves the terrible grandeur of his homeland. But here, in this fertile and abundant place that has been nurturing humans for tens of thousands of years, Connor experiences an unexpected and quite serene sense of belonging. Despite the horrors of today – trauma and violence beyond anything he could have imagined – he feels at home in this land.

Connor's limbs grow heavy as he succumbs to sleep under unfamiliar stars.

CHAPTER THIRTY-SEVEN

*B*loodcurdling screams. A broken line of Turkish soldiers charges across no-man's land.

Stumbling and faltering, they step on the mangled limbs and body parts of dead and dying men, pressing faces, noses, into the ghastly mud. Thick red ooze wells up over the edges of boots, sucking on bare toes bound in rags and worn leather soles. It hasn't rained for months; the dirt is saturated with the lifeblood of thousands of dead soldiers.

There. Like a piece of liquorice wending through the deranged landscape: the Anzac trenches. Almost within reach.

Henry and Ed run like rabbits, ducking and darting as the advancing troops close in.

Art hangs back behind his brothers, heart pounding. He could pass the boys ... longer legs ... has a few years on both of them ... hell, faster runner. In a chase over the flat neither of them could touch him. But he can't turn his back on them. All but holds his arms out, herding them to the relative safety of the trench.

Need to know they're safe.

I promised.

Almost safe. Relief. They're over the edge, beneath the firing line. Out of harm's way.

Now, my turn.

Legs pump, eyes darting. Bloody obstacle course. Barbed wire, severed limbs, bomb craters.

A banshee scream. The ground disappears from beneath his feet. The hot rip of metal through flesh.

Heat, blinding light. Lungs compressed.

Ears hurt.

Can't see. Feel nothing.

White.

Something now. Through the grey.

Whine. Ears buzzing. Something. I hear something. What is that?

'Art?'

'Artie!'

'You all right, Artie?'

No. Go back.

Ed and Henry.

You were safe.

Go back.

They crawl across the mud towards him, clutching their rifles.

'Bugger off, the two of you.' He's poleaxed by the searing pain from where the flesh hangs from his leg in ribbons. Ground tilts, head spinning. Breath catches in his chest. 'Leave me.'

'Yeah, whatever you say, mate.' Henry.

On their feet now. Crouching, zigzagging towards their brother.

Art lifts his head. A trail of bullets spatters in a line towards them. The firing stops.

'Leave me!'

From a nest of sandbags, a Turkish gunner heaves another bandolier towards the barrel of his machine gun. Bends, peers down the sights.

'No! . . . Leave! . . . Go!'

The Turk squeezes the trigger as Henry and Ed cross the last patch of blood-sodden earth and reach their brother.

White hot flashes from the muzzle.

The gun spits bullets.

They hit their marks.

CHAPTER THIRTY-EIGHT

The sun warms Art's face. His eyes close gently against its glare.

Head tilted slightly towards one shoulder, his arms are outstretched, one palm turned down towards the ground, the other cupped and turned towards the heavens, his lips curled gently into a beatific smile. Tiny blooms of condensation form in the chilly dawn air as Art exhales. Slowly spinning on the ball of one foot, the other propels him in a circle, pushing off a small woollen prayer mat.

Art's threadbare tunic has been discarded, exposing his emaciated and ruined torso to the feeble rays of the morning sun. His belly is as hollow as a greyhound's, his ribs and collarbone so prominent they cast shadows on his sallow and scarred skin.

His foot slips. A cascade of gravel and eroded mortar trickles and bounces down the steep sides of the crumbling castle wall. He stumbles, one foot hanging into the void. Instinct kicks in. On the wall top, his toes scrabble for the rug's rough edge. The coarsely woven wool flaps in the wind that eddies between snaggle-toothed ruins.

Art rights himself; looks down from his vertiginous eyrie. Far beneath his feet, the russet-coloured roofs of the houses at the base of the peak look like playthings, the people walking along the winding streets and alleys as inconsequential as insects.

❖

Pale dawn sunlight rakes through the tree trunks as Connor and Hasan follow a narrow shepherd's trail towards the summit of a long range of forested hills. The sappy and invigorating scent of pine fills the air as the horses labour up the slope, crushing the carpet of fallen dark green needles that lie underfoot.

As the sun rises, swarms of industrious bees descend on the forest, crawling over the rough orange bark of the towering pine trees. Connor swats away a persistent few that are bent on landing on his face.

'Where are the flowers?' Connor is curious.

'The flowers?'

'Why are the bees here? I don't see any flowers.'

Hasan looks towards where the insects swarm around the tree trunks. 'No – they are here for that . . .' He points towards a cottony-white substance that sits in patches on the rough boughs. 'The bees use it to make honey. Pine honey. It is the best in Turkey.'

Connor can't help but marvel at the fertility of this country. 'You are so fortunate here. There is so much abundance.'

His companion laughs. 'Yes, so very lucky. People have been fighting to take it all for many thousands of years.'

The irony doesn't escape Connor.

In the distance, a tiered and jagged line of massive mountains stretches towards the pale blue sky, the lower slopes dark with dense forests. The upper reaches are bare

308

of vegetation and thickly edged with something blindingly white; Connor realises with a start that it's snow – something he has never seen before. One peak towers above the others, its summit disappearing into the clouds.

Hasan gestures towards it. 'Mount Dindymus. To the ancient heathens, it was home of the most important god, the Mother Goddess of fertility, Cybele. She rode a chariot drawn by two lions and could cross between the worlds of the living and the dead.'

'They never make it that easy for mortals. I need a chariot like that.'

'I suppose they think it's against the natural order of things, crossing from death to life and back,' replies Hasan.

'What's against the natural order is parents burying children.'

The men reach the ridge, the hill falling away steeply on either side of them. They rein in their horses and take in the spectacular view. The grid-like overgrown streets and semicircular theatre of the ancient city lie far behind them. Ahead stretches the great Anatolian plain, the fields blushing pink and dotted with countless small hamlets. In the distance, the roads that traverse the plain converge like a starburst on a larger town. At its very centre is a steep-sided crag, the most prominent geographic feature in the undulating plain. Fragmentary walls tumble down from its summit.

'There is Afion.' Hasan points at the ruins. 'Your Opium Black Castle.'

Connor laughs. 'You Turks have a lot of ruins.'

The men descend towards the open fields and join a narrow, rutted road that meanders towards Afion. The path cuts through densely sown fields of plants with thick thigh-high stems and lacy grey foliage. Rounded petals as fine as silk flutter in the breeze: carmine red, rose pink and snow white. Where flowers have bloomed and fallen, obscenely plump seed pods nod atop spindly stems, sap awaiting harvest.

Two lone figures – a man and a woman – stand in the opium poppy field, heads bowed and arms extended, deftly cutting slits into the side of the ripe seed pods with curved blades. Hasan calls out a greeting to the man in Turkish.

The old man lifts his head, raising his hand to shield his gaze from the sun, his currant-like eyes buried deep within his wrinkled eye sockets. He expresses no surprise at seeing the imposing uniformed figure before him. He returns Hasan's greeting, and the two men have a short conversation in Turkish. The old man points a pink-stained hand as he speaks.

Hasan turns to Connor. 'The Greeks are moving fast. Last night they were in İscehisar, only thirteen miles away. Come, we must hurry.'

Spurring their horses on, the two men gallop along the dirt road towards the outskirts of Afion, where they encounter a group of Turkish villagers fleeing their homes. Children herd sheep and goats beside women carrying their children, while men push handcarts, household possessions piled haphazardly on the flat trays. The trickle of refugees becomes a deluge and Connor and Hasan are forced to slow their progress as they swim against the tide of the exodus.

Before them, the peak at the heart of Afion looms large; white-plastered homes are clustered about its base. The houses thin towards the outskirts of the town and are interspersed with small fields surrounded by low, rough stone fences that enclose animal pens, orchards and vegetable gardens. Connor looks across the recently ploughed rich soil towards an open plaza which is surrounded on three sides by long, low buildings.

At first, he doesn't register what is right before his eyes. It's a sight so familiar to him that, for a moment, he pays it no heed.

Then, it hits him. Flat wide sheet metal sails turn in the wind atop a spindly frame. A windmill. Just like one of *his* windmills.

Connor wheels his horse around and gallops up the lane towards the square. 'He's here!' he cries.

A hot wind blows from the southeast, kicking up the dust that flies from the heels of Connor's charging horse. Hasan turns back and urges his mount into a canter, in pursuit of his companion.

Connor's excitement and anticipation reach fever pitch. Entering the plaza, he leaps off his horse before it comes to a halt, throwing away the reins as he bolts over to the windmill's base. The sails spin cheerily in the strong wind, a makeshift pump rod rising and dipping, drawing water from the water table below before shooting it out a spout and into a deep stone trough.

Hasan draws his horse up beside the Australian and dismounts. 'What is this thing?'

'It's Art's.' Despite himself, tears well in Connor's eyes. 'Art made this. It's a windmill.' He cups his hand beneath the spout; cool water rushes across his palm. 'It pulls water up from below the earth.'

'Are you sure he made it?'

A wave of relief and certainty washes over Connor. 'Yes. It can't have been anyone else. Art is here. I know it.'

Hasan moves towards one of the buildings on the edge of the square. A thin plume of smoke twirls skywards from its partially open door. In the shadows, an old man sits on a low, rush-bottomed stool with legs outstretched. Eyes wrinkled contentedly over a hand-rolled cigarette, he nurses a rifle in his lap.

'You should retreat to the east, Hadji,' Hasan hails the old man in Turkish. 'You cannot win here!'

'I'd rather die in my own home, thank you.' He rocks on the chair, avoiding Hasan's eyes.

'Then, may Allah protect you.' Hasan smiles. 'Brother, we are looking for a stranger. An Englisher. He came here as a prisoner. Are there any strangers in the town?'

The old man looks into the far distance and lifts his shoulders, eyebrows raised. 'No. Everyone is gone. Cowards. Every last one of them.' Spittle gathers in shining beads on his pendulous, liver-dark bottom lip. 'Cowards.'

Hasan turns from the old man. 'Joshua Bey!' he calls. 'Come . . . we will find someone else to ask!'

Reluctantly, Connor leaves the windmill and follows Hasan into the narrow streets behind the square. The town is ghostly, deserted. For the first time since they fled the train, they can hear the distant sound of explosions. Hasan detects a sense of urgency beginning to build in the Australian, whose breathing has suddenly quickened.

Connor can't restrain himself any longer and begins to cry out. 'Art! Arthur! Where are you?!'

The two men round a corner to find an improbable scene. Perched around a small table set in the shade of an ancient fig tree are four men, cigarettes clamped between lips or clutched in gnarled paws. They are engrossed by the set up of a backgammon board sitting on the table in front of them.

'Peace be with you.' Hasan speaks to the men in Turkish.

'And with you,' the men respond without looking up.

'We look for the man who built the windmill in the square ... the pump for the water. Do you know where he is?'

One of the backgammon players raises his bushy, silver eyebrows and makes a clicking sound with his tongue against the roof of his mouth. 'No. He is gone. He left with the Turks.'

One of his companions corrects him, pointing to a ruined church further up the slope. 'No. The sin-eater is still here. In the old church.'

Hasan nods, places his hand on his chest. 'Thank you.'

The man with the eyebrows shakes his head. 'May this madness end.'

Connor has no idea what is being discussed. 'Everyone has left. So why are they still here?'

'They are Greek. They have nothing to fear.' Hasan nods towards the church. 'Joshua Bey, up there. There, you may find what you are looking for, God willing. But you must hurry.' He looks over Connor's shoulder. 'You see that smoke? The villagers are burning their crops rather than leaving them for the Greeks. They only do that when there is no hope.'

313

With his heart in his mouth, Connor looks towards the church and fixes his bearings on the belltower on the roof. He loosens the reins, gives his stallion a swift kick in the side and the horse explodes up the hill. He steers through the cobbled streets and packed-earth lanes of the town, zigzagging and turning, his eyes locked on the church roof. Connor's steed is bred for battle, calm under fire and surefooted on narrow mountain passes. It gallops through the streets with reckless glee. Its haunches flex and strain as Connor shifts his weight in the saddle to corner, and then pats the horse's neck when they straighten up on the other side.

The streets of Rainbow flash through his mind: wide, dusty and dead straight. Built on the flat, with no cliff-top forts, keeps or walls, peaceful Rainbow seems a distant world away. He turns a corner and the church looms up in front of him behind a stone wall. Brimming with excitement, Connor pulls hard on the reins and guides his horse through a low arch into the forecourt. But then, his shoulders sink.

In his mind's eye this was a living, breathing church, newly painted with a gleaming bell hanging in its tower. He would be greeted by a bearded priest in long black robes who would call inside for Art. But there is no life here, just the dry husk of a building long since abandoned and left to crumble away. Plaster hangs from the façade like a newly-shed snake skin, but rather than glimpsing a gleaming new dermis beneath it Connor sees broken wooden battens and coarse stonework.

He follows the path to the entrance where three arches still stand against the odds. The roof of the atrium they supported has collapsed into a pile of plaster and concrete on the floor. He steps over the rubble to the front doorway, where the last pieces of the ornate marble architrave hang on grimly. Connor hesitates at the black hole where the door once resided, engulfed in a cloud of despair.

His heart sinks still further as he steps inside, whatever faint hope he had harboured in the forecourt now well and truly crushed. The interior is dark and funereal save for the light that streams in through a gaping wound in the barrel-vaulted ceiling.

'Arthur! Art!' he calls into the emptiness.

The room is long, punctuated by small niches. A thin layer of sand and dust has settled on the floor like silt after a retreating flood. The once beautiful tessellated floor is now buckled and broken up by roof tiles and stone blocks that have landed on it from above, scattering the mosaic tiles like loose teeth.

The interior is decorated with a dazzling gallery of frescos. They bleed from the ceiling down all the walls and run side by side the length of the building, all the way to the apse. Many have faded over time; others have lifted off the walls and crumbled to plaster dust on the floor, leaving behind large patches of grey mortar and exposed stone that gape bare, interrupting the Biblical narrative. Near the ceiling, where pigeons nest and coo beneath the eaves, long white dropping trails run down the faces of Christ, Saint George and the full pantheon of disciples, acidic tears stripping away the vivid colour.

Connor steps closer to the wall. His eyes are not deceiving him. All the subjects of the frescos have had their eyes gouged out. It cannot be accidental. Connor runs his fingers across the chipped faces, feeling the powdery trail of the frenzied chisel marks. Someone has gone the full length of the wall and studiously defaced the icons.

'It is because we believe depicting the prophet Jesus is sacrilege, forbidden by God,' announces Hasan from the doorway. 'So the locals blind them.'

In the far corner a rudimentary scaffold made from timber and rope has been erected; a feeble attempt to keep the decay and disintegration at bay.

In the adjacent corner lies an animal pen made from dry branches and pilfered roofing timber. It is now disused and has collapsed haphazardly. Gusts of blustery wind blast through gaps in the wall and blow the dry dung and rotting straw in swirling eddies around the room.

In a darkened niche set into the wall, Connor spies a cluster of odd shapes. His curiosity piqued, he walks over to inspect the collection more closely. A nondescript blanket and jacket lie beside a fire hearth. A jumble of pots and pans are scattered outside the circle of blackened stones, and amongst them is a single plate and solitary fork. Connor's heart jumps and, without thinking, he thrusts his hand into the coals in the fireplace. Cold – dead cold. Whoever built this fire is long gone.

Connor lifts his gaze to the frescos on the niche wall. Jesus stares back at him from the gloom in lively red, orange and blue hues. The religious instruction Connor was compelled to sit through in Sunday School when he was a fidgety student stands him in good stead, and he immediately recognises the figure as the resurrected Christ, showing his wounds to Thomas, who is putting his fingers inside Jesus' bleeding side. But unlike the other figures in the frescos, this Christ has eyes. Newly painted, not particularly well-executed, bright blue eyes. Connor looks at the next panel, and the next, confirming that all the figures at this end of the church have freshly restored eyes.

'That's strange. Someone has fixed these. The eyes,' he tells Hasan, and calls out again impulsively. 'Arthur? Arthur!'

Hasan has entered the church, and takes Connor by the arm, gently leading him to the doorway. 'Come, Joshua, he has gone. There is nobody here.'

Connor refuses to hear him, shaking Hasan off and running back into the nave. 'No! He's here. I'm sure of it.' He shouts at the top of his lungs. 'Art!'

The name reverberates off the vaulted ceiling and peters out to nothing, leaving in its wake the most godforsaken of silences. Connor drops his head. He has nothing left.

As he turns to join Hasan, a voice speaks from the rafters, so hesitant and husky that, for a moment, Connor cannot even be sure he has heard it.

'Who are you?'

CHAPTER THIRTY-NINE

Connor turns as he hears the rattle of wood and peers into the shadowy recesses of the ruined building.

Hasan points to a bedraggled figure slowly descending from the scaffolding in the far corner. The major's hand moves automatically to his holster and unclips it slowly, a reflex action born of a lifetime anticipating trouble. Connor and Hasan can scarcely make the figure out as it passes through the dust and haze, but they can see a brown beard and matted hair. He wears slippers, a pair of baggy Turkish village pants and a khaki shirt freckled with blue paint.

Connor watches the man in silence as he swings awkwardly to the floor and winces. He straightens himself, takes a shepherd's crook in his right hand and begins walking towards them.

He says something again in Turkish, then repeats it in English. 'Who are you?'

It takes Connor a moment to align this broken young man with the memory he holds of his son. But there is no mistaking him.

Connor emits an anguished whisper.

'Art . . .?'

The man stares back querulously, lost in time and space. 'Dad?'

Connor has heard the word thousands of times before but never has he yearned to hear it more than now. Never has it carried such import for him. His breath comes in staggered bursts, his eyes burn with tears.

'Son.'

'Are you really here?' Arthur asks, reaching out, incredulous. He pats his father's face with quivering fingertips as if he does not trust his eyes.

Connor presses Art's hand onto his cheek and kisses his son's open palm. He savours the touch and lets out a colossal sigh that emanates from the no-man's land that resides somewhere between relief and despair.

'It's me all right, son.'

Art rests his head on his father's shoulder and begins to breathe in time with the rise and fall of his dad's broad chest. Connor wraps Art in his arms and begins to stroke his tangled hair. It is unthinkable that this friable collection of bones, held together by wilting skin, is his beloved son. Having found him, the realisation that Art has lost his youth, his life force, breaks Connor's heart anew.

Hasan keeps a wary eye on the father and son from the church doorway, mouthing a prayer under his breath.

'It's time to come home, son,' Connor whispers.

Art suddenly shakes himself free of his father and backs into a niche like a cornered animal, swinging his walking stick at his horrified father.

'I'm not coming home. None of us are coming back. They're dead. None of us are coming home, Dad.' He lets a horrible, hollow sob escape. 'You leave me. You go and leave me here.'

'I know. I know all about it.'

Connor's soothing tone does nothing to calm Art, who has crouched down and is frenetically stirring paint in a pot and talking under his breath. 'You shouldn't have come here. You must go. It's too dangerous here. You shouldn't have come.'

Art stops and points a stick dripping with sky-blue paint at Connor.

'Go now!'

He turns his back on his father, dips a fine brush in the pot, and begins restoring the eyes of the Emperor Constantine, who is holding the walled city of Constantinople in his hands and offering it up to Christ.

Connor is at a loss, feeling his way blindly himself. He stands in silence, helpless. Desperate. He watches Art's brush-strokes as the eyes of the Emperor begin to glimmer and come back to life. As Art paints he looks back over his shoulder spasmodically, seemingly unnerved by his father's presence.

The momentary silence is ruptured by artillery fire in the distance. The walls quiver, and dust, plaster and dry pigeon droppings descend on the three men like snow, settling on their shoulders and heads. Connor looks towards Hasan, who is still standing in the doorway, his eyes gazing inscrutably at the crouching figure of Connor's son.

The thunderclap of another shell, this time closer, jolts Hasan into action.

'The Greeks will be here soon – they are moving quickly. Your son is right. We must go now . . .' His voice trails off when he sees the look of resignation on Connor's face. It is clear that the Australian will not go anywhere without his son, and that Art is not in a fit state to travel. As the Greek artillery fire creeps closer still, the two friends share a knowing look and step out into the forecourt together. Hasan places a hand on Connor's shoulder. 'I would not leave my son either.'

Outside the wind has turned into a rabid dog that claws at their clothes and hats. The sky is black with smoke and airborne sand that peppers their faces and hands like rock salt from a shotgun. As Connor tilts his hat into the oncoming gale he sees a long thin rope of fire unfurled along the horizon as the distant fields burn.

Hasan and Connor shelter against the churchyard wall where Hasan's bay is hitched to a tree. Connor's white stallion has gone. He curses himself, in his haste to find Art he left his horse untethered. Almost certainly the rumbling artillery barrages and escalating storm have spooked it.

Hasan stands by his horse. 'Your boy just needs time.' He says it with hope but little conviction. He and Connor have both seen too many men whose nerves are shredded by shell shock and minds ransacked by their wartime experiences. 'Unfortunately, more time than you have now. But if you take him northeast in the direction of the Black Sea, you can find a ferry that will carry you back to Stamboul. If you travel carefully, that may give you the time you need. I must go to Ankara, I am expected there.'

Not for the first time today, Connor is lost for words. He has no idea why this Turkish major has repeatedly put himself in harm's way to aid him. He has helped him right from the first day at Gallipoli with no explanation and no hope of anything in return.

'How do I thank you?' Connor asks.

'In Turkish – it is easy. "*Teşekkürler*" will do.'

'*Teşekkürler*, then, Hasan Bey. I didn't deserve your help – but thank you.'

The two men shake hands. A strong bond has developed between them despite their differences and both would admit that in a short time they have become accidental friends. Connor bears a lingering shame over his attack on Hasan at Lone Pine. Hasan the Assassin holds no grudge. In his heart he knows he played his part in the deaths of the boys; if not Connor's, then thousands like them. But it was war, so there will be no apologies. The two men are bound by blood: Henry's, Ed's and Jemal's. They also recognise in each other the ability to draw hope from the depths of sorrow and wretchedness.

Hasan holds Connor's hand and kisses him on both cheeks.

'May God give you peace and comfort. Both of you.'

'Goodbye, Hasan.'

Hasan unties his horse, holds it on a short rein and swings into the saddle. He sits upright and dignified, his horse champing at the bit and dancing on the spot, adjusting to the shift in weight.

The major turns to leave then pauses, remembering something. Smiling enigmatically, he leans down out of the saddle and speaks. 'Joshua, tell your son – when he is well – tell him he still owes me a packet of cigarettes.'

Connor looks perplexed, and then suddenly realisation dawns in his eyes.

'The moment I saw the photograph of your boys I recognised him. He is just like you – very brave and very stupid.'

Hasan laughs out loud, digs his spurs into his horse's flanks and disappears through the compound gateway without looking back. Connor doubts he will ever see his friend again. His departure is one more in a painful succession of goodbyes, but this time the farewell is leavened by a miracle of fate that he will never quite believe and most certainly will never forget.

A succession of explosions rocks the ground beneath him and Connor is shaken back to the present. He clutches his hat and scrambles back to the church with the wind thrashing his back.

Art is still obsessing over the restoration of the eyes, unmoved by – perhaps even unaware of – the bombardment or the pending danger. He seems oblivious to his father's return.

'Come on, son,' Connor urges. 'Please, we have to leave.'

Art turns, all of a sudden friendly and engaged. Connor sees a flash of the old Art, a glimmer in his blue eyes and the hint of a smile on his sallow face.

'How is Mum?' he asks matter-of-factly. The two men could have been chatting over a Sunday roast, as if they had seen each other only yesterday.

Connor pauses, deliberating, unsure whether the truth about Lizzie might be too brutal an attack on Art's obviously fragile state. It could unhinge him completely, loosen his tenuous grip on existence even further, or it might just shock him into the here and now. Connor takes a risk.

'She is with your brothers now . . . Art, why didn't you come home? What on earth were you thinking?'

Art is still for a moment, no sign of grief or anguish on his face for a mother he once adored. Connor can see

Art reaching back in his mind for answers, dredging up questions that had long ago slipped from his consciousness. Slowly he responds, his voice devoid of emotion.

'I forgot where it was. How could I have forgotten where home was?'

Without warning an artillery shell crashes through the forecourt wall, hurling rock, concrete and shrapnel across the yard and in through the front door. A dislodged stone the size of a football skims across the floor and slams into the timber scaffolding, shattering the uprights in an explosion of deadly splinters. Connor is desperate and grasps at anything he thinks might motivate his son.

'We can build the farm back up – together. Edith never married. She's still waiting for you. Come now, son. Let's go home.'

Art stands and Connor holds out his hand, hopeful.

'We'll get help. We'll get you right again.'

Art shuffles over to his father and looks into his eyes impassively. He is calm and lucid.

'This can't be put right, Dad. You said take good care of them, and I killed them instead. They won't come home. They can't. How can I?'

Art picks up his walking stick and a small, rolled-up prayer rug and heads for the doorway.

'So you see, Dad, it is all right to leave me here. I want you to.'

He leaves Connor confounded and overwhelmed; to have come this far to find Art and to realise that he has no desire to be found is a painful twist he had never imagined. *I should have known. I should have guessed.*

But now that he has held his son in his arms once again, Connor knows that he is never going to give up on him. His son is all he has left in the world. The guilt and pain that floods through his veins is almost unbearable. He hollers helplessly after Art, 'For pity's sake, I didn't lift a finger to stop any of you.'

He races to the doorway and yells after Art, who limps across the courtyard into the gale. His words are lost on the wind, scattered across the hilltop like dying embers. '*I* killed your brothers, Art – the day I waved you all off . . . Art!'

Without warning a shell whistles overhead and crashes into the corner of the church with a deafening boom. Connor is knocked off his feet, his ears ringing and head spinning from the blast wave. Lying face down, he throws his arms over his head as debris and shrapnel hail down around him. When he surfaces from the blast the churchyard is thick with a tempest of smoke, burning cinders and plaster dust. Everything he hears is through cotton wool: mortar fire, rifles cracking and people crying out. His first thought is for his son.

Where is he? Not now, please. Not after everything we have been through. He must be all right.

Connor struggles to his feet and runs, doubled over, to the gate, coughing and desperate for a lungful of clear air. In the distance he sees a wraith-like figure hobbling along a stone road, staying close to the walls before disappearing between two houses. Connor races to catch his son, listing like a sailor, his balance still thrown by the explosion. He reaches the two houses and discovers a narrow lane and rough stairs leading towards the fortress on the summit.

Connor can see the ancient castle, jagged and crumbling, through the plumes of dark smoke billowing through the now ruined city of Afion. He can see Art's insubstantial silhouette clambering up the stairs with determination and is immediately filled with a sense of foreboding.

CHAPTER FORTY

A rt shuffles along the crumbling Afion battlements, faltering when his walking stick slips on the flat stones or shifts in the rubble. As he moves he looks between the gaps in the saw-toothed crenels towards the town that spills down the side of the hill.

Through the haze of battle he sees his windmill in the square, sheared off at the waist and bent over double, its head swinging listlessly in the wind. The gift he had bequeathed to the village that had taken him in when the prison gates were thrown open is now reduced to scrap. When the freedom trains bound for the ports of Smyrna and Constantinople had eventually come for them, Art's fellow inmates had clambered eagerly aboard, their war at an end. He had chosen instead to hide in a local opium house, which provided a different kind of escape.

Art reaches the highest point of the battlements, where the rampart meets a stone turret that has been decapitated in some ancient conflict. He winces as he kneels and unrolls his prayer rug so that the knotted fringe hangs like a cat's paws over the edge of the tower wall. He pulls himself up on his stick, teetering on his brittle leg as gusts of wind lash at his clothes.

Settling himself, Art inhales deeply and closes his eyes, blocking out the thunder of cannon, the rifles spitting and the wailing of new widows that hangs on the wind. Creeping his toes forwards until they curl over the edge of the precipice, Art raises his right hand, its palm facing upwards, and drops his left arm, palm facing down. He tilts his head towards his right shoulder and waits for the rapture to grip his body.

Art is transported. He opens his eyes, staring out over the ransacked landscape, and is carried to a place in his past he will never escape.

❖

He doesn't feel the shattering pain in his leg any longer. His limbs seem disconnected, detached from his body.

Henry lies beside him, skin now grey and bloodless, his face slack, spattered with mud and gore.

Gone.

Ed lies opposite, face contorted in pain, teeth grinding, eyes screwed into pinpricks of agony. He writhes in the mud, glistening coils of intestine looping out of the gaping hole in his side. Reaching across the blood-sodden mud, Art grasps his brother's hand, squeezes it, wishing he could stop his suffering.

His breathing comes in fits and starts as Ed fights to draw oxygen into his lungs. His body is broken, but still it struggles to survive.

'Art? . . . Art?'

Battling to hold back his tears. 'Yeah, mate. I'm here.'

'I've dirtied myself, Art. Can't tell what's blood and what's shit . . .' Ed's muscles spasm, his teeth chattering and limbs quivering uncontrollably.

Quieter now.

'I want Mum.'

Art weeps. 'Hang on, mate. Someone will come for us.'

Ed's eyes are clear now, blue eyes penetrating the ghastly fog of the battlefield. He pushes his gun across the dirt towards his brother.

'I can't shoot myself. They won't let me in heaven.'

No.

Art's breath catches in his throat. 'You can't ask me.'

'It hurts something shocking. I'm a gut-shot rabbit, Art.'

No. No.

'I can't . . .' Art feels as if he is sinking into the mud, floundering, desperate. 'Please, mate. Don't ask that. I can't.'

'You're my brother. You have to do it. Please?'

No. No. No.

Ed forces the gun into Art's hand and holds the muzzle against his own forehead.

'Please, Art?'

Art looks deep into Ed's sky-blue eyes, and feels his finger resting on the trigger. Acknowledges his brother's calm and peaceful resignation.

'Take me home, Artie.'

Art draws breath.

Cocks the hammer.

'Climb onto the carpet, then, mate. Let's get out of here.'

Art squeezes his eyes shut, tears coursing through the mud and blood on his cheeks. 'It only works if your eyes are closed, Ed.'

As one.

'Tangu!'

The gun fires.

The crack of the pistol in Art's mind becomes the blast of a Greek shell as it crashes into the fortress wall below where he stands.

Art is blinded by his tears. He has lost his bearings, can no longer negotiate the nebulous line between fantasy and reality. Oblivious to the stones and gravel thrown up in the air and the rubble threatening to give way beneath his feet, he lurches forwards.

Connor reaches the top of the stone stairs and is nearly blown back, head over heels, by the blast of incendiary air and flying debris. He steadies himself – his head clearer now – and peers through the dense and sooty smoke for any sign of Art. He lumbers along the rampart, stumbling and clutching onto the crumbling remains of the wall. There. A shape in the gloom. He catches sight of his son, balancing on the edge of a deathly drop with his arms outstretched.

What the devil is he doing?

The realisation comes to Connor before the question has even properly formed in his mind, an overwhelming sense of loss sweeping over him as he watches his son embrace the sky.

'No! Art . . . No, son! Please! I beg you . . . You mustn't!'

Connor runs towards the turret, coming to a halt once he is within reach of his son, fearful that he might startle him. Art hears the fall of his father's boots and turns to him.

'Henry died without a word. Just a shot and then suddenly he was still. Nothing. His head blown away. Eyes empty.' Art lowers his head. 'Then I put Ed down like a dog, Dad. Right between the eyes . . .' He sobs. 'If only I'd waited. I told him, Dad. I did . . . I promise I did. "Someone will come get us," I said. And they did come. The Turks would have picked him up too. He'd be here too. If I'd waited.'

Art's admission cleaves Connor's heart in two, bleeding not for Ed, or Lizzie, or even Henry, but for Art himself. Connor cannot imagine the rings of hell his eldest boy has had to pass through since he left that cursed battlefield. The pain etched in his eyes and the black shadow of guilt that stalks him suddenly make all the sense in the world.

Connor cannot speak. Instead he clambers up onto the turret and picks his way towards his son, blistering wind whipping his face. His boot slips on a loose piece of shale. Flinging his arms back, Connor rights himself. Looking down and watching the stone bounce and shatter on the rocks hundreds of feet below, his head spins.

He looks at his son, toes hooked over the edge of the abyss and teetering on the brink of oblivion.

Art turns towards his father, confused and conflicted.

'Get down, Dad! Go home! You'll get yourself killed!'

Connor smiles madly. Mimicking his son, he lifts his arms. 'You're all that's left to me, Art. If you're not coming, I have nowhere left to go.'

'Dad, don't do this,' begs Art.

'You're the only thing left of your brothers, Art. They are alive in you. In your memories. In your blood. You want to take care of them? You want them to live on? Then get down off the bloody wall and come home.'

Suddenly an artillery shell crashes into the turret, tearing a gaping hole in the wall and spraying stones and debris skywards. The impact knocks Art backwards onto the rampart. Connor is closer to the edge now, closer to danger. A sheet of shale drops out from under his feet and he begins to slip down the face of the tower in a tumble of rubble and dust. As Connor scrambles for purchase, Art's instincts kick in. He throws himself forwards on his belly and locks onto his father's arm.

Connor hangs out over the ancient wall, his feet kicking and scraping for a foothold between the stones. He looks up at Art and stops.

'Let me go.'

'What? No!'

When Connor sees the confusion on his son's face he tries to pull his arm free of his grip.

'If you're not coming home with me, then let me go.'

Art shakes his head, grips harder.

Connor swings out, kicking against the wall. 'I've come halfway round the world, another hundred feet isn't going to kill me!'

As Art takes in the absurdity of Connor's last remark there is the hint of a smile on his lips, a hint of the old Art.

'I reckon it might,' he quips, and begins to pull his father to safety.

The pair scramble back up onto the rampart, chests heaving and muscles screaming from the effort. In the town below they see houses burst into flame as the Greek soldiers overrun the streets and alleys like black ants over a sheep's carcass. Connor recalls Hasan's warning. He turns to his son, still panting from their exertion. 'We must find somewhere to hide. The Greeks won't leave anything standing.'

Art thinks for a moment. 'Come on,' he says, tugging at his father's arm and leading him along the wall. They stumble down a stone stair and into an open court, both crippled and sore, supporting each other as they weave across the paving.

'Over there . . .' Art points to a low structure covered with a partially demolished dome. 'The castle cistern. No one will bother with this.' The plastered exterior has decayed with time and the friable dome looks bruised and on the brink of caving in. Art finds a small doorway. He slides the rusty bolt across and pushes it open.

Inside it is cool and pitch black, but Connor catches the light from the entrance reflecting off the rippling surface and can smell the sweet water. They pull the door shut behind them and fumble in the darkness to secure it with a flimsy latch. Three steps down and Art and Connor immerse themselves waist deep in the cistern, the ice-cold water filling their shoes and soaking through their clothes.

Gradually adjusting to the dimness, Connor smiles as he sees a hint of the old sparkle in Art's eyes, the life reappearing in his face. He dips his hand into the water and splashes it onto his face, washing away the dust from his eyes and the caustic shadow of despair from his soul.

Outside, the din of battle subsides like a train rattling into the distance.

They are in for a wait.

CHAPTER FORTY-ONE

'**I**'m beginning to feel almost human, Dad.'

Connor glances warily over his shoulder towards Art, careful not to disrupt the barber's concentration as he runs a diamond-sharp cutthroat razor in long sweeps down his neck. His son reclines, long legs extended, in another barber's chair beside him, eyes closed and strong chin covered in thick, white lather. The man ministering to Art holds his nose to one side and scrapes the blade carefully across his cheek.

It's difficult to fathom the physical transformation Art has undergone since their reunion. In the church at Afion, Connor had salvaged a dying whisper of the young man he had sent to war. When he'd embraced him, feeling the sharp ridges of his ribs and shoulder blades through the thin fabric of his shirt, Connor had known that life had lost hold of his son. His face had borne the ravages of addiction and deprivation, sharp cheekbones protruding above sunken jowls, haunted eyes recessed in bruised sockets. But now, as the barber goes to work on him, Art's skin glows pink, the lines of his features now strong and rounded rather than gaunt and spectral.

Connor lies back, gazing at the strip of blue sky visible between the uppermost terraces of the tall timber houses that line the street. The cries of the gulls and swallows and the sound of feet ringing on shiny cobblestones conjure a warm and comfortable familiarity within him. What once was alien and disorienting now feels akin to a home.

When they had disembarked from the Black Sea passenger ferry in Eminönü, exhausted and bedraggled, Connor had one destination in mind. But prior to that, there was work to be done. He knew from past experience that facial hair was not something to be treated lightly in Constantinople. As the two men negotiated the thronging crowds on the docks, their bushy and unkempt beards attracted scornful and unapologetic stares. Before doing anything else, Connor knew that he and Art needed grooming. He'd found his way to the row of street barbers in the narrow lane just below the Otel Troya, and the two men had taken their seats, the barbers draping crisp white smocks across their chests with a flourish.

Connor inhales the invigorating tang of the citrus cologne being splashed liberally on the cheeks of the Turkish man sitting in the chair beside him. The barbers exchange pleasantries, gossiping quietly as they ply their trade. During their journey across the Anatolian interior, Art had begun to teach his father smatterings of Turkish. Although much of what's said is still obscure to Connor, it gives him a strange rush of pleasure to be able to recognise some words and phrases as the barbers chatter away.

He lies back and shuts his eyes, trying to keep in check the tide of excitement that rises within his chest when he thinks of where he plans to go next. Connor reminds himself that it's something of a miracle that he's here at all. Many were the times during their arduous journey from the heart of Turkey that the thought of reaching Constantinople became a distant and quixotic pipe dream. Surprisingly, their escape from the cistern in Afion had proved less difficult than he'd imagined as he'd stood in the frigid water as the Greek troops razed the city above their heads. But as the invaders focused their efforts on Afion, Connor and Art had been able to make their escape relatively easily.

At first they'd moved by night, wary of the Greek forces that continued to ravage the countryside. The two men were careful to avoid busy roads, instead following silvery moonbeams through poppy plantations and golden wheat fields and salvaging what food they could from abandoned farms, villages and orchards. But within days of leaving Afion, as the opium accumulated in his bloodstream began to dissipate, Art was seized by the violent and aggressive symptoms of withdrawal, and the men were forced to find refuge in a small, deserted stone farmhouse.

As Art lay on a rough timber pallet that Connor covered with a makeshift mattress cobbled together from empty hessian sacks and straw, his frail and brittle body was racked by brutal convulsions and teeth-shattering tremors. He developed an incandescent fever that caused sweat to pour improbably from skin that looked too desiccated to contain any fluids. Watching his son turn grey, his breath rattling and catching in his hollow ribcage as he was pursued by night horrors and waking phantasms, Connor thought he would lose him. Feeling utterly helpless, he carried buckets of icy cold water from a spring-fed trough set in the centre of the farmyard and bathed his son's face and twig-like, wasted limbs, attempting to quench the fever that ravaged him. As Connor passed the cloth across Art's brow, it tugged at skin stretched taut across his bones and as transparent and insubstantial as yellow cellophane.

Until, one morning, he woke after another night spent sleeping fitfully by his son's side and found Art gazing at him over the edge of his cot. His face was drawn and haggard, but the light of life glinted in his eyes, reflecting the bright beams of the morning sun shining into the room.

They had remained at the farm while Art built his strength, until he was ready to move on. Connor had fashioned a trap from abandoned farm machinery and every other day he went out into the fields where he caught rabbits that he cooked on a spit over glowing coals. Connor knew his son was going to live when he saw Art licking his fingers as he pulled the tender meat off the bones and ate until his emaciated belly swelled beneath his ribcage like a child's balloon.

To the south, they watched as the dull glow of flames left in the partisans' wake slowly disappeared, and the two men knew they were safe. They moved to the east and then headed north through small hamlets where families tended their fields and led their herds into the hills to graze each day, blithely unaware of the conflict that was so close at hand.

Art had tried to explain to his father that they needn't worry; that the people they would encounter were duty-bound to give them succour. It was inconceivable to Connor. If two strangers were to appear on a doorstep in Rainbow, particularly two foreign strangers as moth-eaten and down-at-heel as Art and Connor, they'd be given short shrift. But Art had been right. There wasn't a village they passed through from Afion to the Black Sea where their arrival was not heralded by a rag-tag parade of children and a feast hosted by the *mukhtar*, or mayor, of the settlement. Many was the night that Connor lay beneath a rough woollen blanket, his belly full of rice, marvelling at the largesse of these people who gave without question. When Connor and Art traversed the wide Anatolian plain and passed through the towering forests and craggy mountains that plunged down to the inky depths of the Black Sea at Zonguldak, they did so without exchanging a single coin for the food and comforts that ensured their safe passage back to Constantinople.

The barber dips a towel in boiling-hot water, flicks it and deftly places it on Connor's face, swathing all but his nose under a soft cotton cloud. Connor's reverie is broken as he submits to the ritual. He inhales, feeling plumes of fragrant steam fill his nostrils.

'Hey, Dad! How are you doing under there?'

'Dunno, mate. You tell me.'

His son laughs as the barber removes the towel. 'Barely know you without the beard.'

Connor reaches up and feels his warm, smooth chin. The barber stands before him, splashing cologne into his palms. Connor braces himself as the Turk vigorously slaps his cheeks and chin, the chilly, fragrant balm making his skin burn.

'I need to sort out some accommodation for us, son.' Just the thought of it makes Connor's heart race.

Art looks up the hill to where the turrets and domes of Topkapi soar into the cerulean-blue sky. 'I hear the Sultan's palace is available.' He smiles to himself. 'Tell them the harem can stay.'

Connor feigns an untied bootlace as an excuse to halt in the shadows and gather himself before they round the corner and begin the approach to the pink mansion on the hilltop. Adrenaline courses through his veins and he struggles to control his breath, every cell in his body urging him to run; which way, he's not entirely sure.

'C'mon, Dad. Pick up the pace a little. I'm dying for a little shut-eye.' Art is impatient, eager to settle, take some time to stop and breathe.

'Just a minute, mate. Be right with you.'

Although he has told Art about the Otel Troya and the woman and young boy he met there, he hasn't spoken of the love that blossomed in his heart for Ayshe. The sense of loss Art feels for the death of his mother is still raw, and Connor has no wish to complicate that by revealing his feelings for the Turkish woman. So he has been unable to release the pent-up anticipation that has been building in his gut since they stepped onto the ferry at Zonguldak on the Black Sea coast. It was only then that the sickly feeling of dread and loss that had haunted him throughout their travels began to abate, and Connor allowed himself to entertain the thought that he might, one day, see her again.

He stands, takes a deep breath.

'Up here, is it, Dad?' Art is racing forwards.

'Yep. That's it, son. Just round the corner.' Art disappears up the lane, Connor in his wake.

There. There it is. Unchanged. A closer look. The façade looks less shabby than he remembers, the paint and plaster fresher; the garden brought to order. Then again, he thinks to himself, perhaps he's romanticising it. A thousand questions tug at his resolve.

What if she's not here? What if Omer is running the hotel? What if she has remarried? What if she no longer wants me?

Connor curses himself silently, despising his self-doubt. He hesitates, momentarily entertaining the thought that he should turn, leave, hold on to the precious memories and walk away.

'Dad! C'mon!' Too late. Art has bolted up the street, already has a foot on the stoop. There is no avoiding it. Connor steels himself and mounts the steps. His heart warms as he hears Orhan's lilting patter from within, attempting to recruit another paying customer: Art.

'You want room? Clean sheets. Hot water . . .'

Connor steps into the foyer and finishes his sentence, '. . . and no Australians?'

For a moment, Orhan is rooted to the spot, dumbstruck. Then, his face splits into an enormous smile and he shrieks with joy, racing across the foyer and flinging his arms around Connor's neck. 'Connor Bey! You came back for me!' Connor laughs and wraps the boy in a bear hug, smelling the wood smoke and cinnamon in his hair.

'Orhan, this is someone I'd like you to meet. It's my son, Arthur.'

The boy turns, his face now solemn. He nods his head earnestly, playing the host. 'Good day, Arthur. It is a pleasure to be meeting you. Welcome to Otel Troya. You will be our guest.' Orhan extends his hand.

Connor ruffles the boy's hair as he shakes hands with Art. 'So, you are the patron now, are you?'

A rippling sound comes from behind Connor as a beaded curtain is pulled aside. His heart leaps and he turns.

No. It is not her, but Natalia. She is dressed modestly in a simple, waisted burgundy dress with her hair tied back in a floral scarf, her cheeks lightly powdered and a gentle blush-pink colour on her lips. 'Yes, now he is little patron. I his assistant. Welcome back to hotel, Mr Connor.' She catches sight of Art, who is standing to one side, amused by his father's familiarity with these people and this place. Her eyes widen. 'Your son?'

Connor nods. 'Yes. This is Art.'

The Russian woman smiles. 'So handsome.' She opens the ledger on the front desk and writes Connor's name against one of the room numbers, then turns and takes a key from its hook on the wall behind her. She hands it to Orhan. 'Please show them to our best room.'

Orhan bows. 'It will be my pleasure.' The veil of formality is lifted, and the boy laughs out loud, taking Connor and Art by the hand. 'Come! I show you!'

Connor hesitates. 'You go ahead, son. Show Art the room.' He turns back to where Natalia stands behind the counter. Before he can open his mouth Natalia nods her head and smiles gently. 'She is outside.'

Ayshe walks across the courtyard towards the kitchen, carrying a small tray. She swings the door open and enters, placing the silver salver onto the stone bench. She looks contentedly into the garden, where neatly set tables sit under dappled shade, a handful of them occupied by groups of travellers poring over maps of the city. Her father sits in a chair by the fountain, dressed in a three-piece suit and clutching his cane with both hands, gazing into the indeterminate distance and talking quietly to himself.

341

She stands by the hot coals that glow orange in the stove, tending a tiny engraved copper pot as the silken coffee grounds froth and foam. She is miles away, marvelling at the events that have changed her fortunes. When she rejected Omer's proposal, she was forced to face the prospect of losing the hotel and sending her family into penury. A timely approach from a representative of Thomas Cook & Son then led her to make a spontaneous, albeit desperate, decision. She scraped together enough money to buy an advertisement in Cook's guide to Constantinople. Before the guide had even been published, the company started to recommend the Troya to travellers, and very quickly her investment began to bear fruit. Wealthy tourists from Britain and America were choosing the Otel Troya when they visited the city. Rooms were even booked by telegram and Orhan despatched to meet guests as they disembarked from vessels that moored at the docks, or alighted from the Orient Express at Sirkeci Station.

With the money the new arrivals bring in, Ayshe has been able to afford to pay for some of the repairs the hotel so desperately needs. The fountain at the centre of the courtyard now tinkles gently, its pipes replaced and its ornate fluting scrubbed clean of algae and moss. The tiles have been lifted, broken pavers replaced and fresh mortar laid. The chickens have been banished to a far corner of the garden where they peck at the dirt within the confines of Connor's still sturdy coop. The garden beds that edge the courtyard are once again weeded and planted with neatly pruned rosebushes, bulbs and fragrant flowers. Set against the wall in the corner of the courtyard sits Ayshe's biggest investment. A cylindrical copper boiler sits steaming, its rivets gleaming in the sunlight. Never again will Orhan be caught out lying about the availability of hot water at the Otel Troya.

Ayshe hears the creak of the door as a guest enters the garden. She is intent on pouring chocolate-brown coffee into two tiny bone-china cups decorated with ultramarine blue, carmine red and gold filigree. Placing the cups on the small silver tray along with a glass dish containing tiny, jewel-like cubes of Turkish delight, she looks out into the courtyard. There, a tall figure of a man hesitates by the door, removing his broad-brimmed hat as he glances around the garden.

Her breath catches in her chest.

❖

There is no sign of Ayshe, so Connor moves towards one of the tables, pulling out the chair. He is surprised to see that his rough and calloused hand is shaking. He sits and glances towards the kitchen. There. There she is. Head held high on her graceful swan's neck, shoulders thrown back proudly. He feels his throat swell with longing, his blood pounding in his ears.

Ayshe seems unaware of his arrival as she edges the kitchen door open with her hip and carries a tray towards one of the other tables. She smiles warmly at her guests as she approaches their table, placing the tiny coffee cups before them, full lips curling up at the corners, her translucent green eyes glittering. She turns and looks towards where Connor sits and registers his presence without so much as a flicker of surprise or pleasure. She nods, restrained. Polite, but distant.

Connor is utterly crestfallen, the euphoric rush of reunion replaced by a bitter taint of disappointment that burns behind his eyes. Ayshe moves across the courtyard towards where the Australian sits. She bows her head formally. 'Mr Connor.'

Connor responds in Turkish. 'Good afternoon. I hope you are well.'

If she is surprised to hear him addressing her in her own language, she doesn't show it. She replies perfunctorily, 'I am well. Thank you.'

'You look . . . very well.'

'I have told you I am. You speak Turkish like a villager.'

Blushing, Connor reverts to English. 'Am I welcome here?'

Ayshe shrugs her delicate shoulders, raising her dark eyebrows slightly. 'All are welcome here. It is a hotel.'

'And your brother-in-law, would he welcome me too?'

'He has gone to fight with the Nationalists.' She allows herself a small smile. 'Finally, war has a purpose.'

An uncomfortable silence descends over the couple. Connor is despondent.

I should never have returned. She doesn't want me here.

'May I bring you a Turkish coffee, Mr Connor?'

He shakes his head. 'I still haven't managed to get a taste for it. Even after all this time.'

She places her hands on her hips. 'If you know so much about my country now, then you will also know that it is impolite to refuse such an offer.'

Connor flushes. 'Oh. Yes. All right, then. A coffee, please, but only medium sugar.'

344

Ayshe nods curtly and turns to walk back into the kitchen.

Connor looks down at the palms of his hands, feeling awkward, embarrassed.

The door to the kitchen opens again and Ayshe steps out holding a tray with a single cup on it. She stops at Connor's table and bends to place it by his hand, along with a selection of baklava.

'You don't seem surprised to see me again.'

Ayshe glances up at him. 'It was in your coffee.'

He wrinkles his brow, confused.

'Months ago. Before you left, your cup told me you would return,' Ayshe explains. 'Do you remember what I told you about coffee? The answer to everything is in your cup.'

A customer on the other side of the courtyard signals Ayshe. She turns and moves gracefully across the marble tiles, her hips swinging beneath her slim skirt.

Connor watches her leave and lifts the tiny cup to his lips. Nothing could be worse than the bitter taste of her rejection. He takes a small sip then hurriedly puts it down again, grimacing. The coffee is so sweet it makes his tongue curl. Dipping the tiny teaspoon into the cup, he scoops up some of the coffee, and sees that it is so heavily laden with sugar it's as thick as honey.

Everything is in the coffee. The cup never lies . . .

The shadow of a conversation, what seems a lifetime ago.

Connor's heart soars. He looks over to where Ayshe stands, clearing the plates from a table. She glances up at him, catching his eye, and offers him a secret smile.

The more sugar, the deeper her love.

Connor sits back in his seat, feeling the sun warming his back as a gentle breeze rustles through the ancient trees that shade the courtyard.

He smiles.

Ayshe has made her choice.

ACKNOWLEDGEMENTS

This novel is based on the original film script by Andrew Knight and Andrew Anastasios. Without you, AK, neither of these works would have seen the light of day. As wonderful a writer as you are, to us your friendship will always be your greatest gift.

This story is a work of fiction but it is inspired by true events. Thank you to the unknown father who went looking for his son at Gallipoli in 1919. Your journey continues and we hope you would approve.

To our friends in Turkey, Chris Drum and Bahadır Berkaya, Hasan Selamet and Metin Tosin who welcome us back time and time again, you appear in this book in ways you will never know, and we say *teşekkür ederim*.

This novel is all the better for the encouragement and considered notes from early readers of the script and book, Loretta Little, Jim and Dianne Anastasios, Banu Erzeren, Tolga Örnek, John Alsop, Elise McCredie and Charlie Carmen. Thank you to Andrew Hoyne and Joanna Anderson, for all your friendship and years of gentle nudging.

347

To the word-witchers at Pan Macmillan, including Cate Paterson, Brianne Collins and Paul O'Beirne, thank you for your guidance and keen minds. Our gratitude also to Russell Crowe, Andrew Mason, Troy Lum, Keith Roger and John Collee for bringing this story to the screen and helping make this novel possible.

To Keith Liston, the original water diviner, even though you didn't always find water, when you did you changed lives. Our heartfelt gratitude and affection go to our parents Jim, Di and Loretta for indulging us, sometimes against your better judgement. And to Willie, thank you for showing us how to dream big. Our love and thanks to Irma, Jane, Victoto, Sue, Matt, Katherine, Phoebe, John, Phil, Adrian, AB, Ariana and Sophia for your encouragement and support.

To Roman and Cleopatra, thank you both for the joy you bring us every day. May you find as much love and adventure between the pages of books as we have.